THE CHINESE ROOM

VIVIAN CONNELL

THE Chinese Room

BARRICADE BOOKS

FORT LEE, NEW JERSEY

Published by Barricade Books Inc.
185 Bridge Plaza North
Suite 308-A
Fort Lee, NJ 07024
www.barricadebooks.com

Library of Congress Cataloging-in-Publication Data

Connell, Vivian, 1903-
     The Chinese room / Vivian Connell.
          p. cm.
     ISBN 1-56980-264-5 (pbk.)
     1. Bankers--Fiction. 2. England--Fiction. 3. Married people--Fiction. I. Title.

PR6005.0392C47 2003
823'.912--dc21

                                        2003048143

Manufactured in Canada
First Printing Barricade Books Edition

PREFACE

The Chinese Room and The Heavy Hand of 1950s Citizens for Decency

When Bantam put out the paperback edition of *The Chinese Room* in 1948, the publisher proudly described the front cover as "symbolizing the suggestive allure and glowing intensity" of the novel itself. A somber-toned character study, the oil painting avoided the kinkiest of the details with which the author built his case for what passion means to his characters: adulterous intercourse in beds and meadows, the slapping, biting, and carrying that makes up the sexual foreplay, the Satanic symbols, the decadent trappings and opium pipes of the Chinese Room itself. Although Bantam's front cover blurb provided some clue, one would have to read *The Chinese Room* carefully to find the aggressive sexuality which both male and female characters discover in themselves. A close reading reveals the care with which Connell told his story of sophisticated, class-bound, wealthy Londoners, undergoing late-blooming awakenings to passion. The novel was easily the author's best-selling book. In hardback in this country, it was a steady seller for Citadel Press. Bantam realized more than 2 million in paperback sales when they reprinted from the Citadel edition in 1948.

Though *The Chinese Room* was neither leering nor prurient, the book was targeted for censorship by citizens' and church groups, and the District Attorneys they voted for. The National Organization for Decent Literature (NODL) had been circulating lists of offensive films, magazines, and books since the 1930s. It proscribed Connell's novel, along with other Bantams it thought "glorified" crime, drugs, and licentiousness. These included Uris' *Battle Cry*, Steinbeck's *Wayward Bus*, Schulberg's *Waterfront*, Inge's *Bus Stop*, Ellson's *Tomboy*, and O'Hara's *Ten North Frederick*. Teenagers, blue collar workers, office workers, and especially young women saw and patronized newsstands where wire racks held such paperbacks as well as pulp magazines. In fact, paperbacks, with their dramatic covers and blurbs (those for *The Chinese Room* included "the amazing story of a savage love"), were marketed as a kind of "bookazine." The suggestive advertising was due to the stiff competition for the quarters of millions of readers who bought them at "full line outlets" such as drug stores, cigar stores, bus and train stations, and paperback book stores as well as newsstands. The censorious response gives some idea of the heated moral outrage which energized blacklist-era authority figures as they contemplated the reading matter publishers touted as "good reading for the millions." As one House of Representatives committee member told one of the paperback publishers, getting more indignant with each indictment: "You know darned well you are attracting the young mind, and the lovesick mind, and the sensational mind, and the mind that loves glamour, all tied in with sex . . . .," as if paperbacks like *The Chinese Room* were the reason for the existence of juvenile delinquency, venality, and prurience in America.

In New Jersey and Fall River, MA, local prosecutors harassed news dealers in 1950 regarding *The Chinese Room* and other paperbacks on the NODL list. The Jersey situation surfaced again three years later, when a Middlesex county official requested a New Brunswick distributor remove a similar list of paperback titles that the official, and the NODL, believed would "corrupt the morals of youth." Bantam complained, and while several titles were removed from the list, the prosecutor insisted the distributor withdraw all copies of *The Chinese Room*. The resulting publicity probably drove up the novel's sales, but Bantam felt it had to protect itself from the increasing attacks on its publications, especially after a congressional committee had reported that newsstand paperbacks were a prime cause of juvenile delinquency by disseminating "sensuality, immorality, filth, perversion and degeneracy." The presiding judge ruled that Connell's novel was not obscene by contemporary standards. Further, he stated that local officials were not justified in unilateral assumptions about a book's obscenity or indecency, that citizens' or religious organizations' lists were no valid criteria for prosecution, and that threats to booksellers and distributors were prior restraint. The New Jersey decision provided a precedent for a similar ruling in Ohio that same year.

Connell's work places him in a distinguished company of sexually explicit twentieth century British writers: Norman Douglas, E. M. Hartley, David Storey, Doris Lessing, John Fowles. The dean of these is D. H. Lawrence. Not that the censors cared. The less known about what themes and techniques radicals shared, the better. This is one way institutionalized censorship in a democracy differs from that practiced in a totalitarian society. The offending writer is not imprisoned or deported. Nor do publishers or purchasers of books considered obscene have to worry about visits from the secret police, although booksellers might have been entrapped by undercover agents of the anti-vice societies into selling them copies of it. The machinery of censorship, engineered by authorities acting in the name of the prevailing moral consensus, moves to make an erotic book into just another piece of "hot stuff," and to neutralize the erotic writer. Censors want to foster contempt for a generic malfeasant, not curiosity about a literary outlaw with something original to say.

—Jay A. Gertzman, author, *Bookleggers and Smuthounds: The Trade in Erotica, 1920-1940* (U. of Pennsylvania Press, 1999)

ONE

Nicholas Bude signed his name at the bottom of a page of notepaper that was plain, dignified, and solemn as the Bude Bank. He looked at Mr. Elder and spoke. "Black and white, Mr. Elder, plain black and white. That's how I like notepaper, banking, and life to be—clear and plain in black and white."

"Yes, sir." Mr. Elder paused. "And death, sir. I like funeral cards to have dignity."

Nicholas looked up at the gray stones of Mr. Elder's eyes, at the face blank as a white page. It was seldom Mr. Elder spoke at all. Nicholas indicated the letters.

"That's all, Mr. Elder." Nicholas paused. "Another week done." He looked out at the sunlight over London. "Now for a pleasant week end in the country."

Mr. Elder took up the letters, made a slight bow, said good evening, and went to the door. As he opened it, Miss Coleman came in. Mr. Elder held the door for her, closed it in a noiseless way.

"Face like a tombstone!" said Nicholas.

Miss Coleman did not smile. "Oh, he was an old man long before he was a boy."

Nicholas always saw Miss Coleman for the first time. Now her face painted itself on his eye again. She took him outside his world of black and white for a moment, and then Mr. Elder came back into his mind. "You know, he shut that door like a Chinaman."

"You don't like him?"

"I'm sorry. I shouldn't have said that. It was something he said annoyed me." He paused. "Everything done, Miss Coleman?"

"Yes, Mr. Bude."

She laid down some papers; he nodded without looking at them, and she took them over and locked them in the cabinet. She stood by the window, and Nicholas looked down and saw her on the white blotting pad. He could feel the actual touch of her beauty on his eye. She had green eyes, white skin, a red mouth, and gold hair. Miss Coleman turned the key in the cabinet and the Rossetti lady had gone off the white blotting pad. Miss Coleman came back and bent over the desk, and he saw the gold rope of hair coiled on her neck over her black frock. Nicholas took his hands off the desk, and she looked at the desk with nothing in her eyes, and he felt that she could see his hands underneath strangling his thought. He spoke calmly. "Oh, have those roses come yet?"

"Yes. The page is bringing them up. Your car is not here yet."

"Damn him!" Nicholas got up and looked at the clock.

"Blake won't be late. He never is. Oh . . ." The page came in with an enormous basket of roses, smiled. "Put them down." The page bowed and the smile closed on his face and he shut the door behind him with a tiny snap. She walked over and looked at the roses. "Why didn't you get lilies?"

Nicholas put his hands behind his back.

"Lilies?"

"Yes. Just an idea of mine."

Nicholas thought her face was cold and white as a lily on a tombstone and felt she knew his thought. He pulled out a smile.

"I suppose it does look a bit silly to take roses down to the country. Just a habit. Just a habit."

"Exactly."

She waited, and he knew that he had to say it.

"Would you like them?"

"I don't like roses." She paused. "But I'll take them."

There was something in his eyes that he could not work out of them with his hands. He went to the door, said good evening sharply, and went out. When he had gone a minute, Miss Coleman looked at the clock that pointed the hour and then looked out the window and saw that Blake had come in time. She picked up the telephone.

"Page, please."

When the boy came in she nodded at the roses.

"Take these down, call me a taxi, and put them in it."

What the page was going to say perished on her cold face.

"Yes, miss."

On the white marble stairway Mr. Elder paused as she came down. "They exhale, but do not inhale," he said.

Miss Coleman's eye followed the page. "You do not like Bude?"

"Do you?"

Miss Coleman looked coldly at him. "Did you mean anything about the roses?"

"No. It simply occurred to me—they exhale, but do not inhale."

"Chinese wisdom!"

"Alas, no. All wisdom."

She went down and got into the taxi, and the page

closed the door and copied her silence. He turned to the man with a blue coat and gold buttons who was closing the iron gate of the bank.

"I guess I'm too young to get the hang of her."

"Methuselah," said the man in blue and gold as he clicked the key, "was too young to understand a woman like her."

TWO

Nicholas took up the speaking tube and said into the horn: "Go to Snood's."

Blake nodded in front of the glass window and glided in his clutch. Nicholas dropped the tube and thought it hung like a dead snake, a beautiful green snake with a golden head. His hands working on his lap reminded him that he was thinking of somebody with a golden head and he put them in his pockets to stop his thinking. He tried to relax into the yellow plush and wondered if it was because of his formal blue suit that he could not be comfortable in this car that was like a lounge. He did not notice London passing by and was quite surprised when Blake opened the door and said: "Snood's, sir."

Nicholas, as he went into the flower shop, wished that Blake had not such a smooth voice.

"Good afternoon."

"Good afternoon, Mr. Bude. I hope you liked the roses."

"Yes, thank you, but . . ." Nicholas realized there

was no need to explain. "They were very nice. Could I have some carnations?"

Nicholas watched her supple hands using the gold wire in such a way that it did not argue with her fingers. "Oh—do you do embroidery, or something like that?"

There was no surprise in her calm gray eyes as she looked up. "Oh, I can use a needle." She paused. "Why did you ask, Mr. Bude?"

"Oh, nothing, only—well, I noticed you had persuading fingers. I like people who can get their way with their hands."

Then she realized that Mr. Bude had his hands in his pockets and was faintly annoyed. She did not like men who stood with their hands in their pockets as if waiting for a porter to bring their suitcases. They always seemed to be on the point of moving somewhere and had no time to spend.

When she had done, Nicholas picked up the basket and said: "Now, make up another basket exactly the same."

As he seemed to be going she asked, "To be sent somewhere, Mr. Bude?"

"No. They are for you."

"Oh, thank you, Mr. Bude." When the door had closed behind him she said to the astringent blonde in the office: "Oh, I've got a present!"

"Not a present," said the blonde, "an apology."

"You remember me, my lord?"

Nicholas looked at the shabby cadger who haunted the Ritz arcade. "I do not."

"Times is hard, m'lord."

"I am not 'my lord.' "

"Oh, beg pardon, sir! Mr. Bude!" The cadger's

smile crept over his face. "But I won't be wrong for long, Mr. Bude."

"Don't stand in my way."

Blake was taking the basket of carnations and pushed the cadger aside. The cadger was going to say something when he noticed the look in Mr. Bude's eye.

"Thought Mrs. Bude liked roses, sir?" said Blake.

"Oh—well, I thought I'd make a change for one day."

"Well, these are very nice, sir. I don't think she'll be disappointed." Blake put the rug on his master's knees.

The engine was purring softly and the rug was like a blue Persian cat and Nicholas realized that it had soothed his hands as the green landscape going by had calmed his eyes. He was in a tranquil mood when Blake, sounding his musical horn, reminded him that they had reached the lodge. Blake pulled up and waited for Fuidge to come out of his ivy-covered porch and open the gate, and Nicholas found his eye roving over lawns and woods around Barrington Hall. It was pleasant to be the squire of Barrington.

Blake sounded the horn again, waited a moment, then got out with a frown on him and swung the massive gates on their hinges. When he came back to bring the car he said: "First time Fuidge hasn't opened the gate."

Nicholas nodded, glanced at the lodge as the car glided in.

"What the devil is wrong, Blake?"

Blake got out and looked at the lodge. Fuidge came out on his old stick, and Nicholas thought his soul had gone gray as his beard. Blake was staring as the blinds down in the lodge. They looked queer in the sunlight.

"Excuse me, sir, but . . ." Fuidge did not seem to be able to go on.

"What has happened, Fuidge?"

"Sarah—she—she's dead, sir."

"Dead!"

"Yes. She—she took her own life, sir." Fuidge paused. "She was always a bit . . . But, my own daughter, sir, going against the will of God."

"I'm—I'm very distressed to hear this, Fuidge. What happened?" Nicholas put his hands behind his back.

"I don't know, sir. I—I don't understand it—the doctor, he's up at the Hall with Mrs. Bude, he'll tell you, sir. Excuse me, sir."

Nicholas watched the old man stumping on the porch. "Good God. Come on, Blake. We'll get up to the Hall."

On the broad sweep below the curving steps two cars glistened in the sunshine. Nicholas got out and saw Muriel standing on the stone curb of the doorway. He went up, and Blake brought up the carnations and touched his cap to Muriel.

She looked at the basket. "I am afraid you ought to have brought lilies, Nick."

Nicholas started. He could see Miss Coleman looking down at the roses.

"What on earth has happened at the lodge?"

"Sarah poisoned herself." She paused. "Oh, why have you brought carnations?"

"Oh—I just thought they'd be a change. Whose cars are these?"

"Oh, the doctor and the police inspector. They're talking in the library. I asked them up."

They went in, and Nicholas looked at all the heads and horns in the great hall and suddenly wondered

15

why the hell they should hang there in his house because Lord Barrington had shot them long ago in
Africa. He had a queer feeling that Muriel walked
across the hall as if she were a visitor in a house where
she did not feel quite at home. In the drawing room
she sat by the great silver tray and poured him China
tea. There were more cups for the doctor and inspector when they would come out of the library.

"When did this happen?"

"This morning."

"Why didn't you ring me?"

"I saw no point in it. Friday is the most important
day at the bank, and you would have worried and it
wouldn't have done any good." The maid came in
with the server. "Nick, do you want to wash your
hands?"

"No, ahm . . ."

He looked at her in inquiry.

"Well, you are washing them."

He took a drink of tea and was careful not to let
his teeth bite on the rare china. They wanted to bite
on something. "But why did she poison herself?"

"Anonymous letters."

"Sarah! But what could she do to write anonymous
letters about? Damn it, she was ugly, and—well, no
man would look at her."

"That seems to be it. The letters said she was an
immoral woman."

"But who the hell wrote them?"

"Herself."

"Good God! You are joking?"

"I am not. Ah . . ."

The butler showed the doctor and police inspector
in from the library. Nicholas got up.

16

"Nick, this is Dr. Saluby. You know the Inspector. My husband."

"I'm glad to see you, Doctor. Haven't had time to call on you yet."

"Well, I've only been here a week, Mr. Bude!"

When Saluby sat down, Nicholas had a queer feeling that he did it so perfectly that he was like an actor who had rehearsed sitting in ducal drawing rooms so well that he did it rather better than a duke. His voice was as cultivated as an orchid. The Inspector looked as if he would prefer a whisky, standing up.

"My wife has been telling me an amazing story—something about Sarah writing letters to herself."

"Daftest thing I ever knew. Can hardly believe it yet." The Inspector took a scone in one mouthful as if glad to be rid of it.

Saluby nibbled at his and nibbled at Muriel with his eyes. That voice, Nicholas knew, would explain anything away.

"Not at all daft, Inspector, as you call it. It has happened before. Normal to an abnormal type." Saluby produced a photograph of the dead girl. "When you examine that face you will see that it is that of an inhibited mercurial. She comes from peasant stock, and crude though her feelings might be, her instincts and emotions, from long contact with the soil, are liable to be affected even by atmospheric changes, and . . ."

When he had finished, Nicholas realized that his tea was cold.

The Inspector said: "Well, I suppose that's the science of it, or whatever you call it, but all I can make out of it is that she wanted a man and hadn't got one, and weeds began growing in her mind, and she poisoned herself with them weeds." The Inspector smiled

17

in awkward apology. "Well, I'm peasant stock meself, so maybe that's why I understand it only that way."

Nicholas said nothing and realized that Saluby was looking at his hands. He said: "Have a cigarette, Doctor. They're beside you."

When the doctor looked away, Nicholas put his hands out of sight. When they got up from the table, Saluby strolled out ahead with Muriel. Nicholas said to the Inspector: "He's a bit advanced for a country practice."

"Yay. He's got a head on him." The Inspector paused. "Kind of face that would sell a million bottles of hair oil in a picture paper." He winked at Nicholas. "But he'd never understand Sarah in the way me and you can. He's just a townie. He's got no roots in him."

When they had gone, Muriel said: "I've asked Dr. Saluby back to dine. I'm sure he must be lonely in a new place." She sighed. "I wish you had brought roses. They would have looked nicer on the dinner table."

THREE

In the glow of the log fire, Nicholas felt, one ought to sit in a glow of the mind and forget the world. In this light there was an apricot bloom on Muriel's skin, and the northern pink of the carnations on the table had become golden, like the color of a tropical garden. The Burgundy and the Napoleon were dreaming in the blood, and the odor of the carnations was like an opium. Nicholas fidgeted in his doze. He was growing tired of Saluby's mind working like a mole in Sarah's clay, and he forgot his manners.

"Damn it, Saluby," he said, "the woman is dead, and you've done your post-mortem. You've been eating at Sarah all through dinner and now you're still picking her bones."

Saluby put the photograph of Sarah into his pocket.

"I'm sorry, Mr. Bude. It's a habit of mine to lose myself in my work." He paused. "You see, we have learned in modern medicine that a psychological autopsy can often discover more than a physical examination. Now Sarah is . . ."

"Sarah was," said Nicholas. "Sarah is dead. That's what you forgot. And her mind died with her. It seems to me that the Inspector hit the nail on the head when he said that she poisoned herself with the weeds in her own mind. That's simple and easy to get the hang of."

Saluby sighed and adjusted his bow in his yellow silk collar. "I fear, Mr. Bude, it is not quite as simple as that, nor as elementary. Even at school one goes beyond the A. B. C. Now the letters which caused Sarah's death . . ."

"No letters caused Sarah's death. She was going to commit suicide anyway. If she hadn't thought of the letters, she'd have got up another stunt but she'd have killed herself anyway."

Nicholas put his hands under the cushion on his lap. "Damn it, man, she knew she was writing the letters herself. She wasn't daft enough to forget posting them."

Saluby looked very old and weary, like an Oxford don compelled to lecture in the village school.

"Of course. I cannot argue too far with my host, but . . ."

"Don't let that worry you, I'm not a made-up gent." Nicholas saw Saluby's hand fidget at his tie and took a shot in the dark. "To me, the whole thing is as simple as tying a tie."

Saluby put his right hand inside his dinner jacket as if he hoped to convey that his mind was at rest.

"I think you overlook the power of suggestion—particularly on a peasant. To my mind, if a person like that wrote letters to herself threatening her with death, she would probably get to a state of mind when she'd go to the police for protection." Saluby paused. "Or she might even commit suicide to avert being murdered."

"All that still proves that she was abnormal, so she'd have killed herself anyway. It doesn't apply to a normal person."

Saluby shrugged himself as if he had learned it from a French film. "Perhaps, Mr. Bude, but I still believe that suggestion is the strongest power on earth, to normal or abnormal people."

Saluby paused. "I know I shouldn't like to try an experiment of that kind on myself . . ."

"Look here, Doctor, are you trying to imply that if a person like you or me wrote letters to ourselves—that if I wrote anonymous letters to myself threatening me with death, that I'd begin to take these letters seriously?"

"It is possible." Saluby paused. "At any rate, I'd believe it possible until it was disproved."

Nicholas got up. "Look here. In plain English, without being rude to you personally, that is damned nonsense. Why don't you try it on yourself, to knock this suggestion stuff out of your mind?"

"Why don't you?"

There was a silence, in which the clock ticked five times.

"I?"

"Yes. You can report to me how it feels. You would do me a good turn perhaps. I could write something about it—not saying who you were, of course—in a medical journal."

"That," said Nicholas, "is as good as done." He smiled rather a grim smile. "Anyway, I hope it will end the subject for tonight." He paused. "Help yourself to some whisky."

Nicholas paused for a moment. Saluby had a queer notion that Bude was remembering something, that something was coming into his mind from somewhere outside. Then Nicholas walked over to the window as if he had forgotten they were there and let up the blind. He seemed to be standing apart as he looked out at the moonlight on the landscape.

"Can I pour you a drink, Mr. Bude?"

Nicholas came back from somewhere with a start. "Ah, no, thank you." He paused. "I'm going out for a walk."

Saluby looked at the clock. "Oh, I didn't realize it was so late. I . . ."

"Stay where you are. I often go out for a walk at night. Don't take any notice of me."

"I'm sure you're being polite, Mr. Bude."

"I'm never polite, as you call it." Nicholas paused, said into the air, "Too many damned manners make no manners at all. See you when I come back, I hope."

When Nicholas had gone out, Saluby stood on the hearth and tried to lean his elbow on the mantelpiece. He smiled at Muriel. "You haven't been saying much."

"No. I like to listen."

"I'm afraid I was haranguing a bit. I have bored him out for a walk." Saluby paused. "Well, he'll have to listen to longer speeches in the Lords."

"Lords?"

"Yes. He's bound to go there, isn't he? It's inevitable." He paused. "Some things are inevitable in this life."

His eyes discomforted her, and she moved a little.

"I don't know if Nicholas would take a peerage." She paused. "Please don't think you drove him out. He nearly always goes for a walk at night."

Saluby lighted a cigarette. "No. I didn't really think I did. I knew what took him out. It is full moon." She looked up at him. "I don't know. Perhaps he does understand Sarah better than I can. He is nearer to the soil."

"What do you mean?"

"Well, he is a peasant, isn't he? One can't help knowing about everybody, especially the squire, in a small village. To my mind, he's all the better because his grandfather worked on the land. You can't dig out roots like that in a couple of generations. I'm sorry, do you mind this?"

"No." She paused. "But what did you mean about the full moon?"

"Well, nothing—in a way. But I think it has a certain magnetic effect on a countryman. It makes him want to go out and walk off the unrest in his soul."

"Unrest? Nicholas?"

"Yes. Isn't everybody restless? And he especially. His hands . . ." He saw her slight start. "I mean . . ."

"What do you mean, about his hands?"

"Nothing much. But they are a plowman's hands. And they've been idle for two generations. He wants to work with them—I mean, in a way, he wants to talk with them. They're his—natural language. That's why he's so conscious of them. He keeps them out of the way, as if he felt that his real self was in them, and wanted to be expressed by gripping a spade or an ax, not just in signing his name with a pen. I'm sorry. I'm disturbing you."

"Not at all." She smiled charmingly. "I think you are very intelligent. I think you are right—except that you put too much into Nicholas. I mean—I think he just likes going out for a walk at night, and it is unnecessary to have a lot of theories about the full moon and things like that."

"Well, there is a full moon. Do you feel calm?"

She got up and stood on the hearth and got a cigarette out of the box on the mantelpiece. He lighted it for her.

"What were you saying?"

"Oh, nothing. I just asked you if you felt calm—and you have answered my question."

"Oh—how?"

"Well, you got up, because you are restless."

"I just wanted a cigarette." She looked down into the fire. "I think you get things on your mind too much. Like Sarah. You couldn't think about anything else tonight."

"I wasn't thinking about Sarah at all."

"Oh, I'm sorry."

She kept on looking down at the fire and flicked imaginary ash off her cigarette.

"You look very nice in black. You keep your hair like a very tidy garden."

He paused. "Don't you ever let it down?"

"Let my hair down? No, I wear it up, always."

"I rather meant that figuratively. I mean, let your hair down, go wild, do what you want to do."

"I do what I want to do."

"I see that. Now you want to keep on looking at the fire, so you keep on looking at the fire." She continued to look at the fire, and he lifted the hair off her nape and softly kissed her neck. "You have lovely skin."

She looked up at him.

"Don't you think you are making rather a mistake now?"

"No."

"Well, you are. You are not quite so infallible as you think."

"I don't like it when you shut up your mouth tight like a miser's purse. You make your face a cold, inhibited spinster over the warm bare shoulders of a woman."

"I'm afraid your way of thinking is—rather anatomical for my taste."

"I am not trying to diagnose you. I have already done that."

"And you always believe in your diagnosis?"

"Yes. I believe that human beings are human."

"If you act on a wrong diagnosis . . ."

He kissed her on the mouth, and she slapped his face. He smiled.

"I should know what to expect. I knew exactly what to expect then, and I was right. That was just habit on your part . . . No, don't say it! I know what you are going to say—that you have not had the occasion to slap anybody's face before. All the same, it is just habit—that you learned from books, novels. The woman always slaps a man's face when she is angry with him. However, I have also learned life from human beings, and I know that you slapped me because you are angry with yourself. I don't mind if you hit me with the poker—so long as what you do isn't a damned lie. Why don't you do what you want to do?"

She was pale and her eyes trembled in his gaze. "What do you think I want to do?"

He kissed her on the mouth and twisted his kiss on her mouth as if he were twisting a cork into a bottle. When her resistance stopped, she clung to him in a violent jerk of surrender. Then he put her away and picked up his cigarette.

She stood for some time trying to get control of herself. Her voice was thwarted with anger and emotion. "Well, now that you've got your way . . ."

"I am going to smoke a cigarette." He paused and smiled. "What do you expect me to do?"

"Damn you! Were you making a fool of me!"

"No. You are making a fool of yourself. You have waited about ten years for this, and now you can't wait ten minutes. What do you expect me to do? Make love to you on the sofa?"

"You won't kiss me again!"

"Oh, I will!" He paused. "Do you—live with your husband?"

"You mind your own . . ." Suddenly her face went to pieces.

"Yes, more or less . . . Sometimes . . . I . . . Why are you making me say this?"

"I just wanted to know."

"I have never kissed another man since I was married."

"I guessed that."

"Oh, how?"

"Well, the way you live here, and . . Well, you rather rushed in like a schoolgirl!"

He backed a little from the stinging slap.

"You . . ."

"I deserved that. I am sorry. I know. You're all bottled up inside." He walked over to the window. "Hum, moon-gazing!" She came over, and they saw Nicholas walking on the path below and looking up at the moon. "He'll trip up in a minute!" She could not help a laugh as Nicholas fell over the curb of the path. "I told you. He's magnetic to the moon. You see, it's affecting you, too."

She leaned her body on his.

"It's not the moon is troubling me." She paused. "Please, if you've got me to do this, it's upsetting enough without you diagnosing me as if I were a patient." She gave a little gasp. "Damn it, I couldn't help myself!" He looked at her with scrutiny in his eyes. "Oh, for God's sake, don't look at me as if you were reading a book! I'm just a woman, that's all."

He put his arm about her.

"I'm sorry. I know when to stop reading. But this is not the place." He looked down at Nicholas. "I wonder if he'll write himself those letters."

"Probably. He always likes life proved in black and white." She trembled. "Oh, kiss me, darling. I want love so badly!" She pulled herself away. "Oh God, how can I get to sleep tonight!" There were tears in her eyes. "Now, go home."

```
* * * * * * * * *
*               *
*    F O U R    *
*               *
* * * * * * * * *
```

When Miss Coleman brought in his mail on Monday morning Nicholas was getting his papers out of his case and he looked up and saw her beauty suddenly flushed with the sunlight, like a glass with wine.

"Somebody ought to paint you."

She laid the four letters marked *Personal* by his hand and kept the rest in the tray. "I'm afraid you hadn't a very peaceful week end, Mr. Bude."

"I know. You've seen the papers. Unpleasant business." He paused, worked his fingers below the desk as if trying to unravel it. "Curious case. Don't like these things occurring on my doorstep. Place crawling with newspapermen. Now, the mail!"

"Nothing very much, Mr. Bude."

In the afternoon, when she brought in his tea, the evening paper had a picture of Sarah. He noticed Miss Coleman's eye on it.

"I'll tell you about it, Miss Coleman. Bring in your tea."

"The letters, Mr. Bude . . ."

"Oh, damn, can't you be informal for ten minutes without making me feel guilty!"

When she brought in her cup of tea, he told her the story, and she said: "This doctor sounds more like an actor than a doctor."

Nicholas could see Saluby sitting down with the sharp crease in his trousers and his pointed shoes.

"Damn it, you couldn't be more right if you knew him!"

"Do you really mean to write those letters to yourself, just because he suggested it?"

"Not at all. I'm doing it to amuse myself. My God, it can't be sillier than what I'm doing here all day." Nicholas buckled his hands. "I mean—I didn't mean that, but I just want to get it down in black and white to myself that this doctor is a fool."

"Well, why not! Do you want to dictate it?"

"Ahm—no hurry." Nicholas felt a slight fool. "Leave it until next week." He picked up some papers. "Ahm, remind me."

Miss Coleman picked up the diary and made a note. "I've got it down, Mr. Bude."

Nicholas took the diary and read the entry for next Monday—*Letter on Self.* He smiled at the banking term. "Damn it, you've got a sense of humor."

There was a shadow of a smile on her face. Suddenly he looked at her almost in anger. "Damn it, I'd like to hear you laugh! Don't believe I ever have. Funny as if the Sphinx coughed at you. Now, about this loan to India."

Later, when Miss Coleman came in with the late-afternoon mail, she laid a single letter by the blotting pad. Nicholas took it up, looked at the Chinese stamp, read the address:

> *Manager*
> *The Elder Bank*
> *Pall Mall*
> *London*

"Good Lord!" He put it by and dealt with the scant mail; then he said: "Send Mr. Elder up to me."

When Mr. Elder came in, Nicholas had a curious feeling that in the yellow light cast by the shade of the blind that was down a little to shut out the rays of the sun Mr. Elder himself had something Chinese about him.

"Yes, Mr. Bude?"

Nicholas picked up the letter with a Chinese stamp. "Mr. Elder, I think you ought to open this."

"Out of the mouth of the dragon . . ." murmured Mr. Elder and took the letter. "Do you wish me to, Mr. Bude?"

"Yes."

Mr. Elder opened the letter in a neat way that made Nicholas note how long and thin his fingers were and took out a letter and a fold-over of English bank notes. He laid the notes on the table and slowly read the letter.

"Conscience money, Mr. Bude, from the grandson of a Chinese gentleman in Peking who owed it to the Elder Bank."

"How extraordinary! How much?"

"Nine hundred and forty pounds. The original sum was small, but the interest is there. I am sure it is exact."

"I have no doubt." Nicholas paused. "You must consider that money yours, Mr. Elder."

"Mr. Bude, when you took over our- -the Elder Bank, you took over the accounts."

Nicholas paused for a long time. "Mr. Elder, you said that was—conscience money?"

"Yes, sir."

"I am returning it to you in the same way that this Chinaman returned it to your—the Elder Bank."

"There is no need, Mr. Bude. When your father took over the ruins of the Elder Bank from my father, I was a boy, and I walked along Pall Mall one day with my father, in search of bread at a hostel, and when he saw the plate outside the door with THE BUDE BANK engraved on it, he raised his hat, and said, 'Thank God.' I think I understood then the value of money."

Nicholas put his hands into his pockets.

"I am glad you told me this, Mr. Elder. I often wondered if you—resented being an employee in the bank your father owned once." Nicholas paused. "All the same—do you think, Mr. Elder, that you could—kind of put yourself inside the mind of the Chinaman who sent that money?"

"I think so," Mr. Elder murmured. "Just a matter of mental levitation . . . Oh, nothing, Mr. Bude." Mr. Elder paused. "I think I know what you mean. He would wish me to have it. I feel you are perhaps right. Nevertheless, I do not want it."

"Well, what am I going to do? Somehow—well, I don't want to use it."

"I have a suggestion, Mr. Bude."

"Well?"

"The Crampton account, Mr. Bude . . ."

"Ho! That damned man! My father used to say—never have the accounts of poets or professors. He was right. Crampton is more trouble 'than the India loans . . . But what do you mean?"

"Professor Crampton is engaged on a work, an important work, on the history of the Ming dynasty."

"Oh . . ."

"There are occasions in life, Mr. Bude, when you have to sacrifice your stomach to your conscience. Professor Crampton knows he will not live very long, and he is giving what remains of his life to what he considers is his duty to civilization." Mr. Elder paused.

30

"I could post the money anonymously to his account, Mr. Bude."

"Very well. I'm sorry we have been—that it was necessary to be so harsh with Crampton." Nicholas paused. "You might have told me, Mr. Elder."

"Yes, I see now that I might. I apologize."

Mr. Elder laid the letter down and Nicholas picked it up.

"But, Good God, this letter is in Chinese!"

"And in the most beautiful caligraphy—if that is the correct word to apply to a language which is, if I may say so, more audible to the eye than the ear."

"But I didn't know you could . . ."

"I have the advantage of what is called poverty—in a relative sense, of course—Mr. Bude, so I have time, for a—hobby." Mr. Elder paused. "Money, Mr. Bude, is a child that never grows up, and one's whole life is gone in taking care of it. That is a saying that I cannot quote from Confucius, because he did not say it. But if he had lived long enough, I am sure he would have anticipated my Occidental wisdom."

Nicholas found that his hands had come out of his pockets and put them back again. There was a pause.

"Mr. Elder, please inform Mr. Strood that Professor Crampton's overdraft is not subject to any further stop."

"Thank you, Mr. Bude."

"Mr. Elder . . ."

"Yes, sir."

"I—ahm, your salary, is it . . ."

"Quite adequate. I can walk out at night and draw on the gold bullion in the sky." Mr. Elder paused. "I am sorry that you have had a disturbed week end, Mr.

Bude. The newspapers are busy picking her bones today. They bang like the vultures over the ghats. The Ganges of ink flows down."

"Yes, it was rather a strange happening . . ." Nicholas paused. "You seem rather interested in things like that—I mean the part of life you can't get down in black and white . . ."

"The black and white, Mr. Bude, is only marginal comment on the empty page. I should say, at a guess, that the approach of the full moon disturbed the Scylla and Charybdis in her eyes . . ."

"The doctor said . . ." Nicholas continued, and Mr. Elder listened as the sun came below the blind.

"No. I do not think the idea of experimenting with letters to yourself childish. If it needs the mad person to prove the world sane, why not the sane people prove the odd person mad?"

"I thought it a bit silly myself, but Miss Coleman took me at my word and put it down here." He handed the diary to Mr. Elder. "Didn't know she had a sense of humor, Mr. Elder!"

Mr. Elder smiled at the entry. "Yes, Miss Coleman's beauty is like an Atlantis. You go down in it—and drown."

Nicholas felt his hands clench. The door opened and Miss Coleman walked in.

"I am sorry, Mr. Bude, but I must get these signed to get the post."

Nicholas started up. "Oh, yes."

Mr. Elder took up the money and bowed as he said good evening. The door closed in a noiseless way behind him like a curtain.

Nicholas grunted. "Damned extraordinary conversation." He picked up the Chinese letter.

"Hum, suppose you can read this, too!"

"Yes, Mr. Bude."

Nicholas stared at Miss Coleman. There was no smile on her face.

He took up his pen and signed his name in black and white. He felt outside on the margin.

```
* * * * * * * * *
*               *
*     FIVE      *
*               *
* * * * * * * * *
```

Old Charndale bit the end off his cigar, got a large match out of his waistcoat pocket, struck it on the sole of his boot, and lighted up.

"Cigar, Mr. Bude?"

Nicholas nodded, and Glynde holed the end for him and handed him the lighted taper.

"Too damned fussy for me, Bude. Like torpedo ones. Bite 'em off . . . Hum . . ."

Old Charndale squeaked in his leather chair and picked up his paper again. Nicholas went on counting. Nineteen heads, of which eleven were bald.

"Barrington at nine of the clock, Mr. Bude?"

"Yes, Glynde."

Doubtless when the club tapers had burned themselves out old Glynde would give up saying "of the clock."

"Dammit, why do they shove your picture in, Bude? You didn't commit suicide. Old girl wanted a bit o' love I suppose?"

"That's it, Charndale."

"You ought to go into the Lords, Bude, and get

something done about all this. Introduce a bill for compulsory marriage. Ha, ha! Compulsory marriage. Good subject for a maiden speech."

Old Charndale dandered on. Nicholas counted the heads backwards. Nineteen, eighteen, seventeen . . .

"Barrington, Mr. Bude?"

"Thank you, Glynde."

Nicholas went out and into the cubicle and picked up the elaborately mounted telephone that had a horn attachment for deaf members.

"Nick, whenever you speak to me from your club, even your voice comes right out of the middle of Queen Victoria's age. You've had too much port!"

"No, it was brandy. Everything quieted down?"

"Yes. Old Fuidge has taken to bed after the funeral. If he's not better in the morning I'll send for Dr. Saluby."

"Yes. Good idea. Fine night, Muriel?"

"Lovely. Just looked out at the moon. Why don't you go out and see!"

"Too lazy. When you get stuck in these old leather chairs you just doze until Glynde wakes us all up at eleven and puts us to bed."

"Nick, if you don't give up this Monday-night habit, you'll find yourself an old man!"

"Don't you believe it! Keeps me young. If I were twenty years older, I'd still feel a chicken among the old Methuselahs here . . ."

"Well, good night, Nick."

"Good night. See you tomorrow."

He came out of the cubicle and was amused to see the wagon of great cheeses coming by itself along the corridor. The waiter at the top had given it a push and it rolled down the slight slope. Old Charndale had come out to distill some of the Chambertin he had for dinner, and gazed at the wagon.

"Marvelous thing, cheese! Goes under its own power. Night, Bude."

"Good night."

"Your coat, Mr. Bude."

Nicholas put it on and walked out into the moonlight of St. James.

Old Charndale said to Carraway: "Wonder where he goes?"

"Upon his own pleasure, m'lord." Carraway spoke in a cold and formal way and walked unsmiling to his porter's desk.

Old Charndale muttered to himself. "Damme, the snub royal from old Carraway! Hum, deserved it."

Nicholas scarcely glanced up at the moon over London. He could never feel any communion with the moon in a city, and walked quickly, as if he would be glad to get out of its sight. He wondered if there was a kind of spirit or something which had detached itself from Sarah and gone up to the moon. He had noticed a greenish vapor of light about the silver disk.

Nicholas turned into Mayfair and walked toward Park Lane. Even in the dwindling light, he noted, the geraniums looked fresh in the crescent of Pytchley Court. The commissioners bade him good evening without using his name. When he got into the elegant vestibule, the hall porter merely called him "Sir," and Nicholas felt they must both know who he was by this time, and marveled at the tact in fashionable London. The porter took him up in the lift, and Nicholas walked along the corridor and paused, as he always did, before he rang, to let his mind, as it were, get its breath. He drew in a great nervous sigh and pushed the bell. She opened the door to him, said nothing, and, leaving him in the hall to take off his hat and coat, returned into the sitting room.

When he went in, she was seated at the flat table desk in the corner of the room and continuing to work on whatever engaged her when he came in. Nicholas was used to this, and it gave him a feeling of being at home. He lighted a cigarette and looked around the room. It was the only room furnished in a modern style that he liked, and he wondered if it was some quality in her that made everything come alive. Even that black-and-white design by Ben Nicholson, that he could never think of as a picture, as it seemed more like a proposition in Euclid, now had a queer human feeling, as if it wanted to say something to you. The globes of marble fashioned by Barbara Hepworth, and the shapes of wood like the boles of scale by Henry Moore, had something corporal in them. And all those moons, if they were moons, in that conglomerated sky, if it were a sky, in that painting by Miro, besought one like the eyes of lost children. The Matisse, he realized suddenly, had become as clear as a photograph to him. He looked from the Nicholson design to her, as if he wanted to compare a portrait to the sitter. How strange that it was in that empty white square he saw her face! Good Lord, how very odd! It was like his habit of seeing faces on the white blotting pad!

He knew that she was pondering some calculation of lines and figures as she sat isolated within her mind at the desk. He went to the bookcase and studied the line of books with care. He had never bothered much about her literature. Like the hobby of mathematics, he had accepted these foreign books as part of her total mystery, that he had long given up trying to understand. But now he took down a book with ornamental characters which he recognized as a volume in Chinese. He sat down and opened it, but he found his eyes on her. She was so lost in herself that one could muse upon her now as on a painting. She wore boudoir pajamas of a greenish Oriental silk, a rope of antique crimson, and slippers of Venetian red. He was always fascinated by her elegant slippers, and never had seen her feet bare. He wondered if anybody so beautiful could have ugly feet. These slippers were made like gondolas, and one could almost see them gliding on moonlight canals. It was an enchanting idea, and probably she had designed them herself.

At last, as if a sigh passed in her mind, she moved and then put away her paper and pens, the triangles and squares. She lighted a black cigarette with a scarlet tip and closed the green box. Her fingers were like ivory as they stayed a moment on the marble.

He glanced at the book on his lap and said: "I didn't know you could read Chinese."

"Well, I can."

"I thought you might have been joking today in the bank." That needed no reply; she made none. "Did you manage to work out your problem?"

"Yes, and created another."

He smiled. She did not smile. She hardly ever smiled. Nicholas began to sense a fidgeting in his hands. He wished to God that she would not go on sitting there in solitude, calm, immobile as the embalmed bride of a Pharaoh. His eye dropped on the book. Egyptian picture, Chinese script, something he could not understand. The beauty of a mummy in her face. Suddenly he felt that it would be quite simple to understand her if she were dead. . . .

"Would you like a drink?"

"No. Later." Suddenly he said, though he felt it might annoy her, "You are looking lovely tonight."

There was no motion in her face. My God, had she ever had a soul? He could not stand this intolerable sense of silence and got up and went over to her. He stood behind her and felt his hands coming up and fumbling in the air for her, like the hands of a baby trying to catch the moon. He could not prevent himself speaking.

"Sidonie, if you go on like this, you will soon have me killed inside as dead as I sometimes think you are."

"The choice is your own. If you do not like me as I am, do not come."

"You know that I must come." He paused. "It is not because . . ."

He could feel the cold shudder of contempt in her.

"Must you always explain yourself like A B C?"

"But you do not give me that part of you I come for."

"Is that not mine to give?"

"You mean you are in love with somebody else . . ."

"Oh, don't be a fool!" She paused. "Oh, how easily Elder would understand this."

"Elder?" He paused. "I suppose I ought to learn Chinese!" She was silent. "I am sorry. That was a poor joke." He paused again. "Well, I've known him for twenty-five years and I knew nothing about him until today. Perhaps I shall understand you one day."

"Perhaps."

"I can't stand you holding me away like this. The other night, when Sarah was dead, there was a full moon, and I walked out under it, and I felt a kind of loneliness that made me tear up great sods of earth in anger. . . . I am sorry, I shouldn't have told you this. But I can't stand being here almost touching you and being more alone with you than I am by myself. When you moved your fingers on the table now I could feel them touching my heart."

A shudder went through her that he could not understand. Suddenly his hands came up and rested on her shoulders, and there was no longer any use in trying to keep his voice normal.

"I didn't mind your telling me about going out under the moon and tearing up the earth in anger."

The warmth of her flesh came through the silk into his hands. He touched the coil of golden hair on her nape.

"Sidonie—just for once—let your hair down tonight."

"I am sorry."

"I know you don't like me to ask that, but . . . It's childish, I know, but somehow if all that hair came down I think the wall between us would fall."

"No!"

The word shot into him like a cold arrow. He felt her flinch as his hands squeezed into her shoulder blades.

"Sidonie, kiss me anyway. I can't bear it—the way you keep your mouth away . . ."

"No!"

He started from the noise of the tear as her silk jacket split in his hands down her spine. She did not turn around.

"Oh, God, I am sorry. I couldn't help it. My hands . . . They just did it by themselves without my knowing. I . . ."

"It doesn't matter. It's got to come off anyway."

He looked down at his huge laboring hands that now hung like contrite apes for what they had done. At last he got out the question. "Sidonie—you don't like my hands? I—sometimes I can't help their doing things."

"I have never noticed them."

He knew that was a lie, but it made a sympathy. Suddenly he pressed his face into her breasts. She fastened her teeth in his neck and kept them there until he had seized her and taken her into the bedroom. Then during the fierce, inarticulate conflict of their passion she would grip his shoulder with her teeth and never let go until the end.

When they had done, she was drained and exhausted of color, like a glass now empty of wine. He put on his clothes in silence, went out of the room, poured and swallowed a large whisky, left an envelope on the table, and went out into the night.

When he had gone, she got up, went out into the sitting room, closed the envelope he had left without looking at the contents, wrote the address of an orphanage on it, called the night porter on the telephone, and gave it to him to post as usual in the box opposite the block.

On Thursday, as usual, the anonymous donation of twenty pounds would be acknowledged in the Personal Column of *The Times*.

Then she drank a glass of cold water, did her ablutions in the bathroom, and went to bed.

SIX

Dr. Saluby, Nicholas felt, would never learn to forget about a cigar while smoking it. Perhaps it was impossible to smoke a cigar when wearing a Norfolk jacket. Nicholas pulled away at his old cherrywood pipe and wondered why it always seemed queer to smoke a cigar on Sunday. Saluby had wound himself up like an eight-day clock and was going on and on like a Shaw play.

"Yes, the human body is a complicated machine, but compared to the human mind it is as simple as a wheelbarrow. I suppose one gets something like banking, for instance, down in black and white, but I assure you, Mr. Bude, one cannot get down the riddle of human life in black and white."

Nicholas knocked out his pipe. "You can, Saluby, and in one word."

"Oh . . ." Saluby paused. "And what is that word?"

"Sex."

Muriel gave a very slight laugh at Saluby's disconcerted face. He had an uncomfortable feeling that Bude had thrown a squib at him.

"Well, that is a very simple way of putting it, but that one word hardly contains everything."

"It does, Saluby." Nicholas got up to fill his pipe from the jar on the mantelpiece. "Everything else, Saluby, is just the shopkeeping of life."

"And death?" inquired Saluby, playing for time.

"Just bankruptcy." Nicholas paused. "You think Fuidge is getting along all right?"

Saluby took the hint and got up. "Yes. He ought to be up in a week. It was just . . ."

"Shock," said Nicholas, as if to stop another long-winded theory.

Saluby smiled and thought better of what he was going to say. "Mrs. Bude can be thanked a lot for his recovery."

"And so can his own good hard old countryman's body, Saluby." Nicholas looked at Muriel. "I didn't mean by that you aren't a good nurse!"

"Well, I must get along . . . Oh, I've got the things for Fuidge in the car, Mrs. Bude. I can leave them with the butler . . ."

"No, I'm coming down with you. I want to know all about those bottles myself. One case of poisoning is enough!"

When they had gone out, Nicholas lighted his pipe and smiled.

When they got out onto the steps, the sunset was gold and purple on the hills and the air had almost a reddish glow above the last embers of light.

"It's still hot. I don't think I've ever known hotter weather in England." She laughed. " 'Hot an' rutty weather, ma'am,' as old Fuidge says."

They walked slowly down to the car, and her whole body seemed in tension with the heat of summer.

Saluby laughed. "You know, he rather took the wind out of me when he said sex was everything. Perhaps he was just pulling my leg."

"I don't know. Nick is sometimes unexpected. I was rather surprised myself at the way he said it. It sounded as if he meant it."

They let that die vaguely on the air, and when he stooped in the car to get the bottles for Fuidge out of his bag she leaned over to look at the medical gadgets. There was a pause, and then he said without looking up: "God, I can't stand it any longer! If you don't move away I'll kiss you even if he's looking out the window."

She did not move. "You laughed at me for being—human! And now you just want to rush in like a schoolboy when you've known me only a week."

He jerked himself up as if to get away from her body, his face darkening in anger. "Damn you . . ."

He looked at her and saw the blood gorging her face and he knew she had dropped her guard.

"I know. I can't stand it either. I can't bear—just kissing you down in the lodge with old Fuidge in the next room." She paused. "Well?"

He looked over the lawn at the small village dozing under a blue haze. In a moment he spoke. "You know Dorminster?"

"Yes. I go there sometimes. I have an aunt who lives beyond it . . . Oh, a good way outside."

"I've got a friend there. He's a doctor, too. He goes away a lot as he's got a lecturing job. He's away now. I've got a key to his place. I can't think of anything better than that. We've got to be careful, and Dorminster is nearly thirty miles away. Tomorrow afternoon?"

"Very well. Nick stays in London every Monday night."

"I'll ring you in the morning. How . . ."

"I'll get Blake to drive me over. I can invent shopping."

"All right." He paused. "For God's sake don't wear that frock any more while Nick is there, or I just won't be able to help myself."

She paused, her eyes on the window of the room they had sat in just now. "It seems—Nick was right, about . . ."

"Yes. My God, I could eat you now. You're all made of honey in this light . . ."

"Go away, darling."

When she came in Nicholas was at the bureau, writing a letter over which he seemed to be taking great care. After five minutes she asked: "Your will, Nick? It seems awfully serious!"

"It is. Don't tell the police!"

"What . . ." She laughed. "Don't tell me you're writing that letter to yourself. I'd forgotten about it!"

"So had I—but Saluby and myself got talking about it while you were up changing, and that reminded me. I told him I was taking it very seriously, and that Miss Coleman had marked it in my diary for tomorrow. If I don't write it myself now, I'll have to dictate it to her. No escape from Miss Coleman once she's got it down, even if it's outside banking."

"Miss Coleman sounds grim. I can see her looking at me through enormous spectacles." She paused. "Sometimes it feels rather funny that I know nobody at the bank and that I must have my account somewhere else. The place sounds as grim as a monastery. One day I went in to make some imaginary inquiry, and it was funny that nobody knew who I was."

She was surprised to realize a slight fear of him as his face clouded and he put his hands behind the bureau.

"You went in!"

"I'm sorry, Nick, but—well, I'm just human, and I couldn't resist having a look at the inside of the Bude Bank."

44

"Well, don't do it again!"

"Nick, is all this strictness—necessary?"

"Listen, Muriel, when my father took over the ruins of the Elder Bank, he found out that it had gone bust because it was run as a family tea party and a social club. And if no employee in the Bude Bank can take a private telephone call or keep an account there, and if no relatives are allowed inside the building, it is because it was—and is—necessary."

"I suppose so. But it sounds awful. I wonder anybody stays on there!"

"The point is—nobody leaves."

"Well, I suppose that's the answer!"

"It is. I find it pays to keep banking apart from the rest of my life."

He picked up his pen again and was startled to hear her question.

"Nick, what *is* the rest of your life?"

He dropped the pen and put down his hands. He was on guard. "What do you mean?"

"What I said."

"Well, dammit, the rest of my life is—here."

She lighted a cigarette, and he felt that it took an hour.

"That's what I was thinking." She paused. "It is a funny feeling to stand stock-still for ten years, just in the same place, like a bank."

"I don't quite see what you mean."

"Well, I mean, I always thought of life as something moving or growing."

His hands flexed and unflexed. "Do you mean—children?"

She started. "Well, I suppose I did, though I had never thought of it until you said it. Yes, I suppose they are the growing and moving I meant. I thought I was thinking of something in ourselves. Yes, perhaps it was children I meant."

"Well, we can't help that. That's nobody's fault. We've had everybody in Harley Street." He paused. "I'm not very fond of talking about that."

"I know." She changed the subject with a gay laugh. "Nick, you rather surprised Dr. Saluby when you said that—well, that sex was the whole of life. I couldn't help laughing." She paused. "You didn't mean it, of course?"

"I don't know."

"Oh . . . I'm just thinking, Nick, if sex was the whole of life, then life would be empty without it?"

"Ah—yes, I suppose so."

She moved across the light, and he noticed the silhouette of well-shaped legs inside her frock. There was a slight tingling in the air about her that he hadn't noticed since their honeymoon.

"Well, Nick, is it a very horrible letter?"

"Very. I don't think you ought to see it!"

"Oh—I think I'm going to bed."

He got up. "Good night."

"Good night, Nick."

She went through his dressing room, that lay between their rooms, as she went to bed. Then she closed her door. Their love-making was getting more and more seldom, and it never happened on Saturday or Sunday night. Perhaps love-making was a kind of business, like banking, that one rested from at the week end. She did not worry much about it as she selected the undies for Dorminster tomorrow.

Nick had a curious feeling as he addressed the envelope to himself. He had a feeling that he had made

46

rather a novelettish job of the letter threatening himself with death, and he did not read it again. He sniffed gently at the air. Muriel had changed her perfume. This was somehow like brine on a tropical shore.

SEVEN

Nicholas was opening his personal case that he brought in with him when Miss Coleman came in with the mail. She put two letters marked *Personal* beside him and took up the diary.

"Much today, Miss Coleman?"

"I don't think so."

She began to read over the day's diary and when she came to the note, *Letter on Self,* Nicholas smiled and held up the letter he was taking out of his case.

"You can strike that out. I did it last night." He smiled. "I was damned if I was going to watch your face while I dictated that. Besides, it's outside banking." He took up the envelope. "It's funny, writing your own address on an envelope." He put it down. "Go on, Miss Coleman." When she had read it over he said: "Ring up Symes and tell him I want him half an hour later. Then we'll take the letters."

"Yes, Mr. Bude."

He watched every slight movement of her body as she went to the door. When she had gone he opened the shutter of the direct cabinet telephone to her desk outside so that he could hear her talking to Symes and correct it if the conversation was going wrong. Then

47

he picked up the letters marked *Personal*. The first contained an anonymous donation of nine hundred and fifty pounds for the credit of the Crampton account. Nicholas smiled. Mr. Elder had added ten pounds of his own to the Chinese conscience money. Probably a hint to him. Nicholas smiled as he decided to make it up to a thousand himself. The second personal letter caused Nicholas to put his hands down below the desk. It was typed and short:

YOU HAVE A WILL TO DEATH IN YOUR
HANDS. WHOSE DEATH?

Nicholas felt a slight alarm. He had never before got an anonymous letter. He looked at his hands. He did not like this letter. Then he considered the matter and smiled. It was a legpull from somebody who knew that he intended to write to himself. Four people knew—Muriel, Saluby, Elder, Sidonie. As he read it again the smile left his face. There was something about the wording that did not suggest a joke. He heard Miss Coleman end the talk with Symes and put the letter into his pocket before she came in. He also took up the envelope. His own letter to himself he laid on the desk. When Miss Coleman came in with her pad he was quite normal. But he watched her face with some care.

During the day, Nicholas found that he was somewhat short in temper with Symes and other people, and he was fatigued by the time Miss Coleman brought in the late-afternoon mail.

When they had done, she indicated his own letter to himself and asked: "Do you want that posted, Mr. Bude?"

"No. I'll post it myself."

48

There did not seem much point in posting it now, Nicholas thought. He looked at Miss Coleman and thought she seemed pale and tired. He said:

"I come tonight?"

"Yes." She paused. "If you want to. We can sit and talk."

"Very well. Send Mr. Elder."

When she went out he swore. He wished that she was not in mourning this week end. He wanted something to calm his nerves. He took the envelope of the anonymous letter out of his pocket. It bore a postmark in upper Scotland.

"Yes, Mr. Bude?"

"Oh, Mr. Elder!" Nicholas took up the notes. "I see you've added ten pounds of your own, Mr. Elder. I took the hint and made it a thousand."

"Thank you, Mr. Bude."

"Get it put to Crampton's account. I hope it makes things easy for him. Rather like to see him. Does he come to the bank?"

"Professor Crampton is a cripple, Mr. Bude."

"Oh Lord!" Nicholas paused. "Mr. Elder, you might in future keep me informed about special accounts."

"Yes, Mr. Bude. Thank you." Mr. Elder dropped an eye on the letter on the desk. "I see you are making the experiment on yourself, Mr. Bude?"

"Ahm, yes. Starting today."

"Well, good evening, Mr. Bude."

Nicholas had watched him sharply. When he went out the door Nicholas grunted aloud to himself:

"What the hell could you get out of a face like that!"

"Yes, Mr. Bude?"

Nicholas started at Miss Coleman's voice in the speaking cabinet. He had left the shutter open.

"Oh, nothing, Miss Coleman."

Nicholas took up the letter he had written to himself and put it into his case and locked the case. He looked out at the sunlight. It seemed a damn silly evening to dine in a stuffy club. Damn this woman thing that Sidonie had. He wished he were in the country. On the white blotting pad he was rather surprised to see the silhouette of Muriel's legs inside her frock in the evening light.

```
* * * * * * * * * *
*                 *
*     EIGHT       *
*                 *
* * * * * * * * * *
```

Muriel walked along under the arcade of trees by the cathedral and thought that even in the sunshine there was something sepulchral about Dorminster. The cold slabs of stone in the graveyard looked as if no sunlight could make them warm, and even the green square of grass seemed cold, although the soil was probably warm. Muriel was almost tempted to feel it with her hand. The whole place was a Methuselah bearded with ivy. She turned down from the close into a cul-de-sac road and saw Saluby's car backed into an alley at the end. Anyway, it was a discreet place to meet, and as Saluby got out of the car she felt it was a good omen that they had arrived at the same time. Saluby raised his dark hat that reminded one of the phrase "gents' headgear" and smiled at her.

"Just in time," she said.

"Timing is everything," said Saluby.

Muriel got a slight shock. There was something unpleasant in that remark. She followed him through a narrow gate into a decrepit garden where the last few cultivated flowers were lost within the promiscuous ferns and laurels. He opened a weather-worn door, and they went into a hall that got scant fretted light through the fretted window. Muriel felt it somehow sinister, like the house of an abortion doctor.

Saluby seemed to gather the thought in her mind when he said: "Place is not exactly a sun porch."

"No."

They went into the consulting room that was somehow like the antechamber of death. Books, instruments, furniture, all seemed to sulk in the twilight. Saluby pulled the curtain somewhat wider, and she saw that a large alcove or second room lay within. She walked in and saw a couch for examinations in one corner, a washstand, and, by the window standing upright, set in plaster and wire, the skeleton of a man.

"Hum, we have company!" Her laugh was somewhat uneasy.

"He won't mind us. MacGregor calls him his alter ego. Great bony fellow himself, MacGregor."

"Would he mind—us using this place?"

"No. I've known him a long time."

"Is he—a regular doctor?"

"Good God, yes! One of the most brilliant in England. God knows why he buries himself in Dorminster. Why did you ask?"

"I don't know. This place makes me—uncomfortable."

"Well, it won't talk. And a hotel bedroom might."

"I know. I am sorry."

"You get used to it. I did a month here for Mac-Gregor. I rather missed the old boy when I left."

Saluby walked over and ran his hand in a rather diagnostic way over the skeleton. She noticed the way his fingers lingered, as if they somehow clung to death. She knew that it was going to be difficult to begin anything here and she sat down on the couch and said: "It's cold in here."

"Yes. I'll put the fire on."

He switched on the electric fire, and somehow it was unexpected in this room. She wished steadily that they had gone out into a field somewhere in the hot sunlight. But she saw the drab, overneat dark suit on Saluby and felt that somehow he was wrong for lovemaking in the warm, lusty sunlight.

Saluby lighted a cigarette for her and did not seem too easy himself. "What age are you?"

"Thirty-one."

"Hum. I'm twenty-nine. Why am I older than you?"

He had gone back again to the skeleton.

"I don't know. Perhaps because you are nearer to death."

"What a damn funny thing to say." She knew that he did not like it. He had to say something. "What age is your husband?"

"Forty-six."

"Good God! He doesn't look it."

"No. I don't suppose he does." She paused. "Must we talk about him?"

Suddenly she took off her wedding ring.

"Why don't you take off your stocking? That might be more interesting."

Suddenly something like anger chilled her. "Are you trying to make me feel awkward?"

"Good God, no." He paused. "I wanted you to take off a stocking." He paused. "I have a reason."

She looked at him for a moment in a puzzled way. When she stooped to undo her stocking, he turned his back and looked out the window. When she had got it off she asked with an edge to her voice: "Well?" She gave a little uneasy laugh. "What is it for—a medical examination?"

He ashed his cigarette and came over and picked up her foot and looked at the sole.

"Ah . . ."

"What?"

"Oh, nothing. Just a whim of mine. I couldn't have borne it if I found the geologic wrinkles on the palm of your foot."

She drew away her foot. "Is that why I had to take my stocking off?"

"Yes." He looked at her feet. "They look a bit uneven now. Perhaps . . ."

He began to take off the other stocking. She did not like it very much, but she had come for this. He was a long time getting it off, and her body began to tingle. Then he kissed the sole of her foot and touched it with his tongue. A pang shot through her, and her foot jumped away.

She did not notice the room was cold any more, and everything he was doing seemed careful and methodical and silent and out of tune with the loud pulsing of her heart. She felt a little sweat on her face and finally she stiffened and said: "Oh, for God's sake don't nibble. I can't stand it."

"I see you have been spoiled."

Furious blood came into her face as she felt herself treated like a child, but now she knew there was no escape from her desire. At last she broke from him. "I will not have you torturing me like this."

"My dear, don't be impatient. You are like a child that wants to open a money-box before it is half filled."

In the end she got peace and she supposed that he was right and that the longer one held the fuse, the more fearful the explosion. But she felt exhausted and wished he didn't use his hands on her in the same way that he had on the skeleton, like a cat's diagnosing paw. She said to herself that she would not come here again, but she knew she would. Anyway, she was discovering in herself the animal hunger of the woman and anything was better than being dormant and having one's love-life pigeonholed in Barrington with Nick. She knew that whatever was awaking in her was a healthy thing, but she felt somehow that it belonged to the earth and the hot sunlight and was being interred in the mortuary of this room.

"My God! You are a marvelous woman," he said.

She felt somehow like a prostitute. "Are you always as—surgical as this?"

He smiled in a superior way. "Love is just a dissection of the nervous system, a sensory exploration of the . . ."

He talked on, and she knew that there was not going to be a second dissection today. But his tongue never got tired. The superior smile that had been on his face now began to show on hers as she listened in silence, while he did a post-mortem. She knew the bed was now a slab in a morgue. She made no comment but she thought: "If that's all you think love, or sex, is, you are a bloody fool."

But her body was quite happy now, and she had a curious feeling that it was laughing.

NINE

Nicholas sat with his back to the window and looked at the two letters on his bureau. Then he heard Muriel call to the dogs outside on the lawn and looked at her in the evening sunlight. She walked in a buoyant way along the grass and had the air and carriage of a girl of nineteen. In some way she was resuming her youth, and her skin was all honeyed by the summer and there was a kind of anticipation in that long elastic stride from the loins, as if she were going forward into a delightful world. Nicholas looked at her for a moment and then turned back to the letters. He compared them with care. They were identical in wording.

> THERE IS A WILL TO DEATH IN YOUR
> HANDS. WHOSE DEATH?

Nicholas looked with a curious sense of memory at the notepaper. Somewhere, he felt, he had seen that paper before. It was heavy, a kind of mellow white, with a vellum quality. The top of the page had been cut off with a knife or blade in such an exact way that it had been some time before Nicholas realized that he had not got the whole page. Some address or letterhead had obviously been removed. The setting and position of the typescript were exactly the same in the letter he had received yesterday morning as in the first one a week before. He put down the letters again and decided that he was probably imagining that he knew the paper. It was no different from many brands of good notepaper. But in some way he felt it was old paper. It contained no watermark, and he wondered if that indicated something special. Now he picked up the envelopes, looked at the postmarks, and opened the atlas he had got down, at the map of Scotland. Both were posted from large country towns, the second one about a hundred miles nearer than the first. Nicholas read the wording again and wished that he could feel the letters were a joke. He looked at his hands and then put them into his pockets. Then he heard Muriel coming in and put the letters away.

When Muriel came in, her frock was opened at the throat, and suddenly as she was caught in the golden light Nicholas had an extraordinary feeling that she had come in with her body singing and somewhere in the hinterland of his mind he had a sense of a bird's throat opened in song. The vision had only half formed and had gone so quickly that Nicholas felt it was like something in a dream. Her legs were bare, and when she sat down he noticed how very clean her knees were and how her calves cooled down to her ankles. Everything about her was coming sharply into his eye, but there was also something about her that came in a volume into his whole being. He remembered something like this when he had been courting her, but then it was a kind of vague horizon in his mind where now it had a clear outline in calf and ankle and knee and formal chin and the English syntax of her face that seemed so plain to the eye. And behind all that he felt a kind of expansion of her being into his blood as tangible as the round pressure of her breasts into her frock, and he knew that it was this tactile sense of a woman which really was the woman herself and contained her body and soul and whole being. So long as a woman kept this emphatic in her she could never become a piece of human furniture. And now amazing as the fact that she no longer seemed a piece of furniture was the wonder that for ten years she had been empty of all that quick and sensibility that now seemed so much alive in her dark, golden body. And he knew that it had been for something like this in her that he had married her and into which she had not ripened or grown. There was a silence as if she was subtle enough to give him time to absorb her into his thought before she spoke.

"I've never known a summer so hot in England."

"You're getting a marvelous color. Are you doing a lot of sun-bathing?"

"Yes. I go down to the Wood Pool every day and swim and soak myself in sun."

"Oh, don't you use the bathing pool?"

"No. I don't like sun-bathing in a swim suit. I'm hidden away down there and can lie in the nude. I'm done all over."

"Oh, I didn't know."

"No."

Nicholas put his hands into his pockets. It was very clear why he had not discovered that all her body was golden. He could feel the remark ride off into nothingness in the air, and it left the usual empty feeling. He had an uneasy notion that behind that significant "No" was a sense of amusement mingled with contempt.

She looked at the dark-blue flannel suit with a cream flannel collar and Harrovian tie he had changed into when she said she wasn't going to dress for dinner. "All this dressing-up is silly in this weather—like going into a room and pulling down the blinds and shutting out the sunlight.'

There was a good-humored smile on his face.

"Well, dammit, you can't talk! It is you who have always kept me in uniform, as your father might have put it. I hate this damn dinner-jacketing in the evening."

"Well, maybe I'm getting sense." She paused. "Anyway, I think it's nonsense now." She sighed. "I suppose I got it from Daddy. You know what he used to say—'It's only the white shirt that keeps the Englishman from going black among the natives.' Army, the dear old army. Can't get it out of my system."

"Well, you seem to be changing. I suppose it's never too late."

"Maybe not."

He knew that this was covering a great deal more than the question of clothes. There was a pause, then he asked: "Well, what did you do yesterday?"

"Oh, I went over to Dorminster."

"That's the second Monday! You seem to be getting to like that churchgoers' paradise. Don't tell me you're getting religion!"

"No. I've joined the Conservative Ladies' Club there."

"Good God, politics! That's worse."

"No, it isn't that. But I feel I want something to do."

"Oh . . ."

"I mean—well, just running this house is not a whole-time job, and . . ."

"Has Saluby talked you into politics?"

"No. But I just want something to do."

"Do you mean—you are bored?"

"Perhaps. Anyway, I spent half an hour at the club there yesterday, and the women there were a change

58

from those here. Not one of them said the summer was a damned nuisance because it interrupted fox hunting. I'd rather have a kind of social politics than tiresome village gossip and foxes and stable talk and women with faces like turnips. Most of the women there seemed to wear their own clothes, anyway. Here they seem to wear somebody else's, judging by the way they look on them."

"I suppose it's a case of town bitches versus country bitches."

She laughed.

"Well, you haven't many women friends."

"I don't want them. The best thing about a club so far away is that you can see them there without getting involved in wretched dinner parties and family gossip. It's just useful to drop in."

"Well, if you want town life, why don't we take a house in London?"

"I thought of that—for the winter. I don't want to bake myself in the oven of London now. I'm enjoying it here. The sun is warming my blood—helping me to put off middle age."

"If you ask me, there is less sign of middle age on you now than there was—well, when I married you."

There was a long pause before she spoke. "I wonder if there isn't always something damned old in the kind of people I came from, middle-class army. Somehow I don't ever remember to have been young. Life, as far as I can see, in that crowd, is all spent in behaving properly and going to a lot of trouble to keep on being a gentleman—like making an artificial rose to imitate a real one. Keeping things up! That's all Mummy ever seemed to do. The colonel's wife! A thousand miles from the lower class, and a million miles from real society. Nice and safe in the middle of nowhere."

"Good God, I didn't know you thought all this!"

"Oh, I don't want to talk about it. I thought it was all gone. But now I'm wondering if they didn't play hell with me, and if I hadn't got that paltry social servitude so much into my system that it just ruined me inside in a thousand ways I never suspected. I suppose that's where I got the dinner-jacketing from—that, and some other things." She paused. "And now I'm beginning to wonder if that's all we do here, keep things up, keep a large house and a big place going so that you can sleep somewhere between banking hours. Is this place for us, or the bank? Mummy's life was for the army. Perhaps we're doing the same thing on a bigger scale. Are you shocked?"

"I am not. I'm interested. I don't know why we haven't had this out before."

"There has never been very much communication between us, has there—of any kind?"

"No."

There was another long, uncomfortable pause.

"Well, there's no use in talking about it. A town house in the winter might solve it all."

"That suits me." He paused. "Well, I'm glad you're not going in for politics seriously. A woman only does that when . . ."

"When?"

"Oh, nothing. Yes, I suppose you must do something besides running this house, and . . ."

The door opened, and Oxinham came in, his face grave, and Nicholas saw Muriel frown. Nicholas disliked the butler, who had a kind of careworn pomp on his face, as if he had inherited it from service with

Lord Barrington and just put up with the Budes because they had taken over the place.

"Yes, Oxinham?" Muriel asked.

"Mrs. Biddle again, ma'am. She has returned."

"Yes?"

"In her usual condition, ma'am."

"She brought a drunken sailor home with her, ma'am. Very drunk. The conduct in the kitchen, ma'am . . ."

"Well, put him out, Oxinham."

"He has gone to sleep, ma'am."

"Oh?"

"In Mrs. Biddle's bed, ma'am."

"I see. Well, Oxinham?"

"There is only one thing left to do with Mrs. Biddle, ma'am. She may be a good cook, but she's disorganizing the household, ma'am."

"Very well, Oxinham."

"I shall take the liberty to inform her . . ."

"Thank you, Oxinham."

Oxinham made a slight bow and went out.

Nicholas said: "I wondered why we had a cold supper."

"I'm fond of Mrs. Biddle. I don't want to sack her."

"I don't think you've got very much to do with it."

"What do you mean?"

"You say you run this house. It seems to me Oxinham runs it and always has run it. You might be a guest here."

"Sometimes I feel like that." Angry blood was in her face. "So you think Oxinham runs it?"

"Well . . ."

Muriel got up and rang the bell twice. Oxinham came back.

"Yes, ma'am?"

"Oxinham, I have decided to do nothing about Mrs. Biddle for the moment. I shall talk to her tomorrow."

"But, ma'am . . ."

"Yes?"

"It is impossible to tolerate Mrs. Biddle, ma'am."

"Impossible for whom, Oxinham?"

"Well, ma'am, for any decent person."

"Well, Mr. Bude and I are prepared to tolerate her and give her another chance."

"I see, ma'am. You make my position very difficult, ma'am."

"If you find it too difficult, Oxinham, I will give you a very good reference for another place."

"I understand, ma'am."

"Now, go down and tell Grierson to throw that sailor out."

"Grierson may be unable to obey your orders, ma'am."

Nicholas found his hands clenching. "Oxinham."

"Sir?"

"What height is Grierson?"

"I should say six feet, sir."

"And weight?"

"Possibly fourteen stone, sir."

"Well, if Grierson can't throw that sailor out, I'll go down and throw the sailor out and Grierson after him. I don't want a bloody weakling as a footman in my house."

"Yes, sir."

"When Grierson has thrown him out, send him up to me."

"Yes, sir."

When Oxinham had gone out Muriel laughed. "Well, now, Oxinham knows where he is—at last." She paused grimly. "Perhaps in time I shall find out where the hell I am." She got up and walked about. "Nick, why don't you go in for something? I know you hate politics, and so do I, but surely banking doesn't make a life."

"Well, perhaps not, but . . ."

"I know. I suppose you are going into the Lords?"

"Doubtful. I do not care, and I certainly am not going to pay fourpence to any party fund for a seat."

"That will hardly be neccessary, after the India loan."

"No, I suppose not."

"Do you want a title?"

"No. Do you?"

"I might, if you had earned it."

"What do you mean?"

"Try and think it out."

"I think I know. You mean that Bude's Bank was handed to me on a plate, that I just stepped into it out of Harrow and Oxford?"

"Exactly. It was just something your father left you."

Nicholas got up and walked about. "Do you think I'm not bloody sick of it all?"

"I don't know."

"Well, I am. I wish to Christ I just worked with my hands."

"I suppose that must be a good feeling."

"I'd like to try it anyway. After all, in the beginnings, my father earned Bude's Bank with his hands. If he hadn't swung a pick into the right ore, I wouldn't have had Bude's Bank. He left me everything but the

63

chance to make my own life and career, the chance to swing a pick."

"Hum, it seems to me that being left a lot of money is like being put into a prison with bars of gold."

"You couldn't put it better . . . Oh . . ."

When Grierson came in he had a marked eye and a red ear. Nicholas smiled.

"You wanted me, sir?"

"Is he out?"

"Yes, sir." Grierson smiled. "Right out."

"Bring in the whisky, Grierson. Glasses."

"Yes, sir."

When Grierson went out Nicholas said grimly: "You see! That's the kind of thing I can't do. Grierson's had a whale of a time. What the hell is he doing as a footman?"

Grierson put down the decanter and the glasses. Nicholas in silence filled two large whiskies, added no water, handed one to Grierson.

"Here's to the next fellow you sock, Grierson!"

"And to you, sir"

"Was it all right, Grierson?"

"Yes, sir. When he got awake he was fighting mad. When they sober up at last they're worse than ever then, sir."

"Why do you spend your time handing around dishes?"

"I don't know, sir." He paused. "Just a habit, I suppose. My father was a butler."

"Waste of time. Think I'll sack you—into a man's job."

"Well, sir—I like it here."

"Well, if you want something else, tell me."

"Thank you, sir."

Nicholas put down his glass, spoke to Muriel. "I'm going out for a walk."

When he went out, Muriel looked at the young footman. He had great bony features, fair hair, and whimsical grin. She smiled. "You'll want some iodine, Grierson."

"Yes, ma'am."

She looked closely at his ear. There was still a thumping in his heart after the excitement. Her warm scent came up to him mingled with the salt odor of his own sweat. She said: "Oh, it's not much." She paused. "So you like it here, Grierson?"

"Yes, ma'am." Grierson wondered if he could put down his excitement to the sailor. He said in a hasty way, "I think I'd better go now, ma'am, and get cleaned up. I'm kind of excited after the fight."

"It's no harm to be excited, Grierson."

Grierson picked up the tray. He knew, and she knew, that if he had not picked up the tray, he would have caught hold of her and kissed her. For the first time in her life, Muriel was beginning to take an interest in the staff at Barrington Hall. She remembered the sadistic handling of Saluby yesterday and felt that love-making, to be healthy, must be something nearer to a fight than a five-finger exercise on the body.

**ad** enough to put the headlights on, sir!"

Blake had tapped on the window and then spoken through the tube when Nicholas took it up.

"Yes, Blake, terrible!"

Nicholas let down the window more, and the weighted air came in like a kind of hot gas. One could smell the scorched countryside. Nicholas remembered what old Fuidge said when he opened the gate—"Heat's bouncin' off the ground, sir!" Nicholas wiped his face. The sky was so black that Blake's remark had scarcely been a joke. It was getting worse all the way up to London, and the grimed houses in the suburbs had a dark glint on them. A roof was polished black like a boot. It was like going through a tunnel under this diabolical sky.

When Nicholas got out in Pall Mall, Grover saluted him and said: "Bin saving up for this, sir." He looked at the solid block of thunder in the sky. "Whole sky'll go off like a gun in a minute, sir."

Grover's gold buttons had an ebony shine. Nicholas said to Blake: "Better get back before the whole thing cracks open."

"Yes, sir."

Miss Coleman looked white and exhausted as Nicholas passed through her office. Nicholas looked at her eyes and felt that he would like to go down and bury himself in a green sea from this awful heat. Nothing else seemed cool except her eyes. She followed him and put one *Personal* letter by him and laid down her tray

66

of correspondence and took up the diary in silence. Nicholas got the things out of his case.

"There's a lot for today," she said. "Not a good day for work."

"For two pins," said Nicholas, his eye caught on the *Personal* envelope like on a hook, "I'd pitch the whole bloody day to hell and go and swim somewhere."

What he wanted to do, he knew, was to get away somewhere from that *Personal* envelope.

"Will you take the mail now, Mr. Bude?"

"Yes."

He took up the letters and looked at them and pretended to bend close over one so that he could read the postmark on the *Personal* envelope. He saw that it was Manchester.

Always nearer.

Miss Coleman reminded him: "Mr. Symes, about the Guilfoyle."

"Oh—say yes."

She made a note, and he did not see the mild surprise on her face.

"A letter of thanks from Professor Crampton, Mr. Bude. He says . . ."

Nicholas jumped in his chair, shot down his hands below the desk.

"Good Christ! Must I be bothered with letters of thanks on a day like this! Answer the damn thing, if it wants an answer, and don't pester me."

"Yes, Mr. Bude."

He looked at some more letters, mumbled some dictations that Miss Coleman would put into coherent English, peered down at a handwritten letter from the Treasury about the Indian loan. He wished to God old Dorman didn't carry his courtesy so far as a letter in a script that seemed to be written by some inhabitant of Lilliput. Suddenly he swore.

"Good God, must the blinds be down on a day like this!"

He looked up at her, his nerves taut, and saw her eyes move to the windows. The blinds were up. The black cloud seemed to be sitting on top of the bank.

"I'll put the light on, Mr. Bude."

"I wish the darn thing would burst and get it over." He wiped the sweat off his face. "Is there anything else urgent, Miss Coleman?"

"No. I can manage the rest." She looked at the clock. "Mr. Durrant is at ten-thirty, Lord Ambleside at eleven . . ."

"All right. Get the documents for Durrant, and tell Strood not to keep me waiting if I ask for anything."

"Yes, Mr. Bude."

All he wanted was to get out of the room. When she had gone out he opened the shutter of the cabinet telephone and heard her calling Mr. Law about the deeds. Then she clicked her shutter, and he heard no more and knew she would be busy for ten minutes. He took up the letter and opened it. As he expected, exactly the same as the other three. This from Manchester. Always posted on a Saturday so that they would arrive on Monday from any part of England. . . . There was a buzz on the cabinet.

"Yes, Miss Coleman?"

"Mr. Law says the Durrant deeds are with Oldcastle for engraving the . . ."

"Tell Mr. Law to have them here for Durrant or—may God help him. Why the hell wasn't he ready for Durrant!"

68

Nicholas snapped his shutter. What a nice day to pick for a mistake! And this damn fool Durrant. Every thought coming out of his mind as slowly and crooked as a worm out of his hole . . .

At ten twenty-five Miss Coleman brought in all the documents for the Durrant business. He looked up at her white face. Obviously she had had an anxious time with Law.

"How did he get them?"

"I don't know, Mr. Bude. They are here, anyway."

"Thank you." He gave a slight smile of thanks. "Good God, isn't this storm ever going to break?"

"I wish it would, the . . ."

The page came in with a cup of tea and a box of aspirins. "What's this?"

"I thought a cup of tea and a couple of aspirins . . ."

He looked at her, nodded, thanked the page. When he had gone out Nicholas looked up at Miss Coleman. "Thank you, for thinking of me . . ."

"I was thinking of the bank, Mr. Bude." Her face was cold. "Even on a hot day, Bude's Bank ought to keep cool."

Then she went out, and Nicholas found his hand trembling as he took up the cup of tea. Damn her, she had about as much humanity as a statue.

The cabinet buzzed. "Mr. Durrant."

Nicholas wiped his hands hastily on his handkerchief, got up and steadied himself to deal with Durrant. Miss Coleman, he knew, was right, and now her cold sense of business braced him as Durrant came in.

There was a huge, untrustworthy grin on Durrant's face. He paused on the threshold and said: "Oh, it's nice and cool in here!"

All through the morning and afternoon London

waited inside the black bomb of the sky for the lightning to splinter the cloud and refresh the air with the cool shrapnel of rain. By three o'clock Nicholas felt so exhausted that his nerves twanged like wires at every buzz in the cabinet. He nearly tore the shutter off now as he opened it to Miss Coleman's signal.

"Mr. Symes. I think you'd better talk to him."

Nicholas picked up the hand telephone. "Symes? Yes?"

"Mr. Bude, I don't want to question your judgment, but I was surprised at you granting the Guilfoyle that loan, and . . ."

"Guilfoyle? Loan?"

"Yes, I have just got your letter, and my inquiries about the Guilfoyle Trust make me think . . ."

"Hold the line a moment, Symes, please." Nicholas pressed the button and opened the shutter. "Come in, Miss Coleman." Nicholas put his hands in his pockets as she came in. "Miss Coleman, what the hell is Symes talking about?"

"The Guilfoyle, Mr. Bude. I sent your answer by hand as his letter was marked *Reply Urgent.*" She paused. "I was surprised when you told me to say yes."

"Christ!" He picked up the telephone. "Symes, that letter is canceled. It was a mistake." He paused. "My mistake, not Miss Coleman's." He put down the telephone, stared at Miss Coleman. "I must be going daft. I wouldn't loan those people fourpence."

"That's what I thought, Mr. Bude. It was queer enough that a Manchester trust should have to come to London for a . . ."

"Manchester?" He caught himself up. "Oh, yes."

"You had the letter before you, Mr. Bude, when you told me to say yes to Symes."

70

"It's this damned heat . . ."

She nodded and went out. Nicholas took out the *Personal* envelope and saw the Manchester postmark. "Good God! Must have been that! Mix-up in my mind! Thinking of the letter . . . Getting on my nerves . . . Must pull myself out of this . . ."

Buzz in the cabinet. "Can you see Mr. Elder?"

"Send him in."

Mr. Elder came in, and Nicholas thought he was not looking very well. He completed his business in his usual taciturn and monosyllabic way. Then he made a polite comment on the weather.

"I can't stick this damn compression in the air, Mr. Elder." Nicholas laughed. "I slipped up on something today. First time in my life. No wonder. Lights on in the daytime!"

"I don't like it myself, Mr. Bude." He paused. "How is the experiment getting on, Mr. Bude?"

Nicholas felt every sense in his body taciturn. "Experiment?"

"Oh, the letters you said you were going to write yourself. Or perhaps you didn't go on with it?"

"Oh that! Dull, Mr. Elder."

"Oh, disappointing in a way. But normal. Good day, Mr. Bude."

Nicholas sat back in his chair when Mr. Elder had gone. He looked out at the purple-black sky. Suddenly he spoke aloud. "If this bloody sky doesn't crack open, something in my head will." He opened the shutter. "For God's sake, Miss Coleman, get me some iced water!"

ELEVEN

The storm kept itself bottled up all day, and Nicholas kept his nerves bottled up until dinner at the club. He looked up at Constable, the old waiter, and exclaimed: "Good God, Constable, is this the kind of weather for hot roast pork! For heaven's sake bring me some cold salmon and salad and that hock I like."

"Very well, sir!"

Constable had an offended expression on his face, and there was a slight twitch of his whiskers, but he confined his comment to a survey of the diners. Nicholas looked around and saw that all the members within eyesight were loading up on roast pork and hot vegetables. Nicholas asked himself why he came to this moldering hole for his Monday dinner and knew in disgust that he had no choice from his alibi to Muriel. He nearly sickened on the hot moist odor of the dining room and rushed his dinner. Then he smoldered in impatience in the smoking room until the Barrington call was announced at nine of the clock. The talk with Muriel left him in a worse temper, and she seemed to be in a mood as sultry as the weather. He banged down the telephone and came out to find Carraway looking at him.

"Trying weather, sir!"

"Awful!"

"Better take a macintosh, sir, if you're going for a walk. Might come down any minute."

"I won't bother, Carraway. Hate carrying it. Can get a taxi."

"Very well, sir."

Nicholas turned to the door, then stopped on a sudden. "Good God! Money! I forgot it." He went back to Carraway. "Have you got any money, Carraway, to change a check?"

"Yes, sir. How much?"

"Twenty pounds."

"Twenty pounds, sir? I don't know." Carraway counted the money in his desk. "I can give you eighteen, sir."

"Damn . . . I mean, that will do."

"Yes, sir."

Nicholas wrote the check and felt Carraway watching him with a smile behind his face. That decided him against borrowing two more from one of the members. He thanked Carraway, who had anyway been obliging enough to add three pounds from his own wallet to the fifteen in the desk, and went out.

As he passed through the doorway, Carraway said aloud to himself in a whimsical way: "Blimey! He doesn't walk after all! He goes on a bus!"

There was a red smoke and black ash in the crumbling sky, and Nicholas felt himself accumulating a combustion in his blood as he walked along to Sidonie's flat. A scarlet glint along the side of one street made all the passers-by like red Indians. As he went in the door of the block of flats, the dusk was coming down like a nigger scowl on London. Sooner or later, Nicholas thought, the goddam thing would have to bust. He could feel a cargo of fire in him like in that great red bull in the field behind the lodge at Barrington as he prowled by the border of the wood in a thunder-laden light. He felt that if he did not discharge himself somehow he would burst with his intolerable load.

When Sidonie let him in she wore a kimono of opal silk and somehow was cool and light as that Chinese landscape in the drawing room at Barrington.

There was silence a moment, and then he said: "That damn thing looks silly with your hair up." He suddenly could see her beauty falling down like a golden rain, if she would release that plaited rope of hair, and cooling her skin and cooling him in a long golden shower. He tried to win her with a smile. "If you put that on, you must let your hair down."

"I am sorry."

He controlled his anger. "Well, you look almost cool."

He went over and touched her neck in the open throat of the kimono and somehow was surprised at the tingling heat of her skin. A tremble shot through her from his hand. Then he saw that she had nothing else on except the kimono.

"You look hot and bothered in that suit. I'll lend you a dressing gown."

She shivered again.

"You didn't like me touching you."

"Oh, don't be a fool."

Then he knew what she meant and went and took hold of her and tried to kiss her. She tore away. He swore.

"Damn you. You are not a woman at all!"

She went into the bedroom and brought him out a light silk dressing gown and handed it to him. He went into the bathroom and washed his face in cold water and undressed. His anger gnawed at the way she humiliated him. He went out and found her standing in exactly the same place he had left her, as if she had been nailed there. The words jumped out of his mouth.

"By God, I believe you hate me."

There was not the slightest movement on her face in reply. He went over and caught her by the shoulder, and there was a faint twitch on her mouth. Inhuman or not, she was now strung in tension with desire, and he suddenly picked her up and carried her in to the bed. Their passion was a fierce and exhausting struggle, and her teeth had drawn blood from his shoulder. Her coil of hair had come undone and suddenly he caught it and pulled it out a yard long. She tried to free herself from him in a rage, and he looped the rope of hair around her neck and drew it tight. She tried to cough out a protest and then he realized that it was choking her.

He dropped her and exclaimed in dismay.

"I didn't mean to squeeze it." He looked at them. "It was just—my hands. I couldn't help it. The way you go, you are murdering something in me, and I—my anger got the best of me." She coiled up the long plait and showed no anger. "If you don't want me, why do you let me come?"

"Why do you come?"

"Because I have to come. If you don't want to kiss me, or give me yourself, why do you let me come?"

"You pay me, don't you?"

He sat up in horror. The cold fact spoken in that callous way stunned him. He calmed himself. "Was it necessary to say that?"

"It is necessary to remind you of the plain facts."

"I see."

He got up and dressed himself in silence and went out and left the envelope on the table. He was too disgusted to mention that it was short two pounds of the usual amount and that he would make it up next

Monday. He did not help himself to his usual whisky and went out without looking back.

When he got into the street he walked to the end and leaned on the gate of the square and looked at the pond. He spoke aloud to himself: "Of course she's doing it." He spoke bitterly. "The next letters will be blackmail—whatever the hell these mean." He repeated the words softly to himself: *There is a will to death in your hands. Whose death?* He looked at his great hands drooping over the gate. Suddenly he remembered how they had drawn the rope of hair almost too tightly around her neck. A shock of fear ran through him. God, there was something subtle and dark and sinister in all this. His eyes recoiled from the flash as the thunderbolt glittered in the pond. The thunder clapped down on his ears. As the rain tumbled down he felt an awful sense of relief. Somehow, he felt, if that thunderbolt had not burst in the sky it might have burst in his head. He walked back to the club, his head bared to the absolution of the rain.

```
* * * * * * * * *
*               *
*    TWELVE     *
*               *
* * * * * * * * *
```

Since the storm had burst on Monday night, the countryside had been freshened by some rain, and the sky this Thursday morning had the invigorating blue of a Highland lake. Muriel walked about the garden and saw the green moisture of the plants in the brilliant sunlight and felt the red sap of life running in her. Even old Forsyte, the head gardener, walked briskly among his revived nurslings and looked as if he might even approve a springing weed because it was green and growing after a draught of rain.

She was in a turbulent mood all day, and her humor was not lightened when Nicholas got out of the car looking tired and somehow stifled with the dust of London. She said impatiently: "You look awful. For God's sake, have a swim and freshen yourself up."

He was surprised at the sharpness of her voice: "I might as well."

"You don't swim or sun-bathe. For all the good you get out of the country, you might as well live in London." She paused. "Oh, Grierson's gone."

"Oh, why?"

"He's going to take a ship. He got tired of looking out at the sun from a pantry window. I wish you'd go on a ship, too."

He looked in question at her rather taut face. "Well, I could buy a yacht, and . . ."

"God, I knew you'd say that!"

She swung away with such a gesture of annoyance that her skirt swirled up on her legs and taunted his eye. God, he would like to spank her. It was bad enough to be spun out after London without being mocked by her golden legs. Blast her . . .

He was just going to get his bathing trunks when he saw her from his bedroom window lounging in the cane chair by the swimming pool. He paused in anger. He was damned if he was going down there to be tormented by her. He looked at her for a moment and wondered what the devil was happening to her. Could Saluby have anything to do with it? Or was it this tropical summer? He realized that of late he had been avoiding her because it was impossible to remain negative in her neighborhood. He turned from the window in bad humor and went in and had a warm bath and then a cold shower and put on old gray flannel bags and an open coarse green shirt and decided to go for a walk until dinner.

When he got back from tramping the woodland he found that it was five minutes past eight and he was hurrying up to put on a collar when she saw him.

"Are you going up to change?"

"I won't be a minute."

"Oh, for heaven's sake! Must you put a collar and tie on to have dinner?"

She was still on edge, and he reacted sharply.

"I don't care a damn if I eat my dinner in my skin."

"Well, then, come on. I'm hungry."

He knew that Oxinham did not like his sitting down to dinner like this, and the meal was somewhat unpleasant. They had coffee on the veranda by the greenhouse, and Nicholas was glad enough when Saluby turned up saying that he had an hour to kill whilst waiting on a maternity case and hoping that he wasn't in the way. Nicholas gave him coffee and a brandy splash with ice and thought Muriel held Saluby in a rather narrow grip with her eyes. He wondered if she disliked him and, feeling that, went out of his way to be civil with him.

They were relaxing quite pleasantly into the mellow evening when Saluby said: "Oh, I forgot to ask! How is the experiment going on?"

Nicholas wished that he had somewhere to put his hands. "Experiment?"

"Yes, the letters to yourself."

"Oh—just a waste of stamps, Saluby."

"How disappointing. I mean—I was hoping to get

some kind of report from you that I could compare with Sarah's case and write up somewhere. It might be interesting. Are you still going on with it?"

"Oh—yes."

"Can I ask—do you have to make any conscious effort to impress on yourself that these letters are of no importance?"

"No. None at all."

"Negative, completely negative." Saluby paused. "Perhaps it's too soon yet for a result."

"I think that is nonsense!" Muriel's voice was sharp. "Obviously, the more you get used to them, the less notice you would take of them. I think it's just childish—about as sensible as picking up a stone to show that it is heavy."

"Well, that's the only way you can find out it is heavy."

"That sounds clever, Dr. Saluby, but it means nothing at all. Nicholas is just throwing stones at himself when writing those letters, and that's a damn silly thing to do."

"Yes, I suppose so." Saluby paused. "I suppose, for it to have any result, one ought to get somebody else to write the letters."

Nicholas had taken up a strong wooden rod from the veranda, and now it suddenly cracked between his hands. Saluby looked at him in mild surprise and took the stick from him. Nicholas looked slightly awkward.

"Good Lord, you must have strong hands!" Saluby felt it. "I couldn't break that on my knee, and you cracked it like a match."

"Didn't notice myself doing it."

Muriel had a curious feeling that Nicholas was uncomfortable. Saluby's eye chanced on his watch.

"Good Lord! My case! I must go!"

Muriel got up too. "I'll come down with you. I'm taking out the dogs."

When they had gone down, Nicholas looked at the bits of the rod and fitted the jagged ends together again. He muttered to himself: "I don't like Saluby, and I don't trust him." He went in and got a coat and took up *The Times* to soothe him.

As Saluby walked along to the car, he spoke suddenly: "You're giving off sparks this evening! You jumped on me half a dozen times."

"I'm sorry. But I'm getting sick of Sarah and that letters nonsense."

Saluby paused by the car and felt her near him. "I wish I could see you more often. It's a long time from Monday to Monday."

"Not long enough, if it's going to be like this Monday once more."

He flushed slightly at the steel in her voice. "What do you mean?"

"Nothing—except that I don't like a game of patience in which I lose."

"I'm sorry." He felt that he wanted to get away. He remarked coldly, "I should advise Nicholas to stop writing himself those letters."

She was going to say something and then saw his cold shrewd face. "Why? What do you mean?"

"Nothing very much. Only I know why that stick cracked in his hands. Good-by—until Monday."

She stood watching his car and felt that somehow once again he had made her feel a damned fool.

Nicholas took up *The Times* and put it down again. The letters were turning over and over in his mind,

80

and he felt that he could never get away from them even at Barrington. And thinking of Sidonie he felt a cold repulsion as he remembered her face when she had reminded him last Monday night that he paid. He muttered to himself: "Just a plain kept gold-digger. God, what a fool I am." He looked out the window and saw the easy swing of Muriel's body as she ran along the lawn with the dogs. He spoke aloud: "God, is it her I want, not Sidonie?" This habit of talking to himself alarmed him, and he took up *The Times* and tried to distract himself by scanning the Personal Column. He noted the regular items, and, catching in a subconscious corner of his mind, a minor difference in one of the fixed notices stopped his running eye.

The Aldwycham Orphanage thanks Anonymous
for Eighteen Pounds Tuesday.

For several years now that notice had never mentioned any other sum but twenty pounds. Nicholas laid down the paper with an ejaculation. How very queer. Eighteen pounds . . . Good God, was it possible? Did she send that money to an orphanage? Or was this just a fluke of the eye? Tuesday? It was always Tuesday in the notice. Good God . . . Then how did she keep that expensive flat? And if it was possible, why in heaven's name did she make him pay . . . Questions revolved around in his mind like people caught in the momentum of a swinging door, and he was almost startled when Muriel came in. He noticed that she still seemed in a state of tension. She sat down and rubbed her ankle.

"Those damn midges. They're going mad after the rain."

He looked around for something to say. "Saluby looks as if a game of tennis wouldn't do him any harm."

"Not bad advice for yourself!"

"What the hell use in getting fit and sunburned like you to sit all day on my backside in Pall Mall? Only makes it worse. Always found it did. Once you give your body a chance to get in its say it wants the whole lot of you—when I tried that I used to sit in the bank with muscles busting out my coat and feel like a prize fighter with a knitting needle in my hand."

"Well, some exercise would do you good."

"It might, but"—he spoke impatiently—"I can't do things by halves. If I can't take a thing in both hands I'd rather leave it. I've got to take a thing seriously."

"Nick, are you taking those letters seriously?"

Her inflection alarmed him.

"The letters! Good Lord, no!" He knew suddenly that she was watching his hands and he tried to keep them still. "What in God's name makes you think that?"

"I just wondered—when you said you must take everything seriously." She paused. "I suppose you really aren't writing them at all. I haven't noticed you, anyway."

"I—I dictate them now."

"Oh, I see." She paused. "O curse these midges!"

She scratched herself on her thigh, and he saw a fringe of yellow lace. Suddenly he spoke: "Why the hell don't you have a bath and get rid of them?"

She got up, and he felt that under her tan there was a surge of anger, but she said casually: "Yes, that's an idea. I think I'll go to bed then. Good night."

He said good night, and when she went out the door he swore at himself in his own mind: "Why the hell did I say that, when I wanted to go over to her and . . ." Suddenly he admitted the brutal fact to himself: "I want her so bloody badly that I'm afraid to go near her! Why is that?"

He tried to reason it out in his mind and he didn't know whether it was because of Sidonie or because Muriel had for so long damped down his sexual lust to the inhibition that had been in her that he was afraid in case she had not changed. But he knew in his heart that in some unaccountable way she had changed, and that every intuition told him that she could now answer the healthy ferocity of desire with all her womanhood. But where the hell had she been for the last ten years? And where the hell had she come from now, with that sense of thunder and lightning bottled up in her? Surely it could not be with that thin and dried-up Saluby that she had found herself? He had no more clue to her than he had to the riddle which seemed to lie in the Personal Column of *The Times.*

And he wondered why the hell she had watched his hands while questioning him in that casual guarded way about the letters? He was not so sure of Sidonie now as the writer—if his hunch about the Personal Column was right.

He called his dog and went out for a walk into the twilight to try and work them both out of his system.

```
* * * * * * * * * * *
*                   *
*    THIRTEEN       *
*                   *
* * * * * * * * * * *
```

Next Monday Nicholas felt his heart give a bounce as Miss Coleman laid down the *Personal* letter. He wondered why she had not made any comment on this regular Monday letter, and then he knew that his thought was unreasonable, as no secretary would comment on the *Personal* mail. The postmark seemed to be Birmingham, and he had an unpleasant sense that things were getting closer every week and were being carefully planned.

Miss Coleman went through the diary in her calm way and then took up the letters. Then she said: "Oh, there was a telephone message from Mr. Elder. He is laid up."

When they had drafted the letters that needed a morning reply, she went out, and Nicholas took up the *Personal* letter. The postmark was Birmingham. The letter was, of course, the same as usual. Nicholas dandled the paper in his hand and suddenly wondered if there was anything funny in Elder's absence. And as Elder occupied his mind, something like a tactile memory came into his hand from the notepaper, and instantly he remembered where he thought he had seen this paper before. He pressed the button in the cabinet and told Miss Coleman to send Mr. Law up to him. Nicholas felt an excitement in him as he waited for Mr. Law, who came up promptly and made his polite bow. Nicholas looked at the clerical ledge of Mr. Law's face and said: "Mr. Law, I want to see some documents of the Elder Bank. Would you get the last yearbook from the Records Safe, and also bring me any forms or notepaper with the Elder Bank letterhead. A friend of mine wants to make a short history of the bank, and I want some of the letterheads, etcetera, to photograph into the book." Nicholas paused. "You know the kind of thing I want. Bring them yourself, and you might be able to help me."

Mr. Law went out looking pleased and felt that the unfortunate business of the Durrant deeds had been forgotten in Mr. Bude's mind. It seemed a long time to Nicholas until Mr. Law came back with a leather case full of the Elder Bank properties. Nicholas conferred with him very seriously on the samples to be used and discovered rather a surprising wit in Mr. Law when he relaxed from strict business. At last he got rid of him and then put away the leather case in the bottom drawer and took up the sheet of paper his eye had seized on. There was no doubt about it, Nicholas thought, as he used his magnifying glass. This notepaper was the same as that used in the anonymous letters. He compared the cutoffs in the anonymous letters for height and found that they just eliminated the heading from the rather tall page.

When he left for lunch he did not walk along to his club but went up by Piccadilly to a first-class optician. He said that he wanted to buy a microscope and explained that he wanted a good one to detect fine grains in paper and legal documents. The young man became interested, and Nicholas produced the two sample strips he had cut off and marked, and the young man took him into the back of the shop and compared them in a special light chamber. They were both the same paper beyond any doubt. Nicholas purchased a microscope, was shown how to use it, and said he would take it with him. He produced his wallet to pay, but the young man politely asked him for his name and address as this one had a special lens and it was their custom to keep track of them. Nicholas was somewhat surprised at this formality. He ate a very good lunch, finished the day with a sense of relief, and felt that he was getting on the heels of the puzzle.

In the evening, he left an envelope on Sidonie's table which contained twenty-two pounds. That also, he felt, might answer another question in his mind on next Thursday's *Times*. On the whole he felt that it had been a good day. Even Muriel had been gay and amusing when he rang her at nine of the clock.

* * * * * * * * * * * *
*   *
*   FOURTEEN   *
*   *
* * * * * * * * * * * *

Muriel had not felt either gay or amusing that morning when Saluby rang her up as usual at eleven o'clock. She looked out at the sunlight on the lawn and pictured Saluby dark and slick in his natty suit and narrow tie and parsimonious collar and sleek hair that not once had been ruffled in the love-making in that cold and gloomy room in Dorminster. He somehow became very common on the telephone and she winced as he said: "It's O.K. today with me."

Her mouth tightened in a way that was becoming less habitual with her now. "I don't know if it's O.K. with me, as you put it."

"Oh hell! Why?"

"I may have a cousin coming to tea." She paused. "If I can't come I'll ring you before two o'clock. Good-by."

She just could not go on talking to him. She had invented the cousin as a get-out if she felt unable to go through with it. She sat down in a grim mood and knew that Saluby was playing the devil with her nervous system. Now that she had made up her mind to have a

86

love-life she cursed herself for getting off on the wrong foot. She felt that Saluby in his love-making was not, as he thought, an artist, but an artisan. And her body, she knew, was becoming snobbish about him. But she had a humiliating sense of ignorance about the whole thing, and like so many Englishwomen, she raged at her kindergarten state of mind about what she now guessed was the encyclopedic knowledge of love-making. From the hairy ape of Nicholas she had gone to the bald and bony chest of Saluby. She nearly spoke her thought aloud: "At thirty-one, in the matter of sex, I'm in a cradle, not in a bed." She stretched her legs out like long golden pythons and felt a ripple of sunlight go lazily through her body. She jumped up and said: "I'd better go down and have an affair with a squash racquet!" She played squash singlehanded rather than endure the company of a neighbor at tennis.

She had a bath before lunch, and at five minutes to two went to the telephone to ring Saluby and tell him that she was not going. She took up the instrument and then put it down with a bang. Oh hell! She might as well go. She called Blake and told him that she wanted the car at two-thirty. She thought that she had better spend a formal half-hour at the Ladies' Club in Dorminster before going to meet Saluby.

At the club she met Therese Waldenham for the second time. She was French, perhaps thirty-five, perhaps forty, and had just come to live near Dorminster. Muriel liked this dark and enchanting Parisienne and was fascinated by the contrast of her vivacious face and the somber eyes like pools of amorous oil. She was very formal in black and looked enviously at Muriel, who wore a flowered frock and was, Therese felt, like a tall golden flower in the middle of a garden.

Therese laughed. "Ugh, you make me feel like a black crow! But I must address a wretched meeting in the library! Oh, long lovely golden legs, and no stockings, and no complications to keep them up!"

"All I've got on," said Muriel, "is a Cupid's fig leaf."

Therese tinkled into a musical laugh. "Oh, you're such fun! I'm sure your tongue is a little red imp that dances in your mouth. I think I must not let you meet my husband! You are so adorable I couldn't be jealous of you, and then I could no longer take him seriously. You must come and lunch with me!"

"I'd love to."

"Next Monday week?"

"Yes."

Muriel had to walk hurriedly to meet Saluby. She liked Therese and had talked too long. She hated the gloomy shade about the Cathedral. She stopped and almost turned back. She felt that the something which danced in her today would die in her when she met Saluby. Youth put on mourning with him. But she went on, the shadows of the leaves checkering her face, and turned down from the close into the cul-de-sac road. She stopped. Saluby's car was not there. She felt an enormous relief, but walked on lest it be hidden by the corner of the wall. Perhaps he had been delayed by an urgent case. Then when she got to the gate she saw that the door of MacGregor's house was ajar. So he had come and had perhaps left his car at a garage, or was getting nervous about leaving it here. Muriel got a slight shock of fear. It would be awful and ridiculous if they were caught. She went in the ajar gate and into the house and stood in the hall. Yes, he was in the consulting room. She was just about to go in when her eyes chanced on an old tweed hat and a green macintosh in the hall. My God! She heard another movement inside and wondered if she could get out unseen. But it was too late. The man inside had heard her and came out. MacGregor! She recognized him from Saluby's description. It was impossible to mistake Mac-Gregor. What in God's name had happened . . .

" 'Always leave the door open,' my father used to say, 'and ye'll never know who will walk in!' Ach, he was a wise braw man!"

She suddenly confided herself to MacGregor's enormous smile. She knew it was characteristic of the man to greet somebody like this. Awkward as the situation was, his welcoming smile made things less appalling. She could only think of the obvious thing to say: "Oh, I came to see Dr. MacGregor."

"Dr. MacGregor isn't on duty. He's smelled the buttercups in the meadow and turned himself out on grass, like a wise braw man." He paused. "My name's MacGregor. What can I do for you?"

"Are you Dr. MacGregor?"

"And would ye expect to see a member of the medical profession dressed like this, young lady?"

"I would, if he were you."

He laughed. Then they had a good look at each other. The sunlight struck on his face as if it had gone straight to the living thing in this chamber of gloom. His great red beard and Highland blue eyes made a grand picture in the shock of the light. He had a warlike nose and bony cheeks and his skin was weather-beaten in wind and sun and rain. His hair glistened as though with the brine of a sea. He wore an old stalking coat of a heather mixture spun on a cottage loom, and his eyes seemed to gather up a purple shade from it. His rough shirt was open at the neck and he wore trousers of a kind of green cord. Suddenly he put out his hand and took hers in a clean grip.

"Don't tell me there's anything wrong with you."

"Oh no—it is just a kind of consultation. I'm not ill."

"In that case Dr. MacGregor is staying out on grass. He's only just back anyway from herding a lot of young medical goats in his native Scotland through the sewers of Harley Street hygiene—there I am blaspheming in me own tabernacle of healing—and he's proposing to go down to a quiet bit of river he knows, with a rod in his hand, for the rest of this day and not be bothering himself with a young lady who's probably got toothache in her big toe, and who stands there with her mouth open and her tongue peeping out to laugh at him. So now go back to your ladies' refined teashop in the cathedral town of Dorminster and let him be away to his dallying with the trout."

Suddenly Muriel made up her mind. "Where did you say that river was?"

MacGregor looked at her and saw the laugh rippling in her face. "Just wait one minute."

He went into the room and got a piece of paper and scribbled two words on it and pinned it on the front door. As Muriel read it she laughed. It was like him: BACK SOMETIME.

"Did ye have any tea?"

"No."

"We'll stop on the way down. Women are always a damn nuisance. I had to stick that up because I'm only back a couple o' hours and I rang up a cadaverous scion of a doctor that I know out in a place called Barrington and I suppose he'll be coming in to haunt me like Hamlet's ghost some time today. Now, come on.

90

Me old truck's out at the back. It's ashamed to stand at the front door."

As she went out through the gateway and along the path to the back road her worry about Saluby was lost under the exhilaration of MacGregor's company. She realized that she had left Barrington early and that Saluby had probably tried to stop her coming here. But now she was glad she came. She could not help a laugh when she saw MacGregor's chariot.

"Th' original o' that," said MacGregor, "was a motorcar—speakin', of course, from memory. If she'd only go fast enough to get away from the smell o' the exhaust—the pipe is busted—it wouldn't be so bad. She's just hangin' together by her sinews and she's liable to fall asunder if you sneeze in her. But get in." She was looking at him with a smile. "What are you thinkin' about me?"

"I was just wondering how one tells the age of a man with a beard!"

"I'll be explaining that to ye, as the day goes by. And what age are you, me lassie?"

"Oh—thirty-one."

MacGregor scrambled the clutch.

"Ye're *what?*"

She nodded.

"Don't be daft!" He saw her ring. "Oh, so ye're married! Oogh, the selfishness o' man! If ye want to meet him out o' the office at six o'clock, ye'd better disengage yerself from this chariot."

"Drive on, MacGregor, and don't talk so much!"

MacGregor pushed in the gears and put down his foot, and they went off as quietly as a brass band.

"Pulmonary trouble, by the sound of it!" said MacGregor. Then he did exactly what she knew he would, ignored her altogether and gave over his fine baritone to Scottish ballads. She had a sense of swinging along and around the countryside in an extraordinary rhythm as MacGregor always climbed to a high note and descended again as he swung the car around the grass margins of the corners in the lanes. Once or twice his knee touched hers as he grabbed between his legs for the brake, and she wondered if it was possible to get such a shock and yet for him to be insulated from it. But he gave no sign of being aware of her, except by an occasional smile, as he scraped a corner. After a while she began to find herself borne away in the rhythm of motion and singing and once she had an odd feeling that they were still and the countryside unrolling by them. At last with a fearful turn of the wheel he threw her on to him as he swung down a narrow lane to a farmhouse where they were going to have tea.

As MacGregor pulled up in the yard by the thatched farmhouse a homespun collie ran out and jumped into his lap.

Muriel put up her hand to tidy her hair and said: "I seem to be back from a long cruise—on a stormy sea!"

"Ach, she's got a boisterous motion in her. Why the hell don't ye let down that hair?"

Muriel pulled down her hair out of the formal waves and was combing it out as Mrs. Buchanan came down the steps. She wore a violet-and-red plaid blouse that somehow made her a Highland gypsy under the black cloud of her hair. She had astonishing jet-blue eyes.

"Me daughter, Mrs. Buchanan!" He paused. "The second youngest."

"Welcome young lady. I can see the family likeness!"

92

she said in a forthright way. "The scones are in the oven. I suppose ye got them on the wind, Doctor?" Then she went off, muttering. "Another one o' Robbie Burns' daughters!"

MacGregor laughed. "Best cup o' tea in England here. Come on."

They had tea in the kitchen, and Muriel found it a pleasant change to be treated as a lassie. When she went into a tenant's farm at Barrington she was the squire's wife.

As they left, MacGregor fished out a pouch of tobacco and threw it on the table. "Bit o' baccy, for the guidman."

They drove a few miles and up a cart lane where overhanging hawthorns smothered them with blossoms. Then they pulled up on top of the rise, and through the steam from the radiator Muriel saw the valley twisting along the stream below them. She brushed the hawthorn snow out of her hair and felt herself fragrant with the summer.

"Strictly accordin' to the canons o' punctual medical etiquette I suppose I ought to know who ye are."

"Do you want to?"

"No. In fact, that's just what I don't want to know."

She paused a moment. "Anyway, I live a good distance from Dorminster."

MacGregor got out over the jammed door. "I was goin' to say that it didn't break me heart to hear ye say that, but lookin' at ye now, I don't care a damn if ye're the vicar's wife."

At times, she was discovering, MacGregor could be downright and honest about the things other people side-slipped in conversation.

As they went down the green and twisty path to

93

the river, she was trying to understand why letting her hair down gave her such a sense of freedom. She found herself in a secluded patch of ground by the corner of the stream, and MacGregor walked over and looked down into the pool.

"Aye, it's a lyrical strip o' water, shining along like a line of poetry."

With a sudden throb in her Muriel felt it perhaps had found its poet. MacGregor standing up there was as forthright and natural as a tree in its own ground.

"It's lovely here."

"All the country wants," said MacGregor, "is to be let alone. All it wants is a bit o' trimmin' now and again like that beard o' mine." He joined up his rod, threw a fly on the water, laid the rod on the ground, and sat on his haunches. "That's all the fishin' I do. Just a kind of apology to meself for comin' into the country."

She felt that he was the last man in the world to need an apology for anything. She crooked herself down and tried to see the trout in the pool.

"I can't see any trout."

"All ye can see of a trout is that ripple that breaks over him, like sometimes ye'd see a ripple of sunlight in a woman's hair and ye'd think for a moment 'twas a little tremble o' the spirit in her." MacGregor stretched himself out on his back. "'Tis funny how the character comes out in a person. When I see that twist o' smoky gold in your hair, I know that streak o' wildness away back in you that tells me a grandfather or a grandmother maybe grew up like a bit o' natural corn among the hills."

"There is not much you don't know, MacGregor. On my mother's side we came down from an old coun-

94

try stock—you know a patch of wild acre turned into a nice smooth lawn after a couple of generations of church and army. Am I all trimmed and tidied up?"

"Well, I suppose if ye turned this river into a canal, it would be just a road of water, but 'twould come down all the same from the mountain springs. And just a whisk o' lightning and just a whack o' thunder, up in the hills, and 'twill come down in a flood and burst the walls o' the canal. Two things you can't dam up forever—mountain water and human blood."

He changed suddenly. "Ah, this sun! Bah, how I hate workin' with me head stuck over a jar o' bluidy germs!"

She laughed. She was lying along the ground and turned on her hip to look at him. "I don't know why you are a doctor!"

"Yah, a bluidy germ in me, that's lookin' for more germs."

"You had to do it?"

"I knew you'd know. I like ye for the way ye know things."

"I know them with you, anyway."

MacGregor moved a little to watch a grasshopper. "I've got a wee cottage by the lochs, where ye can see mountains standin' with their feet in the water, and their heads in the sky, and if it wasn't that I can go there now and again, and get out of the laboratory of my mind, I don't know if I could be stickin' it for very long. I'm tellin' ye, 'tis a weary and a laborin' thing, the workin' on the brain. 'Tis like a sponge, that gray matter in the head, that soaks up all the blood in the body to keep it moist, until in the end there's not a drop o' juice left in ye, and ye're like an old withered tree with cerebral sparrows arguin' all day and all night on the top. There's more than one young doctor I know whose work is his wife, and whose wife is his housekeeper, and I'm thinkin' 'tis a scant and monkish thing his life must be. A bluidy dry old attic it is, the scientific head, and it puts cobwebs on a young man's eyes. A kind o' bluidy silent music it is, without a drop o' joy . . . And here am I, as bad as any o' them, pratin' away like a parrot in his cage, when I should be just singin' like a lark with you here in the sunlight." He paused. "I always come down here alone and just lie out in the sun like Adam in his garden . . . There's a kind o' bluidy mourning in clothes over a bronzed and healthy man . . . But that cold white winter flesh is as naked as a plucked fowl, and I'm thinkin' 'tis well out o' sight . . ."

Her long golden legs were sensible to the sunlight and her frock had come up on her thighs, and she said: "You can lie like Adam now, for all I care."

"I'll take me shirt off at your word. I like the hot hand o' the sun on me chest."

He took off his shirt, and she felt a thrilling in her marrow at the unexpected girth of muscle on him.

"Well, you don't look as if you are imprisoned in the great indoors!"

He laughed. "Ah, I got a lot of rowin' when I was takin' those medical goats. The sanatorium was up by the lochs. We practiced a bit o' hygiene on ourselves." He laughed. "Well, I'm a pagan from the waist up, and a chapelman from that down!"

She laughed. It was evident that it wasn't Sunday for the chapelman, and she knew that MacGregor understood the gist of her laughter. Suddenly the bronze hair on his chest seemed electric with light, and she felt sharp twitches in her body.

96

It was a little time before he said: "It's funny how you can lie quiet and silent outside and the blood thunderin' like a red torrent inside you."

"Yes." The word was a whisper. She felt the expansion in her blood to this man, and suddenly had an extraordinary confidence in herself. Some instinct told her that he would respect her more if she began what must begin. With a natural and sudden movement she laid her cheek down on his warm chest, and slowly moved it up with her mouth searching for the warm red mouth inside his beard. When his beard touched her face the hairs shocked her like the tendrils of live wires, and then she felt her breast swell suddenly in the pouch of his hand.

Afterwards, she knew, she would understand the significance to her of that mating in the clear sunlight. But now she surrendered herself to the physical delight of things snatched up like shafts of light into her eyes —the shine of sweat on the muscles that girded his loins, the extraordinary blush of blood that seemed to come like a red undertone through the golden coat of her own skin, the curious plasmatic glint of natural oil, the involuntary twitch of muscles as if they had an individual life of their own. She exulted in the physical man and had a pride in being able to match her vigor to his. All her body ached in the sensual telepathy of the blood, and she cried out loud in the sweet deliverance.

They lay quietly for a little while and then he chuckled.

"What in God's name do you want to see a doctor for?"

"Perhaps I didn't know what the complaint was until I found the cure."

There was a slight alarm in his face. "For God's sake, don't tell me that a woman like you can have that kind of worry."

She sat silent for a time, and like a black cloud in the blue sky she remembered love-making with Nicholas when she had switched off the light. And she knew now that it had been as much her fault as his. She knew that it was a long history and put it out of her mind. She said: "I'm not in the mood for a diagnosis now."

He understood and for a time he talked very quietly of country things, and from his slow, murmured remarks a kind of philosophy formed. She listened, as if she would understand his mind as perfectly as her body understood his body, and then she sighed in content.

"How sweet the air is now!"

There was a kind of loveliness in her simple thanks, and he took her hand and said: "You are a lovely girl." He paused. "You always will be a girl. You have that singin' in you."

Once more before they got up to go they enjoyed love, and when at last they turned up the path to the car she looked back at the little corner by the river and felt somehow like a plant that was being torn away from its bed. They drove in absolute silence homeward as the purple shade of the dusk slowly climbed in the hinterland of the blue light. As they mounted the shoulder of hill that lay above Dorminster she felt a sudden hatred of going back. Some impulse to fight off the parting gave her confidence and she put her hand on his thigh. And as she put out her hand she knew that she had found her womanhood. It was the first confident thing she had done and she felt the blood mantling her cheeks as he turned and smiled. After a

98

time he stopped singing, and as the vale of Dorminster came into gradual view below, an emphasis of her womanhood seemed to command her, and she made very sure that he would stop the car. On the top of the rise he pulled up quietly, and then he got out and lifted her over the door, and they went into a small grove. As the birds startled up from their nestling in the dusk, she felt queer, shy little thoughts fluttering up in her, and their love-making now seemed to gather a gentleness and poignancy from the twilight. They were silent walking back, and he paused with his hand on the lever when they got into the car.

"I'm sorry I'm going back in the morning." He paused. "I only came back to get some gear. I've got to do research in Oxford and then perhaps in London."

"I don't like you going back tomorrow."

He started the car and then stopped it halfway down the hill. There was a gold glint on her wedding ring. He said: "I didn't expect to be saying this—but if you hadn't that ring on, I might have asked you to marry me."

Then he jammed in the clutch and drove homeward in a violent and dangerous way. When they got out in the back street he asked:

"Where are you going?"

"Up to the Ladies' Club."

"Well, come through by the house and go up by the Close."

She knew that he was not going to kiss her or touch her again and she felt a little cold. The door was open as they came round into the garden, and as they turned the corner, Saluby came down the steps. She saw him pause, as if to consider, as he saw them. She felt herself that she didn't care a damn what Saluby thought.

Saluby said to MacGregor: "Where the hell have you been?"

"Fishing."

"Good evening!" Saluby spoke politely to Muriel, as if she were some unknown friend of MacGregor's. Then he turned to MacGregor. "I've been here since five, and I've got to go now. I've got a case waiting."

Muriel moved a step. "I must go now. I'll leave you both to talk."

She gave her hand to MacGregor. "Thank you very much."

"It was a pleasure to help you."

It was curious how MacGregor had changed suddenly into the formal doctor.

"I can't stay to talk," Saluby said. "See you tomor· row, MacGregor."

"I'm going back in the morning."

"Oh hell." Saluby looked at his watch. "No. It's no use. I'll ring you up before bedtime." He said in a casual way: "I'm going up into the town. Can I give you a lift?"

"I'm going to the Ladies' Club."

"That's fine. I'm going to the chemist next door."

"You'll be all right with Dr. Saluby," said MacGregor.

Saluby stopped his car at the other side of the Close. "What the hell happened? I telephoned and you had gone. I didn't know what the devil to do."

"I saw the door open and I walked in thinking you were there. Then I found it was he."

"What on earth did you say?"

"What could I say, except that I wanted to see Dr. MacGregor?"

"Lord, what did you think up!"

100

"Nothing. He began t
me I looked as if I'd got a
advised me to go back to
teashop, and to leave him
frightful surprise when I a
—and then I went down
all about the illness I was

"Well, I'm damned!

"No. He never asked
you."

"I must say you're a
a dither. But what on ea
with him for? He's a damned clever man, but he's a
bit of an old stick."

"Is he old?"

"No. I don't think he's forty. I didn't mean it that
way. I can't understand you wanting to go fishing with
him."

"Well, I'd dismissed Blake and the car for a couple
of hours and I had nothing else to do."

"Well, I hope it wasn't too heavy going." He paused.
"You see, I'm very fond of him, and I know he's going
to do something big, and I'd hate to think somebody
would find him boring simply because he's—well, a bit
Scotch, and puritan."

"I thought he was charming, and I was not bored.
Heavens, Blake will wonder if I'm lost. Better let me
down at the corner."

"You're very quiet this evening," he said, before
he started the car.

"Oh, it was peaceful down by the river."

"Well, I'm glad no harm was done. Thank heaven
you have some wits about you."

She got out at the corner and knew that it was all

uby. The sun was red on the beard of
ıter Raleigh statue in the public garden.

```
* * * * * * * * * * *
*                   *
*     FIFTEEN       *
*                   *
* * * * * * * * * * *
```

When Nicholas sat himself at his desk on this next
Monday he admitted a candid fear of the morning
mail in his mind. Miss Coleman put down the single
Personal letter by him, and Nicholas felt himself
inclined to shout at her: "Why the hell don't you say
something about this Monday letter!" He calmed the
ridiculous impulse and took the mail. There was a
note today from Mr. Elder. Miss Coleman read the
formal and courteous apology. Mr. Elder was no longer
in bed, but his doctor had advised at least another
week's rest. Nicholas heard her vaguely, his eye trans-
fixed on the notepaper.

"Leave it there, Miss Coleman. Let's take the business."

When he got her out of the room he picked up
Elder's note, got a magnifying glass out of his desk.
The same paper! He took up the *Personal* envelope
and saw the Ampthill, Bedford, postmark. Getting
closer to London! Whole thing worked out with diabolical skill. He compared the notepapers. Certainly the
same, and the letterhead also cut off Elder's note of
apology. Nicholas saw Elder's cold bleached face on
the blotting pad, like a pale shadow on the white. A
ghost! An old, evil ghost. Well, he would deal with
Elder.

102

At lunchtime he went around again to the optician and confirmed his magnifying glass in the microscopic cell. He had taken his own microscope to Barrington. The young man in the shop was showing a curiosity, and Nicholas felt that he ought not to go there again. Anyway, he felt, there would be no need. He was confident that he had located the sender of the letters in Elder. He was so relieved and excited that he ate hardly any lunch.

All through the afternoon the matter beat down on his mind as endlessly as the hot sun on London, and suddenly he knew that he would have to clear this matter up today and get it out of his head. It was an insult not less than a threat. A resentful microbe had worked itself out through years of patience in Elder's mind. Well, he was going to end the whole damn thing before he went to bed tonight.

When Miss Coleman had brought him the final letters to sign and he had concluded the day, he said to her: "Sidonie, I won't be round tonight. I have to see old Dorman on the India. Dining with him. You understand?"

"Yes."

He was putting away his things in his case and as he was tucking in his *Times* he remarked: "Don't know why I take this to the club with me. Enough to waste a whole day in this paper." He paused. "Do you take it?"

"Of course."

He smiled. Evidently it was unthinkable that Mr. Bude's personal secretary should not take *The Times*. He ambled on: "I've got a weakness for the Personal Column. Knew an author once who said he made his income out of that. Ever look at it?"

"Oh, sometimes—vaguely. Why?"

"Oh, nothing, just curiosity." He kept on stowing the case. "You don't happen to remember if you read last Thursday's Personal Column."

There was a slightly guarded look on her always-guarded face.

"No. I don't think I did."

Nicholas shut up his case. "Hum, considering you're so vague about it, you remembered that fairly well." He looked up at the clock. "Hum, Blake ought to be here." He pulled an envelope out of his pocket. "Oh, here. Even if I can't come . . ."

"Oh no!"

"Damn it, we've got to keep the orphanage going."

He saw the constriction in her. Then she walked over to the window. He picked up his case, paused, and then went over and stood by her. He spoke quietly: "It was a pure fluke. Last Monday week I left eighteen pounds, and I happened to notice the Personal Column of *The Times*. I knew that the Aldwycham was always twenty pounds on Thursdays, and I began to wonder. Last Monday I left twenty-two pounds in your flat. That was the sum acknowledged in last Thursday's *Times*. Then I was certain." He paused. "Don't you even open the envelopes?"

"No."

"Sidonie."

"Yes?"

"Why are you doing this?"

"What I do with the money is my own business."

"I understand. You are not going to talk. As usual." He paused. "I don't suppose you believe me, but always in the back of my mind I felt there was something very odd about that money on Mondays."

She turned, and he thought she looked very

fatigued, inside, somewhere in her soul, if she had a soul.

"Well, I think we have done for the day," she said.

"Yes. Good evening, Miss Coleman."

"Good evening."

```
* * * * * * * * * * * *
*                      *
*     S I X T E E N    *
*                      *
* * * * * * * * * * * *
```

Nicholas had dined well at his club and relished the very slight current of wind in the hot air that seemed to presage a cooler night as he walked along. He hoped that he would not get there too late, but had determined to put himself in a confident mood with good food and wine before he paid his visit. He felt somehow on holiday as he took a different way this Monday evening. And perhaps Sidonie would let him come tomorrow night—if he could think up a good reason for not going home. He felt somehow that now he could go to see her and leave his money on the table and know that even that strange hostile love she gave him was not tarnished by payment. This afternoon his heart had twinged when he saw her distressed and fatigued, as if she had been trapped into an admission that somewhere in her was a humanity and kindness, and could never forgive him for discovering it. Probably, thought Nicholas, she'll be more arctic than ever now, with that queer twist in her, and . . .

Ah, this must be the place! Nicholas smiled as he strolled down the quiet mews with their green gables and the noise of horses eating in the stables. It was inevitable that Elder should live in a hermit's corner of London. Nicholas thought in a sardonic way that this was quite an honoring of an employee by the great banker, Nicholas Bude, and he thought in a more sardonic way that Elder would feel about as grateful as a stone statue would for roses left at the base. How he had fooled him with his charitable thoughts about Professor Crampton. Probably Crampton and he had split the money. History of Ming dynasty, my eye! Nicholas paused in his stride that seemed to wake the cobbles very loud in the dropping light. Well, certainly Elder knew Chinese, so he had better not jump to conclusions like a kangaroo. He would feel his way.

Over the small green doorway there was a box of red geraniums, and Nicholas wondered if Elder owned the whole house. But a name plate of solid brass in the wall indicated two other tenants, both with foreign names, and Nicholas had for an instant that habitual English feeling of distrust which comes at contact with a foreigner even on a doorplate. There was a notice on the door that bade him not to ring but to walk in. Hum, informal, or sinister? Nicholas went into the hallway and was surprised by the age of the place inside that fresh young doorway. Somehow one felt in the dwelling of learned men or those engaged in mysterious studies. The largest gong Nicholas had ever seen in his life almost covered one wall, and Nicholas knew that it had been left there because no one could get it inside the small door or up the narrow cornered stairway. The gong looked so loud that he felt just to knock on it would send every fire brigade in London out clanging. He felt that nobody in this brooding house would ever dare to touch that gong.

Nicholas found himself walking softly as he went

to examine the name on the doorway in the hall, and then he realized there was no need to walk softly, as the house was carpeted so heavily that even the large gong would ring almost soundless on this pile if it fell down. The name on the door was Indian, Nicholas thought, and then he remembered that Elder's name had been the highest on the doorplate and that probably he lived on the top floor. Nicholas ascended the stairway in a silence that almost unnerved him. In a small niche on the first corner of the stairway there was a flower that somehow was like a blossom of live coral growing or embalmed in oil within a glass vase that was illuminated by an interior bulb. It was delicate and lovely and the glow somehow turned the place into a chapel.

The name on the door on the second landing was in an Eastern script that was only a pattern in Nicholas's eye, and curious Oriental furnishings in the hallways gave Nicholas a feeling that eyes somewhere in this twilight watched him climbing to the next corner of the stairway where there was another lighted niche. Nicholas stopped before the tiny Moorish-looking lantern from which an opal and greenish light dissolved on the open page of a massive book inscribed in strange and beautiful hieroglyphics. So exquisite was this cameo of light and color that for an instant Nicholas lost his fear in the wizardy before his eye. He felt that he would see for a long time that shy and ancient light diamonded on the ivory page, and that somehow the message of that Asiatic script was as legible as if he could read it like plain English. There was something here that came like an aroma into the mind. Nicholas felt the house inhabited, like the air, in a mystery garden. And the silence was like the hush after music.

The top landing or hallway was somehow cold and austere, and Nicholas had a sense of being at a great distance from the light that glowed in the alcove at the end below the parting of two blue curtains. He had a feeling of an Indian sky over the moonlighted Taj Mahal. There was nothing but an ivory globe of light and the blue curtains, and yet he felt his vision of the Taj Mahal had been the picture his eye was meant to see or imagine. He had a sense that later on he would require many hours of meditation to remember and understand this vision.

On the right the door bore a white card with the name: JOHN GREGORIOUS ELDER.

Gregorious! What a queer Latin-chanted name! So that was what the G. stood for that he had noticed today when looking up Elder's address. He looked at the card that was yellowing somewhat with age and sought for the bell. At first he could not discover it, and then he saw what seemed to be a tiny cupboard in the wall, drew aside its door, and found the bell that was a carved animal head. He tried to push it and found that it pulled. When he pulled it out there was no answering sound within, and he waited a moment and wondered if Elder had gone to bed. After half a minute or so he pulled it again, three times, and heard no ringing inside the door. He was just beginning to notice the unusual way the door occupied the frame, and the absence of a doorknob, when to his astonishment the door moved sideways in silence and revealed a small cubicle or hallway across which hung a heavy crimson curtain. Nicholas felt his heart stop. He did not like this sliding door that opened by itself and this small empty cubicle that was ready to swallow him when he stepped in. God knows what was at the other side of the curtain. For an instant he thought of returning down the stairway, but he knew that he could not do that now that the door had opened. He stepped in with caution to the cubicle that was illumined by a light fashioned in a serpent's head that stuck out two glowing fangs from the ceiling. He paused for a moment, and then the door closed behind him and he nearly jumped as something brushed him, and turned to find himself being almost touched by a dragon's head that was attached to the door. He backed hastily from the red fiery eyes that glowed at him and knew that now he was wholly scared. Anything was better than being imprisoned with this diabolical head, and he carefully opened the curtain and stepped into another cubicle. In this he found himself alone with an Asiatic god carved in alabaster that glowed in a green and golden light above the wick that floated in a bowl below it.

"One more cubicle," Nicholas thought, "and I'll yell out loud!" The antique and gnarled smile of the god mocked his fright, and he drew the next yellow curtain and stepped into a Chinese room. By this time nothing could astound him, but it was a moment before he realized that the mandarin or high priest who occupied the thronal chair at the end of the room was Elder. Confused as he was, Nicholas realized the loveliness of the room, and beyond in the alcove the glow of the evening light somehow reassured him of the world as it melted through the windows in a natural harmony with the glow from the lamps and lanterns that made a balcony of shadow over the lighted floor of the room.

Mr. Elder kept his hands within his great silken sleeves as he arose with a slight bow. "Good evening, Mr. Bude. I did not expect this pleasure."

Nicholas realized that he must keep his head. "Good evening, Mr. Elder. I just thought I'd come along. How are you?"

"Very much better, Mr. Bude. Won't you sit down?"

Nicholas looked about for a familiar chair and then placed himself on a low carven stool. He had a feeling that sitting thus with his knees hunched up he was at one more disadvantage with this Oriental seigneur who sat with dignity on his elaborate chair under a canopy of fine tapestry on a kind of dais. He had a curious feeling that all the blood in Mr. Elder's dried body had gone to make the splendid dyes in the robe he wore.

Nicholas looked about the room. "This is a bit surprising, you know, this place, Mr. Elder."

"Yes, it is strange how the very old can seem most new to the eye."

"Hum, yes, I hadn't thought of it that way."

He wondered what was written in invisible ink on the old parchment of Elder's face. It might well be that question he received by post each Monday morning.

"Can I offer you some tea, Mr. Bude?" Elder indicated a great copper urn on the dais. "It has been waiting for you."

At least Elder had a beautiful courtesy.

"Yes, thank you, Mr. Elder."

He watched the ceremonious way in which Elder dipped in some inner well of the urn with a giant amber spoon from which he filled cups that looked so fine that one might think they had been made of beaten air. Elder with tongs pinched out some leaves from a jar and scattered them on the tea which immediately gave out a delicate aroma. Nicholas got up to

fetch his tea, feeling a courtesy imposed on him by this
room. On his way over, his eye paused astounded on
what had been concealed by the dais from his view.
On a long couch on the floor beneath a veil of blue
silk a naked girl lay asleep. Only her feet showed outside the veil, underneath which a golden shadow was
her waist-long hair. Mr. Elder did not appear to notice
the astonishment which had registered on his guest's
face and handed him the cup of tea. Nicholas nearly
dropped the beautiful cup as his eye ranged the outline
of the figure on the couch. He stood for a moment and
then sipped his tea. He realized how delicate the flavor
was, and how the hint of citron was like a faint shadow,
as it were, on the palate, and he smiled in a polite
way at Mr. Elder.

"I don't know Chinese, but I know good tea."

Mr. Elder smiled. Nicholas had a feeling that his
smile was somehow detached from his face, like a
tranquil and luminous cloud from the land, and it
had a singular calm in it. It turned Mr. Elder's bony
face into a boy's, Nicholas thought, and had an uneasy
feeling in his conscience. It was hard to believe that
evil lurked in the spirit of this place. But it was also
very hard to explain this girl or woman or whatever
it was on the couch.

"I think we will shut out the evening," said Mr.
Elder, and moved slowly to draw the curtain across the
alcove. Nicholas watched the last rays of the sun and
felt that it was very curious that Mr. Elder should have
turned to close the curtain at the exact moment at
which the sun touched the solid horizon. Nicholas took
a step or two nearer to the couch and suddenly began
to wonder if this was an embalmed woman. There
was no sign of life or breathing or motion, and although

her head was apparently leaning deeply into the cushion, Nicholas thought that some tremor ought to show in the veil if she were breathing. As if he had just discovered his guest's awareness of her, Mr. Elder dropped his eye on the girl.

"Ah, you are afraid that we will waken her?" He paused. "There is no fear. In the land where she is now, our voices cannot go."

"Is she asleep?"

Mr. Elder indicated the burner and the opium pipe.

"Not so much asleep as gone on a voyage."

"My God, opium!"

"Why say 'My God' like that? A bottle of wine and a cigar do not shock you. Gas at the dentist's, chloroform in the hospital, do they shock you?"

"No, but . . ." Nicholas paused. "Once you go in for that, you're done for, aren't you?"

"So are you if you go in for drink, and it becomes the whole end and meaning of your life. She is not an addict. Sometimes she finds it good as I do, to release the soul from the hibernation in the clay, and let it go from the body like the butterfly from the caterpillar. She is naked simply because it gives more liberty to the air about her body. There is something about clothes that clogs one's parting. I think that is because the soul cannot altogether go and hangs by a last silken thread to the clay. She may be somewhere by the Ganges now, but that thread goes with her, like his life line with the spider when he voyages in air. I put the silk on her simply because you came in. But her body is no more now than a Pharaoh's mummy."

Nicholas was thoughtful, impressed by Elder's calm voice. "You mean, the mind goes away somewhere, on a kind of holiday, and gets a rest from the things that worry it all day?"

"That's not a bad way of putting it," said Mr. Elder. He paused. "As you will have noticed, if the mind is really worried, sleep does not seem to give it any rest." Nicholas nodded. Elder bent and touched the girl's instep. "Touch her, and you will find that your hand is not conscious of the flesh."

Nicholas bent down and touched the girl; and then his eye was startled on her right foot.

"Oh, what a pity!"

Mr. Elder nodded. "Yes, she is a beautiful girl." Elder paused. "I call it the hoof of Pan." He paused again. "I have no doubt that a clever psychologist, looking for the secret of the kink in her, might explore her mind forever and yet discover nothing if she kept that foot concealed from him."

Nicholas was looking in a fascinated way at the curious stump, like a tiny hoof, where the small toe ought to have been. There was a genuine pang in his mind. "I am awfully sorry for her."

"Yes. I know she sees it out of the corner of her mind's eye all day long. Perhaps that is why she gets so much peace and relief from the pipe. That sense of being away on wings makes her subconscious mind forget that contact of the hoof and earth. Would you grant her such an occasional peace if you were me?"

"I would. It can't do much harm."

Mr. Elder courteously dismissed the girl. "Another cup of tea, Mr. Bude?"

"Yes, thank you." He watched the enormous green jade stone on Mr. Elder's ring as his long white hands made a ceremony of movement.

"With that, I recommend this Russian cigarette."

Nicholas took the slender cigarette, and Mr. Elder lighted it with a long green taper from a golden wick in a bowl.

"Have you lived here long, Mr. Elder?"

"For some twenty years."

"It is a curious house to find in London."

"On the ground floor lives an Indian mystic poet whose name I think you will recognize if you read it as you go down. On the floor below lives the most beautiful woman who ever came from the land of Arabia. So, you see, you are in Asia here—if you can believe in this old banking fellow who plays at being a Chinaman!"

Nicholas returned his smile. He realized that he should have recognized the name of the Indian poet. "I suppose it—helps you to get into the East, as you might say, by wearing that robe and having all these Chinese things in the room?"

"Yes, I think just as the perfume hangs around the rose, around each of these pieces hangs still a little of the air Confucius breathed. Perhaps some lotus flowers haunt still this tiny vase. You see how it is like a round blue sky over the lake of water in the bottom. Take it, it is light as the very air. One feels it might be a bubble of air that floated from the artist's mouth. And this illuminated book, when I open it here, the page is like a beautiful window through which one looks into the poet's mind." Mr. Elder paused. "Alas, as you say, I have to have the furniture of my dreams around me, I am not like Coleridge, who can wake up one morning in Xanadu, and a stately pleasure-dome decree. Mr. Elder touched the opium pipe. "This must be my honeydew, and this," he raised his cup, "my milk of paradise. I am only a Marco Polo, who must ride a pack horse into Asia, where Coleridge rode on his pen. I must have my trappings. I am an old man with longings in me, that is all. Ah, but I talk too much!"

"You talk very well, Mr. Elder. I feel outside on what you once called the margin of the page." Nicholas looked at the illuminated page of the book. "On the margin of what you called the empty page. Is this page empty?"

"In a way, Mr. Bude, yes. If you look at the sky, when it is a tapestry of cloud and light, it seems full. When the sun is gone down, it is empty. It was all something conjured out of the air. But nevertheless it was there for the moment, like this solid page. That is as much immortality as we can hope for. But I talk on. My mouth is as full of philosophies as a child's is full of sweetmeats. I crack my teeth on them." He paused. "You have come to talk about something, Mr. Bude?"

Nicholas had an unpleasant notion that a lying story could hardly pass for truth in this room. But he felt a compulsion in him to go on with his mission. "Well, yes, I did. You see, I wasn't sure how long you might be away, and I have something in hand. I know a young author, a fellow called Rogerson, a poet, and I thought I might let him earn some bread-and-butter money, and let him knock up a short history of the bank, that would be a kind of record for us, and that we might publish more or less to mark the India loan."

"An excellent idea, and a better motive. How can I help?"

"Well, first of all, as you are the surviving Elder, I wanted to know if you would mind if we went back to the origin of the Bude Bank in Elder's Bank. The book, of course, would carry no criticism of any kind."

"Thank you, Mr. Bude. I would have known that anyway. Well, how can I assist you?"

"You can help me by letting me have all the old letterheads and documents and seals and crest of the Elder Bank in case we ought to reproduce any in the book. There are some, of course, in the bank, but I want everything available."

"Nothing is more easy. Come with me."

Mr. Elder went over and drew a curtain, and somehow the desk and modern furniture were surprising and almost ugly behind the lovely Chinese room. Mr. Elder opened his desk, went to a cabinet, and produced the various documents and seals and the great crest.

"You can take all these, Mr. Bude."

"Ah, I see you are still using up the old notepaper. Can I have some of the pages?"

"Of course."

Mr. Elder was putting the things in a case while Nicholas examined the notepaper. He looked sharply at Mr. Elder as he stooped over the case. Whatever was behind that white mask of his face, this was undoubtedly the notepaper he had come for. He had made up his mind to probe Elder with some questions, but now he had an instinct to postpone it. If he made Elder suspicious, it would do no good. Nicholas picked up some sheets of the paper and was going to put them in the case.

"Do you mind if I ask, Mr. Bude? How many pages have you taken?"

Nicholas suddenly felt himself grow taut with suspicion. This was a damn curious question. He counted the pages. "I—I've got five."

"That is all right, Mr. Bude. I just wanted to know."

Nicholas realized that the apparently casual piles

of notepaper on the desk must have been counted, and he was tempted to pursue the matter a little, but he was baffled by Elder's air of detachment. They went back into the room. Nicholas felt that he had not better go too abruptly and accepted a cigarette. Suddenly a thought amused him.

"You know, Mr. Elder, one day when I said that I liked to see life down in black and white, I think you were in a way laughing at me."

Mr. Elder looked at him in inquiry.

"Well, it just struck me that, after all, you've got this Chinese room because you wanted to get it down in black and white, if you understand what I mean. It's the same thing, isn't it?"

"Yes. That is quite an interesting thought. It's a matter of actualizing a thing. After all Keats' *Ode to the Nightingale* couldn't exist for anybody else but him until he got it down in black and white. Hum, yes. It's the same with a painting or a sonata. The imagination must take flesh." He paused. "I was just thinking of those letters you said you were going to write to yourself. After all, you could have imagined them, but you felt you had to see them to make the experiment real. Are you still doing it?"

"Yes."

"And I suppose they are as boring as bills?"

"About the same."

"All the same, they have proved something to you, that what affects the abnormal person does not affect the normal. Nothing is useless in a way. They are actual and therefore carry an argument and a proof." He paused. "Hum, I was just thinking. I don't know what you write to yourself, but I often wondered if a thought, once it got down somewhere, didn't have an existence that must affect somebody. I think a thought, or an idea, must have a kind of life of its own. Hum . . . Would you like some more tea, Mr. Bude?"

"No, thank you, I think I must go now." Nicholas got up. "Well, I'm glad I discovered your room, Mr. Elder. If I had just walked in and walked out again, I might have thought I had dreamed it. But now I can see it is the only way you can live. Well, I hope you will be well enough to come back soon. I'm more used to you and Miss Coleman than anybody."

"Good night, Mr. Bude. It has been a great pleasure to me." He hesitated. "If you will allow me to say so, I hope you will consider this house your own."

"I'll take you at your word, Mr. Elder."

"The door will open when you step on the rug, Mr. Bude. I have those curtains to shut out the noise."

When Nicholas got out into the cubicle he felt in some way that he no longer feared the dragon.

As he went down the street he felt the cooling air and wondered if Elder's curiosity could be the mask of malice and design. Somehow his instinct did not believe it. He sat on a bench by the public garden and let it settle down into reflection in his mind. Elder was certainly clever, so clever that suspicious as the question about the number of pages was, it was also not logical to believe that he would give give himself away. But why had he asked that question? And Nicholas felt suddenly that he had overlooked one thing. Surely Elder could not have been such a fool as to write his personal note of apology for absence on the same paper as he used for the *Personal* Monday letters, if he sent them.

"By God," Nicholas thought, "I'm wrong. It's not Elder. And I might have thought it was Sidonie if I hadn't found out about the orphanage. Then who the

118

hell is it? If the anonymous letters were inspired by his own declared proposal, it could only be Muriel or Saluby. But how could they get the paper or get them posted? By heavens, there was some Elder Bank paper at Barrington . . ."

SEVENTEEN

On the same Monday when Saluby rang her up in the morning Muriel lost her temper. She repeated: "I'm sorry, but I can't go to Dorminster today."

"Damn it, we missed out last Monday, and you might have kept this day free."

Saluby was annoyed. He knew also that she was likely not to go next Monday for a natural reason. She tried to keep calm.

"I don't like going in there after last Monday. That made me nervous."

"I don't believe you. You know very well Mac-Gregor won't be there today."

"I don't care a damn whether you believe it or not. I . . ."

"Oh, I'm sorry, ma'am." The parlor maid went out with an apologetic nod.

Muriel felt her nerves more jumpy now and continued to Saluby in a low, irritated voice. "Look here, I can't argue with you now. The maids are about. You must stop ringing me up here."

"Very well. I'm taking it for granted I'm seeing you today!"

119

"You are not!"

She smacked down the telephone and felt she had made a mistake in snapping at him. Saluby would not like being snubbed. She walked out into the garden and lay on the plot of grass in the corner. She loved the sunlight on her limbs and had felt it limbering her mind this lovely summer. She felt that since her ring was no longer a gold shackle on her finger, she had gained a liberty of mind that was more important than sexual freedom only. Now she let her thought range out again as she did when a girl, before she learned that it was better to confine it to the smooth Poona lawn.

She knew that she had been by nature a passionate girl who had felt that love was a wild mustang on the prairie and been given a tame cob who stayed on the lawn. She remembered the vexation in her blood when the subalterns who became human in a fox trot turned from men into dancing partners before they got out on the balcony.

Nothing at all happened for three years as the same day was turned over and over again on the Poona calendar, and then Nick came along to a reunion dance because in his war service he had been attached to her father's regiment. Mrs. Canjole, who always looked as though she would have been more at home in Mayfair and who had constituted herself Muriel's emotional guide, had looked him up and down and said: "Public school one or two generations, but gentleman by instinct. Bored as hell because he's got nothing in his hands but lots of money . . . Ah, his hands! All the rest of him is manufactured, but they are the man himself. Can't make them behave. Hum, a plowman underneath!" Mrs. Canjole had another sip. "Lousy with sex as a bull, and doesn't know it. Wake up like a volcano . . . Oh, you're dancing this with him! Hum . . . You're about right for him, but neither of you know a thing, so who's going to be the schoolmaster? Hum, if you don't get anywhere, I'm going to find out if the rest of him is as hairy as his hands. Bah, these bloody women here!"

Muriel danced with Nicholas, and a strange picture came into her mind in which he seemed to roam about like a dark and brooding peasant on a wet spring earth under a sky congested with black clouds and red dripping light. He stalked through a gloom in her mind, and she could feel his body laboring in desire and his emotions all tangled up in her blood. This strange and troubled picture formed in her mind, and she felt somehow that it was wholly communicated into her body through his hands, and that there was no way of understanding him except by the flesh. Also, there was a kind of coagulating in her belly, as though of a hot and thickening honey, and suddenly her mind sank altogether into her body, and no thought was clear until the dance ended and she was able to get hold of herself again.

"You were just drowned in it like in a sea of chloroform!"

Startled out of her emotion, she looked in anger at Mrs. Canjole's amused face, and her mind cleared in the shock of annoyance. Mrs. Canjole's intrusion into her mood was not less intolerable than the appalling accuracy of her remark.

"Why don't you mind your own damned business?" Muriel snapped.

Mrs. Canjole was not disturbed. "I can see you in a double bed already, my dear!"

"Well, I'll have a third pillow for you, in case you might miss anything!"

Mrs. Canjole smiled. "My dear, I'm going to miss *you*."

Muriel turned away to conceal her smile. There was no use in trying to hide anything from this woman. And somehow Mrs. Canjole had made Muriel's emotion concrete—had, as it were, identified it, and made her look at it. She danced two more dances with Nicholas, and they went out into the garden. It was a lovely night, and Muriel could almost hear her heart knocking on the white silent gong of the moon. Nicholas looked about. Words jumped out of Muriel's mouth.

"Now, for God's sake don't talk about cricket. Why do all you officers dance as though you wanted to polish your buttons on a woman's belly and then come out here and talk about cricket?"

She saw the mild astonishment in his face.

"I wasn't going to." There was a long pause. "Well, are you going to marry me?"

Muriel did not experience any of the feelings that romantics had prophesied for this moment. She said:

"You haven't had much to do with women?"

"No, not a lot. Why do you ask?"

"Well, if you had, I thought you might have suggested something else."

"You are a bit shocking, you know. What age are you?"

"Twenty-one, off."

"Lord, I am about fifteen years older than you!"

"I shouldn't let that worry you. Every man is as young as his inexperience."

He laughed. "You are a bit disconcerting. Well, what do you say?"

"Yes—provided you don't kiss me now, because that's supposed to be the right thing to do. Now you can talk about cricket or the weather, if you like."

"Well, it's a lovely night." He paused. "Are you always as edgy as this?"

"No. But I've had a little too much of the army."

"I don't know very much about you, of course!"

"Do you want a vet's certificate, or a peep over my shoulder at *Who's Who?*"

"I didn't mean it that way."

"Then what *do* you mean? Why do you want to marry me?"

"You know why."

"I do. So what the hell does it matter if you don't know anything else about me?"

"Nothing at all."

"Well, let's go in. I want a drink." She paused. "I'm sorry, making all this scold, but it's only because I know it would be far worse if we had a silly necking party in which you were remembering all the time that you were going to marry me."

"I understand. I'd have been looking up a book of quotations in my mind, searching for all the right things to say."

When he had gone off to dance with a major's wife, Mrs. Canjole inquired: "Are you going to marry him?"

"Yes."

She knew there was no need to ask Mrs. Canjole to keep it to herself.

"It's a date?"

"Yes."

"When? Tomorrow?"

"Don't be silly, for God's sake," said Muriel.

"I'm not being silly. You know the only thing about each other that it's necessary to know, but you'll probably spend four months in quarantine to give your mother time to grow a bunch of orange blossoms and for you and him to get on each other's nerves."

"I've said nothing about orange blossoms."

"But your mother will. She's the kind of woman who thinks a marriage is consummated on the social page of *The Times*. If you were worth a damn you'd have consummated it by now behind the garden hedge, and then everything would have gone all right, instead of getting bitched up, as it will."

"You certainly are very encouraging."

"I'm being truthful. I'll bet you a fiver your mother cries when you tell her . . ."

"Oh, go to hell!"

Mrs. Canjole had got it all right, Muriel thought wearily now in the garden. One way or another the wedding had taken four months to prepare, and in the end, there were eight bridesmaids.

Mrs. Canjole had called her aside at the reception. "Sit down. You look like hell. I don't know why the blazes you got asked in here."

"Damn it," said Muriel. "It's my own wedding. *Will* you let me alone!"

"It's not your wedding. It's the wedding of Mrs. Brampton to the Bude Bank. And your mother's certainly enjoying her marriage. She's as pink and blushing as a debutante in the middle of a menopause. By the way, I hope . . ."

"I wish you'd go away."

"I wish you would. This bloody thing's going on all day. I heard one subaltern call it a fatigue picket, and he's not far out. For God's sake, get out of those nuptial trappings and take Nicholas away. And now I suppose you're going to a marvelous hotel, with flowers in the bridal suite, and you'll eat a long, heavy dinner, all dressed up, and then you'll sit about in the drawing room until it's late enough to go to bed without the rest of the guests suspecting that you might want to go upstairs for some other reason than because you're tired. And by that time, you *will* be tired, and then you'll go into your bedroom and change into something that you can hardly tell from this wedding dress, and Nicholas will tog himself out in pajamas and a dressing gown in his dressing room, and then he'll come in, and cough, and look about the room, and you'll both stand there as if waiting for somebody to introduce you, and . . ."

"Oh, shut up!"

"All right. But if I were you, I'd stop at the first comfortable-looking haystack by the road, and behave like a man and woman, instead of a tailor's dummy being married to a wooden mannequin. But, of course, you won't."

And, of course, they didn't, thought Muriel. The whole evening at the hotel had run like punctual trains according to Mrs. Canjole's timetable. She had yawned five times before going up, and only the first two yawns were caused by nervousness. Nick sat with an expression on his face like a Chinaman playing dominoes. When at last they had gone up, they had separated at her door, and Nicholas had gone into his dressing room. She had sat herself in front of her glass and felt as animated as an exhumed Egyptian mummy. She got up and took everything off but her knickers, and she stood in front of the glass and wished that

Nicholas would come in an tear the damn thing off and throw her on the bed. But nothing like that would happen, she knew, and she wearily put on a beautifully made bridal nightdress and a silk jacket and over that a dressing gown and gazed introspectively at a hat and wondered if she ought to put that on and heard Nick in his dressing room and wondered if he were shaving himself for the third time today and wondered if he had shaved the hair off his chest as well and then when he knocked on the door it sounded like somebody knocking the ashes out of a smoked pipe.

When he came in, he was as correct as something out of a Jermyn Street window. Elegant bedroom attire of English gentleman, correct tailored look upon his face.

He looked everywhere except at the bed.

After a moment she said: "He's not here."

"Not here? Who?"

"Oh, I thought you were looking about as if you expected to find somebody to introduce us."

His laugh was disconcerted. After a certain amount of promenading, his progress brought him as if by accident to her, and he took her in his arms. Things went along in the elaborate way of an elephant on a tightrope, and eventually they got on to the bed. From that point outward, she blamed herself as much as Nicholas. Her body did not seem to be able to release itself from the habit of restraint that she had been forced to impose on it in proximity to the subalterns and then to Nicholas during the long penance or purgatory of the engagement, and her sense of ignorance was made worse by the one abortive attempt she had had to have sex with an elderly colonel who had given himself Dutch courage out of the gin bottle. And Nicholas, whatever experience he had with women, had clearly learned that while one may be a man with a mistress, with a wife one must always be a gentleman, and when they had performed a kind of slow horizontal gavotte on the bed, it remained as smooth as a Poona lawn. Muriel also remained a virgin during a week of some half-dozen gavottes.

It began to take humorous curves in Muriel's mind as she watched a robin flirting his beak in a fern pool in the garden. And then her anger returned as she remembered how all spontaneous instincts of love had vanished one by one from her marriage, until in the end, the business of going to bed together became as formal as going in to dinner. And some worse inhibition than all made it impossible for them to discuss it and prevent its getting worse.

Only once had each of them snapped a nerve and jumped out of the silent morgue of the English mind. One night when he had come back from Edinburgh, he had said: "Damn it, you do nothing."

And remembering that in her mind, she had said later: "Nick, why don't you put your gloves on before you get into bed?"

That closed the communicating door for four months, and repression festered in them. And, her nerves in a tangle, she had from this point lost her confidence in meeting a more gay, liberal, and aristocratic society than the army crowd. Unpleasant memories of failing to held her ground came into her mind now, and she knew that it had worried Nicholas, who, even if he had Cabinet ministers tied to his purse strings, had no more social standing himself than one generation at a public school. In time she had discovered that her lack of humor in taking salt and risque conversation sprang from the same feeling of shame about sex which she had inherited and which she had failed to liberate in her failure with Nick. And now, her mind opened as fully as her body by MacGregor, she realized that every social constraint in a woman sprang from a lack of sexual confidence. Once she had abandoned her idea of giving way to an accomplished Mayfair specialist in cuckolding husbands simply because she lacked confidence in her knowledge of sexual technique. And she remembered how that had given her a feeling of inferiority to women in fashionable society. And not once with Nick had she that confidence to instigate things which is the confirmation of a woman to herself. And now she knew that when she had laid her head on MacGregor's bronzed and thundering chest she had burst a thousand bolts and bars in herself.

Then suddenly Saluby came into her mind, and recalling her bitter talk with him half an hour ago on the telephone, she wondered why in heaven's name she had given way to this insidious leech. And then she knew that it was because he had somehow got inside her with the corkscrew of a psychological diagnosis as tangible as an anatomical exploration. Like a microbe he had conquered her from within. Unpleasantly as she felt about him, she realized that without him she might never have started on this new and rich expansion of herself, although before Saluby had come she had felt herself heavy and loaded with this summer as a peach with juice. It was the old story, he had come at plucking time, and the fruit just fell into his hand.

Resentfully as she thought about him, she felt in another way more resentful to MacGregor. He had just opened a door, let her glimpse a marvelous world, and then shut it again behind his departing heels. She remembered waking on last Tuesday morning with a feeling of happiness and solace in every corner of her being. And in a gradual way her peace had declined up to this hour, until, she knew as her thighs squeezed on her hand, she wanted him badly now. She had several times during the last few days almost written to MacGregor, but instead she had gone out and walked off her desire. Not only was it a humiliating thing to seek MacGregor, but she was afraid of the hold he might get on her. Whatever she felt for him was more direct and touchable than the urgent but inexperienced desire that Nicholas had aroused in her and which had dissolved in marriage. She did not know which feeling was love, or if either of them was love. And she did not know if she wanted MacGregor for himself, or because he gave her love, and she could not tell if she could get that joy only from MacGregor. But that, she knew, as Blake came along the garden, was what she was going to find out by the only known way—comparative experience. She would learn to tell John by Thomas. She wanted love, and the knowledge of love, and she was going to get it wherever she could find it. And she had no scruples. What did Blake want?

"Mrs. Biddle wants some things from the village, madam. If you don't want the car, can I run down for them?"

"Yes, of course, Blake." She paused. "No, I'll go down and get them myself. I'm doing nothing."

"Marvelous how this weather is holding up, madam," said Blake as they walked along the garage. He paused. "I noticed when I was coming over this morning, madam, that there's a good deal of trespassing going on in the Corner Wood by the village, madam."

"Oh, better tell Cantlebye, Blake."

"Well, madam, he don't seem inclined to do anything about it. He says the cold weather will put it right again."

"Cold weather? What are you talking about?"

"Well, madam, it's them young romantic couples from the village that's coming in and spoiling the wood."

Suddenly she stopped and looked Blake straight in the eye.

"Good God, Blake, what harm is that! They've got to go somewhere."

She got into the car and smiled all the way down the avenue at the look of astonishment on Blake's mannered face.

* * * * * * * * * * * *
*   *
*   EIGHTEEN   *
*   *
* * * * * * * * * * * *

As Muriel went round the last bend of the avenue, she put her finger on the horn button and then decided to jump out herself and open the gate. It was ridiculous to make old Fuidge hobble out just to open the gate. A thought struck into her mind—"How damned old money makes us!" Nicholas, too, could never stand a schoolboy giving a groom an order to fetch a saddle while he lounged about waiting in the yard. Ha! She wouldn't have to get out after all! As she slowed down the car, a young man passing on the road saw her, waved his hand in a kind of signal, and came over and pushed the heavy gates wide for her car. She remarked that it was a lovely day, and he nodded and took no notice of her. She could not recognize him as belonging to the village. He looked dark and Spanish, or perhaps had that mahogany color from the sunlight, for he obviously lived in the kingdom of the open air. He wore blue trousers of the cloth a Spanish peasant wears, and a canary-yellow shirt with a V opening. He had a satchel perhaps holding the things he needed for a life on the road, for he had a vagabond look and, one felt certain, a vagabond soul. There was a curious twist running through his dark hair, as if it had been curled just a little on somebody's fingers. He had opened the gates now and came over and looked at her in an amused way, and she had a feeling that his words got warmed on his red lips before they came to her.

"Would you like me to wait here and open it for you when you come back?"

But for his smile that would have disconcerted her.

"Oh no! Thank you." She put her hand on the lever. "Thank you for opening the gate."

"Well, it's as good a way as any of spending the day, waiting to open a gate for a beautiful woman."

Muriel remembered that she was the squire's wife and wished heartily that she was as sure of his social rating. It was as hard to place him as one of those Scotsmen or Irishmen who kept their native accents so that one could not tell in circumstances like this whether one was talking to a lord or a laborer. She felt she had better say something.

"Oh, don't you do anything?"

"Well, it all depends on how you look at it." He

looked up at the sun. "You might think the sun up there very busy, or doing nothing at all."

"Oh, I see. Well, thank you for opening the gate."

She felt in an annoyed way that everything inside her was visible to him, and that she could see nothing behind his green or hazel eyes. He had the air of a gypsy to whom every field is a home and every house a prison. And somehow he now made her feel that her car was a cage and that he was looking in through the bars at her. She could not wholly guard the curiosity in her, and she was forced to answer his smile.

"I'll bet it's got a radio!"

From where he stood he could not see the radio in the car, but he saw the flush on her face. That simple and shrewd remark seemed to be his whole summary of her and her way of living. She was so disconcerted that she started up the engine. As she was about to go, he looked her in the eye, and he looked at her as directly as the sun looked down on the lawn. She stammered out a "Thank you" like a flustered schoolgirl, and as she drove out the gates, she felt she could hear a laughter behind her.

The incident disturbed her, and when she had driven half a mile she found that she had stopped the car by the gable of a wood to let her think. She spoke aloud in astonishment. "God, I ran away from him." She could see his eyes like polished olives. "That's what he meant. I've got this damn car to run away from life in!" His mouth had stretched out lazy as a lizard in his smile. "He's probably not got a penny, and he's wandering about from nowhere to nowhere, and he made me feel a damn fool! Or maybe he's wandering about from everywhere to everywhere, and here am I sitting on a cushion in the middle of nowhere.

132

God, I wonder will he be there when I get back. Good Lord, I just bolted away like a damn dithery girl! I simply can't go back until lunchtime!"

She was astonished to realize how much this had upset her. She was vague and not interested in the shopping, and old Mr. Tynham in the grocer's had to ring up Mrs. Biddle at the Hall to confirm an order. Mr. Tynham had protested that he could have sent the order up with a boy on a bicycle.

Muriel left the shop and found herself in a temper. Damn it, she was the mistress of Barrington Hall, and she knew as much about the kitchen there as if she were a week-end guest. And she had asked that young man at the gate if he had nothing to do! What the hell did *she* do? She got so rattled that she drove the car up to the waterfall in the village park and sat there to kill time and think it over and give that damned gypsy time to go away. And suddenly she pitched pretense to hell and lighted a cigarette and let her fancy roam in much detail about what might have happened if she had also been a vagabond and had met him in a field. "My God, I was just stark naked when he looked at me, and I couldn't do a damn thing about it. What the devil do I know about a man like him? What the devil do I know about anything? Oh, hell, it's nearly lunchtime!"

When she got back he was not at the gate, and her heart jumped up in relief and then dropped in dismay. She looked at Margaret, the young country maid, when she got into the hall, and felt jealous of her. By heavens, if Margaret had met that young man . . .

"Oh, madam, Dr. Saluby has rung up three times, and he has asked you to ring him back."

Not even Margaret's presence could stay the angry

133

blood that boiled up in Muriel's face She kept her voice calm. "Thank you, Margaret."

She waited ten minutes before she rang Saluby, and now he began to shape himself in her mind like a black undertaker mocking the summer on the green lawn. She must keep her temper.

"I'm told you rang."

His voice seemed to cut into her like a cold knife into pink flesh. "Yes."

"Was it necessary to keep on ringing?"

"Well, you snapped down on me this morning, without letting me know if you were coming today."

"I told you I was not."

"Very well, I'll keep on ringing."

My God, he was going to be difficult! "All right, I'll come in."

Her hand shook in anger as she put down the telephone. She had not the least intention of making love to him any more, but it was better to go in and have it out instead of this telephone business between the village doctor and the squire's wife. God, she was getting very sick of being the squire's wife. The gong went for lunch.

She went in and sat herself down in the long dining-room and said to Oxinham: "Oxinham, I'll lunch in the veranda room in the future."

"Yes, ma'am."

"And don't sound the gong."

"Very well, madam."

"I like it better when you say madam, Oxinham, not ma'am."

"Yes, madam."

There was salmon for lunch, and Oxinham said: "Some iced grapefruit, madam?"

Damn it, she wanted something to calm her.

"Don't you think some iced hock might be a little more interesting, Oxinham?"

"Certainly, madam."

She felt a great deal better after two glasses of hock and thought a third might be dangerous in this weather. She had coffee on the veranda, and watched the pigeons flouncing about their crinolines like can-can girls. She told Oxinham to order Blake to have the car at three o'clock for Dorminster and then went down for her after-lunch stroll toward the Wood Pool.

* * * * * * * * * * * *
*   *
*   NINETEEN   *
*   *
* * * * * * * * * * * *

When she went through the door of the close, Saluby was looking at a book, and his face was pale and fatigued with annoyance. He nearly forgot to rise when she came into the room.

"Why on earth are you so late?"

"I got delayed. I'm sorry."

"Damn it, I've got a case I must go back to." He looked at his watch. "I've been here nearly two hours. I can't stay long."

She sat down and asked him for a cigarette. "I only came in to talk."

"Oh." He paused in anger. "Are you suddenly getting respectable, or have you got bored?"

"Now, don't make it awkward." She paused. "It's over, and the less we say, the better."

He got up and paced about the room. "I don't see why I shouldn't have the reasons?"

"Because I don't want to be forced into talking like a bitch."

He was losing his temper, she knew.

"You sound fairly insulting as it is."

"Now I think I am going to go."

He swung about and caught her by the arm. "You are not."

"Well, what do you want me to do?"

He picked her up and took her into the room and put her down on the couch. He kissed her and found her mouth dead beneath his and swore. "What the hell is wrong with you?"

"Nothing. There's not the slightest use in going on, because you can't seduce me. If you want to make a fool of yourself, do so."

He slapped her face and whispered in anger: "You are a complete bitch."

"I told you there was nothing to say. You insist on making a fool of yourself and forcing me to be unpleasant."

He walked over and stood by the skeleton. "Look here, I'm not a fool, and I want to know why you suddenly feel this way."

"You mean you must have your post-mortem, although you know it won't revive the corpse. Can't you understand the simple fact that I no longer want to make love to you, and that I can't help it. I came here hoping that you'd have enough sense to make it easy. We live in the same place, and there is no use in starting a quarrel."

"I see. It's your husband?"

She paused for a moment. "I very nearly said 'Yes'

because it is an easy answer, but if I did, you would feel that it might start again. No, it's not because I'm afraid of Nicholas, or being found out. It's—simply that I know we never had any physical sympathy between us. There is no need to feel angry about it. It might have been you who found it out first, and I just would have accepted it."

"Physical sympathy be damned. It's simply sex. You wanted it and I wanted it, and that's all there is to it."

"Well, I didn't enjoy it."

He flushed in anger. "You are lying."

"I am not." She got up. "Now I am going."

"Not until I have the truth."

"I see. You will nag at it until you make me say something unpleasant."

"I don't care a damn what you say." He paused. "What the hell do you know about love-making anyway?"

"Enough to know that you don't know anything." She paused. "There is not the slightest use in losing your temper. You simply will dissect everything into the bones."

"Good God, you talk like a sophisticated woman! And you're as ignorant as hell."

"That is just abusive." She paused. "Anyway, I am not quite so unsophisticated as when I began with you."

"What the hell do you mean?"

"Well, after all, I've had the benefit of your coaching."

"Coaching! What a word. I should have known better than to waste myself on a damn woman who knows nothing."

She smarted. "Oh, don't be silly. You're about as much of a Casanova as that skeleton there. You're just

137

like a cricketer who has a lot of swagger and can't make two not-out."

Her smile goaded him.

"I suppose you think that's witty. I think it's just damned coarse." He lost his temper finally. "Good God, I might as well have had an affair with the village barmaid!"

She walked out and was not in the least sorry for him.

```
* * * * * * * * * * * *
*                    *
*      TWENTY        *
*                    *
* * * * * * * * * * * *
```

From a Chinese dreamland in the airless bedroom of the club, Nicholas woke on Tuesday morning and decided that he would not ask Sidonie if he might go tonight. After a tiring morning at the bank he returned to the club for lunch and disliked everything on the menu. He had a brandy and soda in the smoking room that was loaded with a smoldering air inside the lobby windows.

Old Charndale spoke to him out of the solid tobacco fog that seemed to muffle voices and make tongues heavy as pendulums. "Might be able to help me, Bude. Got to get down to a place called Champton, in your county, isn't it?"

"Yes. About a dozen miles from me."

"Oh, good. Do you know anything about the trains down?"

"Not much. Hardly ever go by train. Awful service."

"Oh, crikey! Thought I'd get some country air, but

I don't feel like stewing in a train. Mulluigheadly asked me down. Just taken a place there. Know him?"

"Mewdly? No."

"It's spelled like this . . . Oh, I've got a rhyme about it somewhere. Show it to you."

Charndale fumbled out an old flybook printed with rainbow flies, and somehow the fisherman's wallet seemed a surprising thing to dig out of his drab black coat. Nicholas thought that perhaps when old Charndale snored in his leather chair he was asleep by some loch whose waters glinted and laughed below these brilliant flies. He had a feeling that old Charndale was opening a secret drawer when he searched the flybook for the rhyme. At last he found it, and Nicholas read:

One of Chekhov's Russians rolluigheadly
Thumbed his nose at England's Molluigheadly,
And told him very glolmondeley
That his uncle Tsniesakovsky
Died from a sneeze and coughski
Caught in pronouncing Cholmondeley.

Nicholas began to smile as he sorted it out from the phonetic tangle, and old Charndale rubbed his nose and said: "Sent it to old Molluigheadly in the hope that he'd get sense and spell it Mewdly. Ha! No use. Dug into his name like I'm dug into this club. Well, how the devil do I get down to that place Champton?"

"Well, dammit, it's not far from me. Drive down with me. They can either meet you at my village, or I'll get Blake to drive you on."

They arranged that Charndale should telephone his host to meet him at the Barrington post office. Charndale thanked Nicholas. "That's splendid. Might never have gone down if you hadn't suggested this. Can't dig myself out, you know." Now Charndale seemed to be speaking to himself. "Always a bit nervous about going back into the country, you know."

He put away the book of flies, and Nicholas guessed that he was not, after all, a dried-up old stick but an old man with some mortal wound in his soul. Evidently he was afraid to go into the country because he loved it, and it would only touch old chords to a sad music. Nicholas knew vaguely that Charndale had gone bust and sold his country place and had gathered hints that he was a picturesque character in his heyday. But there did not seem to be much sign of fallen glory in the old black-suited man in the chair. But what did the English ever know about an Englishman?

Nicholas looked about the room. By God, no Trappist monks in their silent monastery were so secluded from each other as all these members. What an extraordinary institution the St. James club was! Outside there were Hollywood cinemas and clubs with Negro music and theaters with Freudian plays and Manhattan leg shows and galleries that had paintings with square apples and all the higgle-piggledom of the jazz age as the world closed up to 1939: but in here they lived in a solitude of the past and woke now and again from their slumber to repose their eyes on the old prints of horses and carriages and asked Glynde to shut the windows to keep out the noise of taxis raucous in a traffic jam. And there was old Clibshaw, who insisted that Carraway should take out the carriage step each time he got into his old yellow car that was like Lonsdale's mustard box, as near as a motorcar could be made to resemble a brougham. And sometimes Conkyrie came up from the shire and took down the post horn in the hall and sounded it to call a cab and hailed the driver as

"Coachman!" And it was only five years ago at Ascot that Conkyrie had made his famous reply to an American who said: "Well, Dock, I want to know England!" Conkyrie had cocked up his cigar and replied in his grand manner: "I am England. Why the devil should I let you know me!" It was ridiculous, but grand.

Nicholas looked at Charndale and saw the yellowing skin on his bony face and how even the proud nose was beginning to wrinkle and noticed his eyes closing in his afternoon nap. And Nicholas suddenly thought of Elder and realized that Charndale also had a Chinese room. All of these men had a Chinese room in their minds. They slept, and went into their Chinese rooms, and waited for death in this club as a man might wait for death in his own coffin. The clubs were the coffins of old England. Nicholas looked at the clock. Charndale was down somewhere by a stream in the sunlight, his heart beating faintly underneath that wallet of gorgeous flies. Nicholas got up. England snored, as the world went up and down the street on busy engines.

Charndale was reinforcing himself with a three-decker brandy in an enormous glass when Nicholas called for him just after five o'clock.

"Got to brace myself for the country air. Knock me over if I don't have some brandy in me. Glynde, two more of these!"

"Good God, is this all brandy?" said Nicholas when the drinks arrived.

"Dammit, you don't think I'd order you water, Bude!"

"Lord, I can't drink this at this time of day!"

"Good, God, what is England coming to! You can't drink a three-decker at five o'clock! In my day, we drank by the bottle, not by the clock. Come on, man!"

Nicholas raised his glass. There was no use in arguing with Charndale. There was a nice rosy tinge in the old man's face. Nicholas guessed that he was excited by his adventuring back into the country. He had an awful feeling that Charndale under the influence of the green fields and the golden brandy might open his soul to him on the journey down. Now that he had divined that Charndale buried himself in London because of his intolerable love for the countryside, he feared a disclosure of whatever history lay within the yellow page of his face. But now Charndale smacked home his brandy, and they went out into the hallway to find Carraway ready with an old shabby Gladstone bag.

Charndale sat himself in the Rolls-Royce as if he would have been happier in an old gig.

"Hate that damned fug-hole," he grunted. "Don't know why I live there!"

Nicholas was surprised by the rasp in his voice as he spoke of the club. Then Charndale relaxed into silence as they drove through London. He woke up as they passed a block of stone by the curb of a street in which the old livery-stable sign still gave its name to a garage.

"Hum. Old mounting block still there! Takes a man to get on a horse. Any old woman can get into a car."

There was another long silence, and as they went into the suburbs Charndale grunted again and closed his eyes. Nicholas thought he was going to sleep, then realized that he might have shut his eyes to avoid seeing the ugly houses. Soon the gregarious suburb began to scatter into green outskirts, and at last, as if he smelled it, Charndale opened his eyes and cocked it on the first green field.

"Ha, beginning to feel at home now!"

Charndale rummaged in his old bag and got out a

142

green stalking hat furnished with fly and feather and cocked it over his eye that seemed to get a permanent wink in it as he expanded suddenly into ribald and marvelous tales of moonlight gallops, elopements, wild gig races.

"Pah, these young people think we are fools to keep our horses and traps in the country still. Don't know what they are talking about. Don't know what hoofs say on the road, nor what the wheels of a carriage sing. Bah, this car—don't mean to be rude—is just a glass cage to keep you from the country. Young people today always going somewhere. Never realize that somewhere is where they are. Think England's always round the corner. Like a farmer coming to London to buy hay. Ridiculous. Whole damned world today going to its own funeral. So what the devil is the hurry? Might as well jog along as gallop to a graveyard. Bah."

Charndale let down the window and felt the green oxygen come into his lungs, and somehow old England reddened on his tongue, and Nicholas felt that he could hear the heartbeat of hoofs on the turnpike road. He was surprised to find they had reached Barrington.

"Oh, lovely old village, Bude!"

"Yes."

There was a limousine waiting on the road across from the post office, and Nicholas guessed it was for Charndale. Blake pulled up by the post office, and Nicholas leaned his head out to question the chauffeur of the limousine on the other side of the road.

Then he hear Charndale gasp and exclaim: "By the Lord Harry, a real fizzer! Didn't think they bred 'em like that any more!" Nicholas looked around. "Just gone into the post office, Bude. No wonder you live down here! Going to wait here until she comes out. Hope you know her! Is that the Molluigheadly car? Good? Well, I enjoyed the trip. Damned good of you. Green smell in my nose again. Old heart going for a canter over the fields. . . By Gad, here she comes! The real spunk in her! Just touch her and she'd jump like a trout. Look at the way she swings from the loin like a thoroughbred. Legs that are legs all the way up!" She stopped to talk to old Siddleby, the market gardener, and Charndale kept on talking about her with a ringside look in his eye. "Like a thunderstorm of gold! Mouth that clings to the eye. Moist as a blood rose on a dewy morning. Go through the regiment in my day like a forest fire. Enough to make Byron rise in his grave. God, I wish I had the old rosin in me now. I'd be gone a mile down the road with her already. Take her from my own brother. Good on top, too. Like a woman with something in front. Most of 'em built like a board now. Coffin-chested. Can feel a girl like her trembling like a blood filly on the rein. By Gad, there's something still growing on the green fields of England. O for the young Lochinvar! Haven't seen a woman like that since . . . Oh, she knows you!"

Blake touched his cap and opened the door.

"Hello, Nick, just walked down to get the post."

"Hello. Do you know Lord Charndale? My wife."

"Good God . . . Ahm, how dy'e do, Mrs. Bude." Charndale was trying to get his wind again. "Your husband has just given me a lift down." He turned to Nicholas. "I'll be damned if I apologize to you! You could have stopped me." He looked Muriel up and down. "I stand by all I said."

Before they parted, Charndale had asked himself to lunch at Barrington on his way back from Champton. As he drove away in the Molluigheadly car, he mut-

144

tered: "Whew! Where the hell did he get her! By the Lord Henry God, she'd salt Methuselah's rump and send him bucking like a mustang!"

Nicholas sat almost silent in the car as Blake took them slowly up to Barrington. He looked at Muriel as if he had only just met her for the first time. Charndale wasn't the kind to throw his tongue unless a woman was worth the music. Now she was glowing like a Polynesian girl, and her eyes, catching light from the blue jewel she wore below her throat, burned like Caribbean pools. She was a thunderstorm of gold, as Charndale had put it in his vivid phrasing. And her frock, a gypsy that laughed at Paris, could not burn up her golden skin in all its brilliant flames. Something throbbed out of her like electricity and rippled into his blood. What in God's name was happening to her? Last summer she would not have sprung such an excite·ment in Charndale. Thoughts flared up in Nicholas like the flamenco lightnings in her frock and burned themselves out in air. He was glad when they got home. When he got out of the car he had a curious feeling that he had stepped down into a sudden silence. He wondered if her orchestra of colors had made that sensation of noise in the car. And then he realized that it wasn't that or the humming of the engine. It had been his own tumultuous blood thrumming into his head.

Beyond the hills the sun in a phantasmagora of clouds was an extravaganza of light. Muriel stood on the lawn within its glow, like a Tahitian girl in a tropical garden. Nicholas, standing on the gravel in his blue suit with his case in his hand, felt somehow like a tired clerk waiting for the six-fifteen at Waterloo and looking at a poster of a glorious island thousands

145

of miles away. Muriel ran down the lawn with the dogs, and her frock glittered like a Brazilian bird and soon she was lost under a rainbow of light. Nicholas sat on the rustic seat by the steps and felt that he could no more reach her than he could read that strange Arabian script on the page that Elder had shown him. The woman who had been too familiar now had become too foreign. What the hell more did he know of her than he knew of Elder and Sidonie? They were all like Orientals in a Chinese room. He remembered his remark to Elder that he liked life to be clear and plain in black and white. What a damn fool Elder must have thought him, from his Chinese room. He looked down at the lodge that now was lost under a blue smoke like an opium haze. Whatever was the reason, ever since that crazy Fuidge girl had committed death by her own hand, the whole of his familiar world was revolving under his feet like a magic carpet that he could not get a foothold on. Elder was a Chinaman behind the green door in the mews; Sidonie was an Indian temple girl who purged him of lust; and now Muriel had become a Tahitian beauty with fragrant oils inside her golden belly. And he had got to the stage when he felt he knew as much about himself as he did about that Buddha shining in amber light in Elder's house. . . .

Ah, here was Margaret calling him for his tea! He went into the drawing room and poured out a cup. Then he got up and went over and looked at the Chinese landscape that was as shining and transparent as if it had been got somehow on to a surface of air by a glass blower instead of being painted on cloth or wood or whatever solid the artist used. Then he looked out at the green lawn of Barrington with its single oaks and black Jerseys and suddenly he felt that he knew as much about what lay within and behind the Chinese landscape with its temples and yellow bullocks and languid drover as he did about this English lawn. Suddenly from nowhere a saying of his father's came into his mind: "I must go and have a good talk with myself!" He recalled the old man's hoary tongue and homely wisdom, and went upstairs and sat down in his bedroom and asked himself what the hell he wanted out of life or if he wanted anything at all or if he was getting anything at all or if there was anything at all to get.

After some time it began to sort itself out in his mind. From the time he had gone into the bank until he met Muriel, he had on the whole been content with the job of qualifying himself to be head of an important bank. That meant a knowledge of the Bourse and Wall Street and the City and enough political background to handle those profitable imperial loans and to understand the mind of that honest rogue, the Englishman. He knew that he was the youngest man in England, or perhaps in the world, to hold his position, and he tried to age his mind. After one year in the chair, he had become, like an Etonian after one year at Eton, an old man. One by one he had given up games, as he began to sit on government advisory boards and handle loans, and he had long lost any sense of importance in the fact that he was a Rowing Blue at Oxford. That kind of thing only mattered to one of those thousand-a-year fellows who sculled or batted their way into a good job or a good club. And now, at the moment, he was in Dorman's Royal Flush, as the Council of Five who advised the Treasury was known. He was as good as in the Lords, and he might

147

even get a ministry in the future, as the India loan business had practically bought him a Cabinet chair. In fact, the only thing that made him a doubtful man in the eyes of Whitehall was the suspicion that he was just an efficient robot with no ambition. Whitehall, indeed, had begun to suspect the plain truth that he was bored into his success. He simply did things well because they bored him so much that he wanted to get them out of the way, and thus got a decision out of a Whitehall pigeon hole by the ingenious method of forcing it out by the insertion of his own. He knew what Whitehall thought, and they had guessed the truth. He was bored by the multiplication of the same day over and over again and the piling of one penny upon another. He lived in the cage of Bude's Bank and was as bored as a parrot whose week is seven Mondays.

He had known all this long ago. Before he met Muriel he had tried to find an interest in woman and had put his head on a few casual pillows—and snored. Always he had dreamed of love as a sudden thunderclap in the blood. His soul would tremble like a seismograph at the earthquake in his belly. It would be something terrible and delicate, like a steaming bull in a grove of spring violets. The peasant in him dreaded it like a storm, and he waited for it to come round the corner of Pall Mall and shake the foundations of the world. In the end it came down St. James on a winter evening on a pair of high-heeled shoes and made no more noise than the whisper of pink knickers coming off in a Clarge's Street flat. The next one had a coronet on her handbag and a bedroom striped like a tigress. She had snapped at him like a passionate Pomeranian bitch and thought he had gone out because she had scared him with her tremendous jungle lust.

148

The other five were about the same, and then he had given it up for a couple of years until he met Muriel.

It was the long engagement, Nicholas knew, which had done the harm. But, his parents dead, with no brother or sister in England, he felt like a social orphan, and Mrs. Brampton had adopted him. That extraordinary woman, Mrs. Canjole, had stuck *The Times* notice of the engagement under his nose, and snapped: "Here's the obituary notice of another happy marriage!"

He had been angry, but he knew she was right. As the number of bridesmaids grew from two to eight, the wedding began to expand in Mrs. Brampton's mind until she saw it as the marriage of the Bank of England to the War Office. She moved it from the village church to a cathedral, dropped the parson for a bishop, when, as Mrs. Cajole had said, all they wanted was a special license and a haycock. In the end everything was according to *Who's Who* and *The Tatler*. And Muriel, a spoke in the wheel of the great English social juggernaut, her ribs almost cracked, as Mrs. Canjole put it, by her mother's elbow jogging, became more and more wrought up and crushed every day, until, at last, he dreaded to go out with her alone. She knew that her nuptial bed had become a social tombstone long before they got to the wedding. Even in the bright sunlight of their wedding day, Nicholas had a curious feeling that the confetti fell on them as cold as flakes of Siberian snow. All about them baronial England and banking England laughed on the champagne, and their laughter sounded to Nicholas like the rattle of coins made on those colonial loans to dark and profitable corners of the Empire. All day at the reception he could see nothing but his father swinging his pick and rooting out the natural gold from the earth, with salt drops of sweat falling into his mouth and the muscles humped on his back and polished by the sun. And then a Pharaoh back in Cosmopolis, he built the magnificent tomb of Bude's Bank for the internment of his son.

All that day Nicholas was haunted by the old man who had pioneered with his pick and then pioneered with his loans out into those secret pockets of the Empire until he had got the Colonial Office in the hollow of his hand. Once he had dug for himself, and then he had a hundred thousand black boys digging for him in those blood-red acres on the map of the world where the younger sons of England go. Old Jock Bude would smack his money on the table and spurn the men in the Colonial Office with his tongue and tell them to put their blarney about helping the natives where the Aberdeen men put the sixpence, and again they had to come back to him, for he stood by his saying: "Wherever a pick will go, a pound will travel. Plant money, plow it into the ground, and it will grow." So he sent it out to grow, and it grew in most places, and, therefore, now *The Tatler* man was busy photographing Mrs. Brampton talking to a brace of Cabinet ministers, and Nicholas was enjoying his own wedding as much as a corpse enjoys the wake.

Nicholas moved his chair into the lobby window of his bedroom and lit a pipe. He was trying to see himself in his background, and it was plain that he did not like or believe in this background, or in the social structure of England. Not only did he not like it; he did not belong to it. Barrington belonged to him, not he to Barrington. Did Barrington even belong to him? Surely old Forsyte in his gardens and orchards, Cantlebye in his woodlands, had a sense of proprietorship in

Barrington that he had not. His grandfather, who had once worked here as a plowman, must have had a better sense of owning the fields. If he were away for a year, Barrington would go on just the same. He was the most dispensable person in the whole place. But the bank would not go on the same without him. Therefore, his whole life was in the bank. He did not own the bank. The bank owned him. In what had he a proprietorship, if not in himself? Not in the bank, not in Barrington, not in Muriel, not in Sidonie. He was a millionaire who owned nothing.

He did not believe in this English scheme of things. Old Charndale was not the same. Give him a rod, a saddle, a gun, and he was a rich man. He was the old Englishman, the soldier or the hunter, to whom India was a tiger shoot, England a hunting field, and Europe, when he got bored, a dueling ground on a grand scale. A war was coming along, so he'd polish up his buttons and fight for his tiger shoot and his hunting field. That was what old Jock Bude would say to a Charndale, when he came to him for money to buy guns. Old Jock was never fooled by the parade of glory. He used to put on his topper for Ascot and call it his clown's hat. Nicholas had often wondered if his father had put him in the golden cage of Bude's Bank to see if he had the guts to break out of it. But it was not easy to get out of the money cage of England, or out of the social cage. Old Jock used to say that it was harder to get out of the Royal Enclosure than to get in, so many people were pushing outside at the gate. Mrs. Brampton had got in through the gates of Bude's Bank. Fortunately, it had all been too much for Muriel's mother, and she had burst a blood vessel and had, as it were, bled to death for the pomp and snobdom of England.

Nicholas knew that it was no good. He would never believe in all this antique pageantry, this business of looking through a St. Paul's window over the slums. Worse, he did not care a damn about the slums. Hang a ribbon or bunting over them, and the fools there thought they lived in a palace. Old Charndale had once sharply told a conscientious young Member of Parliament that a charwoman would rather see the changing of the guard on an empty belly than keep her own cakeshop and not have the time to go. That was Charndale's idea, and nothing in the history of England for hundreds of years made him a liar. Oxinham would rather be a butler to a lord than the owner of his own farm. Indeed, Nicholas well knew, he would not stay at Barrington, only that he knew his master was sure to go into the Lords. Oxinham was a snob and a bully and would not be seen dead in the village pub. So what the hell was the good, as Charndale had said to the young Member, of going about with a suffering Calvary look on your face, trying to help people who did not want to be helped. The people of England knew what they wanted. And they wanted greyhound racing and football pools and test matches and cheap beer and a dartboard, and if they went to a political meeting and a dogfight started in five minutes, one dog would be Australia and the other dog England, and somebody in the crowd would be laying the odds on the Kerry blue. So Charndale had advised the young Member to go to Newmarket Sales and buy himself a Derby winner if he wanted to make himself a national figure, and that he would get more votes for that than he would for a social-reform plan. It all sounded, Nicholas thought, a very old story, but now, as the century closed up to 1939, there did not seem to be any reason why it shouldn't go on forever. It had survived the last war, and would survive the next, and he did not see one single way in which he could do one damn thing about it, so it could go to hell.

The only way in which it troubled him was that it had ruined his marriage. The social juggernaut had rolled over their nuptial bed, and Mrs. Brampton stood with a leg in each corner of the bedroom like a sacred cow. They went to bed with all the ceremonial livery on and never got into their own skins. Whatever had been pristine and healthy in their love had been wearied down to a nervous longing while they had waited in social probation. If he had taken Muriel out behind the garden fence on that first night and thrown her down into the dew, nothing would have gone wrong. "Love," old Jock had said, "is war and bloody murder, and a long sleep afterwards." Nicholas had overheard him saying that to a crony one day when he was on holiday from Harrow, and it had shocked him. "Here in England," declaimed old Jock, "it's a kind of social polygamy, and by the time you get down to your muttons, you're so fed up that you might as well have one sheep as another. What with all this dressing up and wedding bells and what not, marriage will soon be as important in England as the mating of a Derby to an Oaks winner. They call it *Who's Who,* but I call it Weatherby's. Now when I was out in . . ." It was at that point that Nicholas, the perfect Harrovian, removed his ear from the keyhole, because old Jock had married his Deborah in a different fashion. "The parson's cob was lame, but there was nothing wrong with our legs, so we didn't wait for him, as we knew the old cob would be sound again in a couple of weeks." This was all very shocking to a young Harrovian.

As he lost confidence in his sexual power with Muriel, he had felt his whole morale going to pieces, and his nerves were in a bad way when some five months after his wedding he and Muriel went to stay at Haylton Place in a house party. There he got the further shock of knowing that Muriel was a social failure in the kind of society to which Laura Haylton and her guests belonged. Although she now had unlimited money she could not get used to the idea of spending forty guineas on a frock, and she dressed in a superior Knightsbridge fashion. And she could not get used to the difference between salted society conversation and the tedious gossip of Poona. Nicholas wondered crossly if she had ever read Shakespeare, who knew that it was a case of "the nearer the king, the nearer the knuckle" in conversation, or had studied the satirical Maugham. She was inclined to sicken on the bitter almonds that society relished on the tongue, and she had a habit of tautening her mouth as if she wanted to say "prudes and prigs." She was an emotional tight-purse, as Laura had described somebody else, adding bluntly: "She's so bloody mean with herself because she's got nothing to give." It was at this point that Laura changed the subject when she saw Adele Copland looking at Muriel with her sharp eyes, and realized that she was by accident describing a guest.

It was here that Nicholas became aware of the habit of hoarding the emotions which is the hallmark of the English middle class but by which society is not so much handicapped. Old Jock, he knew, would agree with Laura on why they had to live within their biological incomes. "You can't spend what you haven't got," Old Jock would have said. "The English are just sexual bankrupts." And Nicholas now began to wonder if not

154

only had he married a sexual bankrupt, but if he were one himself. It might be simply that he had nothing to which Muriel could respond. Surely if either of them had what each had felt in that first night they had met, it would have found itself by now. But Strangbow, an author in the house party, had said at dinner: "Marriage is like a novel. If it starts wrong you can never get it right. If I start a book wrong, I can patch it somehow, and probably can fool my readers, but I will never fool myself or the characters in it. It's the same with marriage. If it begins wrong, you can patch it up maybe, and fool your friends, but you will never fool yourself." That comment had haunted Nicholas, and he had begun to accept it as a hopeless truth for himself and Muriel. He was glad when the house party was over, and when he got back to Barrington he knew that he had given up his marriage as a washout.

It was a fortnight later that he had met Laura in London, and she had told him to take her to lunch at the Ritz. When the coffee arrived, she looked at him and spoke out:

"Well, it's just one hell of a mess with Muriel and you?"

There was no use in lying to Laura. "It's not going very well."

"Gone wrong in the bedroom, as usual?" He would not say anything. "I know." She paused. "Muriel would be all right if she said 'bloody' now and again and learned to spit."

"I know what you mean."

"Why the hell don't you go away from each other for a while?"

"Well, I'm going to Edinburgh for a fortnight on Monday, anyway."

155

"Oh, how odd. I'm going up there too, on Saturday." She paused. "Where are you staying?"

"The Glenbyne. It's near our bank there."

"Well, I'll ring you up when you get there."

Nicholas knew that one could not be certain of anything, but he had a curious feeling that Laura had not had the least intention of going to Edinburgh until he had said he was going. Behind the cloud of cigarette smoke her eyes were heavy black grapes, her mouth was a slice of moist red flesh, and her sooty black hair tangled up his thought in her body. Her mother was a Hungarian of Magyar blood, and now a silence enfolded Laura like a gypsy dusk. She would not talk any more, and got up in a moment, and said good-by until Edinburgh.

Nicholas was only an hour in Edinburgh when she called him up at his hotel and told him to take her out to dinner. They went out and dined and danced.

She had taken a flat, and when they got back to her place she said: "Have you guessed yet why I am in Edinburgh?"

"Yes."

"You are not going to play hell with everything in the usual way of an Englishman?"

"I'm going to play hell with you in a moment. That's all."

For a fortnight they got drunk on each other and stayed drunk. On the last day she said: "It's incredible, to think this is the first time you've really had an affair. Do you know that every woman in my house party wanted to sleep with you?"

"Good God!"

"Is it any wonder!" She paused. "It's going to take some time for me to get you out of my blood."

156

"Why get me out? I'll get a divorce."

"No. I'm not made to be a wife. I'm a mistress. And I'm more moral that way, queer as it may sound." She paused again. "Now go back to Muriel when you're finished with the bank here, and forget about me. If there's anything wrong with your marriage, it's not you anyway. At least you know that."

"Did you do this out of charity?"

"Don't be a damn fool. I did it because I wanted you like hell. But all the same I'm glad you know."

For a week after she left he went around Edinburgh trying to sober up from Laura. He had done almost nothing at the bank while she had been there. They had made love at all hours of the day and night. She had, as old Jock might have put it, roasted him alive on the bed. Now he knew what the whole thing could mean. The casual episodes he had experienced had only disgusted him, and Muriel had been no improvement. But this salting of flesh and scalding of oil had actualized love as something more vital than anything in the world. This was what he had wanted from Muriel and had not got. And why the devil hadn't he got it? All his instincts had told him the first night he met her that she had as much of it as anybody. But now his courage stimulated by Laura, his body cognizant, he began to feel confident that he could do things right with Muriel. On the night before he left Edinburgh he suddenly laughed aloud in his bedroom as he remembered old Jock's phrase——"rip-rarin' for a woman." Now he understood the spirit and gusto of that, and, by the Lord, when he got back to Barrington, Muriel was going to understand it.

When he got home there was a certain excitement at their meeting, and Muriel looked less constrained as she poured him tea. They talked easily by the fire, but, Nicholas felt, they didn't seem to be getting anywhere. The next thing he heard was the dressing gong for dinner, and then he knew the evening had settled down into social habit. When they had dined, they talked until eleven o'clock. By this time he felt things had gone to pieces, and, when they went up, he felt his nerves stick out all over him like pinfeathers. When he got into his pajamas and dressing gown, he knocked on her door, and when he got in, she pulled her dressing gown around her. Then he found her mouth cold after Laura's, and he was glad when she turned out the light, lest she saw his dismay on his face. Anyway, he felt that he now knew how to make love and tried to make her body more confidential to him and to make her happy. Once he passed, and looked at her in the glow of the shaded bedside lamp, but nothing came into her eyes. It was then he realized they were not alone in the room. Mrs. Brampton was there, and with her the four hundred guests at the wedding, and they were all looking on. This was *their* marriage, and they had followed Muriel and him into the bedroom, and it was impossible to be natural under their eyes. They had never got away from them and, by God, they never would. Nicholas resumed his love-making, and, in the end, his frustration escaped on his tongue: "Damn it, you do nothing!"

He felt her shrink up in the corner of the social cage, and then she made some bitter reply about him wearing gloves, that he did not understand, and he knew it was hopeless with her. During the four months' engagement she had had time to remember all the social rules that govern English drawing rooms and then go upstairs and govern English bedrooms. When he got back into his own bedroom, he stood by the window and exclaimed aloud to himself:

"By God, it's as frightful as going to bed with my own sister! I suppose that's what they call being respectable!"

They avoided each other for four months after that, and since then it had got worse and worse. When he realized that they were not going to have any children, he felt the whole inside of his life was empty. She had gone to Harley Street, and Harley Street had said there was no physical reason, except that one of them must be barren. But always he felt that old Jock would have said: "To hell with Harley Street! There's nothing wrong except they put no heart into it!"

For almost five years after that, he had gone sour on women. He avoided social life almost completely, worked so hard that he used himself up that way, and had written love off his books. And then Sidonie came to the bank.

When Miss Olden gave a month's notice before her marriage, he had tried to get Mr. Strood's secretary, as he felt he ought to promote somebody in the bank, but he knew, and Miss Olden confirmed it with her opinion, that Strood's girl was hopeless as personal secretary to him. Then he had advertised, and when he got Miss Coleman's application, that settled the matter as far as qualifications went. It astounded him that a girl with a string of Oxford scholarships and brilliant mathematical honors, holding a good job in the Foreign Office, should want the post at all. And he was still more astounded when she walked in for her interview and he found that she was a beautiful girl. But he was not Jock Bude's son for nothing, and he went straight to the point.

"Miss Coleman, I want a secretary I can keep. How long do you think I can keep a girl like you."

She said nothing that an ordinary girl would say and understood him at once. "I am not going to get married. I think that is what you mean."

He could not help a smile. "Why are you leaving the Foreign Office?"

"Because I'm stuck in a pigeonhole. You know what Whitehall is."

"I do." He paused. "You can work for a week with Miss Olden?"

"Yes. I have given notice anyway."

"Very well. I am quite sure you will do."

After five days Miss Olden reported to him that in her opinion Miss Coleman could run Bude's Bank herself, and, after a month of Miss Coleman, Nicholas had come to that conclusion himself. At first he had thought her cold and detached, but however distant she was in herself, she functioned as a part of Bude's, and her work was as polished and immaculate as the marble stairway that curved up from the well of the bank. Sometimes he began to wonder if she were as cold and inhuman as that pale and shining marble. He had an odd feeling that when she came into the room, the air about her became chilled like the air one felt around a statue. It was not so much, he felt, the classical beauty of her face that made him feel that, as the calm, Euclidean order in her mind. And she had a faculty of keeping things up to a pitch, and Nicholas soon began to guess that the staff feared her more than him if a mistake happened. It was nothing she might say, for she never lost her temper, but her silence isolated one as in an arctic solitude. Her black clothes were plain and elegant, her cool hands manicured, her golden hair was chaste and neat in a coil on her nape.

Once, when she had gone out of the room to lunch, Nicholas had exclaimed to himself: "She's so bloody perfect, something must be wrong." He almost doubled her salary, and she thanked him in a formal way, and handled the minor matters he now began to leave to her without consulting him. Not only did she halve his work, but in some way she halved her own. He took her with him one day to a meeting with old Dorman, and that important man astounded Nicholas by sending her a basket of flowers, presenting his compliments to the most perfect secretary in London. She was a complete mystery to Nicholas, and he knew her value once and for all when she was away a week ill, and the whole damned bottom seemed to drop out of the bank. And, although she seemed so cold and passionless, Nicholas was surprised to feel all that week that he was sitting in a room where the fire had gone out. It was at this point that he noticed that, although he never saw her outside the bank, nor knew her except as an employee, she had made women dispensable to him, and he cared less and less whether he slept with Muriel or not. That gave him a shock, and he knew that he was aware of her as a woman.

She had been almost a year with him, when, spending a week in London while Muriel was away with her family, he met Miss Coleman in the park. There was a greenish light in the sky, and although it was evening, the air had a morning freshness, for the spring rain had fallen, and the grass and the daffodils glistened with drops. She was standing by the lake, in a long green cloak, and, with her golden hair, somehow stood out of the landscape like a golden daffodil on its green stem.

161

She stayed for perhaps fifteen minutes in meditation while Nicholas watched her, and when she turned, her rain-sprinkled hair glittered in the almost horizontal rays of the sunlight. "Good Lord," he thought, "how young she is! I never noticed that in the bank!"

"Good evening, Mr. Bude."

"Hello, Miss Coleman." He paused. "Funny to meet you outside the bank."

That was a silly remark, and she ignored it. "I didn't think you stayed in London, Mr. Bude."

"Only for this week. My wife is away." He paused. "You were looking at the water in a very solemn way."

"Yes, I was just noticing that when the sun is on the water it looks warm, and it turns cold in your eyes when the light goes out of it."

He smiled. "Well, did you get any lesson out of that!"

"Yes. That it's only what you feel about things that matters, not what they are in themselves. The water is only cold when you feel it cold in yourself."

He had guessed that neither her eyes nor mind were ever idle, and that she would not go in for small talk. She made a slight movement as if to go, and he said: "Do you always walk here in the evening?"

"Yes." She paused. "Good evening, Mr. Bude."

He knew that he would come there tomorrow evening, and he did come. He met her at almost the same place and the same hour. He was nervous, but he spoke in an honest way. "I hope that you don't mind. I came down here because you said you came here."

"I do not mind."

Never a smile, always that grave expression, that sense of being absolutely alone with herself, or in the company of a ghost known only to her. They talked

162

very quietly for fifteen minutes, and then she went along.

That happened again on Wednesday and Thursday, and on Friday evening it was cold, and he said: "It's cold here. Would you like to come somewhere and have a drink? We can walk up to the Ritz."

There was no particular sign on her face, but he felt she knew that the suggestion of the Ritz meant everything, that he understood she was the kind of girl Nicholas Bude could be seen with in the Ritz, and that he was not the kind of man who was going to suggest a place where he was not known. In a thing like this, Nicholas never did anything that old Jock Bude would not do, and it was his habit to look life in the eyes and not go in through back doors. Nicholas knew that all this was passing through her mind, and that she understood it, and, he hoped, she would not have expected anything else from him.

"No. Thank you," she answered. "Would you like to walk back to my flat. I can give you a drink."

All the way to Chelsea she got fits of shivering, and something warned him not to comment on it. Inside that cold face she might be trembling mercury. She had a lovely flat, and there were some paintings in it by a man called Matisse, a design by somebody called Ben Nicholson, a piece of marble that looked as if it might have been worn smooth and round by the sea by somebody called Barbara Hepworth, and a couple of vague shapes in walnut by somebody called Henry Moore that reminded one, after a time, of seals in the zoo. It was later on that he learned the names of the people who had worked these, and later still that he found out that they were valuable. But on the first evening he just noticed that they somehow belonged to the room and her and did not get in the way of his eye.

She was very cool and formal and yet made him completely at home. She mixed a hot claret cup in which she put various things that he did not know, and then burned some brown sugar and stirred it in and grated a nutmeg over it, and with some nut-flavored biscuits, it was delicious. She did almost all this in silence, and he began to feel his hands were in his way, and he did not quite know what to do with them, and now, more than ever, they seemed to have an existence of their own, and wanted to touch her much as a child might want to touch a rose to find out if it felt as it smelled. The claret warmed him, but did not seem able to prevent her fits of trembling, and he knew that she did not smoke a cigarette because she could not hold it steady.

"I am sorry," she said, "I can't stop shivering. It's the cold air."

He knew by now it was not the cold air, only her electric nerves, but he nodded.

"I like this place. Can I come again?"

"Yes. Come tomorrow...Oh, it's Saturday. I suppose you're going home for the week-end?"

"I am not."

It was at that instant that he decided to stay in London, and he thought she guessed it, and did not mind.

"Very well. Come at nine o'clock."

The next evening he came at nine o'clock, and she wore a frock that in some way made him less conscious of that feeling she gave of mind dominating body. There was a silence when she gave him a drink, and he seemed to have no control over his hands. She again had fits of trembling and she laughed uneasily.

164

"I am sorry. I am nervous."

"You are no worse than I am."

"Oh . . ."

"I am just wondering if I am in love with you."

She got up and walked about, and one could feel the tension as she calmed herself.

"If you come here, you must not talk about love."

"I am sorry." He paused. "I meant what I said."

"I know."

As she was going back to her chair his hand went out and touched her hand. He took it away as if from a live wire.

"I am sorry. I couldn't help that."

"Yes, I know."

She sat in silence and had gone cold white. Then she got up and said: "I can't stand it. This damned shivering . . ."

When he got up and took her in his arms, it was to comfort her. She kept on shivering, and a sweat came on her forehead, and if one touched any part of her body it jumped. When he kissed her, she seemed unable to kiss him back, and he could not bear her agitation.

"You are all on edge," he said. "I am going now."

"No. Don't go. I must get over it. I couldn't bear all this again. I . . ."

Then he knew that she could only get out of this by letting herself go in passion. Currents seemed to be passing through her body like ripples through a snake. Suddenly she gave him her mouth and began to beseech his body with her hands, and he knew nothing more except that he wanted her and he took her in to the bed. So fierce was their mating that it was afterwards he realized that she was a virgin.

"Yes. I was frightened."

After that, there was no trace ot the frightened girl, and he never got near her again. Their passion was a kind of catharsis that purged their bodies and never touched their minds. For some reason that she could not disclose she left Chelsea and took an expensive flat. Often, he felt that she hated him, but could not do without him, and he dared not approach her with tenderness of speech or touch. Very soon, she gave up kissing him and would never let down her hair, but, sexually, she was completely a woman and had by instinct as much ingenuity as Laura had by experience. In some way, she seemed to let her body love him freely, but withheld her mouth and her mind and her soul, if she had a soul. She began to upset him, because he could not understand this kink in her, and, often, he felt that he would have to give her up. But in some mysterious way he felt that to give her up would be to leave her alone, in that frightened solitude she had in her. She was like a hermit who compelled one to go out into the wilderness and keep her company. Often he felt that she would prefer him to hate her than love her, and when he bought her a diamond clasp, he thought that she had almost accomplished that.

"I don't wear jewels," she said coldly. "If you want to give me something, I would prefer money."

He almost walked out. He was shocked at her plain way of putting it. But he knew by now that he would never understand her, and he supposed that it was no good trying, and on every Monday evening, he left an envelope on the table. A hundred times, trying to compel himself to leave her, he had told himself that she was, for all her beauty, brain, and fine breeding, nothing but a kept girl. And in his heart he had never believed it. He could never feel that when she gave

166

him a drink, he had paid for it. Nor did he ever believe that she stayed at the bank because she got a good salary.

And now, he thought, as the light sank down to the edge of the lawn, *The Times* had proved him right about the money. But it did not bring him one inch nearer to knowing her, or understanding why she did anything.

In a way, he felt now, Sidonie had given him a kind of peace. She stayed cold and beautiful, like a Greek statue, and even when her passion gusted up like a storm about her, it could no more disturb her inward calm than a gale could make any tumult in the silent marble. She had become a habit, and hostile as she was, there was a bond that held them, a curious bond, that sometimes made him wonder if hate did not join in a closer union than love. But, at times, she was so cold and menacing that she alarmed him into something like a physical fear, as on that day, for example, that she had compelled him to give her the roses that he had bought for Muriel in his usual Friday custom, as if she knew that it was a habit that meant nothing, and could not tolerate it.

It was on that day that Sarah Fuidge had poisoned herself, and it was on that day that he had been somehow trapped by Saluby into pledging himself to write those letters, and it was on that day it was full moon, and ever since that day he had lost all sense of location in his world and all feeling of security in his mind. Had Sarah not died, he would not have discovered Elder's Chinese room, that had made him realize that everybody around him seemed to have a Chinese room —even old Charndale, whose Chinese room was in that flybook of small rainbows. Into Sidonie's Chinese room, he knew, he would never go. It might be an empty white room, like that square within the mathematical lines of the Ben Nicholson design that was somehow like a map of her mind. But he had been content to remain outside, knowing that she was inside, and had settled down with her into a kin solitude of his own. She was enough of woman for him, and neither at home nor elsewhere had he been disturbed by other women.

And now the astonishing thing had happened with his own wife, who for years had made no more disturbance in him than Oxinham. And with her, also, it seemed to have begun on the day Sarah had died.

He relighted his pipe and pulled it in long draughts as if he would inhale some oxygen into his mind to enable it to understand this change in Muriel. It was extraordinary that a dull if very nice-looking woman should develop almost overnight into the vital person who had excited Charndale. And nothing struck him more than the fact that Charndale had clearly felt she was a thoroughbred. Unpleasant as the thought was, Nicholas would not have sworn on the Book that Muriel was a gentlewoman in the natural sense of the word, and she had never handled the staff at Barrington with assurance or walked into a room as if she owned it. He had noticed that as lately as the day Sarah died. But now she had altogether a new air, and, Nicholas realized, Oxinham in his own sphere must be almost as puzzled as he was. For it was unquestionable that Oxinham was now afraid of her.

Nicholas almost spoke his thought aloud: "Good God, it must be an affair. Nothing else can explain it." He did not care fourpence if she were having an affair —in fact, after his own awakening with Laura he had

168

prayed for Muriel to have a similar experience—but he could not believe it was with Saluby, although her changing seemed to date from his arrival. That skinflinted neurotic could not have turned Muriel into this woman conscious of her sex appeal. For she knew damned well, she'd got it now, wherever it had come from in this torrid summer. It was amazing, but, after all, he had been thirty-six himself before Laura had enabled him to know what had been asleep in his own body. And, if it was Laura with him, it was somebody else with her, for that kind of thing didn't happen by itself. He did not care who it was, or what her secret was, but he cared a great deal about its effect on him, for she had shaken him out of his content with Sidonie, and she was beginning to trouble his sleep. He was afraid of the whole thing. His instinct told him that if he slept with Muriel now, it would murder Sidonie, and he had a strange feeling that he was more necessary to Sidonie, and that he somehow belonged to her. But he knew very well that Muriel would get him if she wanted him now. By God, it was a ridiculous situation, when a man hesitated to be unfaithful to his mistress with his own wife! That had not troubled him during these last years when his infrequent and dismal sexual attempts with Muriel had only made Monday nights with Sidonie more real. But now it would be something very different with Muriel, and she would not, like Sidonie, keep her mouth away and shut like a Chinese room.

He stowed away his pipe. It was smoked out. And his mind was filled with ashes. Going over it all, as he tried to find himself in the social structure of England, in his banking life, to find himself with Muriel and Sidonie, he knew that he was only going about the outside of that Chinese room that was the interior of Nicholas Bude, and that was a place of mystery and shadow and strange lights, that Elder might guess in him, that Sidonie might guess, but that only somebody like Sarah Fuidge could know. When he dreamed at night, he went down into the earth like a badger into his warren, when he walked by the full moon his soul moved like a fish in a mesmeric field of water, and whenever in the daylight his hands got beyond his mastery, they were fumbling for the door of that Chinese room, to open it and let him go in there alone. He guessed that everybody had a Chinese room, and that many, like him, were afraid to go into that haunted chamber.

He could not get the Chinese-room notion out of his mind, for it seemed to make everything clear, and he seemed to know what his hands were always doing, trying to open that door. He had always known that Nicholas Bude was in his hands. They were the hands that for generations had worked the soil of the Highlands, and then the English earth of the shire when his grandfather had come down from Scotland, and they were the hands that had swung his father's pick into the gold. They were the peasant's hands that had to grip something—an ax, a plow, a spade. Clenched on the oars, tight on the bat, they had been occupied at Harrow and Oxford. Since then they had been empty, and they ached like an empty stomach, in a continual hunger for the handle of the spade, the iron of the plow, hard loaves of rock, the wet dough of yellow clay, the moist wool of lambs at birth, corn sprinkling through fingers, for the whole sensual flesh of the world. They wanted to build with stones, to pack earth about stalks and make things grow. And they wanted to do these things themselves. It did not satisfy them to know that Forsyte was planting in the garden, that Cantlebye was lopping in the woodland. And they never left him alone. He could never forget his hands. Some things gave them a curious peace. Whenever Sidonie was out of the room, he would pouch them about the Barbara Hepworth sphere of marble, and they would be somehow cooled. And couching Sidonie's breasts in his hands they would be soothed and healed by that white flesh. But even then he had not forgotten them.

Only once in his life, he realized, had he entirely forgotten his hands, or, perhaps, they had forgotten him. And that was last night in Elder's Chinese room. It was an hour after he had gone to bed, waking up in the hot club bedroom, that he had woken up out of a kind of coma and known that all the sense of peace in Elder's had come from the absolute forgetfulness of his hands in that room.

He looked at his great hands. He did not think they were ugly. They never fully opened and, even when hanging, kept in the position in which a man walking behind a plow might bend them to hold the reins loosely. They wanted to carry things and to close about shafts of wood and make them instruments that turned the earth and built and made chips fly from the boles of trees. They simply wanted to work, and to earn their own living. There was nothing very lunatic about that. At this moment, his uncle, Christian Bude, lived in a small cottage in Northumberland and earned his living as a farm laborer because he liked to work with his hands, and had never accepted one penny of the unlimited money that was available to him for the asking. And at sixty-five, Jock Bude had pensioned himself off on three pounds a week and ended his days in a wood cabin, and had come in, aged eighty, from a hard day's work in a nor'easter and sat down in a straw-rope chair that he had made himself and looked at the peat fire and gone to sleep forever.

These men, his father and his uncle, would nod their heads quietly now if he said that he was going to do the same thing, and they would not have stared in wonder had they seen him, the night of the day on which Sarah Fuidge had died, suddenly tearing up sods of earth, as a bull might tear up the ground when the light of the full moon sent tides through his blood as it sent tides through the sea. They might not understand these things any more than he understood them, but they would not laugh at them, but ruminate in their minds about eggs in thunderstorms and such mysterious phenomena. His mother would have said: "Aye, he's got a bothering in his hands, and he'd best be getting a spade and keeping them from thinking." Even in her Ascot gown, Deborah had a habit of dropping into speech like that. And once, listening to her Harrovian son talking about his match at Lords, she had muttered to herself: "It be a bad thing for the corn to come up too quick."

Perhaps that was the trouble, they had come up too quickly in the world. There was not yet enough distance between him and the soil. He was as ridiculous as a shaggy Highland colt in the social harness. It was ridiculous that because he wanted a spade and an acre of ground, he should be shut into the spacious enclosure of Barrington. He felt like a muzzled horse in a grassy paddock. All around him was food, and he could not eat . . .

Ah, here was Muriel, coming up in the shadow of the laurel wood. A golden pheasant went up like a bright rocket in the evening light, and the dogs barked. Then it was tranquil again. He must put this history away from his mind and look at the page before him, that green page of the lawn under the golden lamp of the sun. It was something like this he had pictured at Barrington when he had got engaged to Muriel. She would come up by the woodland with the golden summer in her, as she was coming up now. In God's name, why hadn't it gone like this? It was pleasant now to forget the fretful Sahara of the past ten years and at least imagine paradise, and let his eye meditate upon her as she came up in the glow . . .

Then a clanging awoke the house. It was the dressing gong. Anger jumped up in him. It was this bloody gong and all it symbolized that had ruined things. His life was just an empty gap between gong and gong. Whatever happened, one obeyed the gong.

If he obeyed his impulse now and ran down and threw Muriel into the grass, in ten minutes Oxinham would be out on the steps looking for them in case the chicken got spoiled in the oven. He spat out of the window in anger. He was a millionaire, and, by Christ, he was earning his money. He was paying for it, and had paid for it, and would go on paying for it, with the whole of his life. He was Atlas, with the Bude Bank and Mrs. Brampton's England on his back.

When Nicholas got up from the window and turned into the room, his case on the table reminded him of what he had managed to forget for the last hour or two. Now it immediately returned and occupied his mind. Once and for all, he felt, he must clear up the mystery of these letters on Monday morning. In some way, he knew, he would never get clear about the future until he got rid of this tiresome business. Now he was beginning to remember his hands again and he stuffed them into his pockets. Whoever was writing these letters was shrewd enough to know his obsession with his hands. He considered Saluby. This doctor was possibly clever enough to know that he was unsatisfied in his life and it might appeal to his macabre humor to forestall him by writing the letters himself. But how the devil could he get hold of that notepaper? So far as he knew, the only Elder Bank paper at Barrington was some in his own desk in the library, locked in the bottom drawer, which he had just kept as a curiosity. And Muriel? Why on earth should Muriel, assuming that she had got the key and taken the paper, write letters to him, even as a joke? And the wording did not seem to be the kind she would invent. Also it did not seem a joke. It worried him. He felt that somebody knew hidden destiny in his hands.

Nicholas felt that even Elder's curious question about the number of pages he had taken last night did not convict him. There was nobody else but Sidonie—unless, by an extraordinary fluke, the letters came from somewhere outside his circle. He had considered Sidonie, until his mind had gone round in a drunken spin. Sidonie could have got the notepaper in the bank. She had the use of his keys and enough authority to open the Records Safe herself. Yes, she could easily have got the paper. And, Nicholas shuddered a little, she had some reason to fear his hands. More than once, in a black frustration, he had squeezed them too tight on her, and once he had, when he had wrenched the rope of her hair in anger, pulled it in a kind of knot around her neck. He had been thoroughly frightened by these happenings, because his hands seemed to be acting by themselves, tormented by that terrible hunger for her that she would not satisfy. In the most violent embrace of passion, she never yielded anything but her body to him. Nicholas wiped a little sweat off his forehead. He was afraid of this business, and he did not seem to have any way of tracking it down to Sidonie, if it was she. Once he could find the sender, he knew, his fear would go.

My God, he must have his bath and forget about it until dinner was over and he questioned Muriel in as casual a way as he could manage.

Somehow he got it out of his mind while having his bath, and his thought returned to Muriel. When he had dried himself, he looked at himself in the long glass and thought that his body, once glossy and muscular, was now like a lump of white plasticine. There was not a gray hair on his head, and the dark shag all over his body still showed the strength and vigor which had stroked the eight home against Cambridge, and which, as Laura had said, turned the bed into a gymnasium of lust, but his muscles had gone into mere flesh, and he put his thought bluntly to himself: "By

God, I'd want a month's holiday and hard rowing before I could have anything to do with Muriel." He realized that he had flushed in anger in the humiliation of knowing that his body had become too old for her. Like any man who has been an athlete, he had a strong physical common sense, and, once again, he remembered how old Jock would have put it: "A man who isn't fit to go into a boat isn't fit to go into bed!" His mind struck out at random in anger, and he blamed Muriel for the scowl on his face, and then he saw that this was a ridiculous attitude of mind and began to wonder if he could get away for a month, and then the gong went and he pulled on his clothes hastily and went down to dinner.

All during dinner she disturbed him, and she glowed like an orchid at the end of the table. They made the usual small talk that seemed somehow nothing more than a keeping up of appearances before the servants, and he said nothing personal until they had got their coffee in the veranda room. Then he said: "You knocked over Charndale today."

"Oh—how?"

"Well, I mean, the way you look." He paused. "You look about nineteen this summer."

Somehow this acutely embarrassed him.

"Oh, well, I'm getting a lot of sun."

"I wish I could get some."

"Why don't you take a holiday, before the summer is gone?"

"It's not very easy now. I'm on a thing with old Dorman."

"Well, it's up to yourself."

That seemed to mean a lot. Once again, they couldn't seem to get anywhere. He had a very strong feeling that she was getting sex somewhere and didn't care about him. It annoyed him, and he went over to his desk. After a moment he said: "By the way, you haven't seen any of the Elder Bank notepaper about the house?"

"Elder Bank paper? No. Why?"

"Oh, I just wanted a few samples."

"I thought you had some. I remember you showed it to me."

"I don't seem to be able to find any here. I thought you might have used it up."

"Good heavens, no. I've got our own paper. Why on earth should I use that?"

He pretended to rummage in the drawer. "Oh, I've found it. I knew I had it somewhere."

Well, it certainly wasn't Muriel.

"By the way, are you still writing those letters to yourself?"

That startled him. Was it a fluke?

"Ahm, yes. Why did you ask that?"

"Just curiosity." She paused. "It seems a waste of stamps."

"Oh, it's just a joke."

"Dr. Saluby thinks it's a mistake."

"Saluby? It was he suggested it. Why?"

"I don't know. He thought they were beginning to worry you."

"What the devil made him think that?"

"I don't know. But I got that idea."

"Well, it's nonsense. Saluby isn't the Bible, you know."

"I know."

"Do you like him?"

"No."

"Oh, have you seen him lately?"

"I met him yesterday."

"I suppose Saluby hopes they are worrying me just to prove him right?"

"Perhaps. But I didn't get that impression when he told me you ought to stop writing them."

"He told you that?"

"Yes."

There was a silence after that, and then she got up.

"Oh, are you going to bed?"

"Yes, I'm sleepy. Good night."

"Good night."

He sat for ten minutes at his desk. The puzzle was worse than ever. What the devil did Saluby know? Why did she mention those letters? He breathed in the perfume she used. Everything else went out of his head. He would either have to go out for a walk or go upstairs and throw her on the bed.

He opened the window and whistled for the dogs.

My God, where the devil was he with the lot of them?

* * * * * * * * * * * *
* TWENTY-TWO *
* * * * * * * * * * * *

On the next Monday, as Muriel rested in her room before going over to lunch with Therese Waldenham, she felt somewhat relieved at being today her own worst enemy. In her heart she had never believed in Harley Street's opinion that she was not meant to be a mother, and had safeguarded herself through Saluby, and therefore had been able to enjoy herself with MacGregor.

She pictured him in his cottage by the lochs in the Highlands. He did not have a pantechnicon of luggage rumbling at his heels, as she and Nicholas had. She had never got Nicholas away by himself from the bank and Barrington. Since their talk on the evening that Grierson had thrown the sailor out, she had guessed that Nicholas was tired of the heavy gold shackles that buckled him to old Dorman and the bank. But she wondered if he would, when they offered him a peerage, answer as old Jock had: "D'ye think I want to lift myself up by me golden bootstraps into the Lords!"

Nicholas had annoyed her all the week. He was, she thought bluntly, getting old. He was letting himself get old. And he was dull. He had let himself grow dull. He seldom laughed, and laughed out of his belly only when he recalled a crusty saying of old Jock's. She felt that Nicholas was a good deal more intelligent than he knew himself and that banking was not enough to use up all his mind. And he was developing kinks. This business of writing himself letters, even as an idle experiment, was nonsensical for a grown man. She guessed that Nicholas wanted her now, but she could not give herself to him. It was his own fault. He had let his body go into putty. Soon he would have a pillion backside. The realism of sex was giving her thought a realism, and she no longer dodged away in her mind from physical considerations. When she thought about MacGregor she thought about the whole man. She was being sharpened into an impatience by the feeling that she had been tricked out of her youth. She had wanted a Byron and had been landed with a one-pip subaltern. She was now beginning to understand the implication of the way Mrs. Canjole used to say "one-pip" when she spoke of army youth.

She looked at the clock. It was time to put on something to go and see Therese. In a few days' time, she knew, she would have a fresh problem—to find a new lover. A lover who would somehow remind her of MacGregor or of Nick as he might have been. Her mouth hardened. It was a pity that Nicholas could not simplify his vague existence to one plain need like that. She snapped open her hygiene box. She was damned well sick of English sexual bumbledom. She nearly spoke her angry thought aloud: "What a bloody idiot I have been! My God, how Therese would laugh if she knew that I never had any real fun out of my body until I met MacGregor! What a fool I have been!"

Therese, Muriel felt, was not quite happy as the chatelaine of Waldenham Court. This elegant Parisienne simply could not put on tweeds and become a country gentlewoman. And she did not try the impossible. She had dressed for lunch as she might in her London house, and one could know that her eye was pleased that Muriel had clad herself in such a way that she need not change for lunch in the Ritz. Muriel guessed that she was getting tired of buxom English-women in brogues with a dog at their heels.

They had gone into a small room for coffee, and Muriel noticed at once the special atmosphere of this room that was an angle of the house. One had the curious feeling of sitting outside in a green arbor, since half the floor made the lobby of the French window, and shadows of leaves seemed to rustle in the corners of the room. The books in the cabinet were dappled in gold light.

"Oh, how lovely!" Muriel exclaimed. "You'd expect to find a bird singing in here!"

Therese looked at her in a quick pleasure. "Oh,

how funny you said that! This is called the Nightingale Room. Nobody knows why. Perhaps somebody used to sit in here and listen to the nightingale. At night you can turn off the lamp, and the room is full of stars. The birds often come in here."

Muriel knew that her spontaneous remark, which had jumped out of her mouth, had somehow made a friendship with Therese.

Suddenly Therese said: "I think perhaps I can marry an Englishman, but I cannot marry his castle. So I live in this little room. You do know what I mean?"

Muriel laughed. She knew very well. This French-woman had quickly discovered that everything in England, this England of money and position, became a kind of castle in which one got lost. One was only a caretaker of a heritage, as Nicholas was a caretaker of Barrington and the bank. She rather wondered what George Waldenham was like. He must be fairly interesting to have gained a wife like Therese. Muriel was used to his photograph in the newspapers since he had got the Foreign Office post. She felt that perhaps Therese might have been happier if he had stayed at the embassy in Paris.

Therese began to talk about herself. "London is so hot, and George becomes so tired, he thought it might be a good idea to live down here for a few months. He gets so tired with always the crisis in Europe, and he thinks also it is good for me to have a rest from London. And I am glad, because I think I am going to live with myself down here, and be alone to refresh myself with my books and my thoughts. But never am I alone. I discover the English neighbor. In London, in Paris, I do not know who lives next door, as you say. But down here the person at *quinze kilo*—at fifteen miles perhaps

is *a côte*. I see all these empty fields and I think I have
solitude. But no. Behind each group of trees there is a
house, and in the house are people, and all these people
think I wish to see them because I can see the smoke of
their chimneys." She sighed. "So I think now I cannot
stand all this company in the English country, and I
must go back to Grosvenor Square to find myself alone."
She made a face. "They come, the big clop-cloppety
women, and they talk of nothing I can understand, and
when it is time to make the excuse, they say they must
go because I do not ask the dog in to call on George's
dog, and sometimes I wonder if they ever go unless the
dog wait in the car. Am I being rude to your English-
women? I am sorry. But you are not the same. You like
so much to be a woman. And they feel ashamed to be a
woman, I think—I mean the women in the English
country. Of course, in London, they are so different, in
the superior houses of the arts and diplomacy, that I
say to George I think these London women as much
foreign as I am to the country England women."
Therese paused. "I suppose you live nearly all the time
in London."

"I don't. I live always in this country. But I do not
see many neighbors."

"Oh, how do you manage?"

"They got tired of me, and I got tired of them."

"Oh, so that is the way! And how long time does
it need?"

"Oh—years!"

"That is what I have guessed. I feel I do not wait all
that time. So I go back to London when the summer
goes, pouf, in a rain shower . . . Oh, you think of
going! Do not, please! I mean you to stay at least for
tea!"

"I'd love to stay."

"It is so pleasant to meet somebody . . . You understand . . . Oh . . ." In a calm dismay Therese watched the car coming up the avenue. Muriel knew that Therese was tempted to move out of the lobby window, but Muriel's car waited outside, and, moreover, it was somehow ill-bred to avoid guests. Muriel thought it was a perfect *Tatler* picture as the car pulled up on the gravel. The woman who got out wore tweeds, of good cloth but Dorminster cut, a hat that looked as if it belonged to somebody else, and low-heeled brogue shoes. She was built like a heavyweight hunter—the kind of woman, as old Jock might have said, who could carry home the horse if he went lame. Muriel noticed for the first time that a woman of this kind did not stand on her feet, but sat on them. No other word could describe the way she was planked down on the earth. Now she was talking to the terrier in the car before she closed the window on him. Immediately she left he barked. She avoided looking toward the lobby window, but, Muriel knew, had remarked them before she got out of the car.

"I suppose I must be at home, as you call it?" Therese said.

"I think so. She saw us and has noticed my car."

"You can stay here. I will see her in the drawing room and come back."

"Yes, I think I'd like to be lazy."

The maid came in and said that Mrs. Henderly had called and was in the drawing room. Was madame at home?

"Yes. I will come. If I ask for tea, bring two cups. Madame Bude remains here."

"Yes, madame."

"If you want anything, please ring the bell," said Therese to Muriel.

When she had gone out, Muriel listened to the barking of the dog that somehow put her mind on edge. For two years, until she realized that the wife of Nicholas Bude could be distant, or rude if necessary, Muriel had endured this dawdling social bumbledom of English country life. At that stage she discovered that she liked really fashionable clothes, and discarded Knightsbridge tailoring and parochial hunting society at the same time. But she was punctilious about medical and clerical society, and the doctor and the parson felt they could drop in at Barrington at any time or call upon the Bude money for anything charitable. The Saluby affair was unfortunate, but she was going to ask him to dinner in spite of that. But now, as the barking of the dog irked her ears, she wondered what on earth right this frumpish wife of some obscure country gentleman had to come in here and unload the clods in her mind onto the carpet of the Waldenham drawing room as a carter might unload turnips in the yard. This greenwood *Frau* was not doing it out of friendship or sincerity, but simply because she wanted to prove her social position by calling on Lady Waldenham. Looking out on the great sweep of lawn, Muriel began to feel that English social life was a Ruritanian show of which the libretto was the social page of *The Times*.

Often, watching a play in London which showed this kind of life, she had a dreamlike feeling that she was looking at something as old and vanished as the court of Versailles. It was hard to believe that this was a contemporary world, and she had noticed that many petulant Chelsea young men wrote notices of plays and novels which showed this life, and referred to them as period pieces which portrayed a world that was as dead as Queen Anne. Sometimes Muriel wondered if these young men considered that their own parish of a few thousand people comprised contemporary England. Period piece or no, this was contemporary England nearly halfway through the twentieth century, and it did not seem to Muriel that it got one anywhere if you pretended it was not there. The young men might own Chelsea, but Mrs. Henderly owned England. The social page of *The Times* was Mrs. Henderly's bible as it had been Mrs. Brampton's. There it was, every day, as actual as this lawn in front of your eyes, and somewhere stuck away in a corner of that voluminous journal was an item about Chelsea, and somewhere else, nicely cleaned and polished up in tranquil prose, some news about those distant lands, India, and the slums, and tomorrow India and the slums would be gone out of the corners, but the social page would be there to chronicle inch by inch and name by name and lawn by lawn the history of England.

The young men who lived in the ivory tower of Chelsea looked out at England through a blind telescope and announced that it was not there, and that it must be something that somebody remembered and that had gone out as soon as Noel Coward had arrived. One of them said roundly that he wanted a map to show where Galsworthy's England lay. It seemed that in all his travels from Chelsea to Soho he had never come across it. Muriel had read that looking out over the lawn at Barrington, where nearly sixty horses stood down at the corner while their riders watched the foxhounds draw the woodland, and she thought how ridiculous the young men in the ivory tower seemed, until she was disturbed by that curious feeling that she had in the theater when looking at presentations of this England, and she had an odd sensation that all these horsemen were ghosts, and wondered if the young men had not perhaps some kind of premonition of death in this England.

At lunch today, Therese had in her a sense of disquiet, and it was clear that George Waldenham expected a new European war. Muriel looked hard at Mrs. Henderly's car, as if she thought it might vanish suddenly, and heard the dog's ironical bark. She began to wonder if a new war was going to make any change and suddenly remembered that when she had come back from school on holiday, when the whole country seemed to be grumbling about something going wrong at Passchendaele, she had found her mother in bed with a nervous breakdown because she had to sit below the wife of a ranking colonel at a dinner. Mrs. Brampton, if nobody else did, knew what victory was going to mean to England. It was going to mean a demobilization in which, thank God, they were going to get rid of the T. G.'s. And from Mrs. Brampton to Mrs. Henderly, Muriel could not discover one real change.

Now Muriel wondered if England always belonged to the last generation. Muriel's own youth had belonged to her mother, and after that to the Bude Bank and Barrington Hall. Even her body had not been her personal property until that day she met MacGregor. She flushed a little in anger. Therese took her for a sophisticated woman, and she felt somehow a liar in this room. She was just entering on the kindergarten stage of sexual education at the age of thirty-one. It was ridiculous. And somehow or the other, new workings in her mind linked up that failure in her life with Mrs. Henderly's car outside there on the gravel. It was

186

a safe bet that Mrs. Henderly went to more trouble about the sex life of that pedigreed terrier than she had ever gone to about her own.

She fidgeted in the chair. She had a sense of disturbance in her. It had been somehow communicated to her from Therese, whose whole mind was impregnated by the political and social thought of Europe. Therese lived in a world inside which things happened. Nothing at all ever happened in Mrs. Henderly's world. Her years began at the first day's cubbing and ended at the last point-to-point. Her calendar was on the social page of *The Times.* The only thing she would notice about Therese was that she was called "madame" and not "my lady" by the servants. She would put that down to the unfortunate kink in every foreigner. Somewhere between Mrs. Henderly and Therese, Muriel felt she herself was lost in nowhere.

When Therese came in, she looked as if her patience with Mrs. Henderly had fatigued her. "You must excuse me," she said. "I have ordered the tea." She watched the car go down the avenue. "You must permit me to be a little angry. All the time she talk of dogs, of horses, and people I do not know, and about the bullocks of her husband. Tell me, what is a bullock?"

"A bull with the pips taken out," said Muriel, who had acquired that much knowledge at Barrington.

"Ah, yes, I understand. It is amusing to know these things. It helps me to understand Madame Henderly. And a heifer, what is that?"

"Oh, a cow which is a *jeune fille* and not yet a *dame.*"

"Ah, thank you. I can understand from you. I think Madame Henderly goes to much trouble to arrange the marriage of her cows and horses and dogs. And she explain so carefully that her cousin is Lady Somebody,

187

I think she nearly take as much interest in arranging the classes of people as she take to arrange the animals."

Muriel laughed.

"Ah, here is the tea! Now, you must stay to dinner!"

"I can't. I'd love to, but I must get back. Why don't you come over next Monday and stay the night with me?"

"Monday? Ah, yes. George always stay in London from Monday until Thursday. I would like to so much."

Muriel knew the only reason she did not stay the night was that she felt she must get away by herself and think. She knew that she had reached some kind of crisis in her mind today and wanted to get alone with it and understand it. They sat rather quietly after tea, and Muriel felt that she was absorbing the atmosphere of Therese. She did not quite know what it was that made it different from the atmosphere of an Englishwoman. It was somehow as if her mind seemed to inhabit her whole body. There was a kind of continual flux in her. One felt the flowing of the blood, the breeding of the mind. Muriel suddenly knew what it was. She was growing, she had never ceased to grow, and would never stop growing.

TWENTY-THREE

The same Monday, on his way to London, Nicholas tried to concentrate on the leaders in *The Times*. Then he realized that he was not reading the words on the page, but those engraved on his mind—*There is a will to death in your hands. Whose death?* He tried to fold up the paper, cursed as Blake swerved to avoid a cart, then tore the pages in a violent way. "My God," he thought, "my nerves are gone to hell. I can't get these damned letters out of my mind." The only escape for his mind seemed to be Muriel, and that was like throwing a hot coal from one hand to the other to avoid getting burned. His mind was beginning to wrestle with itself in an alarming way when he dreamed at night. Once he had woken up in a sweat to find his hands about his own neck as if they wanted to strangle him.

Blake swerved the car again to avoid another cart whose driver was lost in a daydream and threw Nicholas almost into the other corner. He shouted to Blake as he looked back in apology: "Get off this bloody road!"

Blake opened the glass shutter and slowed down to ask: "What did you say, sir?"

"I said get off this bloody road. Take another."

"Very well, sir."

Blake drove with caution, and that finally snapped the tension in Nicholas. He rapped on the window, made a sign to stop. Blake pulled up. Nicholas got out.

"I'll drive. Get in the back."

Blake looked puzzled, then somewhat hurt. This had not happened before. "Yes sir."

"It's bad enough having to go to London on a day like this, without being pushed off the road by those bloody yokels."

Blake felt somewhat alarmed as Nicholas pushed down his foot. When they had gone a mile, trimming the corners of grass, Nicholas saw a cart loaded with hay, in the middle of the road. He sighted along the

189

road and felt rather like a hunter who had at last got his gun on a lion. He guessed there was just room. He pushed down his foot and Blake shut his eyes in the back and did not open them again until the whorooosh of hay against the roof showed that Nicholas had got by. From that point, until they reached the traffic controls of outer London, Blake kept his arm up ready to shield his eyes from splintering glass. When they pulled up at the bank, Nicholas felt somewhat better. He gave Blake five shillings and remarked: "Buy yourself a drink. You look as if you wanted one."

"I could do with one, sir."

"I'll bet that hayseed doesn't drive in the middle of the road again."

Blake smiled and touched his cap as Nicholas went up the steps. He wondered what on earth was happening to Mr. Bude and hoped profoundly that it would not happen again. He got a chamois and brushed the hayseeds from the car under the amused eye of Lord Cluricawn's chauffeur waiting at the club across the street.

"You're early, Mr. Bude!" Miss Coleman looked up in mild surprise.

As Nicholas went through into his room, he realized that all he had done was to arrive ten minutes earlier to get the damned letter. He had seen it on her tray. He kept his eye from it until she had reported the mail to him, and then got a shock as he saw the postmark was Edgware. "Good God, the damn thing is getting into London now!" A thought struck him. He opened the shutter.

"Miss Coleman, is Mr. Elder back?"

"Yes, Mr. Bude. Do you want him?"

"No. Just asked."

Later on, when they took the letters for reply, Miss Coleman suddenly stopped writing and said: "Mr. Bude, aren't you well?"

His hand jumped out and took up the Edgware letter that he had not yet opened.

"Miss Coleman, do you know anything about this letter?" She looked at him with cold eyes. "No, why should I?"

He felt that he was making a fool of himself, but he had to go on. "Have you noticed that it comes every Monday, the same envelope?"

"I have." She paused. "Why?"

"Oh, nothing, only I just wanted to find out something about it."

"Well, why not open it? That's a good method of finding out."

His voice, he knew, was a bark. "Because I know what's in it!"

She looked baffled and annoyed.

"Well, what were you saying to me?" Then he remembered. "What the devil do you mean by asking if I'm not well?"

"Would you like me to read you back the letters you have dictated?"

He realized that his mind must have been slipping. He felt nervous, and said angrily to conceal it: "Miss Coleman, why the hell don't you answer them yourself? A bloody counter clerk could deal with most of what I waste my time with!"

"Certainly, I can answer them."

She picked up the letters and her pad with a look of contempt on her face.

"I suppose you think you could run this bloody bank," he said.

"Certainly."

"I hope you approve of the way I do it." He knew that he was now being childish.

"I do not approve of the India loan."

He knew that he must either laugh or strike the desk, but his laugh was uneasy. "Oh, don't you? Why?"

"Because I'm not sure if you'll ever get the money back."

"By God, so you go in for high finance!"

"This particular loan is not finance. It is politics."

She picked up the papers and went out. By God, she was shrewd. More than once he had felt uneasy about this loan which had no government security on paper, and was really guaranteed by private enterprise, although it had got itself decked up with a lot of Whitehall blessings. He wondered if old Jock would have said: "My name's Bude, not Carnegie!" if they had come to him with a similar proposition. My God, he had made a damned fool of himself in asking her about that letter!

There was a buzz in the cabinet. "Mr. Elder."

"Send him in!"

Mr. Elder, he thought, looked very white and empty of blood. He put the letter away in case he made a fool of himself again. Mr. Elder went into the business in his usual monosyllabic way.

For a moment, Nicholas wondered if he had dreamed the Chinese room. When they had done, he said: "Perhaps you ought to have taken another week, Mr. Elder."

"Thank you, Mr. Bude, but I feel much better now."

"Well, go off, if you feel shaky."

"Thank you, Mr. Bude."

192

As Mr. Elder went out, closing the door in a noiseless way, Nicholas had a feeling that he didn't know a damn thing about any of these people associated with him. And he had lived with two women for years and was just as wise about them. Muriel in her own way was now as much of a mystery as Sidonie. Ah, here was Miss Coleman. She was still somewhat angry he knew, and that somehow made her more desirable. Thank God, anyway, he would get off the physical tension Muriel had set up in him all last week, tonight, in her flat. He had an unpleasant feeling that he was somehow using Sidonie as a proxy for Muriel. Everything in his life was somehow a substitute for something else. Even this enormous bank was only a substitute for the humble pick he wanted to swing in his hands. By God, he'd like to root up the whole building and see if he could find any real gold underneath it.

TWENTY-FOUR

When he left the bank, he had a cup of tea in Stewart's, and then decided to walk in the park. The afternoon was freshening into evening, and he felt somewhat braced as he reached at last the place where he met Sidonie for the first time outside the bank. Only once had he walked by the lake since, as if he wanted to avoid the memory of that April evening when she had stood gazing into the water and then turned in the golden light with the rain on her hair. Now something of that poignant emotion he had felt then returned, and

193

he thought bitterly that the whole thing had been rather like a love song by Herrick that had been turned into a satirical lampoon. Somehow he had lived in the cold green water of her eyes and had been denied the warm golden sunshine of her hair. Suddenly it was all unbearable, and he turned and walked smartly to his club, took a warm bath, then had a cold shower, and ordered Burgundy with an early dinner. He had dined by eight o'clock, and surprised Glynde by saying: "Get me Barrington now."

He told Muriel on the telephone that he had to go out to meet somebody in the Treasury and discovered that she had enjoyed herself lunching with Therese Waldenham. Then he ordered his coat and set out to walk to Park Lane. He hoped that Sidonie would not mind his coming early and wondered if she, like him, had missed the lost Monday. This evening, somehow, perhaps because he had gone back to the lake where they had met, he felt he wanted not only sexual relief, but the total sensation of love. He was strangely alone with these two women, and now, since this extraordinary blossoming of Muriel's personality, he felt lost between them and could not tell which he wanted the more.

When he gave the usual three rings on Sidonie's bell, it was a moment before she opened the door. She was clad in a green dressing gown of Turkish toweling and had a yellow towel bound like a turban on her head.

Evidently he had caught her at her toilet. "I'm sorry. I just came early."

She seemed slightly off guard. "Oh, I was just washing my hair."

There was a slight flush on her face, and he knew that she had told him a lie. It was intolerable that she

194

should lie, because, somehow, there was not a lie in her. Also it hurt him, and he said angrily: "Goddam it, you needn't lie to me!" She flushed again. "Go on, and do up your hair, if you don't want me to see it!" Suddenly his hands seemed to jump out by themselves and she backed away from him. "By God, for two pins I'd pull that damn towel away!"

Now she went pale, and he knew she was ashamed of herself, and all at once, as if she had got tired, she said: "You don't need to pull off the towel." She paused. "You can change in there."

As he went into the bathroom to take off his clothes and put on the towel dressing gown that he used, he wondered what she had meant by her remark. Was it possible that she was going to let her hair down? He felt nervous and bathed his face in cold water. He wanted her very badly this evening, and yet his physical desire seemed only to be expressing another and stranger need. He dallied in the bathroom, and put his hands in his pockets, in case they jumped out again in anger and wrenched the towel off her head or the rope of hair down. He felt that she could not have meant that she would let her hair down herself. She would be sitting as usual like the dead, beautiful bride of a dead man . . .

He stepped in the doorway of her bedroom, and his eyes took in the picture as the lungs might take in a long drink of air. She sat motionless in front of the glass, her hands shut as if to hold a prayer, her hair falling in a golden Niagara to her waist, upon the white garment. At last he went over to her and knew that his heart was beating like the heart of a youth. He saw now that what she wore was not a dressing gown but a nightdress that was made like a cloak and that fastened

195

with a girdle of gold. She wore satin ivory slippers closed like the wings of swans upon her feet. Her breasts, in the opening of the nightdress, seemed to have the soft pink flesh of clouds, and he had a strange sensation that if he picked her up she would not weigh more than air. As she waited there in stillness, one could imagine that if she suddenly shook out all that hair,. it might chime like a carillon. He took a step near her, and saw himself in the glass, with the black hairs curling on his chest in the V of his scarlet dressing gown, with the black hair on the backs of his hands, and his dark eyes looking out from under the shaggy hairs of his eyebrows, and he thought suddenly that he was like some animal that had roamed in from the jungle and had no right to her beauty.

At last she looked up, and her face was flushed with emotion as a rose with color, and he knew that she had made herself a bride for him. He felt that to say anything would disturb the air about her.

Her voice was only a whisper. "I got tired—of arguing."

He knew that she was only trying to say something more than this in a casual way, and he smiled. "Well, I'm very glad I came early."

She sat very quietly, and he wondered if by any chance she was as frightened as he was. He had to know whether this meant anything more than a sudden weariness of argument, and he kissed her hand, and then looked up as if to question her eyes, to know if he might touch her mouth. But her lids guarded her eyes. Then he softly kissed her. She did not kiss him back, but he knew now that she did not mind. He put his head into her breasts, inside the golden shawl of hair. It was a long time before their emotion changed itself into desire, and he could hardly remember anything until he laid her gently on the bed. When he wanted to undo her nightdress, his hands suddenly were helpless as a baby's, and she had to open the girdle herself. They made love in silence, but no longer in a hostile silence, and as he cherished all her body with his mouth, he saw how the blue veins lay inside her skin like watermarks in a translucent paper. It was as delicate as the glow on the book in the stairway niche in Elder's house. She kept her mouth closed in a virginal way, not because she any longer wanted to withhold it, but because it was in mood with the delicate courtship. Only her fingers, now and again sweetening his body, showed that she was answering his love-making. In the end, emotion had so translated the flesh that he was surprised to find they had come together in the marriage. Afterwards, he did not, as he always had done, release her because she wanted nothing more from him, but stayed in the reminiscence that is like the sunlight cooling to moonlight. He knew that they must have been there some hours before he said: "This is what I've always wanted from you."

She said nothing, but he did not mind her silence any more. All her body had the gratified blush of love on it, and he began to wander over it with his lips, but no longer in desire. He sensed that she was somehow gone apart, with her soul asleep in that golden field of hair. He kissed her on the instep, and suddenly felt that she was now so much his that he could not bear even her feet covered, and gently took off the right slipper that divided off the foot like wings opening into flight. . . .

"Oh, my God, I'm sorry!"

His eye rebounded from her foot like a hammer from the nail. She awoke out of her trance to his shock, but did not start up. He felt the shiver coming down along her body to him. Her whisper was as lonely and tragic as the last whisper in a theater.

"I am sorry you did that."

He could not say anything for a moment. Generations of peasants looked out through his eyes in superstitious horror at that ancient stump of animal hoof. My God, why hadn't he guessed that she was the girl in Elder's room. The hoof of Pan, Elder had called the stigma. He could feel her waiting, waiting up there on the pillow for him to come up and say in his eyes that it meant nothing to him. His hands trembled as he closed the innocent wings of the slipper over that ghastly thing. He mustered his control and gently kissed her instep, but she moved her foot, as if she knew it was no more than a gesture now. He made an enormous effort to sound natural. "Why didn't you get that operated on?"

"I don't know. My father was superstitious. He wouldn't let me."

"It makes no difference, anyway."

There was a silence, and he still could not pull himself up and take his eyes up to her.

"Doesn't it?" She paused, then also pulled herself together. "It's been a nuisance. I couldn't go to school, or anything." She was silent a moment. "I didn't want you to know about it." Her voice seemed to be going. "Get me a glass of water, will you?"

He got up and took his dressing gown and brought a glass of water from the bathroom. When he came back she had closed the nightdress. She was as white and bloodless as Elder looked.

"Thank you. I'm so thirsty."

He smiled back, that dreadful, friendly smile that is

198

an obituary on something and that is the most ghastly of all things that register on the human face. Thoughts now began to pound in his head, and he felt that he had to get away to think about this. He said in a conversational way: "You ought to get that operated on." His distress produced a kind, awkward jest. "It will tear all your stockings."

"Even if I got it down now," she said, "it would still be there."

He thought of Elder saying: *"She sees it out of the corner of her mind's eye all day long."* Now she looked like a child in her pillow of golden hair. He thought of her lying in that opium sleep at Elder's to get away from it in a distant enchanted sleep. It was clear that Elder had not told her that he had been in the Chinese room. Also it was clear that Elder did not know that she was his mistress, or he would not have talked about her foot. My God, they all had their Chinese rooms, to hide away in from each other. Heavens, he could not bear to stay here any longer.

"I think I must get my clothes on," he said.

He bent and kissed her on the mouth. She accepted it as a child accepts the good-night kiss.

"You can let yourself out," she said. "I don't think I'll get up again."

"Yes." He smiled. "I won't forget to leave your payment on the table. You're a very expensive kept woman, you know!"

His smile suddenly died out in anguish. He could not bear to see her pride humiliated in tears. She was so beautiful now, her face a white solitude in the golden hair. He must get away. Once he got over the shock, it might be all right. He knew that never in his life again would he touch the exaltation he had reached

199

with her tonight. If this was not love, it was something greater than love.

He smiled at her and went out, having touched her hand with his lips. He put his clothes on in the bathroom without being aware of one movement he made. When he came out he forgot to leave the money for the orphanage. He avoided looking into her room. If he found her crying in there, by Christ he'd break down into sobbing himself and let his heart bleed out through his eyes.

TWENTY-FIVE

The next morning in the bank was ghastly. When he had got back from her flat last night, he had felt so upset that he got a bottle of whisky from the night porter and made himself drunk in his bedroom before he went to sleep. Nicholas had not been drunk for a long time, and this morning vinegar seemed to be coming up through his blood from his stomach to his mind. The page had already brought him up a second jug of water, and now he drank another glass before she came in with the letters that needed a reply.

He tried to avoid looking at her, and she avoided looking at him. In some way she reminded him of a young widow who had the ghost of a dead man in her white face. The light seemed to have gone out inside her. They both had to make a desperate effort to deal with the mail. When they had done, he felt he could not stand it any longer. "My God, must I see Ambleside?" he said. "Can't Strood see him?"

"Lord Ambleside is an old man, and he might feel hurt."

"Very well." As usual she was right. "For God's sake, get me some strong tea, and some for yourself."

When she had gone out, he wiped the sweat off his face. He sat back in his chair and watched the faces dilating and then disappearing on the white blotting pad. He had never worried much about this trick of his eyes, but the number of faces and the strange looks they had this morning, the way they had of delaying on the pad when he tried to banish them, began to alarm him. He clenched his hands and stared at the white pad and tried to see it empty. But he could not stop his eyes throwing pictures onto the white pad like a projection machine throwing pictures onto a cinema screen. He turned the pad upside down and took out *The Times* from his case. He decided to try the crossword puzzle to calm himself for Ambleside, but in each white square of the puzzle a small hoof appeared. He gave it up and shut his eyes and got his mind away from the hoof on to the letters.

What on earth was the connection between her and Elder? He had never guessed they knew each other outside the bank. Well, that was not extraordinary, because Elder obviously did not know she was his mistress. They all seemed to have their private Chinese rooms. Had Elder also a secret hoof of Pan of some kind? Was their connection only because of her need of the opium pipe? Of course they had a cultural communion in their knowledge of Chinese. And they both inhabited that world of literature and painting and science and philosophy that was like a forbidden temple of Asia to him. Nicholas knew that he was afraid of that interior world as he was of that Chinese room in his own mind that held these pictures that came on the blotting pad or occupied the huge mirror of the full moon. He did not like these transshifting images that came into his mind. He feared these haunting faces. And above all he dreaded that plasmatic face of Sarah Fuidge clinging to his eyes. He could feel its Stygian damp. Suddenly now he could see Sarah's face looking out at him from the window of the lodge as he passed in and out the gate of Barrington. Her long yellow tooth stuck into her lower lip like a hoof into the ground. There was always a hunger in her face, and a nostalgia in it, like one saw in the face of an ape at the zoo. Now he wondered if her sexual longing might not have caused her to imagine him as her lover. She had named no one in those letters she wrote accusing herself of having love with a married man, but it might as well be he as anybody. He tried to squeeze this thought out of him between his hands. He did not like it, and hated the thought that in her imagined lust she might have clung her falling dugs to him. Somehow he was able to inhabit her and feel her abnormal moods. He wondered if her ghost could haunt him, trying to pull him away from any other woman. My God, how he hated being able to understand her and to feel the apprehension in her as she waited for those letters. . . .

"Some tea, Mr. Bude!" He looked up at Miss Coleman's white and exhausted face. "Oh, were you asleep?"

He pulled himself out of the subterranean world of his mind. "No. Just thinking."

When she went out of the room, he sat up rigid and tried to shake this other world away. His mind seemed to have become helpless since that shock last night. He must take a holiday when this Dorman business was done. The trouble was that he could not lose himself in his work. It was outside him; he was not interested in it. He knew that she had been right yesterday about the India loan. He had let that be wished on to him simply because he was bored. He would be more careful with the Bude money if it had been his own, not just a gift handed to him on a golden plate. He never had had a chance to dig life out of the ground for himself. In a vague way he knew he was looking for a root to plant himself in the earth and feel a growing up through him. He had that sense of the earth in him. He knew, without caring, that it was that which made him wanted by women. They wanted to get back into the jungle with him. He was not really afraid of this dark jungle world which Sarah had inhabited. If he could once get inside it, he could fight a way out through the tangled undergrowth of his mind into the sunlight. But he was shut up in a cage with gold bars that his hands wanted to wrench asunder. Perhaps it was some ancestor of Sidonie's who had felt the same and had grown that hoof to kick down the door.

My God, here were those faces on the white pad again, with a hoof sticking out of each mouth. His hand had turned up the pad because his mind had wanted to get those faces out somewhere that were haunting that dark inside room. Now he even knew why he kept that pad always unused and clean. The faces kept on painting themselves on the white pad until Lord Ambleside was announced.

TWENTY-SIX

Nicholas was only vaguely aware of how he got through that day and through that week. His mind seemed to sleep all day at the bank and wake at night as he roamed the countryside under the moon growing round. Quite suddenly he got into a kinship with the earth. Listening to the mice as they rustled in the cornstalks; lying on the ground by a heap of earth that erupted from a hole, to hear the moles in their tunnels; starting at the hysterical chirp of a squirrel at dusk; marking the shush into the water of an otter; all his senses sharpened into attention like players in an orchestra waiting on the baton for the entry. So innumerable were the sounds, he noted, that it was the silences that had the most inflection. He began to stay out very late and dread the return to a slumber tenanted by those visitors who came and went on the white blotting pad by day and passed through a turnstile in his mind all night long. Muriel this week was not a bother in his blood, and his body in some way seemed to be only a corporal shell inhabited by his mind. He had a sense of being in a pause, and as Monday came near, he realized that all his existence now seemed to be a pause between those letters.

He had done all the obvious things to locate the sender. He had compared the typescript with samples from Elder's machine and Sidonie's under the microscope, only to convince himself that here lay no clue. He guessed anyway that neither of them would be fool enough to use an office machine. If Elder had not his kink of the Chinese room, if Sidonie had not the kink of that hoof, he could not have believed it possible that either of such two intelligent people could do such a thing. They might be eccentric, but they were not abnormal. A neurotic like Saluby, whose clever brain seemed not to belong to his mean character, was more capable of such a sinister attack on a man's mind. But there was no way on earth that he could think of in which Saluby could obtain that paper. Nicholas had tried to get the paper matched in nearly every shop in London, and had failed. None of them seemed to recognize the maker, and most of them guessed that it was a very old paper. Saluby could obtain it only in complicity with Muriel, and it was impossible to believe that anybody so normal as she was could lend herself to such an idea. Besides, she now seemed fully occupied by herself and to have discovered a new existence that gave her the feeling of excitement she communicated to him.

He was thinking over all this on Sunday night and, unaware, had come back from the upland by the lodge path. Always he had avoided going near the lodge on his nightly walk, inventing to himself reasons why another way was more interesting. But now he found himself almost in the plot behind the lodge and was startled to see what he thought was Sarah's ghost. His heart gave a wild jump, and then he resolved himself and went up and saw that it was her long white nightdress which old Fuidge must have washed out before he gave it away in charity. Nicholas almost laughed aloud at himself and turned down the path to the Hall. His boot slipped on something, and he bent down and picked up a small hoof that must have belonged to a baby deer who had got killed perhaps by jumping at the wire as they sometimes did. He did not know why, but this tiny hoof, not much bigger than Sidonie's, seemed 'a bad omen. It was queer that he had come down here by accident and found it by the lodge. He had a queer feeling that Sarah might have dropped it there out of her hand. For some unaccountable reason he put it in his pocket and wondered if any of his peasant forefathers had regarded such a thing as a sign. He took it out of his pocket, but his hand refused to throw it away.

He looked up at the empty white moon and thought that Sidonie's face had become like it. He remembered a queer remark that old Fuidge had made: "The moon was aching up in the sky that night before Sarah died." And in the same way all this week Sidonie's face had seemed to be aching in loneliness. He wondered now if she perhaps loved him after all, and because of that stigma had feared to let him know. She could never marry knowing that it would be discovered. He knew that much as he hated fuss, he would have divorced Muriel for her, if she had shown she loved him. There was no reason why she should marry anybody. She had beauty and brains and breeding, and people like Ambleside always talked to her as an equal. And she had made herself a bride for him that last Monday night. He guessed that she had, as she said, simply got tired and given in, taken off guard by the accident of his coming early, and ashamed of herself for telling him a lie. He knew there was no lie in her. And in his heart he knew that she had never given herself to another man. Good as her salary was now, he did not know how she could afford that flat, but he knew there was nothing sinister in the explanation. But whatever the sight of that hoof had done to him, he knew that he only felt bound to her now by something like that last silken thread that Elder had mentioned as holding the soul to the clay.

TWENTY-SEVEN

When Nicholas got to the bank on Monday, he had so exhausted himself by anticipation that now he felt almost empty of fear. He sat at his desk waiting for Miss Coleman to bring in the mail and felt like a person on the operating table. In a moment the doctor would come in, and there was nothing to be done about it. He drank a glass of water and wondered what was delaying Miss Coleman and wished to God that she would come in and give him the letter and get it over.

When she came in, he saw that she had somehow regained herself over the week end. There was that sense of coldness in her again. She put the tray of letters down and handed him the *Personal* letter. Usually, she laid his personal letters by him, but today she handed him the single letter and watched him closely, and, although he knew she was watching him, he could not hide the unwillingness of his hand to receive the letter.

"Put it down!" he said sharply.

She put it down and said distinctly: "I wanted to ask you about it." She paused. "You asked me last Monday if I knew anything about this letter."

"Yes."

"Why?"

"Oh, nothing."

"There must have been some reason."

"It doesn't matter."

"Very well." She paused. "But you don't seem to like getting that letter." She paused again. "I was just wondering."

"Wondering what?"

"Well, I thought first it might be that letter you said you were going to write to yourself as an experiment, but I can't understand why it has been postmarked from all over the country."

"You seem to have been taking rather a lot of notice of it."

"There is no need to be nasty. You know I am not interested in your personal letters, but I can't help noticing one that comes every Monday morning."

"Why the hell shouldn't it come on Monday?" said Nicholas in a random way.

"I know nothing about it, but it just occurs to me now that Monday is the one day on which it would arrive regularly from any part of the country."

"Anything else you have noticed?" asked Nicholas in what he hoped she would think a sarcastic way.

She took up the letter and paused for a moment. "Yes, now that I think of it, the postmarks have been coming nearer to London." She looked at the envelope. "This one is S. W. I.—right on the doorstep."

Nicholas knew that she had seen his start. He put his hands out of sight, and continued in what he thought was a sarcastic voice. "Do you pay this attention to all my personal letters?"

She was too disgusted to be annoyed. "That is a stupid question. You know it is my business to note everything in detail." She paused. "I have paid attention to this letter because after it comes on each Monday you don't seem to be able to concentrate on what you have to do." She paused again. "Besides, you brought it up yourself by asking me if I knew anything about it."

"Yes. I wasn't thinking of what I was saying. It doesn't matter. If you don't mind, I think we might get on with the mail."

"I'm sorry." She took up the letters. "But I think if you are making this experiment on yourself, and this is the letter, that you ought to stop it." She opened her pad. "Will you take the New York mail first?"

Nicholas found difficulty in dealing with a tricky mail, and as soon as she got out of the room, he drank another glass of water. So she had noticed the letters and the effect on him! He lighted a cigarette and through the blue smoke saw faces looking at him from the white pad. He tried to keep his brain cool. Was her curiosity a blind? She was clever enough to put up an alibi of ignorance in this way. But, my God, it was out of character with that clean intelligent mind and that flat she had with good paintings and fine books and her genius for mathematics. But what did that opium smoking signify? Was it possible that she became another person when she went away in that smoke from the pipe? But, even it it was, she could not write letters in her sleep and would be her normal self when she came back from that Asia of dream. Suddenly his mind became very acute. *Was* it possible that she could write the letters under the hypnosis of opium? By God, Elder had paper in that very room! What was that kind of writing mediums were supposed to do in a trance? But how could she be capable of movement under a drug that could only liberate the mind by stopping the functioning of the body? He knew that he had not enough knowledge to know if all this was possible and thought suddenly that he might consult a book or a doctor. The whole damn thing was getting him down. All he had to understand it was the colossal encyclopedic ignorance of the average man. But he would do something about it. He might see old Hames in Harley Street and consult him with discretion. Also he might mention this curious habit of seeing these faces on the blotting pad.

Nicholas sighed and picked up the *Personal* envelope. Somehow the S. W. I. postmark made the whole thing as actual and near as the sound of the traffic outside in the street. In a way it became less frightening as it came close. He remembered that in France when one got used to the Germans in a trench a hundred yards away, they somehow felt less dangerous than when more distant. Well, he had better look at the damn thing. It would of course be the same as usual. . . .

Nicholas got a shock. It was not the same as usual. One word had been added to make it read now:

YOU HAVE A WILL TO DEATH IN YOUR
HANDS. WHOSE DEATH? WHEN?

The word *when* was like the clang of a bell in his mind. Suddenly his vague imaginative fear of the letters became an actual sense of physical danger. By God, he was dealing with somebody to be feared. Was this person intending to kill him. Something hardened in Nicholas. He felt his mind tautening to the danger as his muscles used to tauten for a spurt in the boat race. By heavens, was this something he could fight? Now it seemed more concrete, not an intangible suggestion coming from somewhere or anywhere. It was a live message from somebody who had posted it in this very district of London. But what had he to arm himself against this psychological weapon?

He considered again whether he ought to call in a detective agency. But he feared a disclosure would turn out to be something ridiculous. Moreover, this person was clever enough to have left no fingerprints on the paper. It would be easy to get the fingerprints of Elder and Sidonie from the documents they handled. Whose else? Muriel's? My God, he could not allow somebody to take the fingerprints of these people simply because he was afraid of these damn letters. Why was he afraid? Was this person trying to get him to kill himself? He wished to God that he had not mentioned the idea to Elder or Sidonie. If he had not, the letters would be located in Muriel or Saluby, and it would be easier to investigate the affair. He considered the four of them again, and there seemed to be a good reason against each of them as the sender. Then was it somebody outside? But who? He had not, so far as he knew, a single enemy. It couldn't be anybody like Charndale. It couldn't be anybody like old Fuidge. . . . Damn it, the fact was, it could only be somebody who could get hold of this paper.

He picked up the letter again and put it away in his case with the others. He felt that he must do something concrete about it. Action of any kind was better than waiting in a negative way. There was one obvious thing he could do anyway, in case it was a physical threat. On his way to lunch he would go along to St. James to buy himself a pistol. Deciding that, he suddenly felt better. He put his hand into his pocket to get his cigarette case. He felt a hard shell. He took it out and looked at it. It was the small hoof of the deer he had picked up in the moonlight last night. All at once the whole damn thing was mysterious again, and he felt the pistol was about as much use as it would be when that yellow fog of gas crept along to you while the moonlight was still in the dawn and death was not something that hit you in the chest but was breathed in the very air. Nevertheless, he was going to buy the pistol.

In some way the pistol in his pocket reassured him when he came back from lunch, and for a moment forgetting about the letters, he faced the other problem. He was looking at Sarah's face on the white pad and thinking how like a long hoof was her yellow tooth that rooted in her underlip, and found that his hand in his pocket was rubbing the deer's hoof around the palm. And, any moment now, Miss Coleman was going to come in, and he would have to force himself to say what he did not want to say. She came in with the afternoon mail, and he had an extraordinary feeling that she was overhearing everything that he was saying to himself in his mind. They dealt with the few letters, and then he paused, trying to keep his eyes frank and his voice calm: "Oh, Sidonie, about tonight . . ."

When he paused, he knew, she had decided to lessen the embarrassment for him, and she said quickly: "Oh, I meant to tell you, I've got to go out this evening."

"Well, I've got myself tied up too, so"—he laughed uneasily—"it will have to wait until next Monday."

"Yes."

When she went out he discovered that he had some sweat on his face. He was ashamed of himself, but he could not do anything about it. He knew that it was some kind of animal reflex in him that made him recoil from a deformity that, after all, did not affect her beauty or her mind—unless, of course, she was writing the letters. But what he could not bear was the emptiness of death in her face just now when her generosity had made it easy for him. He saw her face on the blotting pad now and it was only a faint shadow upon the white. Always he saw faces either in color or with a sense of color such as the eye always has on a face. Even Sarah's face had a kind of phosphorescent mildew on it that was like a tinge of color, but Sidonie's face now was only a shadow on the pad. In some way, she seemed to be going away from him, and he did not like the feeling.

The pistol in his pocket irked his leg, and he changed it into his coat pocket. It reminded him that he was perhaps facing an actual danger, and suddenly he felt that he ought to see his family solicitor. He had made up his mind to leave Sidonie an income and now quickly he decided on the amount. He would leave her fifteen hundred a year. She would never marry. She liked fine things and would do good to artists and people like that. He opened the cabinet and told her he was leaving at four o'clock. He would go round and get a codicil inserted in his will. After that, he would have an early dinner and go to a theater and try to forget about it all.

TWENTY-EIGHT

Nicholas had eaten hardly anything at dinner, and Muriel, who had tried to make a conversation, based on Therese, who had stayed at Barrington last night, found herself becoming more annoyed each moment.

213

She realized that in ten years of life together she and Nicholas had never succeeded in having a thorough conversation about anything. The influence of Therese, and the sudden flowering of her own life, enabled her to see clearly that they had come through life together with little more contact between them than was forced between two guests in a hotel. Often she had wondered why they got married. Now she was beginning to wonder why they stayed married. Nicholas was obviously obsessed by some worry and had no more notion of communicating it to her than he would to a fellow guest at a hotel. By the time they got into coffee, she had almost decided to broach the whole question and see if something could not be done to reconstruct their lives. But he was so distraught in himself that she felt it was an unhappy moment to force an important subject upon his mind. At last, having spilled his coffee and got into a temper about it, as if to calm his nerves he went over to his desk and opened his case.

She watched his face above the desk as it became unguarded in his poring over whatever he had taken out of his personal case, and she realized that he had the hunted look of somebody who could not escape in any corner of the world from whatever haunted his mind. Whatever this worry was, it was like a ghost that never left him, waking or sleeping. Lately there had seemed to be nothing else at all in his face but this unknown ghost. He shut up the case in a baffled way and left the key in it, as if he knew he must return to it later. He came back and sat by the fire and looked into the red glow and left the cigarette in his mouth burn on to his lip until he jumped up and smacked it away with his hand. He used a fearful oath and apologized to her.

214

In a moment she said: "Nick, what is on your mind? Your nerves seem to be in pieces."

"Good Christ, can't I burn myself with a cigarette, without being considered a nervous wreck!"

"I didn't mean the cigarette. I mean—everything."

"You're just imagining things."

"Perhaps you are." She paused. "Are these letters still going on?"

She saw that he immediately became on guard.

"Letters? What letters?"

"The ones Saluby suggested."

"Ahm, yes."

There was a pause, and he seemed to have gone away by himself again. She was trying to feel her way into him.

"Are they worrying you?"

He pulled himself back again. "Worrying me?"

"Yes."

"Lord, no!"

He was going away and coming back, and her instinct told her that she would force him off guard by taking it slowly. She paused again before she spoke. "Well, I think they must be. Something is, anyway."

He was annoyed at being called back again out of his introspection. "Oh, don't talk damned nonsense!"

She knew that she was making him angry and understood that her best chance was to make him angry.

"Why don't you stop them?"

Now she had got his tortured mind in the middle of its seesawing away and back, and his anger jumped out at her.

"Good Christ, what do you want me to do! Employ a bloody detective."

He saw her eyes on his face and he realized what he had done. He thought it an hour before she spoke again.

"Employ a detective? What on earth do you mean?"

"Oh, nothing. I was thinking of something else."

She waited again. Then said in a persisting way: "Good heavens, has it got to the state when you must employ a detective to stop you writing letters to yourself? If it has, Saluby was right, and you are taking them seriously."

"Look here, I wish you wouldn't go on nagging me with silly questions. I'm tired of . . ."

Oxinham came in. "A trunk call, sir, from Northumberland. Will I put it . . ."

"I'll take it outside."

Nicholas got up as if glad to be rid of the conversation. Muriel almost was tempted to pick up the telephone in the room, to listen, if the line was open. The room bells never rang, as the servants had to inquire before passing a call. Now she wondered if this Northumberland call had anything to do with his worry. Perhaps he only wanted an excuse to get out of the room. When he had done talking, he would probably go out for a walk. His unguarded remark about the detective had astonished and puzzled her. What on earth did he mean? It did not make any sense. She must . . .

Nicholas came in with a bustled and yet relieved look on his face.

"It's my uncle, Christian. He's dying. He's asking for me." Nicholas paused. "I must go. I'm the last Bude." He spoke almost bitterly. "My God, he had to be on the edge of the grave before he wanted to see me. I must go."

"Of course. When?"

"Now."

She got up. Obviously he was glad of something to do, to get his mind off his worry.

"Well, what am I to do?"

"Telephone Blake. Tell him to get that village taxi and come round at once. Ring Dorminster and see can I make a connection with the night train to the North. If I can't, Blake must take me on. Tell him to bring his sleeping things. If he can't get a taxi, fetch him. I'll shove in a few things."

He went upstairs, and she quickly got things in hand. There was a sporting chance of making the train connection. She rang Nicholas in his room and told him Blake would be up in ten minutes and that he must be ready. She ordered a picnic basket of food from the kitchen and ran out to fill up the car with petrol and found the tank full. That was like Blake. She came back to the house, having pulled out the car, and Nicholas was ready with his suitcase. He was excited by the prospect of doing something different. He told her to ring Mr. Strood at the bank in the morning. She gave him all the money she had in the house. God knows what it would be like up in that peasant's cottage in Northumberland. He could hardly understand what his uncle's wife had been saying . . .

Ah, here was Blake. Nicholas looked at his watch. "Blake, will I drive? Or can you make it?"

"Sir, what this car can do, I can do in her."

"Very well. I leave it to you."

He jumped in, and Muriel watched Blake going down the avenue with some surprise. She realized that Blake could meet an emergency. She paid off Blake's taxi and went back into the house.

She sat down to consider things. She could not understand the mystery that lay behind his remark about the detective. All she knew was that the clue was in his case . . . Heavens, had he left his case! She went over to the desk.

Muriel sat down at the desk and felt a slight flush in her face. She would not dream of looking at anybody's letters or of interfering in anything somebody wished to keep private. But this, she felt, was something that Nicholas could not handle himself. She took a long breath and turned the key in the case.

It took Muriel a long time to puzzle it out. She recognized the unposted envelope as Barrington notepaper and realized it must be the letter she saw him writing on that Sunday evening Saluby had been here. Though the address was in inked capitals, she knew it was his writing. Therefore he had not posted that first letter. Then, as she took up the file of letters, postmarked from various parts of Scotland and England, she remembered that he had said that he had decided to dictate the letters to his secretary. But it was remarkable that he should have gone to so much trouble to get them posted from so many places. Then she came on the two marked strips that he had got compared under the misroscope, saw that one strip was cut off one of the letters. Good Lord, this was extraordinary! Why should he have gone to so much trouble about these letters that had such a strange implication in the wording? She sat in thought and then remembered how he had questioned her about the Elder Bank notepaper. An idea struck her, and she opened the drawer of the desk and found the Elder Bank paper. It was the same paper obviously as in the anonymous letters. But what did this signify? Unable to comprehend it, she opened other drawers in the desk, and then in the well of the large middle drawer found the microscope. Good heavens, had he bought that microscope in connection with these letters? She examined the letters and saw from the dates how they had been systematically getting closer to London. And then she saw with a shock that the word *when* was added to the last one, posted in S. W. I.

She lighted a cigarette and began to reason it out. At last it dawned on her that Nicholas might not be writing these letters himself. That would explain the remark about employing a detective. She felt an unpleasant shock going through her. There was something ominous about the wording of these letters. She wondered if she ought to steam open the unposted letter that she knew for certain Nicholas had written himself, and then considered the microscope and the care with which Nicholas was watching this affair and decided that it was too risky. Besides, she felt, the letter he had written himself had nothing at all to do with these letters that were written on Elder Bank paper. But who was writing them, and why? Who knew of his original idea to try the experiment? Herself, Saluby, and, according to Nicholas, Miss Coleman, his secretary. Were these letters prompted by the original suggestion? If they were, either Miss Coleman or Saluby was writing them, unless, of course, somebody else knew about it. Obviously, Nicholas did not know, since it looked as if he was trying to trace the sender. Then she recalled his question about the Elder Bank paper, and she realized that he might be suspecting her . . .

Heavens, this matter was going beyond a joke. She must do something about it. But where was she to begin? She thought it over for a minute, and then knew that the first step must be to find out if he were dictating these letters to Miss Coleman or not. She would go to London tomorrow. She would have to take a chance on being able to handle Miss Coleman. She wondered what she was like. She sounded fairly grim, from the way Nicholas had spoken of her . . .

Muriel looked out the window at the noise of a car. Saluby! What on earth did he want? Or perhaps he was just dropping in. She had not seen him since that unpleasant last day at Dorminster. Well, she would be civil. Barrington was too small a place for a feeling of unpleasantness between the doctor and the Hall. She closed up the desk and the case and waited until he came in.

Saluby was perhaps slightly nervous, but she immediately got him a drink and put him at his ease. After a moment he said: "Where is your husband? Out for a walk?"

"No. He's just rushed off up North. He got a telephone message that somebody was dying."

There was some more small talk, and then he said: "I've come to be a nuisance to you. I've got a case over at Yeoman Spire." He paused. "Poverty is the real sickness. I . . ."

"Of course. How much do you want? I'll give you a check."

"That's very good of you. Jimpson told me when I took over that I should always come to you."

"Yes. I'll get my checkbook." When she came back with the checkbook and began to write the check, she paused. "How funny, I don't know your name."

"Oh, are you making it to me?"

"Of course."

"The initials are 'H. D.' "

"Say fifteen pounds. You can have more if necessary."

"Oh, that's rather a lot, but . . . Well, there's a baby on the way, and . . ."

"I'll make it twenty-five." She gave him the check. "Always come here without hesitation."

"It's awfully good of you."

"I don't think so. That's the least we can do if we've got some money, to help people."

Saluby looked introspectively into his glass. "Of course, it doesn't help them, really."

"Oh?"

"Do you think that really helps people, to have a social system based on charity?"

"Oh, I wasn't thinking about it that way. I see what you mean."

"I don't want to sound ungrateful."

"I understand." She poured herself a drink. "Tell me, have you ever noticed any special desire among the English working people to help themselves?"

"No. I can't say I have."

"Nick's father was a self-made man, and he never gave a penny to charity. He said that no human being was worth helping who couldn't help himself." She paused. "He despised the workingman in this country." She paused again. "Nick might have gone in for politics, but he has the same idea about the English working people. Of course, this kind of charity is different, so I don't mean that. When I came to live here, I tried to do something myself. But I could never be five minutes inside any house before they tried to entangle me in local gossip of some kind. I realized the feudal wars were still going on between doorstep and doorstep in the English village. I had no intention of being turned into a Napoleon to find the parson's wife was a Wellington, just to gratify the jealousy and bitterness of yokel wives. I am not interested in Women's Guilds, or giving out prizes at the local flower show. Barrington and Yeomen Spire look very pleasant under their thatched roofs and green creepers, but there are plenty of the weeds that poisoned Sarah Fuidge in every front garden. I imagine old Jock Bude knew that charity was the best fertilizer of those weeds in the working-class mind. I am sorry, if you are shocked."

"I am not. I'm rather surprised." Suddenly he spoke in a bitter way. "I ought to know all about what charity does to the human mind. It's like being fed on maggots that stay inside and eat the belly out of you." He paused. "I'm sorry, to have to put it that way."

"It's all right. I don't like genteel talk."

She knew that he had some personal feeling about charity and thought that perhaps his kinks came from having a hard time.

He looked at her and said: "You know, you don't seem to be the same woman you were the first day I saw you."

"I suppose I am not."

There was a silence, and then he changed the subject.

"Oh, that place in Dorminster is closed up. Mac-Gregor has left his practice there. He's caught a bug."

She was surprised to find that her heart leaped. "Caught a bug?"

"Yes. You'll probably see about it in the papers. He's in London now, working it out in the lab. He'll probably wind up with an O. M. It was lunacy for a man like him to waste his time in Dorminster. Now he's got endowments and what not to enable him to work."

"Oh, I'm so glad." She hesitated. "Is he an old friend of yours?"

"Yes, I suppose so. I sometimes wonder if he doesn't use my mind as a kind of lab to catch unpleasant germs in."

She smiled. "I can't imagine anything like that with him. He's not insincere. Are you fond of him?"

"Yes. About the only person I like."

"You say it was stupid of him to waste his time at Dorminster. Is Barrington a very profitable place to be in, for you?"

"Why?"

"Well, you have a good brain, haven't you?"

He gave a slight shrug. "I don't know. I just don't seem to be able to get hold of the helm. Maybe I've got a drift in my mind." He paused. "I like human guinea pigs. The peasant is the best psychological guinea pig of all."

Somehow that made her shudder. She realized that his face, which had the kind of good looks one saw in those young men who posed for multiple store advertisements, somehow had a twist in it, so that one always seemed to catch it in a half profile. It was a curious slanting face, and he had that detestable trait, habitual to the café prostitute, of looking at one by moving the eyes and not turning the face. He never liked to be caught looking at you. He peeped around a corner at the world. Now he lighted a cigarette, and there was a lull, and she wondered how on earth she had given herself to him.

"I suppose I ought to be going?"

"What is the hurry?" she smiled. "Surely you don't feel you have to go because Nicholas is away!"

"No." He paused. "How is he?"

"Oh, he's all right." She felt an instinct to be guarded. "I think he needs a holiday."

"Why doesn't he take it?"

"Oh, he's tied up on some Advisory Council or something."

Saluby was looking out into the twilight on the lawn.

"Is he still trying that experiment on himself?"

It was a moment before she replied. She felt her senses feeling for his mood like inquisitive antennae. "I think so."

"I was hoping he'd tell me his reaction. That kind of thing is useful to a doctor."

She had meant to consult Saluby on her anxiety about this, and now she found herself guarding it from him. "Don't you think it is rather a silly idea, for somebody in his position?"

"What do you mean by 'his position'?"

"Well, one hardly expects a person of affairs to go in for that kind of thing."

"Why the hell not!"

She was astonished at the venom in Saluby's voice.

"Why the hell shouldn't he be a guinea pig as some damned pauper? What the devil is he, anyway, except a kind of toll gate that money goes through?"

"Good heavens, you needn't get so worked up about it! Anyway, whatever you say, it seems ridiculous for him to waste his time on that kind of thing." She paused, and said sharply: "I'm not sure I like the way you use the word guinea pig."

"What the hell are we all but guinea pigs? That's all I am to MacGregor, although he doesn't suspect it. He just likes me with him to watch whether the bug in my brain will kill it or be killed."

"So you see Nicholas as a guinea pig to make an experiment on?"

"Yes, a valuable one. Outside, he's a phlegmatic normal. Inside, he's just a superstitious peasant with a mind like a dog that bays at the moon. That's why his hands are always arguing, the peasant is wrestling with the sleek and wealthy banker, one of them is trying to kill the other. He's just as valuable as a guinea pig as he is as a banker."

There was a curious glint of light on Saluby's face in the dusk that made it phosphorescent and cold, so that one could feel it damp on the eye.

She felt a tendency to shiver. "It's getting dark. I'll switch on the light."

When she put the light on, she felt more comfortable. "Well, if you talk like that, you seem to think that the letters might have an effect on Nicholas?"

"Well, that's the idea, isn't it, to find out?"

* * * * * * * * * * * * *
*   *
*   TWENTY-NINE   *
*   *
* * * * * * * * * * * * *

Nicholas had just caught the Dorminster connection last night, and Muriel ordered the car for ten o'clock. She rang Mr. Strood at the bank to let him know that Nicholas was away. She did not ask for Miss Coleman. She had made her own plan to find out if Nicholas was dictating the letters. Then she rang Fantoine and made a hairdressing appointment and next booked a room at the Clarendon. She was going to stay a night or two in London. As she packed her suitcase, she sang gently and smiled as she put in her hygiene box. A couple of months ago she would not have done that. She had never used it, indeed, until she had made love with Saluby. And now, remembering how, in spite of her physical dislike of him, he had almost hypnotized her last night, she realized for the first time the compulsion of the mind over the flesh. Saluby had become so confident of himself in his analysis of Nicholas that he almost had been able to dominate her by sheer mental power. She would not forget the lesson of what the working brain could do. She had read somewhere that no woman can in the end resist a man with a brilliant mind. It seemed to her now that it was true.

She enjoyed herself in London. When she had got her hair done in Dover Street, she walked down to the Berkeley, lunched by herself, and enjoyed the play of her beauty on the South American at the next table. His companion, however, did not enjoy the way he kept looking at Muriel, as if he recognized in her the kindred blood of a tropical clime. Muriel was beginning to feel her power over men. She sighed. It was a pity the young Frenchman who had done her hair in Fantoine's was not right about a rendezvous very special for this evening!

After lunch she bought a flask of perfume in Bond Street and then went to Grosvenor Square, where Madame Ranel agreed that a garment cut as simply as an Athenian tunic, of ivory silk, had a most enchanting moonlight effect on madame's golden skin. After an amusing conversation, Madame Ranel, with French candor, said that Madame Bude seemed to have exchanged herself for somebody else and remarked how pleasant it was to dress somebody who had learned to grow, not merely wear, clothes on her lovely figure. Muriel left in good humor. She knew how significant it was that this keen Frenchwoman should have noticed the change in her. It was too early for tea, and she decided to walk about London.

She turned into Piccadilly and walked along toward the Circus. The faces of people, she noticed, became very naked in the sunlight. She observed women in an acute way now. It seemed to her that the only women whose minds and bodies were alive were in society, or girls who, working in smart shops, were in contact with the fashionable world. The emptiness and worry in the faces of the women who had come in on the bus to shop in the cheap stores alarmed her. Their whole lives obviously went into keeping an eye on the saucepan, the baby, and the housekeeping money. Nearly all of them had bitter eyes. Busy with livelihood, they had no time to live. They appalled Muriel. Their faces were alike as the dials of clocks. Each day was yesterday again. She walked along and stood near a famous tea-shop and studied the wives going in the corner door. They were the wives of the major, the parson, the lawyer, the tea planter—in a word, the women of the world known as Poona, whether they lived at the end of the P. and O. or in Knightsbridge. They were as distant from Mayfair as from Surbiton. They read *Punch, The Tatler,* the social page of *The Times,* came up for the new Cochran show, enjoyed a Dodie Smith play, thought Noel Coward modern. They were bound to know somebody who knew somebody in Malay about whom Maugham was supposed to have written. That somehow made them a part of the world of literature. Muriel remembered her mother and the garrison wives and felt a crawling on her skin. Where had she felt this sensation before? Suddenly she remembered. She had felt like this once before, when after reading Darwin she had stood by the monkey house in the zoo and asked herself: "Was I once one of these?"

She took a long breath. If money did nothing else, at least it got one away from them. Once again she had that uncanny feeling that she was watching ghosts walking in from the past. They seemed no more contemporary than the Boer War and Rudyard Kipling. The smart revues and novels mocked them. But the incredible thing was that they were nearly the whole of England and apparently were ignorant of the fact that they were dead and had been interred years ago by the Bright Young People. Muriel left the corner and walked up Bond Street. A fashionable and lovely girl that Muriel knew to have written books on surrealism and the origin of swing music came out of Asprey's and bumped into a lumpish country gentlewoman in tweeds who almost certainly had never heard of Dali or Duke Ellington. Muriel had the notion that she could not have been more surprised at a collision between a ricksha and an airplane. Somewhere in the gap between those two women something was lost. Muriel wondered if it could be the future of England.

She felt somewhat ashamed of herself. In ten years she had not done very much with the advantages of money. This was the first time she had walked about London and really seen something. She had grown up more in the last two months than in the last ten years. She had an uncomfortable sensation that she had damn nearly missed the whole thing. She looked at her watch. It was time to go to the Ritz and have tea and make her telephone call.

She ordered tea in the Ritz and went along to the

telephones. It was almost ten minutes past five. She had decided to ring the bank at that hour, hoping that Miss Coleman would have gone. She guessed that everything could be sharp on the clock at Bude's and that Miss Coleman would leave at five. She seemed to have got a minor clerk or a porter at the bank, and it was some time before they found the address book of the staff. She took down Miss Coleman's address and smiled. So far everything had gone all right. The bank had said that Miss Coleman had just left. She would go round to Miss Coleman about six-fifteen. She would probably have not gone out, and she was almost certain to have got back by then, even if she had tea somewhere on her way home. Muriel looked at the address before she put it into her bag. Suddenly she realized that Miss Coleman lived in a very expensive place and began to wonder if she was going to be the brilliant but dull person she had pictured. She thought she had better ring up Barrington and learned that Mr. Bude had wired that his uncle was dead and that he did not expect to be home for some days.

She had tea and then went back to the Clarendon and found her box from Madame Ranel had arrived. She went upstairs and had a bath and decided to wear the moonlight garment. Then she stood in front of the bathroom glass and smiled. Damn it, one never knew what was going to happen. She clicked open her hygiene box. She went to a great deal of care in dressing and eventually had to ask the taxi driver to hurry to Park Lane when she called a taxi. She had noted going out that the cocktail bar at the Clarendon was beginning to look gay already, although the fashionable world was supposed to be in Scotland or abroad. She decided she would come back there and have a cocktail.

Muriel's first thought when Sidonie opened the door to her was: "Thank God, I'm looking smart." Her second thought was: "Surely this can't be Nick's secretary!" She was careful from the first question.

"Is Miss Coleman at home?"

"Yes. I am Miss Coleman."

"Oh . . . I am Mrs. Bude. May I come in? Am I disturbing you?"

"No. Do please come in."

Muriel photographed the room in one glance, noted the sculptures and paintings, saw within the alcove of the room, in the parting of the curtains, that the table was laid for supper or dinner for one with exquisite glass and fine silverware. She saw that Miss Coleman's frock was expensively simple, that her hair was dressed in a fashionable salon.

"Do sit down. I just must turn off something in the kitchen. I shan't be a moment."

Muriel did not sit down. She looked at the bookcase, saw at once what it signified; went to the window to look over the park; remarked as she turned back a drawing of a kangaroo on a large sheet of paper on the desk, saw it was enclosed in a geometrical design, gathered from a quick glance that Miss Coleman's mathematical knowledge was complicated and abstruse; then she stood in front of the Matisse and was looking at it when Miss Coleman came back.

"I was just admiring your things."

"What will you have? Sherry or a cocktail?"

"I'd love a cocktail. But—am I being a nuisance?"

"Oh no. I'm doing nothing."

Miss Coleman handled the cocktail things with lovely articulate hands. Muriel noted the glasses and almond dishes and the biscuit tray were elegant and expensive. She thought abruptly: "Either she's got an enormous salary, or somebody is keeping her. Good heavens, can it be Nicholas!" She said: "I've been shopping all day. This cocktail is just what I wanted." She smiled.

"What are you giving me?"

"One I make up myself."

There was an easy silence until she gave Muriel her glass.

"Oh, this is good! Yes, I'd love a biscuit." She paused. "I suppose I ought to apologize for coming to see you here, but I didn't want to go to the bank."

"That is all right. How did you get my address?"

"I rang the bank"—Muriel smiled—"after five o'clock." Now Miss Coleman smiled very slightly, as if to convey that she knew she was dealing with somebody clever. Muriel smiled at her and said spontaneously: "I must say I didn't think you'd be like—well, this!"

Miss Coleman paused, then decided to give a little of herself in response. "Well, I've got a bit of a surprise, too, from you."

Muriel paused for a moment and looked her in the eye. It required a certain candor in oneself to look into those cold, lucid eyes. Muriel decided that it was no use in being overguarded. This girl was clearly well bred, reticent, and her sensitiveness was safeguard enough without a somewhat vulgar caution. Muriel said in a forthright way: "I've come to see you because I'm worried." She paused. "I had meant to ask you if I could have your promise to keep this visit confidential" —Muriel smiled—"but, now, of course, I can see there is no need to ask you that. Now, I'll see if I can get to the point at once." She looked straight at Miss Coleman.

"Miss Coleman, is my husband writing himself those letters he gets every week?"

Miss Coleman looked thoughtful, as if she were making up her mind. Then she said: "Why should you expect me to answer questions like that?"

"This is not Bude's Bank business, Miss Coleman. I am worried. It is only last night I realized that there was something very curious about all this letter business. I know, of course, that you knew about my husband's original idea to experiment on himself with these ridiculous letters, because he told me that he was going to dictate them to you. It was a kind of joke then, but now it seems to be something more than a joke. Of course, you know what I am talking about?"

"Yes." She paused. "He does not dictate the letters to me."

Muriel took her drink as if she needed it. Miss Coleman refilled her glass without comment.

"Then the letters he is getting are coming from somebody else. Have you noticed anything special about this business?"

"Yes. First I noticed that he was beginning to fear getting this letter, and then, I think it was yesterday week, his nerves got out of hand, and he asked me if I knew anything about it." Miss Coleman looked cold and disgusted. "That is all I know."

Muriel paused for a long time. "Do you know what is in the letters?"

"I do not."

Muriel got out her cigarette case, but Miss Coleman gave her one from the green box. Muriel said at last: "I am puzzled. Do you know of anybody connected with the bank who might write him those letters?"

Miss Coleman paused for a moment. "No."

Muriel looked at her. "You seemed to be hesitating in your mind then, as if you were considering some person who might possibly write them?"

"I was." Miss Coleman paused. "But I cannot believe that person would."

"Well, I must trust your judgment." Muriel paused. "As far as I can see, you can't help me about this."

"Well, you haven't told me anything I do not already know."

"I see. I haven't told you what is in the letters." Muriel looked at her for a long time and began to feel her face warm slightly under Miss Coleman's cold, ironical gaze. "Well, the message is the same in all of them, except in the last, postmarked S. W. I." Muriel flushed in embarrassment. "It says: *'You have a will to death in your hands. Whose death'?"* Miss Coleman tautened. "In the last letter, postmarked S. W. I., the word *'When?'* was added at the end." Muriel paused. "It all seems very curious and unpleasant."

Miss Coleman, Muriel guessed, had an anxiety inside that cold, judicial exterior.

"Yes," Miss Coleman remarked, "and clever." She paused. "Are the letters typewritten?"

"Yes . . . Oh, I forgot. There is something else I can tell you. They are written on the Elder Bank notepaper." Miss Coleman could not conceal her start. "Why did that give you a shock?" Miss Coleman was silent, thoughtful. "Do you know of anybody who has this paper, or who could get it?"

"Almost anybody in the bank could get hold of that paper. How very . . . Do you mean that they come with the Elder Bank address on them?"

"The address is cut off. But it is the same paper."

233

"Does Mr. Bude know?"

"I assume he does. Yes, he must know."

"Why are you in doubt? From what you say, he has discussed this with you."

"No. I asked him, but I couldn't get anything out of him. So, last night, when he went away, I opened his private case that he brings in every day to the bank." Muriel paused.

"You would have done the same thing."

"Yes. I understand. I wasn't thinking anything— nasty."

"Well, I have told you everything I know. Do you really think this is worrying him badly?"

"Yes."

"Well, it seems to me that the letters must be coming from somebody in the bank, and from somebody who knows Nicholas well." Muriel hesitated. "You must have noticed that his hands—well, they get in his way."

"I have," Miss Coleman answered. "It looks to me as if the letters were inspired by his own idea of writing to himself."

"That is what I thought."

"Well, who knew of that idea? You, myself . . . Oh, and, of course, the doctor who suggested the idea."

"Nobody else, so far as I know," said Muriel.

"What is the doctor like?"

Muriel felt herself under the X ray of Miss Coleman's eyes. In some unaccountable way she feared that Miss Coleman might discover her own connection with Saluby.

"Ahm, well, very intelligent, but—I'd say he has some kind of kink."

"Hum. Not a likely thing for a doctor to do. If it was found out, it would be the end of his career."

234

"Well, can you help me, Miss Coleman?" Muriel paused. "I wondered if I ought to call in a detective."

"I don't think you can do that without letting Mr. Bude know."

"No. I suppose I can't. He'd be furious, and God only knows where it might end. We might be making a fuss about nothing at all. Somehow, though, I have an uneasy feeling about the whole thing." She looked hard at Miss Coleman. "Most people would say that Nicholas is an ordinary stolid man, I suppose, but I think he is the kind of person who might easily get obsessed by a thing like this." Muriel gave a kind of half smile. "We seem to be getting very frank, at the first time of meeting."

"Well, it's necessary."

"Yes. Well, is there anything we can do?"

"Nothing, except to wait. Perhaps the letters will stop. The one on Monday came from the doorstep, as you might say." Miss Coleman paused. "That seems all that can be done, to wait and to watch. It is still possible that he might be writing these letters himself, but unlikely. I can't believe they would be affecting him like this, if he were. Anyway, I'm glad you told me about the Elder Bank notepaper. It might help. You must leave that to me. I'll let you know, if I can find out anything—unless it is something I can deal with myself. You can have my telephone number. It's not in the book." Miss Coleman got up and took the cocktail shaker. "Now, let us put it away for the moment and enjoy a cocktail. Are you in a hurry?"

"No, I could have several of these cocktails." Muriel smiled. "I can't tell you what a relief it is to me that you turned out to be like—well, the way you are. Good heavens, Nicholas is lucky to have somebody like you."

Muriel looked around the flat. "You've got a lovely flat.

"Yes, it is expensive, isn't it!"

Muriel looked up in astonishment and wondered if she saw a smile on Miss Coleman's face as she bent over the cocktails. What a devil of a remark. Suddenly Muriel laughed, and said: "I'll bet you haven't got any women friends!" Again she thought Miss Coleman smiled. "You know, when you came to the bank, Nicholas was so astounded by all your what nots at Oxford that he mentioned it to me, although he's nearly always an oyster about the bank. But I think the other kind of cleverness you have is more fun!" Muriel took the glass. "Yes, I'll let you have it! I *was* thinking that you must get a very good salary to have this place. What bitches we are!"

"Well, I get a very good salary, although I'm not supposed to tell you or anybody. But that's not how I have this flat. An uncle who lived as if he had about a shilling a week died about five years ago and left me quite a lot of money. Until then I lived in Chelsea. I think I was happier there, in a way."

"You know, Nicholas told me all about your scholarships and honors, but he told me nothing about your looks. Bude's Bank seems to be a general kind of mystery. Anyway, I didn't expect you!" Muriel paused. "Why did I surprise you?"

Miss Coleman had all her reserve again. "Well, you did. I suppose one always imagines the wife of somebody you see every day dull."

"Oh, is that because you think Nicholas dull?"

"Oh, no!"

"He's bored to death, of course, with banking."

"Yes."

Suddenly Muriel looked hard at her. "Look here, I'm staying in London. Will you lunch with me tomorrow?"

Miss Coleman looked very thoughtful. "I think I ought not to."

"Because you work at the bank?"

"Yes."

"What absolute nonsense!" Muriel smiled at her. "I come here and drink your cocktails. Why shouldn't you lunch with me?"

"Well, if Nicholas finds out we know each other, and we don't tell him, he will wonder why. And he will want to know how we met. He's certain to guess that it has something to do with the letters."

"I see . . . Well, Nicholas won't be back for some days. He can't see us across England. Come and dine with me at the Clarendon tomorrow night." Muriel paused. "I really lead rather a lonely kind of life. I'm afraid I don't like women as a rule. I haven't talked to a woman for ages until lately to Therese Waldenham."

"Yes. I know her."

"Oh, do you?"

"Yes, I worked at the Foreign Office. When she came over from Paris the first time, when she worked at the embassy, we used to do theaters together. She hadn't met George then."

"Well, then, we're old friends. You must come and dine with me. Come early and we'll have a cocktail first."

"Very well." Miss Coleman hesitated. "I seldom go out now."

"I'd ask you to dine this evening, but I've really had a hectic day and I'm going to retire early."

"Yes, I guessed that."

"You know, I think it's ridiculous. I don't know why I haven't met you before. You could come down and stay."

"It's awfully nice of you."

"Well, I'll see you tomorrow about seven. Come up to my room, if I'm not downstairs."

"Yes."

"And thank you for the cocktails."

When she got into the street, Muriel thought to herself: "My God, what a surprise!" She stopped dead. "Is it possible? Is it possible?"

She had never been so astonished in her life, as every instinct told her that Miss Coleman knew Nicholas well outside the bank. Was that what he did on Monday nights? Good heavens, Nicholas must be interesting! That girl, she knew, was like a volcano inside an iceberg. She was as proud and independent as the devil. She would not dream of having an affair with a man for any other reason than a fondness or passion for him.

Muriel called a taxi to take her to the Clarendon. She could do with another drink. She had an unpleasant feeling that Miss Coleman could get something out of Nicholas that she could not. Lord, perhaps he was in love with her! Why not? She was as beautiful as they were made, with exquisite taste, and that indefinable air of the complete sophisticated woman in the elegant world. She was, in fact, a gentlewoman, and, a great deal rarer, an educated one. What an extraordinary person to be a bank secretary. Why on earth did she stay on there? Good heavens, was she in love with Nicholas? Anyway, she called him Nicholas in conversation about him. She could easily not have done that, but, Muriel knew, Miss Coleman would despise the use of her mind for petty concealments. Muriel felt herself flushing. Was it possible that Nicholas felt his own wife a fool compared to this woman? Why had Miss Coleman been surprised to find she herself was attractive? Obviously because she was having an affair with Nicholas and had thought his wife must be dull. She remembered now how attractice Nicholas was. She thought of his hairy black chest and his big hands . . . and she knew that she wanted her own husband. Muriel discovered that she was forgetting about the letters.

THIRTY

Nicholas arrived back in London on Friday morning at twenty minutes past eleven in a black humor. He stepped out of the hired car at the bank and was so tired that the hot pavement came up with a jolt through his exhausted nerves and seemed to bang against the ceiling of his head. The driver looked done in after the long journey in the sun, and Nicholas gave him a very large tip and thanked him and shook hands.

"You look dead beat, sir."

"Christ," thought Nicholas to himself as he looked up at the smoldering sky, "if I only had time for a bath!"

He put his hand into his pocket to get his handkerchief, and the deer's hoof came out with the handkerchief and rolled from the pavement into the road, and the bank porter nearly got run over by a car as he bent to retrieve it for Nicholas.

"Blimey, that was a narrow shave, sir!"

"Why the hell didn't you look before you stepped out . . ." Nicholas took the shell of hoof from him and regretted his ingratitude. "Thank you, Roberts." He laughed nervously. "I got a bit of a fright when I saw that car coming at you."

Nicholas put the hoof into his inner coat pocket and swore as he hurried into the bank. It was this damned hoof that had caused his terrible journey by whistle stop and junction trains and hired cars down from the North. At the local station in Northumberland he had thrown away the hoof, as if throwing away all that it symbolized, into the waste bin on the platform, and, then, because he could not help it, he had got out from the train at the second-next station and gone back to recover that damned hoof. He knew that it was ridiculous, and that it would cause him to lose the night sleeper. Since then it had been a nightmare journey through a sleepless, sweating night and under a morning sky with the sun looking out through the smoked blind of yellow dust that gathered for the harvest thunderstorm. The fields of grass scorched almost the same color as the stubble reeled past his eyes, as the car hummed along with tires squealing on the melting tar of the road by the early harvesters that were racing the approaching storm. He had taken the wheel for about twenty-five miles to rest the driver, and his eyes had burned in the solid opaque glare of light, and now he had a headache that clanged on each step of the marble stairway on the bank.

Miss Coleman looked up as he came into her room, and he spoke without wasting time on a good morning.

"Get Dorman. Tell him I'll be round in ten minutes."

Miss Coleman pushed in a connection and said:

"Have a pot of strong tea up here in five minutes."

"I wish you'd stop being a bloody nurse!"

Miss Coleman took no notice but asked for the treasury and made the connection and said: "Tell Mr. Dorman that Mr. Bude will be in the Council Room at eleven forty-five."

Nicholas looked at the clock. "Christ, can't you obey orders?"

She got up in silence and went into his room and got a glass of water and found two aspirin tablets in her handbag and handed them to him without a comment.

He gave in. "I know. I'm all in." He sat on her desk. "I missed a bloody train, and I've been tangled up all night in milk trains and hired cars and God knows what. Couldn't sleep."

"Can't you manage to have a bath?"

"No . . . Oh, here's the tea."

She nodded to the page. "I'll let it draw a moment."

"Anything much?"

"Yes, a heavy afternoon. The delegation about Egypt."

"Good Christ! Can't it wait?"

"No. Whitehall has been giving me its confidences. They want to get it out to forestall anything in the Sunday papers. I've made all the appointments. I've given you until three to lunch and have a rest."

"In the bank itself?"

"Routine." She poured out the tea and put in four lumps of sugar as he made a face. "It's a pick-me-up." She remarked in a cold way: "Strood is an inconsequential fool. He fusses like a bitch monkey in a heat wave over nothing at all."

Nicholas suddenly relieved his tension in a roar of

laughter. The pompous manager would have been surprised to hear this conversation. He sipped the tea and said: "I must have a holiday." He looked at her. "It's you who ought to run this bloody bank when I'm away. Old Dorman won't even talk in person to Strood, and he'll let you sit in his lap." He paused. "You'd better come over with me now."

"Very well. Let's walk. I'll stay for ten minutes in case you want me to take notes. Then I'd better get back and do something on the Egypt for this afternoon."

They had waited for him in the Royal Flush, and old Dorman ceased to be in any hurry at all when he settled down into a chat with Miss Coleman in the anteroom. The great man was going to have the perquisites of office, and he was pretending to bribe her to leave Nicholas and work for him. Nicholas was almost normal again as he took his seat in one of the comfortable chairs in which the Advisory Council sat and strolled into business by easy roads. But this morning Colonel Bogey, as Lord Cluricawn was nicknamed, began to make his ethical apology for this business at length, and Nicholas lost his temper.

"Good God, Cluricawn, can't you keep this for your Saturday-afternoon speech in the constituency? Let's get down to figures and forget La Fontaine or whomever you're talking about!"

After this, business proceeded in a not very genial mood, and Nicholas tried to soak his evil humor out of him in a long hot bath at the club and to brace himself with a cold shower. He drank too much brandy at lunch, and his head had a slight noise in it as he walked to the bank. He wondered why in God's name he had rushed down in this headlong manner to the Advisory Council. For nearly three months now they

242

had dawdled over a business that he and Miss Coleman could settle in less than an hour. He thought angrily: "The whole of this bloody country has its backside anchored to an armchair. Christ help us, if there's a war around the corner."

Mr. Strood, also returning to the bank, joined him and began to fret about somebody's overdraft.

Nicholas stopped dead and looked angrily at his bank manager. "For God's sake, Mr. Strood, don't bother me with this. Take it up to Miss Coleman, and she'll decide the whole damned thing in one minute."

Mr. Strood went pale, raised his hat, and walked on. Nicholas knew that he had done wrong. He looked up at the smoldering tawny clouds in the sky. This damned thunder! It always clogged his blood and made the nerves in his legs twitch. My God, what an afternoon to tackle these bloody rogues from Cairo! If he told Whitehall that he knew this money was going to be reinvested in a hostile country, they would never forgive him for revealing them as fools. What the hell could he do with them?

At ten minutes past four, finally goaded by an Egyptian who insisted on speaking French, although Nicholas knew he could speak English, he told them to go to hell and elsewhere for the money. Miss Coleman had looked up in warning, but he ignored her. This made a consternation, as the delegation well knew the City would look askance at anything he had refused. The annoying Egyptian began to conciliate in English. Nicholas snapped: "If you had talked plain English all the time, instead of your puerile French, I might have listened to you. Now, the matter is closed."

Nicholas got up. They left hardly able to muster a farewell politeness.

Miss Coleman gathered up her notes. She said: "I imagine we'll have a telephone call from Dorman."

The call came half an hour later. Old Dorman sounded very puzzled. Nicholas said bluntly: "Your advisers are either fools or rogues. It's your job to find out which and why. I'm done with it."

Although he knew he had done the right thing, Nicholas worked himself up into a nerve storm. Outside, the heat that seemed, like the glass, a solid leaned against the window, and he felt that his head was like a drum on which at any moment thoughts would begin to pound like hands. He looked about for something to occupy his mind, and then his eye fell on his private case which Muriel had sent in with Blake. As if he could not help himself, he opened it with the key which Muriel had sent in an envelope with a note asking him to ring if he were not coming home to dinner as usual. He noted that her writing had changed somewhat. It was more compact, tauter, and the points of the letters had sharpened. Nicholas had frequently noticed how any sharp development in character at once showed in a more economical handwriting. Yes, she had changed rapidly. Then he saw the file of anonymous letters, there was a gap in his pulse, and he knew that suddenly he was back again in the middle of it all.

As if it had somehow to discharge itself, his mind at once began to project faces on the white pad, and his eye occupied itself with them. Underneath each face now was the image of Sarah Fuidge with that mildewed light on the skin. Suddenly the other faces began to jump up and down on her face in a staccato rhythm, and Nicholas shifted uneasily in his chair, clenched his hands on the arms, and tried to abolish these faces that shot out at him like the close-ups he had seen in Russian films. As if to get away from them, he jumped up from his chair and went and took a glass of water. He wondered if they would vanish if he pulled the blind down. He walked about the room, felt calmer, sat down again, and found that the faces now came and went more slowly and that watching them was a comfort to his mind. So long as he kept looking at them, he was able to forget about the letters . . .

"Mr. Elder."

"Send him in," said Nicholas, and closed the shutter.

During the week, Mr. Elder had accumulated documents, and Nicholas groaned as he saw the file in Elder's hand. He asked unreasonably: "Mr. Elder, must I go on all my life scratching my name on these damned documents that I know very well you've got in order?"

Mr. Elder looked at the taut white face of his chief and said: "Well, Mr. Bude, you can depute it to Mr. Strood."

Nicholas looked up and tried to consider him. "But you don't want that, Mr. Elder, because Mr. Strood will fuss like a damned hen over each one and then probably send it up to me because he can't make up his own mind."

Mr. Elder looked at him with nothing in his eyes.

"Miss Coleman often signs your letters for you. Perhaps . . ."

"All right, I'll do them this time, but the system here is going to be changed." He looked sharply at Mr. Elder. "Mr. Elder, I want a quick answer. Who is the most competent person in this bank?"

"Outside yourself, Miss Coleman."

Nicholas took up one of the pens Mr. Elder had brought him. Mr. Elder always brought his special pens and special inks for these transfers involving large sums. Nicholas signed his name again and again and got more and more irritated with the pointed nob that Mr. Elder brought for the interlineal signature that was a Bude Bank safeguard against forgery in foreign transactions. He blotched the last deed and swore. Mr. Elder forgot his own blotter and turned the documents hastily on the white blotting pad on the desk. Nicholas jumped in his chair and hit the desk and overturned the pot of red ink so that the whole pad was incarnadined.

"Jesus Christ! You fool!"

Mr. Elder was startled. He stared at Mr. Bude.

Nicholas looked furiously at him, and said: "Don't you know damned well I never use that blotting pad!"

"I'm sorry, Mr. Bude. I forgot myself." Mr. Elder was a little pale under the onslaught. "After all, Mr. Bude, it *is* a blotter, isn't it?"

How the hell could he tell Elder that he wanted the thing to see faces on and kept it there for that? He gripped the arms of the chair and tried to calm himself. "I'm sorry, Mr. Elder. I shouldn't have lost my temper." Nicholas knew he was sweating. "It's this goddam thunder in the air, and—I got no sleep last night."

"It's quite all right, Mr. Bude."

Mr. Elder got his own blotter and mopped the splashes from the desk and then saw that the letters in Mr. Bude's private case were reddened by the ink and took them in his hand to blot them.

"Leave those alone!"

Mr. Elder looked in some alarm at Mr. Bude's face.

246

Nicholas had shouted at him. Mr. Elder dropped the letters and said: "I'm sorry. I simply wanted to dry them."

Nicholas was too confused to explain.

"Mr. Bude, I hope you don't think me impertinent, but if I were you, I'd have a holiday."

"Why?" Nicholas barked the question.

"Well—you seem overworked, or worried, or something. I'm sorry. Perhaps I ought not to have spoken."

Nicholas looked at him in a way that made Mr. Elder flinch.

"Mr. Elder, why did you ask me how many pages of that notepaper I took the night I went to your place?"

Mr. Elder paused for some time, as if trying to understand what lay behind this question. "Mr. Bude, I don't know why you asked me that question. Must I answer it?"

"I would prefer if you did."

Mr. Elder seemed very uncomfortable. "I am afraid you will think it rather childish, Mr. Bude, but I have a certain number of pages of that paper, and each day I use one page, either for a letter, or sometimes for a kind of diary I keep, of my thoughts, and . . ."

"Go on," said Nicholas as Mr. Elder paused in some embarrassment.

"Well, I know it is perhaps stupid, but I always have had the idea that I have just so many days of life left as there remain pages of that notepaper." Something like a spot of color came into the old face. "So, I had the queer idea that you had taken five days of my life away."

Nicholas looked hard at him. He was feeling awkward under this disclosure and suddenly remembered the uncanny way in which Mr. Elder had arisen from his chair in the Chinese room to draw the curtains at the exact moment when the sun, behind his back, had touched the horizon.

"Well, perhaps that is the truth, Mr. Elder."

Mr. Elder seemed to be all bone and skin suddenly, and his voice had got thin. "Mr. Bude, that is a very unpleasant thing to say. I do not see why you should expect me to tell you a lie. I do not understand why you asked that question, anyway."

"Well, it's no dafter than the answer you gave, is it?"

"No, perhaps not. I suppose my culture, such as I have, ought to protect me from a superstition of that kind, but . . ."

"So, I suppose, you keep that notepaper counted?"

"Yes."

Nicholas looked at the desk and asked: "If that is so, you would know if any pages were missing?"

"Yes. At the end of each box. I can check them by the calendar."

"Have you missed any?"

Mr. Elder was obviously startled. Nicholas looked full at him suddenly. There was a pause.

"Extraordinary! Why do you ask me that?"

"Never mind. I want the answer."

"I have. Eighteen pages."

"You have no idea who took them?"

"No. I have been puzzled. And annoyed."

"I see."

"Mr. Bude, I don't understand how you could come to guess that I have missed this paper."

"I'm not a fool, Mr. Elder."

"I don't think you are. But I still don't . . ."

"You say you write letters on this paper. To whom?"

"Almost invariably to Professor Crampton."

"When you were ill, you wrote a note of apology on it to me."

"That is correct."

"Hum . . ."

There was a pause.

"Mr. Bude, what is all this mystery?"

"That's what I want to know from you."

"Well, I have answered some very personal questions, but you do not explain your reason for asking them. It's all very queer."

"Very queer, Mr. Elder, with you living like a Chinese mandarin, and somebody else in the bank smoking opium, and . . ."

Mr. Elder looked as if he might faint. Nicholas had not meant to talk about Miss Coleman, but it had slipped his tongue. Mr. Elder was upset.

"Has Miss Coleman told you?"

"She has not. She doesn't even know I was in your room—unless you told her."

"Of course I did not." Mr. Elder paused. "Then how do you know it was her. You could not recognize her under that veil . . ." Mr. Elder was startled. "Good heavens . . ."

"I hadn't meant to say it, Mr. Elder." Nicholas hesitated. "This conversation is private."

"I understand. Well, is there anything else you want to know?"

Nicholas took up one of the anonymous letters. "Have you seen this envelope before?"

"No."

"Do you use envelopes of that kind?"

"No."

"That is all, Mr. Elder."

Mr. Elder now looked obstinate. "It is not all, Mr. Bude. I don't understand all this. But I want to know how you knew I missed that paper."

"Very well. You see these letters?"

"Yes."

"They are written on Elder Bank notepaper."

"But . . ."

"They are anonymous letters."

Mr. Elder paused. "The ones you are writing yourself?"

"I am not writing them."

"Good Lord! What do they say?"

"Perhaps you already know, Mr. Elder?"

"Mr. Bude, even if I am your employee, I cannot permit this."

Nicholas hit the desk. "I don't care a goddam whether you permit it or not." He suddenly stood up. "If you repeat a word of this conversation anywhere, by Christ, I'll . . ."

Nicholas took up the blotting pad and tore it across. Somehow the ink looked like blood on his hands. He saw Mr. Elder looking at his hands, and swore.

"Is there anything wrong with my hands, Mr. Elder?"

"No."

"Are you sure you have never noticed anything wrong with my hands?"

Mr. Elder looked in alarm at the sweating white face of Mr. Bude.

"No, Mr. Bude, except . . ."

"Except what?"

"Well, you don't always seem to be able to keep them under control."

Nicholas sat down as if exhausted. Mr. Elder got him a glass of water. The clock struck five with its almost noiseless chime. All the fight had gone out of Nicholas. He said: "I've got my Chinese room, too, Mr. Elder."

"Your car will be here, Mr. Bude."

"Very well. Send somebody up to clear up this bloody mess."

Muriel felt angry when Nicholas got home after his confession to Mr. Elder. He looked so exhausted that one felt the blood could not move in his body, and he stumbled as he came up the steps. He was too fatigued to utter the curse on his lips. He mopped his gray, damp face and looked up at the incubating thunder in the sky.

"My God, what a day."

Muriel, who had gone to much care to make herself look nice, realized that he did not notice her at all. He had that awful, absent-minded look on his face.

"You look dead tired."

"I am. I got no sleep last night. I missed the train and got down somehow." He paused. "I stayed for the funeral."

"When did he die?"

"About an hour after they telephoned me on Tuesday."

"You'd better have some tea, and a bath."

"Yes." He said in a polite, random way: "What have you been doing?"

"Oh, I spent the last two nights in London. I came down early this morning. It's like an oven up there with all this thunder about."

"Yes."

He was taking no interest in anything. She felt she could not bear this any longer and said: "I'm just taking the dogs for a walk. Margaret is bringing tea. I've had mine. Why not have a sleep until dinner?"

"I might."

Muriel put on a new frock for dinner, but he hardly seemed aware of her coming into the room. She began to get annoyed. She had not been able to get him out of her mind since she had discovered that he almost certainly had affairs with Laura and Miss Coleman and maybe other women. Now, as he sat like an old man in his chair, in some world of his own, she felt the whole thing was hopeless. Oxinham brought in the sherry.

"Bring in the cocktail things, Oxinham."

"Yes, madam."

When they came she made a very strong cocktail and said: "Better have this, if you are tired. What about some Château Yquem for dinner? I've told Oxinham."

"Yes."

She thought he seemed to move, as well as talk, in monosyllables. She took up the *Evening Standard* he had brought and gave up any attempt at conversation. He obviously was not inclined to talk about what had happened in Northumberland, or else was too fatigued to mention anything at all.

After dinner he apologized for being tired. He opened the window and stood by it to get some air, and remarked that it was terribly stuffy. She knew that it was, and said, as if to make it easy for him, that it had got her down all day. Nicholas came back from the window

252

and gave it up and sank into his chair. His eyes closed, and his face seemed to hang in dejection, and she wondered if he was turning that file of letters over and over in his mind.

With the sunlight of the wine in his blood, and the glow of the fire in his eyes, Nicholas had felt tides of sleep submerging his mind, and he shut his lids and was like some medium into whose liquid glass pictures and memories glided like bright fish in a sunlighted room of the sea. He could see the blue peat smoke climbing into the sky from the chimney of his uncle's cottage in Northumberland. He could see the widow in her cheap black clothes that looked urban and cold on her strong peasant body. He counted again with her the old shabby bank notes that she had taken from a cupboard, and calculated with her again if they could afford a name plate on the coffin. And there he had sat, in the kitchen with the stone floor, Nicholas Bude, the millionaire, a future member of the House of Lords, knowing that he dare not offer her as much as a one-pound note to help with the burial, lest he offend the ghost of the proud and humble man who now lay on the bed with his mouth forever closed upon whatever last word he had wanted to say to his nephew, the great London banker, and his clean, muscular, and bony hands clasped upon a Bible on his breast.

Nicholas remembered how he had stood by Christian's widow by the graveside and in some way had felt closer to her than he had ever been to anybody save his own father, although they had spoken few words, as if she understood that they inhabited different worlds and there could be no communication between them. And she had said nothing personal until the last moment before he left for the country station. Then she had looked out at him from her clear eyes and said: "I'm glad he was gone, before you came, for he would have known that you had no happiness." Then she had put her hands on his shoulders. "Kiss me, Nicholas. I'm thinking you are as lonely as I am, and my man dead."

Then the door of the car had banged behind him, as it banged now in his memory, and woke him up, and he saw Muriel, suddenly beautiful, and as distant as some golden girl in a technicolor film. The hot air of the room seemed to choke him, and he felt the pressure of the accumulating thunder outside, and he wanted to pull the clouds asunder in his hands and then bang them together and burst the rain out of them. He saw Muriel's long lovely legs and under the silk could feel in his hands the live, beautiful breasts. And her mouth was the red meat of the rose and her flesh the golden meat of the honey. And now he knew that he was admiring her like a painting, and a vague surprise came into him that she was his own wife, and it seemed like some accident that had nothing to do with him, and all he wanted to do was to get away by himself and sleep. Somewhere filed away in his mind were the letters, and Sidonie lay asleep in a corner, with a blue veil of slumber hiding her, and Elder's Chinese room was hidden inside that Chinese painting on the wall. He knew that for the first time for ages he had got into a peaceful mood and wondered if he could slip away inside it to bed.

Suddenly light cracked in the room, and the flash was followed by a tremendous bang, and both were repeated almost simultaneously.

"God, it's burst right over here!"

The lights, of course, went out. Nicholas knew from long experience that every shaft of lightning in the district aimed itself at the Barrington electric plant and got it the first time. Muriel got up in the light of a flash and closed the window. Oxinham brought in an oil lamp and blinked at the violent flashes.

"For God's sake, draw the curtains," said Nicholas, "or this damned lightning will blind us."

When Oxinham went out, Nicholas felt the electricity shooting through his body and swore in anger.

"Goddam it, I want a night's sleep. And now we'll have this bloody storm all night long."

Muriel listened to the fierce pant of air that would soon develop to a hysterical wind and said calmly: "Take a couple of aspirins and a large whisky and you might sleep through it all."

"I dream like hell in a thunderstorm." Nicholas suddenly picked up *The Times*. "By God, it's full moon."

Muriel looked at him with some alarm. She knew that he dreaded sleep tonight more than he would hate sitting down here awake and listening to the tumult around the house. She would not have hesitated for a second in doing what her woman's sense told her to do, seduce him to her bed, but she knew that it was quite useless, so deranged was his system, and all she could think of was to pour him a large drink and have one herself. She persuaded him to have a couple of tablets and then went upstairs. She could feel that every flash of lightning jammed into his mind.

She did not undress for half an hour until she heard him come into his dressing room, and then she knew that he would at least get some sleep. She did not get to sleep herself for a long time.

Nicholas put his head on the pillow and plunged into the nocturnal world of dream.

In the jungle, faces that sat like white owls on the bough had moons for eyes. A flash of lightning rico-

255

cheted on the faces, and the page of his child's nursery book flipped over and each face had become a square that was the Ben Nicholson room inside the black lines and also the white blotting pad in the bank. After the flash, he waited for the bang of thunder, but it alighted noiseless on his head like a white owl, and the huge gong in Elder's hall was lying on the silent carpet. Then the gong jumped up and was hanging on the wall of darkness again and multiplied itself out in Saturnine moons that balanced on their rims along the bough, and one had to be careful not to let a thought knock against them lest they topple off their edges, for the moons had visages closed yet open like windows. He could not stop his thought looking into them, and suddenly they widened as if to shout in agony and they had become swans, and he saw that it was a gust of wind which had blown open their wings and each swan had a hoof cloven instead of a beak and suddenly the hoof slammed together and a long yellow tooth stuck into the underlip and Sarah Fuidge was looking out the window and stayed for a long time until a bottle of red ink on the sill jumped at his fist hitting the desk and Sarah's face was blotched in blood and sank into the blotter until it was far away in the sun outside Elder's room that turned crimson as it balanced on the horizon. Then Elder pulled the curtains and the wings closed on the swans and made them round, smooth Barbara Hepworth marbles. He put out his hands through the blue veil on Sidonie but he could not lift the marbles although they looked very light and had the soft pink flesh of clouds and then he collapsed from the effort and lay under a golden shawl of hair and he could feel the beating of her heart and when she breathed out he pulled her breath into him and when she breathed in the breath was pulled out of him and his sides were shutting and opening like a bellows and each time he ached until he could not stand the pain and had to put his hands up behind his neck and rend himself asunder down the middle but she said it did not matter as the silk jacket had to come off anyway. A notch slipped in space and his sundered halves had joined him whole again and he was in the bank and one of the swans flew in the window although its wings were shut and fell on his desk and he got a paperknife and opened its wings where they locked in the clasp and he read on the vellum instep a message saying he had a will to death in his hands and then he took up the envelope and the hoof fell out and Roberts ran over the edge of the desk and picked it up just as the car screeched aside and he carefully thanked Roberts and put the hoof in his pocket and looked back to see the moonshine on Sarah's nightdress where old Fuidge had hung it behind the lodge and there along the boughs again were the faces like owls that had moons for eyes.

He awoke sweating and with his mouth parched, but he could not get up for a glass of water because he had to lie motionless and keep the dream motionless in the thunder that was shaking the world in case it damaged the pictures in the lunar mirror of his mind and made the glass fly into shrapnel around his head. But he could not get the dream quite the same again and at last the hoof somehow kicked out through a cloud of white swans and clanged the gong in the hall of Elder's house and the noise awoke him into a shout and somehow switched on the lights that searched him out through the dark. . . .

"Oh, I'm sorry. I thought I heard you shouting."

Muriel was ghostly behind her torch and wore a dressing gown with a hood that somehow made her fully dressed.

"Shouting?"

"Yes. Perhaps you had a nightmare!"

"I believe I had. It's nothing."

She paused for a moment, and he resented her mind trying to probe his mind along the shaft of light.

"Oh, very well. Good night."

"Good night."

Now he knew that he would not get to sleep again. If she said in the morning that he ought to have a holiday or see a doctor, by God, he would kick her on the backside.

He might be a damned fool, but he knew that long before the letters had ever come, it was the inhibition she had put on his sexual life that had caused this nightmare. To hell with her, coming in like a bloody nurse!

THIRTY-TWO

Some fitful bouts of sleep in the dawn hours only dislocated Nicholas' rest, and he got up in the morning with a cold, empty headache. He felt somehow that the gale blowing through him during the night had gutted him of all the fears and pictures and even feelings, and he was only a husk. He let up the blind and contemplated the dreary landscape under a rain that slanted from the southwest. The room was cold, and he hoped to God there would be a good fire in the breakfast room. He knew that for days now there was going to be an intolerable nagging rain. Often, at night, when it rained, he could feel the rain drumming down on his.

head as one heard it on the roof of a conservatory. Last night behind this curtain of rain was the full moon, and even old Fuidge knew what a storm on the night of full moon did to the worried mind. Now he was gutted by the wind and swabbed out by the rain, and the bathroom was cold and aching and white as a hospital washroom and he wished to God that he did not have to shave before going down. Then hunger began to attack him and he left his razor uncleaned and hurried down to the breakfast room and thanked God that Muriel was not there. He could not look at the porridge but ate three fried eggs and two juicy slices of Virginia ham and swallowed a pint of hot coffee and sent Margaret out of the room on some errand so that he could enjoy a couple of enormous belches. Then Muriel came in looking as happy as a Tahitian girl at the North Pole and looked out the window and shuddered and helped herself to porridge, and he looked at the yellow cream on the porridge and without a word of apology got up and went into the smoking room and found that the fire was not lighted. He rang the bell and a maid came in and he asked why there wasn't a fire there, and she said the logs had got wet because the roof had blown off the timber shed, and she knew that he never liked a coal fire in this room, and she was trying to dry some logs in the kitchen. He walked about the house while she tried to make a fire and felt like a guest having a look over a new hotel. This house was everything but a home, and he supposed the only reason he had bought it was that some homing instinct had made him come to the neighborhood of that small farm over past Yeoman Spire where his grandfather had worked first as a hired man and then as the owner; if a tenant farmer could be called an owner. Barrington had cost

259

eighteen thousand pounds, and he still did not know more than two of his tenants by sight and still took a doubtful turning if he went into the north wing. When he was away, he could hardly place the furniture from memory, but now he could remember the place and texture and personality of every chair and cup and utensil in the small cottage in Northumberland. There was something one put into a house that made it come alive, and no one had put it in here, and this morning the house was damp and hollow, and a gooseflesh was coming on his skin as he stood by a window and looked at the tunnels of water upon the vinehouses.

Suddenly it began to get him down, and he felt a kind of nausea of loneliness in the empty world of his life, and he knew that he did not care a fundamental damn about Muriel or Sidonie at this moment. He was like a mouse in the bottom of an empty barrel and he did not know how he could get out of it. He wondered if old Jock was watching him with a cynical eye in the empty barrel of Bude's Bank. He thought of all the men he knew in Lombard Street and in the City and how busily they went about their lives, dictating hastily in cars and taxis, or signing some document that changed pounds into dollars or francs, and he wondered if they fancied they were doing some urgent work in the world, when they were no more, really, than money-changers in a bureau who, handling millions, could not buy anything for themselves.

He wandered about the unused rooms for an hour, getting cold and damp, and returned to the breakfast room to find Muriel reading the morning papers. Last night, suddenly, he had come almost to hate her. He looked out at the rain and said in an irritable way: "I think I'll go out in the car. Do you want Blake?"

"No. Where are you going?"

"Oh, I just thought I'd go over to the Roebuck and have lunch." He paused. "I want to get away from myself."

"Why don't you go for a walk?"

"Well, goddam it, I can get away faster in a car, can't I?"

She looked up at his sharp, ridiculous remark, and he wondered if she had guessed that the annoyance in his voice was a resentment against her. He was getting damn tired of living this separate existence in the same house.

"Well, you would get away still faster and farther if you took a holiday." She got up and looked testy. "Don't snap at me as if it is my fault, if you can't make up your mind to leave that wretched bank for a month."

She paused. "*I'm* going on a holiday, a good long way."

Then she went abruptly out of the room, leaving him in a bad temper. Blast her, her anger only made her sexual power all the more potent.

He was in very bad humor when he got into the car and said to Blake: "I'm going over to lunch at the Roebuck Inn. Take any road you like. It's such a lovely day, we might as well enjoy the country." Blake smiled carefully, as if unsure whether to laugh or not. Suddenly Nicholas stopped as he was stepping into the car and looked at Blake. "Blake, if you had this car, and somebody to drive you, what the hell would you do with yourself on Saturday?"

Blake was surprised by the question, and confused. "Blessed if I know, sir."

"Then it's bloody hard for me to know. Never mind the run, Blake. Soon I'll have you putting on my pants for me." Nicholas saw that he was discomfited. "It's all right, Blake, I'm not annoyed with you. I'm just sick of this weather."

"So am I, sir. It's knocked all my apples down. Had a lovely crop."

"Never mind. You can get some here."

"Thank you, sir, but"—Blake smiled—"your apples are all down too, sir."

Nicholas laughed and felt a little better. Forsyte and Blake had at least something tangible to worry about. Nicholas looked out in a despairing way at the ruined and disheveled countryside. Where the farmer had not beaten the storm, the stooks lay tumbled on the stubble, lashed by the ceaseless rain. It was like a March day strayed into August.

Blake had taken the road through the hamlet of Yeoman Spire, and now they turned out into the bleak countryside, and Nicholas felt in him the hopeless frustration of the farmers who looked with sullen eyes at the rain and had to suffer it as a man suffers blows with his hands tied behind him. Over that hillock was the farmhouse where his grandfather had lived and where his father had been born, and Nicholas wondered if it was on such a day as this, looking at the ruined harvest, that Jock had made up his mind to swing his pick in another country and strike something harder than the mushy clay. Now they were coasting down to the valley of the farm, and Nicholas had a feeling that he was somehow driving back into his ancestry, and a curious subterranean longing arose in him to fight somehow this weather as the peasant tried to fight it with his hands. And all he could do with himself was to get rid of his boredom by lunching at the Roebuck Inn with others as bored as himself.

Down in a hollow by the roadside, where the earth was yellow marl, a peasant was hacking out a drain to carry away the flood from the adjacent field of roots. Wet in rain and splotched by the yellow mud, he swung his grubber to work out the roots and allow him to use the spade, and, as if he knew that the mangolds would soon be naked and afloat if he did not stop this river of water, he worked in a kind of fury, like a bull rooting at the ground.

Nicholas tapped on the glass shutter behind Blake's head and told him to pull up. Unaware that the car had stopped, above him on the road, the man continued to hack away as if he were digging a hole into the bottom of the world. Nicholas had a feeling that he was working in the way a man might work who felt his pick near gold. Now he saw that he was almost an old man, perhaps sixty, but his whole body was an instrument of sinew and muscle almost as hardy and virile as that of a young man. Blake looked around for the second time and then realized that his master had stopped merely to watch this man working.

At last the man straightened his back to take a spell for a moment, and then he saw the car. He looked up in curiosity, wiped the rain and sweat off his face, and thought of something. He shouted up to Blake: "Got a match, mister?"

"Yes."

Blake had delayed a moment before replying, as if he wondered if he should answer him while driving his master. Nicholas felt a jerk of annoyance in him and opened the door and got out.

"I'll take him down a match."

Blake was rather surprised to see Mr. Bude get over the gap in the hedge and walk down through the mud as carelessly as if he were on the pavement in Pall Mall. Certainly Mr. Bude was in a queer mood this morning.

The old man, who Nicholas now realized was perhaps seventy years, touched his sopping felt hat, and said:

"It be a nasty morning, mister."

Nicholas looked down into the honest eyes with time's stitching about them. Up to the waist in the drain, one might almost think he was digging his own grave.

"Yes. You want a match?"

Nicholas had pulled out a box.

"Thankee, mister, I do." He had a look of apology. "It be your driver I called at." He looked at Nicholas in his Savile Row suit, St. James shoes, Jermyn Street silk shirt and collar and tie. "I didn't want ee to come down slammerin' in the mud."

Nicholas handed him the box.

"I'll take a couple, sir."

"Keep the box. I've got a lighter."

"Oh, thankee, sir."

Nicholas looked about and surveyed the distance needed to allow the drain to cut off the water from the channel it had broken through into the mangold field.

"Do you expect to get up there today?"

"Mebbe. I be goin' to work on at it, though it be Saturday, unless the flood go rollin' down them mangolds like billiard balls. Mebbe, I'll have driven her up by the dark, or mebbe no, for them blasted roots be like my old teeth that won't stop in nor come out. This one be a sally and it be fair hooked up and all hingy. I be once an' I'd get so mad with the bastin' at it that I'd fair haul it out by my teeth, the way it's

264

gainsettin' me. But I be no younker now, like when I was quarryman to old Bude."

"Bude? Is this Bude's farm?"

"It be, a long time back, but now it be Maclew's, since the old Simon himself be gone, for that son of his had no use for danderin' about on the land." The old man chuckled. "I'm tellin' ee, 'twas no sally root Jock Bude struck his pick into, but grains o' gold, and they be after growin' now into Bude's Bank, if ee have ever heard the name. Aye, it be a long story of some goin' up, an' others goin' down, but old Simon, he bided by the land." The old man paused. "There I be danderin' on, and the rain soakin' in to ee." He touched his hat again. "Well, thankee, sir."

Nicholas knew that he could not go. "Go on working, I'll see that root come out."

The old man hacked away, grunting as the roots sank from the edge of the grubber into the clay bottom. Nicholas measured the run of the drain and wondered if this old man could ever cut all the way up before dark. He had a feeling that it would heartbreak him if he did not, having given up his Saturday halfday, probably not because he wanted to earn the extra-time money, but from his instinct to fight the weather and save the mangolds from the water each moment heavier in the flood as the rain swathed down. The old man cursed in healthy anger and straightened up again.

"It be tough, and fightin' at me."

"Give me that grubber!"

The old man was alarmed as Nicholas grabbed the implement.

"Heigh, sir, ee can't be slip-sloppin' and sliverin' them clothes in the mud . . ."

"Come on. Get out, and let me get in."

Bewildered, the old man took hold of Nicholas' hand and was hauled out of the drain. Nicholas handed him his overcoat and took the grubber and jumped into the drain. For about five minutes he whacked at the roots and felt it was about as much use as trying to decapitate an eel in the water. There was no backing in this clay to cut against. He straightened himself up, looked down at it, realized the cynical, shrewd eyes of the old man watching him, and worse, saw that Blake had come down. Then he bent over the root and began to wrestle with it. For the first time in his life he felt that he had something in his hands. They singled out the main rootholds through the mud which had already plastered Nicholas from head to foot, and, settling himself, he got a leverage with his knee against the side of the trench. Then he hauled. For about two minutes he tried it in every direction, until, at last, he felt that he discovered the angle from which he could wrench out the anchor root. Then to get a long pull of breath, he stood up.

"Aye, this be tougher than drivin' about in a car." The old man smiled. "Ach, ye made a good try."

Nicholas smiled. Now he stopped, got down as far as he could through the mud to the claw of the root, gripped it, forced it around, and then heaved. After a fearful struggle he at last tore it up with a jerk that threw him on his back. Now all he had to do was to wrench away the secondary roots, and he took a long breath and looked at the stump.

"Come out, you—bastard!" said Nicholas, astounding Blake, who jumped aside as the heavy root was slung up out of the trench. Nicholas got out and felt good. His clothes were ruined.

The old man looked at the root. "Aye, 'twas a good

266

bit job, but ee wouldn't be able to do that after a day's work."

"Wouldn't I?" Nicholas paused. "Blake, get my wallet out of the inside pocket." He turned to the old man. "Go on, get your overcoat." The old man obeyed the command in Nicholas' voice and went down to the bush where his overcoat was bundled. "Take out a fiver, Blake. My hands are muddy."

"Yes, sir."

"Drive him to his house, let him change his clothes, then take him over to the Roebuck and tell Mr. Hillson to give him the same lunch that I have. Come back for me at five o'clock."

"Yes, sir."

"Don't tell him who I am, Blake."

"Very well, sir."

The old man came back with his coat.

"Have you any lunch in your pocket?" asked Nicholas.

"Aye, a wee bit bread and cheese."

"Leave it there. I'm going to finish this drain. You can do my job for the rest of the day."

"But, sir . . "

"Never mind. Do as I tell you. Blake will look after you. I want a holiday. You call this work. I call it pleasure."

"But, sir, I be planning the lie of this drain all the morning, and . . ."

"That's all right. A blind man could see how to cut this drain. Go on, Blake."

Blake nodded at the old man who was too bewildered to resist. Then he looked back at Nicholas. Unaccountably Blake found that he had winked at his master. He saw him take up the grubber, having spat

267

on his hands. He knew that the drain would be done at five o'clock. Blake suddenly realized that it was raining like hell. He had forgotten it.

Nicholas watched the car vanish around the corner of the lonely byroad and looked about the landscape. There was not a house in sight. He was alone with his labor. He felt alone as a cow does that goes away by herself to calve in the corner of a field, alone as a man does who goes into the wilderness to let his soul in the pangs of birth come out before his eyes alone. Out here in the whisking rain and the skirling wind he was alone with something to do. He stuck the grubber in the soil and went and folded up his overcoat about the bread and cheese wrapped in a red handkerchief and laid it under a bush. Then he stood and examined the lie of the drain. He wondered why the old man had cut it so deep and then he realized that the flooding came from a blocked underground drain at the level of which he must junction with this cutting, and he saw also that this drain, the way it slanted, would clear once and for all this boggy corner of the field and make it plowable. The old man had reckoned it all out and was not going to temper it in a temporary job and let perhaps a fortnight's rain turn the subsoil into a winter sponge.

Nicholas was slightly surprised to find how he could understand the old man's mind and see it mapped out here in the field. He pulled off his collar and tie and stuffed them into his pocket. In an indifferent way he felt that those who knew him might think he was doing something odd. He did not care a damn. This was about the first thing he had really wanted to do, and he was discovering that once something really got its hands about one's heart, all doubts and problems had gone. They were gone away with those clouds and blown away with those shocked leaves, and somewhere at the other side of the hill were Muriel, and Sidonie, and the Chinese room, and the anonymous letters, and they had lost all their meaning. The only thing here and present was that drain, and now, by God, he must get down to it, and he'd better cut a stick, not having the old man's training, so that he could keep it at the same depth all the way up.

Now, the root out of the way, he could take the spade for a while, and he picked it up and found the handle was a skinned limb that had not been planed, and he felt for the natural holds between the knots, and familiarized his hands with it as a blind man might try to apprehend the face of somebody with his fingers. Then he rubbed his hands on his buttocks, and spat on them, feeling that in some way he was consecrating them to labor.

He got down in the drain and began to dig.

He found there was a sensual delight in the slicing of the moist clay, and he cut clean oblongs and piled them on one parapet of the trench, feeling that later on they would be useful to build a fence or clamp into a dam, because, he knew in some way, this drain ought to be closed by large stones upon a floor of flagstones, and, realizing that, he made four-inch shelves on each side a foot above the bottom to support the flagstones. Each time he came to a root or a stone the beauty of the job was spoiled, but he packed each empty warren of a root with clay, and remedied the gapped shelf with this plastic stuff that one could shape on the potter's wheel. Under an old cart track, he ran into a gravel bottom of flints and clinkers once laid on the surface to bear the wheels and now sunk down, and here he had to use the pick arm of the grubber, and for the first time felt the sting of point on stone going up through his arms and down his spine. This was something, by the Lord, that one could take a shoulder swing at, and something that one smacked one's teeth at, and cursed, and basted, until one felt the pick was a geologic hammer making the bones of the world fly in splinters. This, by the Lord, was something like *work,* and Nicholas felt the salt of sweat pickle his eyes and the handle beginning to stick to his hands as if it were scalded onto the skin. He stopped for a moment and felt the hinge of his back bending as in a cramp, surveyed his foreground, and, as the old man might have, spoke aloud to himself: "Christ, the bloody carts on this track must have been a mile wide!"

He loosed the pick in his hand and realized that a patch of skin had come away on the handle. "God, I'd forgotten about the blisters!"

He made up his mind to clear through the track before he took a spell for the bread and cheese. The wind, going high, had blown the rain away, and he could take off his coat, and now he began to experience the real slog of physical work. He was getting tired, but that knowledge did not alter the fact that he must work on until the job was done, and suddenly he knew that he was jailed here in this drain, and that there was no way out until he cut his passage through to the water. He found somehow that a job like this insisted on being done and that that insistence had no bearing on payment or the love of work or anything outside the internal necessity of the job itself to get done. The drain had jailed him in itself as a painting or concerto or novel jails the artist and contains him there in the manual execution. All he knew was that the job

270

somehow had to get completed and would have confined anybody else there in the same way it confined him. Getting tired was not going to be any escape, nor would Blake at five o'clock allow him to get away if it were not done. There he would have to stay and finish it, as certainly the old man would have stayed. Once, as he straightened up to ease his back, he nearly dropped the spade in surprise as he realized that he would not have the slightest notion of leaving this job to rush into a meeting of Dorman's Royal Flush, although he had come down through the length of England like a man in a panic on yesterday, simply to arrive in time for that *conversazione*. Then he almost slapped himself in impatience for standing here and wasting time in thought with at least another yard of this cart bottom to get done before lunch.

His hands had become very sore before he got through the track, and he was dog-tired when he sat down to the bread and cheese. There were four great slices of bread, and a hunk of red cheese, and a pinch of salt in a twist of paper, and there was a slight taste of tobacco over everything. Nicholas would not have cared a damn, he knew, if there was a taste of urine. All he knew was that four enormous slices of bread now looked to him no larger than a snack for some bored epicure in Lilliput, and certainly not a meal. He ate it as slowly as he could, then went up and knelt down and drank water from a spring. He got his cigarette case, and found his lighter and he hoped it would work.

Before he snapped his lighter, he paused in thought. Now the only problem in life was whether his lighter would work or leave him stranded here without a smoke. He took a deep breath and snapped it and thanked God for the flame. Then, over his cigarette, he pondered on the fact that the fate of the Indian loan was not his problem at all. It was a headache he had inherited with Bude's Bank and that did not concern his personal existence or happiness. But the lighting of this cigarette was something important. He wanted it for himself, was doing it for himself, not for a lot of bloody fools in Whitehall or for the satisfaction of the Bude Bank staff, who would probably get more personal kick out of the India loan and his peerage than he ever could. So what the hell was he doing it all for? He was doing it simply as Grierson had been doing his manservanting at Barrington Hall, because he had inherited it, and it had deprived him of all personal volition. Grierson had kicked out of an existence that did not belong to him, so why the hell shouldn't he? He knew that now was not the time to consider it, but he also knew that what he was doing now would make the decision by itself, and his own decision later would simply be the royal rubber-stamping of a bill and nothing more. It would all have happened here. It irritated him now, even to waste time thinking about it, because he had the immediate labor before him, that was more urgent each moment as the water began to swirl over the corner of the mangold field. And, my God, his hands were red and sore and raw as a baby's bottom, and, the moment he touched that rough, unplaned handle, they were going to sting and burn and whatever skin was left to peel off would be gone soon.

He almost leaped from the contact of the grubber. Heavens, this was the hell of a root in front. It seemed to have been sewn into the earth, and it was all knuckles, as if it had to fight its way through the hard soil below the cart track. He dropped into the trench and began to whack at it. After some moments, for the first time, he began to wonder if he could stick this out and bear the scorching on his palms. But his instinct as an oarsman told him one went on through the unbearable to the end, and that it was useless to contemplate giving up. The tears smarted into his eyes as his hands stung fiercely in the hacking. God, it was raining again, and he must put his coat on. Even the silk lining of the sleeve was painful on his skin. He used his handkerchief to insulate his forehand, and wished to God that he had not left his gloves in the car. And then he stood up and saw the old man in his mind's eye coming back and seeing him working in gloves, and he stuck his handkerchief furiously into his pocket and drove the grubber as much as possible from the palm of his thumb. At last he got the root out and had some ease in cutting with the spade. He rubbed his forehead with the palm of his hand, and the salt of the sweat stung his now almost skinless palm. By God, this was hell . . .

It was hell, and he was enjoying it.

He kept his eyes off the goal of the drain, and worked on steadily, his sense of the architecture of the drain now becoming almost instinctive, so that he seldom glanced back to confirm his lines with the eye. As he tired, at each sag his body mustered new power in his muscles that now were beginning to breed their own energy, so that they could almost work on without the ordering of the brain, the body excelling in its own genius. Now he had established that rhythm and circulation that goes on inexhaustible as the blood, and he felt that to stop would somehow jar the automomentum, and he did not even look at his watch until he found himself within a yard of the end. Then he stood and saw that he would have to cut another short temporary drain above to divert the water while he joined the entrance. He looked at his watch. It was half-past four less a few minutes. He thought he could just do it before Blake arrived, and he hauled himself out and began furiously to hack out another drain to take the erupting flood. That took him fifteen minutes, and he ran to the spring for a drink before he tackled the last yard. He realized that it had again stopped raining and wondered when it had. He threw his coat aside, opened his shirt, and took the spade.

When he had cut the last piece of clay, and cleaned out the bottom, that came in just two inches below the gravel floor of the underground drain, Nicholas had a feeling a man might have who has joined two continents in an undersea tunnel. It was something done. This was a new drain. Not a new investment of old money. It was his drain. Not somebody else's drain. He had made it, built and smoothed up the sides, made those exact and intelligent ledges to take the flagstones. Somebody called Maclew might own for an hour or a hundred years this land that was once his grandfather's but this drain was his, just as it would have been the old man's drain if he had made it. And the old man would know that very well. Bit by bit, plow sod by plow sod, seed by seed, sapling by sapling, fence by fence, stone by stone, building, sowing, opening gaps in nature, directing the flow of water, the old man had made England his own. Not England, the earth itself. That was owning land. He did not own Barrington. Forsyte and Cantlebye did. One could not own anything one bought, only what one made. Deed and lease signified nothing. That was what old Christian

Bude knew, whose tough hands would not be bleeding now after this labor. That was what old Jock knew when he pensioned himself off back into the real ownership of . . .

He looked up and saw the car sliding into a pause. Good Lord, he had been daydreaming. Had the old man come back? Nicholas smiled. He had done the job. The recognition of that from the old man was more important than a peerage. All one wanted to be a successful peer was a double seat to one's pants as there were no beds in the Lords.

Blake came down and did not touch his cap, and in some way showed more respect by not doing it. He said nothing but walked to the edge of the drain and looked along it. He stood for a moment and then said: "Are you going to let the water in now?"

"Yes."

Nicholas found that it was now quite natural to work under the eyes of Blake. He took away the shield of sods, and the water rushed down into the new drain, and Nicholas felt all the blood rushing through his body and for a terrible instant thought it was going to rush out through his eyes.

Blake kept watching the water in a silent way. Then he turned and said: "He wanted to come back, but he was—kind of sleepy, and I put him down at his house."

"Yes." Nicholas paused. "Was he all right?"

"Yes. I didn't take him to the Roebuck. I thought he'd only be out of place. We had a steak in the Short-horn Arms and plenty of beer. Then we went and looked at a football match in the rain, and what with the beer and all he got tired. So I put him down."

"You did the right thing. I knew it was silly about the Roebuck."

Blake was somehow more sure of himself. He knew he had been sensible. Nicholas pulled on his coat and found his pipe. He sat down on the bank of the drain and said: "I think I'll have a pipe." He paused. "I'd like to see the water come clear. Oh, Lord, this looks in a mess."

Nicholas looked at the tobacco pouch and sighed.

"Have some of mine. It's cut flake, but you won't mind it in the open air." Blake looked at the water and said in a considering way, "They ought to stop the water and put the flagstones down on Monday before the ledges get washed."

"I was thinking that."

"I'll drop over tomorrow and tell old Hampton you've cut the ledges."

"Does he know who I am?"

"Yes. He found out in Morton Syme. They know your car."

"Oh, it doesn't matter." Nicholas pulled at his pipe, and Blake smoked his in a leisurely way.

Blake had sat on a large stone and had speculated on whether his master had managed to get it out. He said: "Was this stone in the way?"

"Yes."

"Humph."

Nicholas was looking quietly at Blake. He realized he had just met him for the first time. They were silent for some time, and then Nicholas said: "It's getting clear now."

"Yeah."

They sat in complete silence for some time after that, and then Nicholas said: "I can see bottom now. I think we might go."

Blake got up. Nicholas went along and fetched his

overcoat, and Blake did not offer to help him. They walked up to the road together when Nicholas had put the tools where old Hampton would find them. Just before they got to the road Nicholas stopped and looked back.

"You know, Blake, this used to be our land."

"I know."

When they got out on the road, Blake opened the door of the car for him and said: "Home, sir?"

"Ah, yes."

Nicholas knew very well why Blake had not called him "sir" or commented on the drain. He was treating him as a man, not an amateur who had just enjoyed a prank.

"Coat, sir? Apt to chill after work."

"Very well."

Blake was closing the door on him when he paused and suggested: "Like to keep this to ourselves, sir? We can go in the stable yard, and you can cross over the bridge straight to your room."

"Yes."

Blake got in and, Nicholas thought with a sigh, had become the smooth and debonair chauffeur to Nicholas Bude, the great banker, again.

When they got home, nobody was about, and Blake said: "If you'd like to put those clothes on your window sill, sir, when you've changed, I could get rid of them for you. Beyond cleaning or anything now. Leave your shoes, too. I'll clean them and put them back in your room."

"Thank you, Blake."

"Oh, here's your change, sir."

Blake gave him the change out of the fiver. Something told Nicholas not to offer it to him.

"Thank you, Blake. Pay for your own meal out of it?"

"Yes, sir. Thank you, sir."

"Thank you, Blake. Come for the clothes in about ten minutes. Good night."

"Good night, sir."

Nicholas crossed the wooden bridge from the stable yard over the garden lake and stepped onto the upper floor of the house. He went along to his own room and had a pleasant feeling that thanks to Blake he had managed to keep the whole thing a secret. He undressed quickly while his bath ran and put the clothes in a bundle around his shoes on the sill of his window and felt that he could leave the rest to Blake. He hastened along and locked himself in the bathroom and felt safe. Then he put his hand in the bath to try the water and leaped into the air.

"Christ Almighty!"

My God, how could the water be boiling like that? He thought for a moment and put his other hand under the cold tap and leaped again. Good God, he would not be able to do anything with his hands for a week! How on earth was he going to conceal them? His hands got used to the water and he had a slow, luxurious bath. When he got out he felt clean. He had not felt clean for years. All the poison had been sweated out of his mind, not only out of his body. He swore in good humor as he had to hold the towel between his thumb and forefinger to dry himself. Lord only knows how he was going to dress himself or do anything with these hands. He found some ointment in the bathroom cupboard and dressed them and saw they were in a shocking state. He could hardly bear the telephone in his hand when he rang the servants' hall.

"Margaret, call me with a cup of strong tea at twenty to eight. I don't want any tea now. I'm going to sleep until you call me."

"Yes, sir."

"Is the mistress in?"

"I think so, sir."

"Very well. I am not to be disturbed until twenty to eight. I've had my bath."

Nicholas had warmed his silk pajamas in the bathroom hot cupboard and now when he put them on he found that all his skin was conscious of them as if it had come alive again. It was marvelous how even one day's work had slimmed and tautened his belly. Now he was relaxed, but later on he knew his muscles would discover themselves, as if each were an individual, and brace themselves with involuntary movements and he would have again that peculiar feeling that he used to have as an oarsman, that his body had a personality independent of his mind. But, now, here was the pillow, and until dinner he would have a beautiful sleep, that kind of beautiful sleep which made a cushion of down out of the flesh until at last . . .

Margaret had tapped gently four times and not awakened him and then she came into the room and woke him by saying, "Your tea, sir," over and over again until the message got into his sleep and gently opened his eyes. He knew by her cap that it was not morning.

"Had a good sleep, sir?"

"Yes, Margaret."

She poured out his tea for him. He liked this girl with her cool-gray eyes and finely cut face and unexpectedly warm mouth.

"The mistress is changing, sir."

"All right."

He swore softly to himself when she went out. Good heavens, what dear old middle-class memory had decided Muriel to change for dinner this evening? He thought she had given that up. Well, he'd better shake a leg. Hum, he had woken with his body rejuvenated! He had a feeling that if Margaret's eyes had been blue, he might have pulled her down and kissed her.

She had, of course, laid out his dinner jacket in his dressing room. Gosh, he'd better be quick. Lord knows how he was going to make the bow in his tie. Even the tips of his fingers were blistered. His hands did not hurt now so much, but he knew that if they got hot and sweated, as one always sweated after exercise, the salt would sting him. He took up everything as if he were picking up a pea. He funked washing his hands again. Almost anything was bearable but water on the sore patches. He dressed himself quickly and looked at the clock. Five minutes to nine! Good God, had Margaret made a mistake? He picked up his watch. It was seven minutes to nine by that. What the hell had happened? Dinner was at eight. What the devil? Anyway, he had got a good sleep in and now he felt absolutely fine. He'd better get down.

THIRTY-THREE

When he got down, the decanters and glasses mirrored the glow of the log fire. Sherry and cocktails. Pleasant. He was glad now he had changed. The fine clothes after the long hardship and mud had a special luxury. He would like a very dry sherry, to get away the taste of the tea. Yes, this one was exactly right. Better wait until Muriel came down. There was some kind of glow in the room tonight. He looked about. Everything was the same. He felt good, that was it. But some curious instinct told him that was not all of it. The room was waiting for somebody to come back. It waited like a chair made warm by somebody just gone out. The clock struck nine. Hum, nobody was in any hurry tonight. Well, he wasn't. London papers. Have a look at the Londoner's Diary in the *Evening Standard*. Hum, paragraph about the Egyptian to whom he had refused the loan. Always knew somebody who made a paragraph in the Diary. Family feeling of London about it. Ambassador-just-dropped-in-from-across-the-street kind of atmosphere. Slightly surprising always to find he came from Brazil or somewhere. Cosmopolitan page. *Evening Standard* was London. *The Times* was England. Hum, he hadn't felt amused like this for ages. Oh . . .

The one clear thing Nicholas realized was that a perfect stranger had come into the room. For the last few months Muriel had been changing over her personality to somebody else, and now, in a click, the whole thing was complete. She came in with a formality, and Nicholas knew at once that she was not going to lose it for the rest of the evening. That meant she was conscious. And she wore a conscious dress. It seemed some kind of Spanish affair and from the waist down was only black lace over a Castilian pink underskirt through which, vaguely, her legs were silhouetted against the glow of the fire. Nicholas realized that this was a very subtle dress. It was formal and chaste enough for an ambassadorial dinner and yet as tantalizing as something one wore in a bedroom. She wore a red comb like a cockerel's crest in her hair, which seemed to be almost black tonight. He wondered how she made her hair look so dark. She had come in and stood in front of the fire for six or seven seconds before Nicholas could get enough acclimated to her to speak. She stood on the hearth, and the whole room had come alive and knew that this had never happened before at Barrington.

"Ahm, what would you like?"

"Sherry."

When he caught hold of the knob of the decanter it burned like a red-hot coal. God, how was he going to eat his dinner?

"Ahm, we're a little late, aren't we?"

"Yes. Margaret told me you had gone to sleep, so I thought you might as well have a good rest, and I put back dinner an hour."

She raised her glass with a very slight nod of acknowledgment that made the correct half-formal toast that one might exchange over a sherry. He was slightly flustered by her and forgot to answer it.

Oxinham came in. "Shall I serve dinner now, madame?"

"In about five minutes, Oxinham."

Nicholas was trying to feel his way into what was happening. He said: "I don't think I heard a gong."

"No. I am not going to use the gong any more."

Nicholas had a feeling that he wanted to get to know this woman. When she turned on the rug she gave just a slight swing to her frock, and her legs suggested themselves in the firelight. She knew perfectly well they did, he knew. She was dead sure of herself.

"New frock?" he asked.

"Yes."

How the devil had she got out of herself and gone into this new woman? What did she intend? He had vaguely proposed to himself that he was going to invent work and retire to the fire in the library after dinner and let the long day drift over him in the smoke of a cigar. But if for no other reason than the social compulsion she exercised this evening, he knew that he must share it with her. But that was not the reason. No sane man was going to leave a woman like this. She gave a slight nod, and he got up and opened the door. He knew perfectly well this was going to be a marvelous dinner, with matched wines and dishes. One had the feeling that the smallest error of taste was impossible with her now. As she spoke to Oxinham he realized something else. Her voice had changed. Now how could the voice change and the accent remain the same? She now had the trick of making the ear pause for each word before it came.

Nicholas waited for each dish with some alarm. The handle of the knife made his eyes smart, so acute was the contact on his palm. The worst thing would be the meat, but, thank God, the veal was tender. She seemed quite unaware that he was scarcely able to hold his knife. She had chosen Burgundy for the meal, and, Nicholas knew, that above all wines could best restore the body from fatigue. She was not in the least hurry and carried the wine over to the biscuits. Oxinham, like every born servant, obviously liked the feeling of being commanded and, for the first time, exercised that subtle knack of sharing the success of a meal, while yet remaining apart by the sideboard.

When Nicholas got back into the drawing room

he was surprised to find that it was ten minutes past ten. Time had sat lightly as the wine, and the clock, as it should, had abolished itself. She gave him coffee, had a cigarette, and somehow decided him to have a cigarette instead of a cigar. She was very cool, remained at a distance, then asked him if he would mind some music. She got up and found a program of Spanish music from Paris. Nicholas, every sense acute, had a feeling that she might have looked up the program and tuned herself and her dress to this music. She stood by the fire, and he had a curious perception that she had somehow made herself fluid and was absorbing the music into herself and was being charged by the waves. As she drank a liqueur she compelled the eye to watch every movement. She exercised the mind so much now that she made no physical disturbance in him, and, again, he had the feeling that she wanted that mood, and was able to command it.

She listened for forty minutes to the end of the program and then got up and turned off the radio. As she turned from the cabinet, there was a slight whisk in her gesture, as if she had been filled by the rhythm like a dancer and wanted to express it. She went and stood on the hearth, paused a moment, and then said: "I think I am going up."

Nicholas got a fearful shock of disappointment. The violence of his disappointment astonished him. He realized that he had been completely occupied by her, and now that she was going, he would be left empty. Instinct warned him to let her have her way, and he stood up, and said: "I'm going to bed too, in a moment." He paused. "I've had a long day in the open air."

She seemed to be very careless as she said: "Oh, I should have a cigarette and a drink and then go up."

Then, somehow, she was gone out of the room. When the door closed, Nicholas stood in front of the fire and tried to sort out his thoughts. What the devil was she playing at? She must know that she had got him into a state of excitement. Yet, whatever mood she had been in, it was not a mood of bitchiness. He recalled every gesture and syllable since she had come into the room. A woman like that demanded a subtle apprehension and somehow she was going beyond him. She had suggested a cigarette and a drink, and still feeling her compulsion, he poured himself a drink and lighted a cigarette. Sleep was going to be impossible. He was not in the least tired. His whole body was alive and tingling as if she had touched him all over with her fingers. Once again he tried to remember if there was anything significant in what she had said about having a cigarette and a drink. She was so different tonight that nothing she did seemed to have happened before. What else was new in her way of leaving the room? What was that sense he had of something unsaid . . .

Good God, he realized it now. She had not said good night.

Nicholas compelled himself to smoke his cigarette slowly. Now that he had begun to suspect the evening might not be over, his body had come alive in desire for her, and he did not try to control his longing. All this evening she had been exercising the total vocabulary of the sophisticated woman and had played on all the keys of his mind and senses, and now he began to feel a slight impatience. He had not the Latin or Gallic finesse that delights in thinking of a woman as an orchestra of emotion in which one by one each instrument must be awakened into music to achieve the crescendo of passion. There was something that exhausted him in that sensual epicurianism, and suddenly he remembered the brutal remark of a young man at Oxford who had said: "These bloody dons! They spend their whole lives nibbling the fat off Falstaff's rump!" Now suddenly he understood that queer remark. He had something in him that was the Elizabethan sense of flesh and blood. Again that gaunt and powerful young Oxford intellectual spoke in his memory. "You can't suckle babes on Shelley's bosom. That ignorant and hairy lout of an oarsman over there has a better sense of Shakespeare in his blood than all of you have in your minds that smell of orchids and Walter Pater." Nicholas almost flushed now. The hairy lout had been himself, and he had often wondered since why he had not punched Geoheghan on the nose. He was amazed to find himself recalling Geoheghan and now he began to see that he hadn't punched him because he knew that Geoheghan had understood him. Geoheghan would have known now why he was beginning to resent that complicated and subtle mood Muriel had imposed on him all the evening. He hadn't that patience in him that could stay at that pitch. He admired her, and she had given a beautiful performance, but it was distant as something on the stage.

Good heavens, he had finished his cigarette, and his body had stopped thinking about her. His mind had not been so acute and untroubled by worries for a long time, and now he had got to the stage when he would almost like to sit down here for an hour or two and enjoy the clear functioning of his own mind. He got up and stood on the hearth and suddenly in the warmer higher air he caught the perfume she had left behind, and the whole room was flooded with her being, and he was conscious of her again. His hand trembled a little as he finished his brandy. His instinct told him that to stay down here was wrong. If she had given him a cue, he would be a coward if he did not take it. He felt rather ashamed of his thought and churlish. After all, she was a really lovely woman now . . . Oh, damn it, he was probably imagining the whole thing anyway, and when he went up into his dressing room, her door would be shut as usual. Good God, he was nervous about going up!

When he got into his dressing room, his heart jumped a beat. Her door was ajar. He was conscious of a red glow of light and a throb of music. Then he paused a moment before he closed the door behind him. He wondered why she had turned the radio on. He could only just glimpse the reddish glow in her room. She had changed the lighting. He listened to the music. It seemed to be a Mexican rhumba. One saw dancers in the twilight under the shade of mountain-wide hats. There was a kind of excitement of color and noise inside that door. He closed the door of his room, and his hand was so nervous and smarted so much on the knob that it made a little bang. Silence. The music inside was quiet now as the throbbing of his own blood.

Suddenly he heard a chuckle. Then she laughed. He moved over nearer to her door. He said, without having the least intention of saying it: "What are you laughing at?"

She gave another chuckle. "Oh, a joke that occurred to me. I was just wondering what the definition of a husband is in the dictionary and I thought it must be— one who husbands himself!"

He could not help a laugh. He had now reached her door. Now, curiously enough, it was impossible to go back without being a fool.

"You won't find that in the Oxford, I'll bet!" he said.

He had to raise his voice slightly over the music.

"Must you talk through the door?" She was in good humor. "If you must, I'll turn the wireless off."

He knew now that it was all right to go in.

This was the second surprise he had got in a bedroom within a few weeks. She had changed the positions of the lamps, and now they had apricot shades and one lamp on the dressing table had a green shade, and somehow or other she was glowing like an Indian girl as she sat in front of her table mirror with her back to him. The music, too, belonged to the mood in the room. Nicholas knew that he would be astounded if his mind was able to work, but nothing operated but his sense of instinct, and his instinct told him to take all this just by the feel of it. For a moment he just listened to the music and kept his eyes on her. It was nothing more than a stupid habit of mind which had been astonished by the fact that a woman sat there naked above the waist and took no notice of his being there. In the mirror he saw that she was making up her mouth heavily until it looked a huge, moist scarlet sweetmeat on her golden face.

"Would you like to turn off the wireless?" she said quietly.

288

In silence he went over and turned the knob. Then he moved back to her and stood behind her. Her hair still looked almost black, and he saw that she had moistened it with oil and it somehow clung to her neck and shoulders, and all her skin looked moist as if soaked in honey. He said nothing because he suspected his voice had gone. Now she used the soft lipstick on her nipples, and he had never known a woman did that and he nearly exclaimed in surprise. She touched the leg of the stool that was by her dressing table and said. "Why don't you sit down?"

Now he was in front of her and confronted with her golden body and her red mouth and the whole enigma of what she was doing as she touched her breasts with scarlet. On her legs she wore, almost to the tops of her thighs, curious trousers of red silk with a green and gold braid like the fringe on a cowboy's trousers, and they were held up by plain green cords that hung loosely on her waist. He saw the significance of these trousers that were only separate legs of silk and obviously were of no purpose for sleeping or anything. They explained boldly that they were there, like the lipstick on her mouth and lips, for seduction, and they somehow only increased her nakedness. He felt curiously at ease, in spite of his fearful excitement, and he realized that in some way she had managed to tune him into her mood, and that so long as he did not lose the pitch, nothing would go wrong. He saw that she had put an indigo shading on her eyelids, and now the purple tinge in her eyes, that always indicated passion in a woman, had become a solid color.

She had sat in silence, and now he had become unconscious enough of her body to look down at her trousers and say: "Did you get these in London?"

"No." She smiled. "I made them myself." She smiled again. "They just haven't any excuse at all."

She moved her legs slightly, and he felt their heat in proximity to him. All her warmth was now moving in his blood. She took a jar and rubbed some kind of cream into the skin above her waist and suddenly looked up and smiled in a nonchalant way. "I'm just amusing myself."

He knew that he had to wait, and she indicated a jar on the table and said: "Will you open that?"

When he tried to twist off the top it scorched his hand. He was now sweating in excitement and his hands had begun to burn.

"Oh, your hands are sore!"

"I—ahm, yes."

He did not know how to explain about his hands.

"You seemed hardly able to hold your knife and fork at dinner."

So she had noticed it. There was a silence while he tried to think of something to say.

"I know why your hands are sore," she said.

"Oh?"

"Yes. I saw you coming back. I'd gone up to the box room and saw you on the bridge. Then I got it out of Blake. When I saw him taking your suit away, I stopped him. He didn't want to tell me anything but I"—she smiled—"blackmailed him. I told him I'd call up the police and report him for stealing your clothes. He was furious with me for making him tell me. I thought he'd slap my face once. I didn't know Blake had such a temper." She paused. "Did you enjoy yourself, Nick?"

"Yes."

"I knew you'd want a good sleep, and—I didn't want you to wake tired." Now her voice was very soft. "Let me see your hands."

She took his hands and he felt that she could somehow feel the pain of them in herself as fearfully as he felt the heat of her body come into him through her hands. She blew softly on the palm and he felt it.

"Even my breath hurts you. I'll rub in a little cream."

As she rubbed in the cream gently he wondered how long more he could stand this desire for her without seizing her in his arms. When she had done his hands she touched the palm of one with her tongue and he leaped from the touch.

"They taste nicely now."

She took his hand in hers and turned it over. The palm was raw and red like the inside flesh of the body, and the black hairs on the back stood out as the hand became tumescent in the heat of her hand and the soft, agonizing cold of the cream. For the first time she looked up at him with her emotion in her eyes, and he knew that she was feeling the symbolism of the hand with the black hairs and the red, tender flesh. Her face was now slightly swollen below the eyes and he felt that her blood was clogging in desire. She murmured, having awakened his eyes in hers: "I've always liked your hands, Nick."

He felt that somehow this was the truth, although perhaps in an oblique way. "God, I can't bear water on them. I could hardly get my clothes on."

She put her cheek down on his hand and then looked up with eyes that now had a slumberous light on them, like purple grapes in the shadow of leaves.

"I'll undo your tie for you."

She moved near to him and undid the knot, and he found every muscle in his body clenched in the effort to restrain himself. Now they were both beyond speech, and she very gently got all his clothes off. Then when he stood up, he felt a pressure on his eyeballs and felt they might burst out of his head if this were delayed any longer. She stood in front of him, with her lip held between her teeth, and her whole body tensed, and then suddenly felt that strange impersonal, almost hostile look of sexual desire leap out of her eyes into his. Then her hands jumped up and caught his shoulders, and, as if released from a spring of intolerant compression, she leaped off the carpet and seized him around the waist with her legs. He was nearly overborne by the shock, and then somehow sank to the floor with her, was conscious of two violent turns on the rug in conjunction, and knew they had rolled asunder after the mutual accomplishment.

He felt giddy and empty for a moment and knew that the whole thing had been over in less than ten seconds. There was a trickle on his neck, and he put up his hand thinking it was sweat and found that it was blood. She must have unconsciously bitten his ear or he had cut it against the stool. He could not remember. He looked at her as she lay panting. It was a long time before he spoke.

"In God's name, why had we to wait ten years for this?"

She did not speak for a moment. Now the emotional onslaught was upon her, and she was unable to think or reason or do anything except rest herself in an obliteration of ten years in ten seconds. At last she said: "I don't know."

This, he realized, was the wrong time to try and sum up ten years of disaster in a few words. After a while he got up and sat on the edge of the bed. She still lay on the rug. He knew that this violent explosion had been necessary to discharge the repression of ten years. It was incredible that it had happened at last. It was incredible that it had not happened before. It was incredible that an external barrier of social and sexual inhibitions could have separated them all this time from each other and their own natures.

For a little time he felt empty in the shock of the emotional concussion and watched her lying on the rug. Then, at last, she gave a long sigh, and pulled herself onto her haunches . . . and removed the trouser leg that had not been torn away. She gave a slight smile to herself as she flung the pieces of silk onto a chair. Then she moved over to the dressing table and sat herself on the stool and combed down her hair and made up her mouth again. There was a red glint of light on her golden skin.

"You look like a red Indian girl," he said.

Her smile communicated itself to him in the glass. After a moment she stood up, and he saw how clean and shining and slim were her loins and flanks and how she was able to go naked without being nude. She was everything that a man wanted and hardly ever got. Her bosom had a lighter shade of gold and he guessed that she had protected her breasts from the sunlight with a silk bandage. And all about her hair and skin was that sense of moisture, as if her whole body breathed freely and was soaked in the dew of breath. She paused for a moment and then came over and sat on the rug and laid her head on his knee. She said nothing, and he knew that she wanted to shut the mind away and let the body use its own language.

"How have you got like this?" he asked.

She gave a little laugh.

"Maybe the question is how I stayed so long like I was." She laughed. "Does it matter now?"

"No."

Now there was a jerk of anger in her voice. "God, what a fool you must have thought me."

He pulled her face up to him and kissed her. "Don't let's talk about it now."

He pulled her slowly onto the bed because it was exquisite and luxurious to delay, and now that they had got rid of ten years on the rug, they could begin a new lifetime up here on the bed.

An hour later, when they had rested, and the heart had slowed down again to its regular beat, she moved her head on the pillow, and said: "Nicholas, you must go on a holiday." She paused. "Why don't you give up the bank altogether?"

"That's what I intend to do. Every time I dug in that spade today I dug a stone out of Bude's Bank. It was like digging my way out of jail."

"Let's go down to the South and sun and run away from the winter."

"Yes."

She suddenly gave a little gasp and kissed him. "I've always been like this inside, darling, but I didn't know it or something."

"I know. I knew that the first time I met you."

"I thought you were going to take me in the garden that night."

"I wish to God I had. If we'd been ourselves nothing would have gone wrong."

"I know. We got locked up in the social cage. Mummy did that. I'd always been locked up." She spoke bitterly. "So I was a bitch, Nick, a rather common little bitch, but I didn't know it. I didn't know I was being one. I suppose you must have felt like raping a nun when you tried to make love to me in a natural way."

"Yes. Something like that. But it's all gone now."

"I'll make it up to you now, darling. I'll show you what a woman can be when she's not afraid to be a woman."

"Well, you've shown me a lot in the last hour."

"It's not very late yet, darling."

Nicholas smiled. She reached for a mirror on the bedside. "I must get my lip salve. My mouth's gone all over you. You'll be like a red Indian long before you go to sleep, darling, if you don't stop me."

"I'm not going to stop you."

She made a large, juicy mouth, and he had the feeling each time she made a new mouth it would refresh them to begin again. She smiled as she laid down the lipstick.

"I like it when we can't unstick, darling."

Now she began to make love to him again, and at last she knew by his face that she had relaxed his mind into his body. His face was no longer, as the face nearly always is, the photograph of whatever thought is in the mind. All it registered was the emotion in him. When moved, it shaded from one mood into another. His mouth softened into a smile, as her hand moved on his body, in a natural reflex. When she startled him with a pinch, the nostrils of his strong, courageous nose twitched in protest. When his eyes answered hers, the look in them was not directed by the mind. She managed to loosen him into the forgetfulness that allows the body to breathe and heal itself. For even as she saturated him in her oils, her woman's instinct working told her that the important thing in all this was not the quieting down of lust, but the fact that it let his mind go away to heal itself of the fatigue, the frustration, the interminable fear of the anonymous letters. She knew now the woman's real secret, that she must keep always secret. Soon he would be only a child sleeping by her side.·

She only hoped that she was not too late in being a woman.

* * * * * * * * * * * *
* THIRTY-FOUR *
* * * * * * * * * * * *

When Nicholas awoke at dawn he got up quietly from her side and went into his own bedroom. There was something in him that could not bear the sentimental hang-over of the morning. He wondered why he felt so buoyant and realized that he had enjoyed a dreamless sleep. His fears and worries had gone away. He lay in the cool sheets of his bed and felt happy and calm. What gave him this confidence was the knowledge that his first instinct about Muriel had been right. This was the woman to whom, without any hesitation, he had proposed a few hours after they had met. She had generosity in her blood. And, also, she had an imagination about love. She had been clever enough to know that she had to change from the sophisticated woman into a bold and naked gypsy to find the mood natural to them both.

Suddenly he thought of Sidonie when she had made herself a bride for him and somehow had glowed like a waxen light before her glass. His mind was very clear now and he knew that Muriel had not the spiritual reach of Sidonie. She could never travel out beyond the light of day. When he lost himself in passion with Muriel he would be drowned in a red ocean of the blood. But that last night with Sidonie he had gone aloft and dreamed in the balcony of the moon. Never with Muriel could he have that sense of holiness that he had with Sidonie. Never could he know with Muriel such a terror of the soul that made his hands helpless to unbind the girdle from Sidonie's waist. Never would he feel that Muriel's soul had gone away into that electric light beyond the mountain spires. Never could she make him feel a monk and a vampire at the same time as Sidonie could. Nor ever lying beside her would he have that curious notion he had when lying by Sidonie, that he was like an empty mirror into which her mind projected beautiful pictures and images always in profile so that he wanted to go round the corner of the world to look at them. Never with Muriel would he see the gleam of that delicate and distant light like the ancient glow on the luminous page in the niche on Elder's stairway. What was that queer remark that Elder had made about Sidonie? *Miss Coleman's beauty is like an Atlantis. You go down in it—and drown.* Yes, Elder understood all this, too, this interior world that was his Chinese room, that mysterious world the sense of which settled on you like a cold dew on the skin, like the plasmatic glow on the face of Sarah Fuidge . . .

"Your tea, sir!"

Good Lord, he had fallen into a doze, gone back into that world that was his own terrible secret. Ah, it was good to see the sunshine on this windy morning! Just for a moment he had slipped back into the Chinese room, that chamber of twilight that belonged to the other side of the world. He drank his tea and for the first time in his life wondered if he were two persons, one which belonged to Sidonie, one which belonged to Muriel. Somehow it seemed a sharp solution that cleared up everything in his mind. Psychologists, he knew, had some name that defined this dualism in a human being. But now, with the sun shining in, as if it were a light blown along the clear wind, he felt that he said good-by forever to that mysterious Nicholas Bude who was linked up with Elder and Sidonie. He stretched himself and sat up and slapped his chest. Blast it, he had forgotten his sore hands Never mind, it was good to feel the ridge of muscle from shoulder to shoulder again. By the Lord, he felt braced and fine this morning, and his body was seasoned by the salt and oil from Muriel. Hum, he wondered if he might go in and say good morning to her. No, he would have a fresh cool bath and spend the day in the open air. He went over to the window, and the wind whetted his appetite. By George, but he wanted breakfast!

Muriel came down late to breakfast, gave him a slight smile, and took up *The Sunday Times*. She had a stimulating air about her, and she somehow embodied the spirit of this morning. She was as fresh as if she had climbed out of a lake of spring water and had been dried by the wind and polished by the sunlight. Before he left the room he bent and kissed her on the mouth, and she made a little snatch with her mouth at his, and he went out of the room laughing. Something very important had happened to him. He had just got married.

He looked through the newspapers over the library fire and then went out for a walk. He felt that Muriel wanted to be left alone. He went over the fields straight into the wind and felt his hands swing at his sides in muscular freedom. He knew that the fresh air would heal them. He had walked about a mile when suddenly he stopped. He had felt the wind streaming through his fingers like cool water. He looked down at his hands. They were hanging open. By God, the hard labor of yesterday must have done that. His hands never hung open. And then suddenly he knew that it was not merely the hard labor in the drain. Some great internal tension had gone. It was that which had kept his hands cracked. And it was Muriel who had undone the psychological knots in his mind.

THIRTY-FIVE

Nicholas enjoyed his breakfast on Monday morning. There was a glow in the log fire, and he felt a glow within him. He was looking at the morning paper, and Muriel heard him chuckle. A social and political diarist had commented on the fact that the Egyptian to whom Nicholas had refused the loan had complained of the English cold over dinner last Friday. That paragraph would be understood by everybody in Lombard Street and the City. Nicholas had a peculiar feeling that he was enjoying it as an outsider, and from a distance, much as he might laugh at something in an English paper from a veranda in Honolulu. That somehow made him certain that he had done with banking for good and all.

"What are you laughing at?"

"Just a bit in the paper." He saw the car coming around the steps outside. "Oh, here's Blake! I must shake myself up." He got up. "Going to get my case."

The mention of the case suddenly reminded her of the letters and she got up and strolled into the drawing room after him. She felt it was all right now, but she wanted to make sure. He came out of the study with the case. Then he looked at her, and something jumped between their eyes.

He went over to her and said: "Well, until tomorrow. Thank God this will be the last Monday night I'll sleep at the club for many a long day. I'm going around to Cook's today to make a few inquiries. The sooner we get away the better. Let's just hop a ship without too much choosing and planning."

"Hau! Hau! That's what I want." She paused and said almost shyly, "It's fun being married, isn't it, Nick?"

"Yes." He sighed. "God, I've just lost count of this week end!"

She chuckled and said: "I lost count, too, darling!"

He smiled at her and then laughed: "You're coarse as well as being immoral." He paused and said with emotion, "God, you're looking lovely this morning!"

That seemed to have jumped out of his heart, and

she was touched and suddenly kissed him. She teased him with her body enough to make sure that he would want to come back to her. Then she said: "Nick, you've had something on your mind, haven't you, for some time? I mean, some worry."

"Yes."

"Is it all gone now?"

"Yes."

"Did—this week end take it away?"

"Yes."

"Oh, I'm so happy about that." She added with a little snap: "God, what damn fools we've been, all these years. It's—it's like being cheated out of ten years of one's life."

"I know. We'll make up for it now." She kissed him with a long, searching kiss. He pushed her away. "If you do that again, I'll put down this case and send the car back and stay here all day."

She laughed. "Go on, darling. You must go up. The sooner it's all cleared up, the better." She framed his face in her hands. "Oh, it's so nice to see you now. I couldn't bear you all these weeks, with that awful kind of absent-minded look you had on your face."

"Had I?"

"Yes . . . What are you doing?" He laughed. "Gosh, I'll never wear a blouse like this again in the morning."

"Are you mad with me?"

"Go away, damn you!"

He went out of the room with a laugh. As she closed her blouse, she felt herself aching all over for him at this very moment. Then she smiled to herself. Therese would take very good care that her husband left her this way every morning. She trembled into the marrow of her being as she remembered last night. Perhaps because she wanted him to master her, she had found herself in an unaccountable mood of sulkiness, and, then when she had resisted, he had got out of control and awakened red hell in her. She had fought, and cried, and used her teeth, and snarled, and had been astonished at the animal she had discovered in herself. Afterwards she nearly wept in remorse, knowing his hands were sore and she had chafed them between her body and the bed. Then she felt that he might have been annoyed and apologized.

"Heavens, I didn't know I was such a wildcat, Nick!"

"That's all right. You've got to go right down to the ends of the roots to get at it and get it out of you."

"Get at what?"

"Oh, the animal in man. The thing with hoofs. If you don't go into the jungle and get hold of it and tame it, it's always likely to come out and kill you."

How very strange and absorbed Nicholas had looked when he had said—*The thing with hoofs.* But she no longer felt alarmed by her own animal fury, now that she knew that the mind could understand what the body was doing. Perhaps it was some animal with a hoof that she had killed in Nicholas this week end. Perhaps when his face had been absent-minded, he had been looking into a darkness at that animal. She could feel an instinct in him that understood the fundamental things that one could never quite understand by the mind. She went over and sat by the window and let her mind probe into the week end. It was all somehow extraordinary. But nothing was quite so strange as that moment when, by accident in the box room, she had seen Nicholas on Saturday coming in

302

over the footbridge after his day's labor in the field. Plastered in mud, a steam coming from his body, his legs heavy with clinging earth, he had seemed, under the congestion of black clouds and red dripping light, a dark and brooding peasant on the edge of the world. But the amazing thing was the sense of memory that it awoke in her. And then she had suddenly remembered. In the very first dance she had had with Nicholas, a curious picture of him like that had come into her mind. She recalled even now how the picture had somehow been transmitted into her through his hands.

Muriel was not used to these experiences outside the chronometrical plane of time, and she had sat in the box room with a queer sensation going through her. For her time was the face of a clock, a face that one learned to know well day by day. But now she had glimpsed the ghost behind the face. How funny, that this strange picture should come to life ten years later! And now that it lived and breathed in her eyes, she felt in some way that she had got back to the beginning with Nicholas again. She felt again that strange disturbance in her blood. She looked in her mother's trunk and found the book she had come up here to seek. And then her hand dropped on the piece of Indian silk shawl with the fringe. It was very curious, but she began to create the trousers out of it in her mind. And she had cut and sewn the silk while Nicholas slept before dinner. She knew quite suddenly that she wanted him badly. She wanted that earthly man who had come over the footbridge out of a strange world. That was the man she had wanted the night she met him. She was possessed by instinct, and it was by instinct that she had made those trousers, had oiled the hair on her head and body, had put scarlet on her nipples, and had rubbed grease into her stomach, had done everything to rouse a primal lust in him, as if she had wanted to destroy in one stroke the inhibited Englishwoman she had been to him.

And the curious thing was that she felt cleansed now in every corner of her being. There was something of the Turkish bath in sex. It sweated you in every pore and let you breathe. And it somehow washed out the room of the mind as it cleared the windows of the eyes. She was not able to understand how, but she had known by instinct that this week end of sex would purge the poison of worry from Nicholas' mind. His face this morning was as human and healthy as a boy's in the open air. He had lost the sense of being shut up behind the walls of inhibition that had made their marriage a jail. She felt certain that he had lived with Laura and Miss Coleman, but they had not been able to discharge him wholly of that animal in him. Well, she had let it out of the cage at last. In her smile there was a secret triumph. Not every woman would be able to take Nicholas. It was no wonder she had been afraid of him before she had got rid of her inhibition. Last night he had lost himself, and had made her lose herself, until it was no longer him and her, but the male and female in the violent generation of love. That was what she had wanted, to abandon the mind and feel nothing but the thunder in her blood and the thumping of her heart. That was what the woman wanted, and to hell with the namby-pamby talk that was supposed to be going on in the mind. There was nothing at all in the mind. One shut one's eyes and plunged into the darkness and came out at last on the other side of the world with sweat and oil dripping off one like the ancient slime. And afterwards one felt purged and clean. The animal had been let out into the jungle. The lion only stank in the cage. But it was no wonder it scared hell out of people.

It was funny, but she had no feeling of age about Nicholas. It was impossible to believe he was forty-six. Both of them had plenty of youth left to enjoy. She guessed that he was staying in London tonight to say good-by to Miss Coleman. She would not resent it if Nicholas slept with Miss Coleman tonight. After all, while she had starved him, Miss Coleman and maybe other women had given him peace with their womanhood. Why on earth wasn't she feeling all that jealousy a woman was supposed to feel? And love with Nicholas only made her memory of MacGregor more tender. All she felt about Miss Coleman was that she hoped it would somehow be possible to make her a friend. Over dinner at the Clarendon she had felt again the beautiful clearness of Miss Coleman's mind. Miss Coleman was infinitely more educated and cultured than she was. She felt ashamed of her stupidity in living down at Barrington and letting her mind become a grass field.

She got up. She would go out and have a walk. Her bosom was a little sore. She laughed. She was glad of it. She guessed that perhaps a woman liked bearing that in the same way that she liked bearing the pangs of birth. Her face softened a little. That was something she did not want to think about yet. She called the dogs.

She came back at noon and had some hot chocolate. She was resting, calm and happy, when she heard the noise of a car. She looked out. It was Saluby. Damn. Somehow she loathed him when he came in, and got annoyed by his dithering about whether he would or would not have a cup of chocolate. In the end, he said he would have coffee.

His small talk was frightful. At last he said: "I just dropped in to tell you about that case over at Yeoman Spire that you helped."

"Oh, yes?"

"Well, the baby has arrived, and everything is going on fine. I'm just going over there now."

"Oh, I'm so glad." She paused. "Do they need any more help?"

"No. One of the family has got a good job. They are awfully grateful to you. You must go over and see the baby. I'll call for you one day."

"Yes, I'll go with you."

She looked at Saluby. She felt sure he was a good and compassionate doctor. What the devil was wrong with him?

"Oh, did you see about MacGregor in today's *Times*?"

"No."

"Well, he's finally proved his discovery in hospital experiments."

"I'm very pleased."

"I'm just going over to Dorminster this afternoon, to get some things he left."

Vague remark. Why did she feel that it was not vague?

Saluby got up. He eased his taut face into a smile. "Well, thank you for the coffee." He paused. "Oh, how is the patient?"

"Patient?"

"Oh, I mean your husband."

My God, she must control her temper! "What on earth do you mean?"

"Well, from the way you talked about the effect those letters have on him, he's a patient in a way."

She tried to keep the angry blood out of her face. God, Saluby gave off a most peculiar feeling.

"Are you trying to be funny?"

"Well, no."

What damn impertinence!

"I think you have a peculiar sense of humor. It is a wonder you didn't ask for the guinea pig." She paused. "As a matter of fact, I think he's given up that ridiculous experiment."

"Oh." Saluby paused. "Well, he's cured then."

She got up, and Saluby took the hint.

As she watched his car going down the avenue, she felt every sense tauten. Why on earth did she feel so uneasy? She had a curious feeling that this visit was planned. Why had he been so insulting? She knew that he would never forgive her for finding out his failure as a lover. My God, he was unpleasant. And he had a diabolical skill in his sadistic mind. He knew that Nicholas was a peasant, not an urban banker. She could not explain or understand her conviction that Saluby had made this visit with a purpose and that still more peculiar feeling that the casual remark about going to Dorminster today had some significance that had nothing to do with what had happened there between them. She felt some internal scheming in his mind. She wished he had not mentioned the letters. If another came, it would come today. An hour ago, she would have been confident that Nicholas would just sit back in his chair and laugh at any letter this morning. But now she had this vague, sinister, damp feeling about her, that came like some unhealthy fog or ectoplasm off Saluby. She sat down and took up *The*

Times to read about MacGregor. She found the piece and read it. When she put down the paper she realized that she could not remember a single word of what she had read this very moment. Good heavens, she hated this feeling.

She was astonished to find that she had pressed the bell. It was Oxinham who came in.

"Yes, madam?"

"Tell Blake, when he comes back, that I want the car to go to London after lunch."

"Yes, madam."

Good heavens, why had she done this?

Suddenly she cheered herself by planning a night in London with Nicholas. She would take a couple of rooms at the Ritz or Clarendon and surprise him. It would be fun to have a night out with him at a play or something, and . . .

Why had Saluby come?

Once in London, in the noise of Piccadilly, gregarious in the sunlight, she forgot this queer feeling that was like somebody behind one's back. She went up Dover Street and saw about some clothes for her cruise with Nicholas. For the first time she felt that she owned a husband. It was a pleasant feeling. When Nicholas got himself away from the bank, she knew that she could make him happy. But one did not live by love alone. When they got back, he would have to find something to do that was worth doing. Love wasn't much good if it didn't drive something. What it had done for her was to open her faculties and senses to the world about her. With an English detachment, she contemplated the fact that it was unlikely she would confine her sex life to Nicholas. The life of the world was hardly monogamous. Nick's life in the bank was monogamy. It was like locking oneself up in one room.

She went back to the Clarendon and ordered tea. Then she went into the telephone box and asked for Mr. Bude's private secretary when she got the bank. It was very pleasant to hear Miss Coleman's calm, full, measured voice again.

"Hello? Oh, hello, Mrs. Bude."

"Hello, Miss Coleman. How are you?"

"Oh, I'm very well."

"I want you to give a message to Nicholas."

"Yes?"

"I'm in London. He doesn't know. I don't want you to tell him I am, until he is leaving the bank. Then tell him I'm here at the Clarendon, and I want him to come round. I don't want to bother him until he's done the day."

"I understand."

She knew now that she would like to see Miss Coleman again and said: "Well, when am I going to see you again?"

"I don't know. Ring me at my flat when you're in London in the evening. I'd love to see you again, too."

"I will. Well . . . Oh, has there been any anonymous letter today?"

"Yes." Miss Coleman said. "It came just now. I've just taken it in to him."

Miss Coleman did not seem inclined to say any more. It must be all right. Oh, there was something she wanted to ask Miss Coleman.

"Oh, there's something I want to ask you. I know you go to the theater a lot. What is the play at the Apollo like? I thought we might go tonight. Have you seen it?"

"Yes. I've seen it. It's quite a good play. And it's got a last act you remember."

"Good. Then I'll book the seats and hope Nicholas will come. I haven't seen a play for ages. They all seem awful unless they are French or American." Muriel paused. "Well, you must have dinner with me again soon!"

"Oh, no! You must dine with me this time. Well, good——" There was a noise like the loud slam of a door, then a pause. Then Miss Coleman said: "Hold the line a moment, please."

Muriel held the line. Miss Coleman seemed to be some time. Then she was back. She seemed a little out of breath, as if she had been running. She asked: "Are you there?"

"I am," said Muriel. "Was that a door banging?"

"No." There was another slight pause. Muriel had a feeling that Miss Coleman was trying to steady her voice before she spoke. Then she said: "I think you ought to come round to the bank."

"Come round?"

"Yes, please—now."

Miss Coleman had put down the telephone. Muriel's heart missed a beat. How funny that Miss Coleman had asked her in that urgent way to come round. She hastened out without paying for the call and called a taxi that was passing.

"Down to Bude's Bank, Pall Mall, quickly."

She slammed the door of the taxi. It did not seem to make the same kind of noise that came over the telephone.

THIRTY-SIX

Nicholas fancied that Blake looked at him in a curious way as he opened the door of the car. After a slight pause, Blake said: "Did you cut yourself shaving, sir? There's blood on your face."

Blake closed the door and got in himself in front, Nicholas rubbed his handkerchief on his face. Lip salve, by God, after all these years! No wonder Blake had looked somewhat puzzled. Nicholas had often wondered if the staff at Barrington knew how futile family life was upstairs. Probably they did. Although most of them were of the family-servant type who knew that a public-school Englishman would prefer to let his butler find him kissing a parlormaid than his own wife, nevertheless they had an instinct about bedroom affairs. Nicholas rubbed off the salve and opened the windows to let the nostalgia of Muriel's scent blow away. His body was still reminiscent about her. He smiled. He felt a hell of a long way from forty-six on this fresh morning. And charged with the restorative juices of sex, he felt a desire to use his new energy in something creative. When he got back from the cruise he must find something to engage him in heart and soul. He would not waste time in the tomfoolery of the Lords or the hoofling in the Commons. He began to plan out a future. It must be something in which Muriel could share. He knew that she now, too, was determined to use her personality. He became so rapt in the prospect that he was surprised to find they had arrived at the bank.

As he went up the marble stairway, easing the case in his sore palm, he realized that not once on this journey in had he thought about the letters. The Monday-morning nightmare had passed him by. The work on Saturday had opened his lungs, and now he got to the top of the stairway with no hastening in his heartbeat. The sunshine was on Miss Coleman's hair, and she looked cheerful. Nicholas avoided dropping an eye on her tray to see if there was a letter. He honestly did not care a damn if there was.

When she followed him in with the mail, she laid a personal letter down by the pad. He saw that it was from old Dorman, probably about the Egyptian hand-off. Miss Coleman did not look at him. She said: "I have some calls to make. Will you look over the mail?"

"Yes. Come in when you are done."

How understanding and delicate she was. She had wanted to let him alone with his relief at getting no anonymous letter. Hum, she didn't know that it didn't matter a damn to him now. He picked up Dorman's letter. Then he felt a tickling on his forehead, put up his hand, felt the sting of salt on his sore palm. Sweat was pouring down his face, out of his body, down his spine.

Good God! So it had been in his mind all the time!

Nicholas got a shock. He had no idea that a fear could lie waiting in the mind like that. He had been unaware of any apprehension as he waited for Miss Coleman to come in. But it had been there, curled up asleep in his mind, and now it was weeping in relief through every pore in his body. Nicholas found that he had taken several long drinks of air into his lungs. Then he knew he had a fearful thirst. He got up and drank two glasses of water.

Well, the letters had stopped.

Why?

Nicholas took a good look at the new white pad on his desk and saw no faces there. It was all right. It was over now. He made a grim face. By the Lord, it was just as well it was! He did not like the discovery that it had been in his mind. Now he felt inclined to laugh in relief.

Miss Coleman came in, and he saw that her eye went straight to the water jug. She looked down and said: "Good heavens, what have you done to your hands!"

Nicholas looked at them. One of them was bleeding. My God, his hands must have been fighting while he awaited her coming in with the mail! It was incredible.

"Oh, I got them sore on Saturday. I went out and did some work in a field."

"Oh." She paused. "I wondered why you looked so fit this morning."

He felt somewhat guilty. It seemed unfair to her, after all she had given him, after so much time, that he should have found himself with Muriel. He had a sudden curiosity about how she and Muriel would get on. He had a feeling they would like each other. Well . . .

"Look, would you get me old Dorman before we do the mail?"

"Yes."

He glanced hastily at Dorman's note while she got the call. Hum, old Dorman had seen daylight. It was a note of thanks for opening his eyes. Here was the call.

"Hello."

"Hello. Is that the Dormouse?"

"In person."

"Just got your note."

"Yes. I've got my eyes opened this week-end."

"Well, I want you about something else."

"Yes?"

"Would you like to buy something?"

"If Miss Coleman is for sale . . ."

Nicholas chuckled. "She's not. And don't try to buy her off me with baskets of flowers." Nicholas paused. "Would you like to buy a bank?"

"A bank? What do you mean?"

"I mean this bank."

"Well, go on, explain."

"I want to give up banking."

"Good Lord! Why?"

"Well, I'm getting tired of running a slate club for you and the Colonial Office."

Old Dorman laughed. "I must tell that to Cluricawn! What's happened?"

"It's a long story, and I want you to lunch with me."

"I can't . . ." Dorman paused. "If you think it necessary, I'll put off my engagement and lunch with you."

"I'd like you to."

"Very well." Dorman paused. "I hope, whatever this is, you are not doing anything before you see me."

"I am not. But I've got to get out of this bank, sell it, put in a board, or some damn thing, and I want your advice."

"All right. I'll be at your club at one." Dorman paused. "It all sounds—damned odd." Now a kindness came into his voice.

"Nothing wrong—Nicholas?"

"No."

Human old man, thought Nicholas. So long as he didn't let anything go cold, he could make all his

314

decisions today. Damn Strood. He had no confidence in him.

Nicholas was lost in introspection when Miss Coleman came in. She woke him up. "What are you think-. ing about?"

"Strood. Just wondering if there's anything at all in him." Nicholas paused. "I must talk to him, try and get at his mind, if he's got one. Now what the hell can you invent for me to see Strood about. . . . No, I'll wait until tomorrow." He looked up at her. "Can you dine with me tonight?"

"Dine with you?"

"Yes. Let's dine at the Ritz and talk. I've got something on my mind—about the bank. It's serious. I'm lunching with Dorman about it—remind me to leave here at ten to one—and I want you to dine on it." He smiled. "Strictly a business engagement! If I can't damn well get you out to dinner any other way, I'm ordering you now to work overtime, at the Ritz."

"Very well."

"Now, let's go ahead."

Suddenly she seemed very young and lonely as she bent her head over her notebook. Sometimes, too, old Dorman looked very old and lonely, making a decision about millions, with his mind on his crippled son. Nicholas put his hand in his pocket to get his cigarette case and found it enclosing the deer's hoof.

In the afternoon, when Mr. Elder came in, Nicholas was in good humor. Dorman had surprised him at lunch by taking his decision for granted and had confessed that he too was resigning at the end of the year. The importance of the India loan made it necessary to avoid a public change in Bude's Bank, and Dorman and he had worked out a satisfactory plan. Nicholas felt

315

that at last he was a free man, and now even Mr. Elder noticed at once the change in him. Mr. Elder, remembering the nerve storm of last Friday, was both anxious and distant, but Nicholas put him at ease.

"Mr. Elder," he said in a forthright way, "I owe you an apology for last Friday." He smiled. "My nerves were in pieces, I'm afraid."

"That was easy to see." Mr. Elder paused. "I take it the cause of your—disquiet has been removed?"

"Well, the letters have stopped. But—" Nicholas paused—"I don't think it would have mattered much if one had come today. I—well, I think I managed to get it out of my system over the week end."

Mr. Elder noticed his hands and smiled. "There's nothing like a good sweat to get anything out of your system."

"Yes. I—ahm, I had a bit of exercise over the weekend." Nicholas could see the water running bright and clean in the drain and taking the poison he had sweated out of his mind down to the sea. "Well, what have you got for me?"

Nicholas signed the documents and, making a blurred signature on one, turned it hastily onto his blotting pad. Mr. Elder smiled.

"That's the first time I've seen you use that blotting pad, Mr. Bude!"

Nicholas laughed. He remembered that Mr. Elder's use of the desk pad had caused the explosion on last Friday. What the hell of a long way back last Friday seemed! He could hardly explain to Elder that until today he had used that pad as a mirror in which to see faces. He said in a casual way: "Just a kink of mine, to keep that pad clean. Suppose everybody gets these kinks."

"Yes." Mr. Elder paused. "They usually signify something more important, though, than the kink itself."

"Hum, yes. Well, Mr. Elder, that's all, I think."

"Thank you, Mr. Bude." Mr. Elder paused. "Well, I'm glad to know that the letters business is no longer worrying you. I was very surprised to know of it. I don't suppose you are making any inquiries, but if you are, and you happen to find out who took that paper from my house, I would be grateful if you let me know."

"I will, Mr. Elder. But I am not making any inquiries. That kind of thing only flatters the fool or the blackguard who is sending them." Nicholas paused. "He seems to have got tired at last."

Mr. Elder looked thoughtful as he remarked: "He— or she."

Nicholas looked up sharply. "Why did you say that?"

"Well, there's no reason why it shouldn't be a woman."

Nicholas discovered to his annoyance that his hands were restless under the desk. "No," he said. "Do you suspect anybody?"

Mr. Elder looked him in the eyes but showed nothing in his. "Well, you suspected me, didn't you?"

"Yes, but . . . Well, the facts rather pointed to you, and I was upset last Friday, and I was ready to suspect anybody."

"But you suspected me long ago—the night you visited me, for instance."

"Yes. I was uneasy. I am sorry. But you can hardly blame me."

"No. It is reasonable to suspect anybody who could get hold of that Elder Bank paper." Mr. Elder paused.

"Well, I'm glad you are not letting it worry you any more." He paused again. "I hope those crests and seals I lent you are being of some use in getting out that history of the bank?"

"Yes, thank you, Mr. Elder. I'll let you have them back when I'm done with them."

"There's no hurry, Mr. Bude. Well, good afternoon, Mr. Bude."

"Good afternoon, Mr. Elder."

When Elder went out, Nicholas thought: "Damn it. He knew I was lying about that bank history." Nicholas frowned. "Good God, does he suspect Sidonie? After all, she could have taken the paper out of his room. God, I just can't believe that!" Poor old Elder had probably got a shock when he had been fool enough to let him guess last Friday that Sidonie was his mistress. Since then Elder probably felt he could trust nobody. Hell, here he was thinking back to the letters again. He must get them out of his mind. Suddenly he got an idea. He opened the shutter and told Miss Coleman to get him a Bond Street sweetshop. As he waited for the call, he felt certain Miss Coleman would not listen in, although it was seldom he made a call of this kind. And realizing how certain he was of this, he knew that it was impossible to suspect her of sending anonymous . . . God, here he was still thinking about them. Ah, here was the call.

"I want a five-guinea box of the Madame Pompadour to be delivered at Barrington Hall by seven o'clock."

"Certainly, Mr. Bude. A card with them?"

"Just address them to Mrs. Bude."

He put down the telephone. He knew the chocolates would be there, even if they had to hire a car.

318

Bond Street was expensive, but they got things done. He chuckled, as he realized that his body was actively thinking about Muriel. She had shown him a sweet and tantalizing way to eat slices of peach on Sunday evening. She might have another idea about chocolates. He chuckled again. It was interesting to speculate about whether she had been taught the *tendresse* about the peach, or had invented it, or perhaps read about it. He did not care very much. All he knew was that it was exciting to have a wife like Muriel. By God, when one came to think of it, he was on honeymoon! He would be darned glad to get a warm brine on his skin in some tropical bay and get bronzed to match her color. He'd have to be pretty good to keep Muriel.

Suddenly he had glided away into a daydream of golden seas and blue glooms of dusk and dawns in green leaves, and pausing in his vision he knew why he felt so happy. *He was no longer alone.* Somehow the realization was a shock. And then he knew why it was a shock. The shock lay in the fact that he had found out that he had always been alone. And all at once loneliness seemed a desolation more horrible to contemplate than being lost in the Sahara. If anything happened to Muriel now, he would feel like a man turned alone into the wilderness again, there to be haunted by the wolves in his mind, those wolves that haunted the nocturnal caves of his sleep. Only in Muriel, somehow, could he make a home. By heavens, in the end, it must all come down to the fact that he loved her, had always loved her. My God, what fools they had been! Suddenly he felt in a violent spasm that he wanted to get her away. He would like to pack up this very moment and go down to the docks and get on a ship and sail out into the new world they had found on last Saturday night. God, he had nearly missed it all. If he had not gone into that field and worked and somehow found himself so that Muriel was able to give herself to him, he might have gone on forever sitting in this bank.

He felt a shiver in him, and then, as if he had cast it all away like an outworn skin, he gave a sudden laugh, and put his hand to the shutter to call Miss Coleman and get on with the business of the afternoon.

"I'm just coming in," she said.

Nicholas had a smile ready on his mouth to greet Miss Coleman, but it died when he saw her face. She looked white and empty, as if everything had suddenly gone out of her, and he felt everything go out of himself. She paused as if to collect herself, then came over and said as calmly as she could: "Nothing in the mail except acknowledgements." She laid down the letter. "This came out of the bank letter box."

Nicholas nodded. She hesitated, as if to say something, then went out, and, in the sunshine, as she turned, Nicholas saw the glint of sweat on her forehead.

Nicholas looked down at the envelope. It had no stamp. But there was no mistaking it. For a moment there was a complete gap in his mind. He could not make his hands function and pick the letter up. When at last he got in the paper knife to slit the envelope, his hands were numb, and he could not feel the knife or paper even on the sore skin. The letter opened in his fingers as by itself. The message read:

THERE IS A WILL TO DEATH IN YOUR HANDS. WHOSE DEATH? WHEN? NOW?

For a few seconds, his head was like an empty skull. His mind was numbed like his hands. From somewhere outside he felt that his heart had stopped. And then it began to thump. His left hand went out by itself and turned over the flap of his case on the desk, and he saw the other letters neatly filed in the pouch. As if his thought had suddenly found a point of beginning again, his mind began to work, moving slowly like limbs coming out of sleep. The first coherent thought was a question. *Whose* death? Somehow he wanted to know that. It would help him. Now there was another blank in his mind again. Then, suddenly as if one had dropped a coin into an automatic gramophone, there was a clash of noise in his head. Thoughts seemed to be banging like cymbals and glittering as they struck. Clap! And lightnings and sparks flew between the cymbals. And then he realized that his hands had clapped together and seized each other and were trying to murder this panic in their hold.

"Christ, the bastard!" His tongue had whispered the thought. Now he had begun to fight it. A fearful hate of the sender of these letters possessed him. He saw the diabolical skill behind this delayed message. His mind had been lulled into peace all the morning and then leaped at suddenly in this letter. Now sweat began to pour out of him and relieve him, and he put his hand into his pocket to get out his handkerchief and felt the hard thing. He pulled it out and threw it on the desk. Somehow the sight of the hoof upset him. The curious thing, he knew, was that it was upsetting his blood, not his mind. It seemed to act in some queer way. He stared at it in horror. He felt an itching on his skin, and knew that it was fear and hate. It was the hair rising on the dog. Then his hate began to gnaw his stomach. He felt an acid eating into his mind. By God Almighty, if he could know the sender at this moment! He wiped the sweat off his face on his sleeve. Then his mouth closed like a pincers. He opened the second drawer in the desk and took up the pistol. The cold steel burned into his sweating palm. He liked the scorching. It embodied his anger. His thumb clicked on the catch. His finger softly closed about the trigger, as gently as it might curl into a ringlet of gold hair. He pulled the shutter with his other hand and spoke into the cabinet. "Come in."

When she came in, he watched her as carefully as a polecat might watch a snake. Her face was like the globe of a lamp when the wick has gone out. It had no color, no light. He pulled her over slowly with his eyes, like a huntsman drawing a hound. She was so held in his eyes that she walked into the desk and stopped at the contact. His eyes continued to search into her until, he felt, she was on the point of screaming. Then he said: "Who sent that letter?"

"I don't know."

There was a kind of cold agony on her face. She knew that his question meant: "Did you send it?"

He looked at her for a moment and then said: "I am sorry."

She nodded and turned to go. Then her eye caught on the hoof on the desk. She seemed to leap away in horror, although she did not move. He thought she would faint, but she walked out like somebody walking away from a deathbed. When she went out, his mind collapsed.

He knew it was not she. If it had been, he would have killed her. But he was being attacked by a ghost. The gun in his hand was useless. The gun was scorching his hand, stuck to the palm like a stamp to an envelope. It might be the pain of the steel that made his mind want to shriek out through his forehead. There were stabs like needles in his eyes. His mind must escape from this transfixion. Where? How . . .

The pad!

Christ! How could he see faces with that damned inkstain on the pad! He could not let the gun go that was stuck to his skin and he held the edge of the pad between his teeth and tore away the blotted sheet with his left hand and exposed a new clean sheet. He saw that his teeth had bitten nearly through the leather edge. God, he was drawn out like wires that sang in the wind. And now there was a kind of whistle through his mind that became a screeching.

He could see nothing on the pad. It was white and empty. My God, if he could only see those faces and occupy himself by watching them. He could not stand this intolerable whining in his mind. Then suddenly the pad was a pane of glass, and Sarah Fuidge looked out the window. He felt a gasp in his mind, as if the air had got in again. Now it was all right. The faces had returned. They came one by one, and then came faster, and suddenly began to spin up like shining dishes from a juggler's hand. They whirled up through the pad and into his eyes and they made a slight whining noise and suddenly he wanted to stop them. God, if one of them would only fall and make a wham, this mad Catherine's wheel might stop. Now they were moons, empty. Then they were moons with a shadow of Sarah's face on them. Then they were gongs, gongs that whanged up noiselessly, and fell through a long space in his mind down on Elder's carpet that was silent in the bottom of his head. Ah, they were back into faces again. Sarah, Jock, Muriel, Sidonie, Elder, Saluby, the old man in the drain on Saturday, Dorman, people he did not know or had lost in his memory. And then, his own face, 'at last, for the first time, lonely, aghast, shining like a fungus in the moonlight . . .

My God, his mind must be going. He was alone, with a gun clung to his hand, and he was inside the blotting pad, and looking out at himself, and wanting to know whom he had to kill. He had to kill somebody. The letters said so. Who? He felt that he was spinning away out from himself, like a spider on his line, and that he must get back. He must get back to somebody. He wanted company . . .

He heard the click in his mind and was astonished not to hear the noise of a shot. He thought it must be the trigger, but he looked down at the gun and knew that he had not pulled the trigger. The click was in his mind. And suddenly he had got back to his desk, was thinking, knew what to do. He must ring Muriel, talk to her on the telephone, and that would make him feel safe again. Then he would go home at once by a hired car and fall on her with kisses and comfort his hands on her bosom and be healed. And then immediately they would pack and go away. He was alone with everybody but her. He sweated again in relief. He had just got back in time and knew what to do. He pulled open the shutter of the cabinet to ask Miss Coleman for the Barrington number. She was talking to somebody. Nicholas listened.

"Yes, Mr. Strood? Oh, perhaps it had better wait until the morning. Mr. Bude is very busy. Very well, Mr. Strood."

Hum, she was saving him from Strood because she knew he was upset. He heard the buzz on her desk and realize that she was taking another call. Damn! He listened to her.

"Hello? Oh, hello, Mrs. Bude!"

Nicholas gave a start. What a queer chance! Or had Muriel guessed him in trouble by some telepathy? She had never called him at the bank before. He reached his hand for the receiver, expecting Miss Coleman to put Muriel through. But Miss Coleman was going on talking.

"Oh, I'm very well."

Very sociable conversation, Nicholas thought, considering Muriel had never before rung up Miss Coleman. Miss Coleman was still going on.

"Yes?"

There was a pause.

"I understand."

There was another pause.

"I don't know. Ring me at my flat when you're in London in the evening. I'd love to see you again, too."

Good Christ! Muriel and Sidonie knew each other! What did this mean?

There was another pause.

"Yes. It came just now. I've just taken it into him."

Nicholas felt a click inside his head. My God, it was Muriel who had sent these letters! Muriel! His mind dropped down like a stone into space. Now he had nobody. They were in a conspiracy to get him.

The last things he remembered were the hoof on the desk and the skin hurting on his palm where he held the gun. Then his head fell over with a thud.

THIRTY-SEVEN

At last they had got rid of everybody and were waiting for the doctor to come out of Nicholas' office. Sidonie took Muriel into the small waiting room between Mr. Elder's office and Nicholas' room. It was a yellow room with blue armchairs and now the sunlight came in and made it warm. Sidonie thought it was the only human room in the bank, and that was why she had asked Muriel to come in here. She opened her case and offered Muriel a cigarette. Then they both sat in silence until the page brought in tea.

"Oh, tea! How nice of you!"

She smiled at Sidonie, who said quietly: "I think we both need it."

Muriel watched her pouring out the tea and said: "I am afraid I was rather rude to Mr. Strood. I just couldn't stand him any longer."

"I know."

There was another silence before Muriel said:

"And you have found out nothing about the letters?"

"No."

Muriel could not prevent the edge on her voice as she said:

"Well, I wish you hadn't taken in that one today."

Sidonie's voice was cold and formal and distant.

"I am sorry. I had to take it in."

Muriel looked up and spoke gently.

"I know. I shouldn't have said that." She waited for a second cup and then remarked: "Can't the doctor tell us how Nicholas is, without keeping us in this suspense?

This strain must have done fearful things to his heart, but he is a strong man." She looked again at the closed door of the room in which the doctor was ministering to Nicholas, then turned with determination to Sidonie. "Miss Coleman, I want this mystery cleared up. If Nicholas pulls through, I want his mind at ease."

"Of course."

"Is Mr. Elder gone?"

"I don't think so."

"I'd like to see him."

Sidonie got up and said:

"I know why you want to see him."

"Do you suspect him?"

"Well, the letter that came today has vanished."

"How long was he alone in the room with Nicholas?"

"Half a minute, while I called the doctor."

"Why did he come in so quickly?"

"He heard Mr. Bude fall. This is his office next door."

"I see. Now can we see him?"

Sidonie went out and brought Mr. Elder in.

Muriel let him stand in silence a moment before she spoke. "Mr. Elder, have you got anything you want to give me?"

"Yes, Mrs. Bude."

Muriel was slightly surprised. Mr. Elder put his hand in his hip pocket and produced the letters.

"Why did you take those out of his case?"

"In case he was dead and we had to call the police in."

"Why didn't you want the police to see them?"

"Because I don't want a scandal in the bank."

"How did you know what those letters were about?"

"Mr. Bude told me, last Friday."

327

Sidonie looked sharply at Mr. Elder. She did not know that Nicholas had talked to him.

"I see. Why should Mr. Bude discuss them with you?"

"Because he suspected me of sending them," Mr. Elder answered. "I presume he told you that?"

"Mr. Bude does not know I knew about them," Muriel said. "I found out about them, but he doesn't know I know. Miss Coleman does. I went to see her about them. I wanted her help to find out who was sending them."

Mr. Elder looked at Sidonie. This had surprised him.

"I see." He looked again at Sidonie. "Why didn't you ask me to help you?" Sidonie could not answer him. "I see. You suspect me."

Sidonie now looked cold and hostile.

"If you knew about them, Mr. Elder, why didn't you ask *me?*"

Muriel knew now that they suspected each other. She tried another line. "Mr. Elder, why should it affect the bank even if it were found out that my husband was getting these letters?"

"The letters are written on the paper of the Elder Bank. Whoever wrote them must be connected in some way with the Bude Bank. A matter like this might end anywhere."

"I am glad you had the presence of mind to take them, Mr. Elder. That is not my point. What I want to find out is who wrote them. Do you know if Mr. Bude suspects anybody else?"

"I can't answer that question, Mrs. Bude. I am sorry."

"Well, I know he suspects me," said Sidonie.

Mr. Elder looked sharply at her.

Muriel went on: "What did you say to Mr. Bude when he told you about them?"

"I told him that I did not know who was writing them," Mr. Elder said. "I also was able to inform him that eighteen pages of Elder Bank paper had been taken from my desk."

"Good heavens!"

Muriel and Mr. Elder glanced sharply at Sidonie as she made the exclamation. Muriel tensed herself and spoke. "Do you know who took them?"

"No."

"Do you mean from your house?"

"Yes, from the desk in my house."

"Well, Mr. Elder, you can at least know all the people who *could* have taken them."

"I am afraid, Mrs. Bude, that I cannot feel convinced in my heart that anybody who comes to my place would have taken that paper or written those letters, no matter how bad the facts look."

"Does anybody from the bank go to your house?"

There was a pause. Mr. Elder waited.

Sidonie said: "Yes, I do."

Muriel looked worried. "Has anybody else from the bank been to your house?"

"Nobody, except Mr. Bude himself. He came to see me when I was ill."

Sidonie started up. "Mr. Bude!"

"Yes," said Mr. Elder. He paused, then said: "I think that is perhaps why he suspects you."

Sidonie stared at Mr. Elder.

"Why should that make him suspect me? I didn't know Mr. Bude had been to your place. Did you tell him I go there?"

"You were there the night he came."

There was a kind of pause in Sidonie's face. Then at last she understood. All the blood went out of her face. "Oh, my God!"

Muriel stood up with her nerves on edge.

"Mr. Elder, what is all this! I don't understand it."

Sidonie looked at her with a distressed face. "That— is something besides the letters. Please don't ask. It doesn't matter."

"Then I wish I could get something out of one of you that might explain something!" There was something like anger in Muriel's voice.

"I'm sorry, Mrs. Bude, I'm as puzzled as you are."

Muriel looked at him with her patience gone. "Mr. Elder, let us be frank. You suspect Miss Coleman, don't you?"

Mr. Elder looked distressed. Sidonie now looked cold and disgusted as he spoke.

"Mrs. Bude, I don't know what to say. I know that Miss Coleman could have taken the paper, but . . . Well, I have known Miss Coleman for some years, and I—I can hardly believe . . ." Mr. Elder's voice died away unhappily.

Muriel looked at him. "I see, Mr. Elder. You can't be sure." Muriel looked at Sidonie and said: "Well, I am sure, Mr. Elder. Miss Coleman could not possibly write those letters."

Mr. Elder looked at Sidonie and wondered if she were going to cry. This was the first time he had seen her moved.

"I'm glad to hear you say that, Mrs. Bude. It's a weight off my mind!" Mr. Elder paused. "Does that apply to me, Mrs. Bude?"

"I don't know," she answered. "Those letters are

clever. You are clever. You were clever enough to take those letters. It might have been for your own sake. Don't be offended, Mr. Elder. I am just taking the facts." She looked carefully at him. "Somebody very clever wrote those letters and planned the posting of them. Only somebody who knows my husband well could have worded them that way. You will agree about that, Mr. Elder?"

"I don't know. I haven't read the letters."

Muriel got another surprise. "You don't know what's in them?"

"No. Mr. Bude did not tell me. Surely you don't think I would look at somebody's letters?"

"Oh, I'm sorry. I wasn't thinking that. I thought my husband told you. Well, you'd better look at them now."

When Mr. Elder opened the file of letters, Muriel started at the red splashes on them.

"Ink stains, Mrs. Bude. That happened last Friday."

"Oh . . ."

Mr. Elder examined the letters and said to Sidonie at last: "This was posted by hand in the bank today?"

"Yes."

"Diabolical . . . Can you get me the magnifying glass?

Sidonie went out to get the glass. Mr. Elder looked at Muriel.

"I'm glad you know she couldn't have done it, Mrs. Bude."

"I know she couldn't." Muriel smiled gently. "I'm afraid I don't think you could either, Mr. Elder." She was astonished at the beauty of his smile.

Sidonie came in with the glass, and Mr. Elder used it several times on the corner of the sheets of paper. At

331

last he said: "I can't swear, but I think this paper came from my desk. The corner of the box got jammed in the drawer, and there are some very faint wrinkles on this paper." He paused. "Now, that was the last box I used." He paused again. "After all, I could hardly have missed eighteen pages without some reason behind their disappearance." He paused for a long time. "Yes, this must be the paper I had stolen." He looked at the text again. "Somebody very clever and—abnormal."

"Abnormal?"

Muriel looked hard at him.

"Yes. Nobody normal could have planned that out. Merely sending anonymous letters is abnormal, but I mean something deeper." Mr. Elder frowned. "I can't think."

Muriel sat up tautly. "Now, Mr. Elder, tell me everybody who goes into your house. I want them all. After all, it must be some one of them."

Mr. Elder looked thoughtful and spoke slowly. "Well, Miss Coleman, as you know. Professor Crampton used to come until he got crippled—nearly a year ago. He's absolutely out of the question. He's a distinguished scholar. The people who live in the flats below me, an Indian poet, his wife, and a Persian woman who lives in the other flat. There's absolutely no possibility of these people writing the letters. Lord Tyrnode, who, like myself, is a Chinese scholar. The woman who does out the flat. Nobody else." Mr. Elder paused. "I assure you, Mrs. Bude, not even by a miracle could one of those people be connected with these letters."

"No, it doesn't seem likely," Muriel said. "Now, are you absolutely certain that nobody else has been in your place during the last few months?"

Mr. Elder put his hand to his forehead and was

silent for a moment. Then he said: "Yes, I remember now. My nephew came to see me one day, I think it must be a couple of months ago. "I can't see what he's got to do with it, either. He came to borrow a book about old Chinese medical practices . . ."

"Medical practices?" The question leaped off Muriel's tongue.

"Yes. He's a doctor, so . . ."

"A doctor!" Muriel stood up.

"Yes, Mrs. Bude. Why . . ."

"What is his name?"

"Well, as a matter of fact, he's got two names. He changed his by deed poll. It's rather a long story. He was ashamed of the name of Elder, since the crash, and . . ."

"What is his name now?"

"Oh, Saluby."

Muriel went over and picked up the letters. She turned to Mr. Elder. "Mr. Elder, I don't know if you will get the book back he borrowed, but here are some of the eighteen pages of paper he took from your desk."

"Good God! Harry! But, why . . . ? I don't understand this!" Mr. Elder stared at Muriel's drawn, angry face. "Do you know him?"

"Yes." Muriel felt herself tauten and looked hard at Mr. Elder. "Mr. Elder, how is it you don't know I know him?"

"Good heavens, Mrs. Bude. How should I know you knew him!"

"Mr. Elder, did you read the report in the papers of the suicide of our lodgekeeper's daughter?"

"Yes."

"You mean to say you read that and did not notice the name of the doctor who did the post mortem?"

Mr. Elder searched his memory.

"I don't think I did. A name like that never makes any mark in my mind. It's simply a doctor attending a case, and doesn't matter. I was interested in the girl herself . . . Good heavens, I remember now. Mr. Bude told me at that time it was the doctor who suggested that he should send himself letters. He did not mention the doctor's name. But . . ."

"Look here, Mr. Elder, it's very hard for me to believe that you didn't notice the doctor's name. Did you know he was practicing down there?"

"I knew he was in the country, that's all."

"And you didn't know the name of the place where he was?"

"He did tell me. But I wasn't taking much notice."

"Even if you had forgotten, surely seeing the name Barrington in the papers would have reminded you?"

"I suppose it ought, but . . ." Mr. Elder frowned. "Somehow I don't think he told me it was Barrington. I thought it was a place with two names. Something to do with a church. Yes, I remember now—Spire. Something Spire."

Muriel started. "Was it Yeoman Spire?"

"Yes, I think so."

"I've just remembered. Yeoman Spire is only a place of a few houses. The village is Barrington, but I've suddenly realized that the medical parish is Yeoman Spire. You're quite right, Mr. Elder."

"Anyway, I didn't notice it, Mrs. Bude. I hope you believe me when I say I simply don't understand all this. Are you sure it was he?"

"Almost certain. Now I want to ask you some questions, and I want plain answers."

"Yes."

"Is Dr. Saluby your nephew? Is that what you said?'

"Actually he's my second cousin, but when he was a boy he used to call me 'Uncle,' and . . ."

"Yes."

"Well, I sort of adopted him, and helped him with his schooling, and . . ."

"I see, Mr. Elder." Muriel paused. "And he always resented getting—what he called charity from you?"

"Yes. How did you know that?"

"Never mind. Why did you say he changed his name?"

"Well, his father did, because the family were ruined when Elder's Bank went, and Harry had a hard time because of that, and he—well, he never forgave things."

"I see. But, come—he must have had somebody he could trust to post those letters for him. Have you any idea who could have posted these from all over the country?"

"Good Lord, Cecil!"

"Who is Cecil?"

"His half brother. He's a commercial traveler . . ."

"I see. Now, Mr. Elder, can you remember the date when he came to see you? I assume he could have taken the paper?"

"Yes. He was there when I got back. My door is not locked. It opens on a secret catch, but Harry knows that."

Muriel took up the letters and found the first date. "Now, Mr. Elder, can you place that date?"

Mr. Elder got out a diary and made some calculations. "I think so."

Muriel compared the dates. Saluby had taken the paper five days before the first letter was posted.

"I don't think there is any doubt about it," she

said. "I felt uneasy about him even today. He came to see me before lunch about something, and I felt it was a planned visit. I see now it was his alibi, to show that he was at Barrington today, when the letter was dropped into the box here. My instinct was right. That's why I came to London. I felt uneasy when he had gone." She paused. "He worked it all out. The Elder Bank paper would be recognized and would cause Nicholas to suspect everybody in the bank and increase his worry and fear . . . I see it all now."

"It's hard to believe a doctor could do that," said Mr. Elder.

"Doctors are the same as any other men. He knows damn well we can't expose him even now that we've found out. We wouldn't have the scandal in the bank. My husband won't expose him when he learns that he was an Elder, and a relative of yours."

"Yes. I suppose that's right." Mr. Elder's mouth hardened. "He'll have to consider the India loan and the effect in the City of a long-drawn-out newspaper story." Mr. Elder was white with anger. "But I should not mind an exposure. I don't see why a blackguard like him should be left at large to do something like this again. Good God, he's a doctor. He might poison a patient he disliked. We ought to be able to bring it home to him."

"I doubt it. I don't believe there's a fingerprint on those letters. I'll bet everything was handled with rubber gloves on. He wouldn't make a mistake." Muriel paused. "I don't think I'd worry, Mr. Elder. He may never do it again. He tried to get rid of a hereditary grudge against the Bude name. You know, like the Corsican vendetta."

"Corsican! How queer! His grandmother—no, his

336

great-grandmother was a Corsican. That's why he's got that slight Latin look." Mr. Elder paused. "But it's such a long way back."

"That's not a long way back," said Sidonie. "It's not even an inch of the journey to the ape."

Mr. Elder nodded.

"I suppose so. I see what you mean." Then he paused. "My God, if he ever puts a foot in my place again . . ."

"If he does, Mr. Elder, I would prefer that you let him know quietly that we know everything. Just that, or he will try again. But if he knows that we know, he'll be afraid to try again."

"Very well, Mrs. Bude."

"Mr. Elder," said Muriel suddenly a little on edge, "I want you to do one thing. Keep Mr. Strood away from me. He's trying to look sad, but he just looks sick."

Mr. Elder almost smiled. He took up the letters to tidy them into the case. Mr. Elder was very surprised to find that Mrs. Bude was a young and beautiful woman. He took out *The Times* and the case. As he picked up the case, the deer's hoof fell out on the table. Muriel saw Mr. Elder stare at it, then look in a strange way at Sidonie, who did not seem to be able to say anything.

Muriel had a feeling that there was something very queer about this hoof. "That was on his desk, wasn't it?"

"Yes," Sidonie answered without looking at the hoof.

Muriel picked it up. "It seems to be a deer's hoof, or a lamb's. It's a deer's, I think. I suppose he picked it up at Barrington."

Muriel saw Mr. Elder close up the case. She moved the hoof about in her hand and then left it on the table.

"I'll go in and see if the doctor is finished," Mr. Elder said. "I'm sure Mr. Bude will be all right; I have an intuition about such things."

"Thank you. And please, please hurry."

Sidonie said: "I won't be a moment."

Muriel nodded, as Sidonie went out with Mr. Elder. Muriel noticed they went into Mr. Elder's room rather than into Nicholas' office.

When Sidonie got into Mr. Elder's room she said: "Why did you let him see me in your room?"

Mr. Elder looked upset. "I am sorry. I covered you over with that blue veil. I did not know who was coming in. It should have been perfectly safe with that blue veil. I didn't feel well enough to carry you into the bedroom when I heard the ring, so I covered you over." Mr. Elder looked distressed. "Unfortunately, I did not cover your foot."

"I still don't . . ."

"He lost his head last Friday and hardly knew what he was saying to me. He said he didn't know where he was, what with Chinese mandarins in the bank and people who smoked opium. I knew that escaped from him." Mr. Elder paused. "Well, I knew that he must have seen your foot somewhere else besides my room."

"So you know?"

"I can guess," Mr. Elder answered. "Does she know?"

"I don't know. She is very clever."

"And beautiful," said Mr. Elder. "I got a surprise."

"I like her. I dined with her the night she came to see me about the letters."

338

"She likes you very much. Not everybody would have trusted you and believed in you as she did just now."

"I know that. I think Mr. Bude will be happy with her now—if he lives." Suddenly her eyes were wet and she turned to Mr. Elder. "Will he live? Will he?"

Mr. Elder nodded. "He'll pull out of it." He did not go at once, but put his arm around her shoulder. "You're in love with him, too, aren't you?"

"Yes. He lived with me. It's all over now and I'm glad I like his wife. I'll feel better when I go away knowing he's happy."

"I think you are very wise—and very compassionate. I agree it's best for you to go away."

"Thank you for understanding. I'm going back to his wife now."

They went out, and Mr. Elder opened the door of Nicholas' office and shut it quickly behind him. Sidonie sat down with Muriel.

Mr. Elder was back in the room in a second. His face glowed, and as Muriel looked at him she was no longer afraid. "Nicholas is all right?" she asked.

Mr. Elder nodded. "He's going to be as good as ever. He's coming around now, but the doctor suggests that you wait another few minutes before going in."

"Oh, thank you." Muriel got up and grasped his hand.

"I'll go tell the others. You and Miss Coleman can wait here by yourselves—without being bothered by Mr. Strood." He was smiling when he went out.

Muriel said: "I like Mr. Elder."

"Yes. He's a very cultured man. At home he lives and dresses like a mandarin and his room is a Chinese room."

"Oh . . . How interesting." Muriel paused. "How funny, that Nicholas did not tell me about that, if he went to see him. But he never talks much." Muriel paused. "I couldn't quite understand about your being at Mr. Elder's place when Nicholas was there and not seeing him."

Sidonie looked at her and said: "I was asleep."

"Oh."

Muriel did not understand it, and Sidonie had conveyed to her in some way that she could not explain this. But Muriel had a feeling that it was all right and did not concern her.

Suddenly Sidonie seemed shy as she spoke. "You don't know how glad I am that you trusted me and knew I would not write those letters."

"Anybody would have known that."

"No. Not even Mr. Elder was sure."

"He was, in his heart, as you were sure about him. You've got to believe in something and somebody."

Muriel got up and walked about the room. Then she came back and looked at Sidonie. "What is your name?"

"Sidonie."

"May I call you that?"

"I'd like you to."

"Well, you know mine." Muriel sat down. "Sidonie, let's have it all out. I don't want to lose you as a friend. Let's ask each other anything we want to know."

"Very well, I'd like to get it over, too. Go ahead."

"Have you been living with Nicholas?"

"Yes." Sidonie paused. "If you call every Monday living with somebody."

"For how long?"

"Oh—four or five years."

340

"Did you love him?"

"I did, when he was unhappy. We had that in common. Now he'll be happy again, and he'll be free of me and I of him."

Muriel blushed. Then she smiled gently, and said:

"Now what do you want to know from me?"

"I want to know why Nicholas wasn't happy with you. He never spoke of you. Since the evening you came into my flat, I simply have not been able to understand it. I don't know why, but I pictured you as somebody inhibited and rather middle class and completely unable to understand Nicholas. You were the last person I expected to see."

"It's a very queer story. I was inhibited, and I did almost ruin the marriage because I was middle-class, and knew nothing about sex, and was afraid of it."

"I can't believe you are like that."

"I think I had better tell you the whole thing."

Sidonie listened in a quiet amazement, until Muriel ended:

"So you see, our honeymoon began ten years after we were married. That's only two days ago."

Muriel paused and then asked Sidonie:

"Did you think he was in love with you?"

"Yes, in a way; I might have said 'yes' if I didn't know you. I think he must have been in love with you always."

"Does he know you were in love with him, Sidonie?"

"I don't know. I kept it from him. I never even— let him kiss me until a few weeks ago."

Muriel sat up.

"You mean, he was living with you, and you never kissed him?"

"Yes. I—only gave him my body. I—was afraid to

let him know I loved him. But I gave in—just a little time ago. I suppose he must have known then."

"But why, but why, in God's name? Why shouldn't he know?"

Sidonie began to tremble, and Muriel saw she could not speak.

"Were you afraid he might want to marry you? Is it because you didn't want to break up my home?"

"No. I never even thought about you."

"But—good heavens, people divorce, and you would be a perfect wife for somebody like Nicholas. Damn it, you are probably much better bred than I am."

"It's nothing like that. Please don't ask me."

Muriel got up and put her hand on the trembling shoulder.

"Sidonie, I must know. It's not because I want to know, but there's something inside you that's killing you, and I can't bear it. Please tell me."

A long, silent sob shook Sidonie and then she began to perspire. At last she said:

"Please don't look at me."

Muriel turned away and fixed her eyes on the hoof on the table.

It seemed an age until Sidonie said: "I have a deformity." There was a pause. "It's that, what you are looking at. I have that instead of a small toe on my right foot." There was another pause. "If I got married to anybody, I could not conceal it. I always wore slippers when—Nicholas came."

Muriel let her hand slide back into Sidonie's.

"Oh, you poor darling! So you thought a man would mind that if he loved you."

"He would. The last time Nicholas came to see me, when I gave myself to him at last, he pulled off my

342

slipper and saw my foot. He tried to hide it, but that ended it." There was another pause. "You see, he picked up that hoof, because—because it was like mine, and . . ."

"Don't talk about it any more."

Sidonie looked faint and had to lie back a moment. "I'm glad I told you."

"So am I. I knew something was eating you up inside, and I was—afraid. Who else knows?"

"Only my family—and Mr. Elder. I go to his place to get peace sometimes. I get it from opium."

"Oh, my God."

Muriel had swung round with horror on her face.

"Please don't be alarmed. I am not an addict. Mr. Elder would not have given me the pipe if he were not sure that I was safe. But it releases my mind from this worry—about my foot—and I think it's better than having something shut up in your mind like Nicholas had."

"Nicholas?"

"Yes. I think he had something in his mind that none of us knew about."

"He used to have nightmares—and he was affected by the moon."

"I knew about the moon. He told me."

"Saluby said he was a superstitious peasant with a mind like a dog that bays at the moon. That haunted me."

"This man Saluby must be very clever."

"He is. He saw Nicholas as a guinea pig to experiment on. He said so openly to me. He pretended, of course, that he thought Nicholas was writing the letters himself. He knew that Nicholas had moles underneath his mind like Sarah Fuidge had—that's the girl who

343

committed suicide. And he knew that Nicholas was in his hands."

"Yes, I know that."

A curious memory came into Muriel's mind of that first night when Nicholas' personality seemed to go into her blood from his hands.

"Sidonie, dont let's talk about it any more. I'm going to have something done about your foot."

"No, it's too late now. It's inside of me, not just on my foot. I think I'd rather not."

Spontaneously, they gave themselves to each other in their eyes. Muriel exclaimed: "Oh, I'm so glad I met you. And I'm glad it was you he went to. Let's always be friends."

"We will be . . . I'll go now before you go in to him."

"When will I see you again?"

"Soon." She knew she would never see either of the Budes again. She went quickly before the door to Nicholas' office opened. She was not there when the doctor came out and smiled at Muriel.

"He can see you now, Mrs. Bude," he said. "He's ready to go home."